QUARTET ENCOUNTERS

## SHORT STORIES

Pirandello's short stories are among the greatest writings in that genre. There are over two hundred of them, and any selection can hope only to tantalize the reader with brilliant examples from so immense an oeuvre. The twenty-one stories included in the present volume reveal Pirandello's astonishing and varied genius. As Frederick May writes in his Introduction: 'The outer world of Pirandello's stories – the appearance of its reality – has a deceptive monotony and a deceptive variety. The monotony is the mask which society exacts from us; the variety is the pathetic series of fragmentary masks in which we strut about the world: the peasant, the clerk, the editor, the landowner, the prostitute, the pseudo-veteran of Garibaldi's campaigns, the member of Parliament, the submissive daughter, the criminal, the usurer.'

## LUIGI PIRANDELLO

Born in Sicily in 1867, Pirandello was particularly fortunate to have a mother who encouraged his artistic sensibility despite his father's wish that he should have a technical education. He studied at the Universities of Palermo, Rome and Bonn, and after settling in Rome became prominent among a group of young writers and artists who challenged D'Annunzio and his cult of the superman. His marriage to Antonietta Portulano, the daughter of his father's partner, though initially happy (she bore him three children) ended in a disaster which was to influence him greatly. After the financial collapse of his father-in-law's sulphur mines he was compelled to make writing his profession. His private life was devastated when his wife, after a severe illness, developed paranoia and grew steadily more insane. Her manic jealousy made his life utter torment until 1919, when she entered a nursing-home. This undoubtedly led him to concentrate his work on themes of exile and the search for the unattainable woman. Despite his novels and short stories, he is best known for his highly acclaimed plays, *Six Characters in Search of an Author* and *Henry IV*. After the collapse of his Teatro d'Arte in 1928, he became a voluntary exile from Italy, and even his love for Marta Abba, his leading lady and chief inspiration, failed to mitigate his sense of spiritual estrangement. In 1934 he was awarded the Nobel Prize for Literature, and in 1936 he died in Rome. His wife died in 1959.

LUIGI PIRANDELLO

# Short Stories

Selected, translated from the Italian by
FREDERICK MAY

Quartet Books London New York

Published in Great Britain by Quartet Books Limited 1987
A member of the Namara Group
27/29 Goodge Street, London W1P 1FD



British Library Cataloguing in Publication Data

Pirandello, Luigi
Short stories.
I. Title
852'.912 [F] PQ4835.I7

ISBN 0-7043-0037-0

Reproduced, printed and bound in Great Britain
by The Camelot Press plc, Southampton

TRANSLATOR'S DEDICATION

*In Memoriam*

ANGELO CRESPI
TULLIO SAMBUCETTI
VIOLET M. SAUNDERS

# CONTENTS

of communication; the possibility of a religion of compassion that springs from our common anguish; the ineluctable struggle between form and flux—and our inability to forgo the luxury of ideal images; coming to terms with and living out our aloneness; defining the role of paradox; and the unreasonableness of hope. These are universal problems, implicit in the human situation wherever man finds himself on the social scale. Pirandello refuses to allocate them by class or context, so that it is pointless to speak of middle-class or peasant *novelle*. True, he makes his characters elaborate their dialectic according to context, but he never allows us to believe that the central argument is generated by that context.

I have stressed the importance of dialogue in Pirandello because I feel it to be his especial contribution to the art of the short story. All but a few of the tales are shifting areas of conversation, either between Pirandello and the reader, or between character and character (or character and community). As a consequence, Nature, class, region, profession, and social institution are valued only in so far as they make it possible for him to thrust the sense of the debate tellingly upon us. It is not worthwhile simply to portray the melodrama of adverse fate cruelly defeating man; we must also comprehend and absorb into ourselves the irony beyond the operatic thunder; which means that we must see man as man, and not as a level of society or peculiarly touched by the region that begets him. The conflict in 'The Jar' is not between man and nature, or master and man, but between two artists, each caught in the trap of frustration, each the agent of the other's imprisonment. Only incidentally are we invited to delight in nature in 'The Black Kid',[1] 'Bitter Waters', or 'Cinci', though the passages are wholly satisfying and evocative; our main concern is to be with the symbolic representation they afford of that transcendental farce (Pirandello's term) which we play out.

Pirandello cuts through the picturesque (in whatever disguise it gets into) in order to strip man to those myths by which he organizes his life. For him every story is fundamentally a vision, a journey in search of the unattainable. Frequently, he juxtaposes

[1] Where a title is given in English, it refers to a story in this volume.

# CONTENTS

# NOTE

The number in italics at the foot of the half-title to each story refers either to *Translations* (pp. 242–51) or, where the number is greater than 91, to the order which these tales, now translated for the first time, occupy in the chronology of the English versions.

# INTRODUCTION

Oserei definire la civiltà: la perfetta
[arte] di fingere.
E la virtù: il secreto di mascherare
tutti i volti.
UGO FOSCOLO, *Sesto tomo dell'io.*

Un sogno ancora, una menzogna, e
poi la nera e fredda eternità del
nulla.
LUIGI PIRANDELLO, *Mal giocondo.*

WE are so used to thinking of Luigi Pirandello as a dramatist that it is salutary to recall his own wish—that his work for the theatre should ultimately be seen as a parenthesis in his progress as a short-story writer. There is, of course, no clear-cut distinction to be drawn between Pirandello the playwright and Pirandello the *novelliere,* any more than we may separate his poetry, his novels, or his essays. His writing is one interpenetrating whole. Undoubtedly, the stories and plays are most closely related; often, indeed, a play comes from the refashioning of a story or from the uniting of elements from several tales. The dramatic feature of the *novelle* which is most immediately impressive is their dialogue. Here is an author who has mastered the secret of speech that can carry with ease and cogency plot, narrative, atmosphere, and character; here is an author who knows what pace is.

Pirandello's sureness of control issues from his perception that life—in which he always includes death, since that also is a state of being—is argument, a ceaseless polemic. He has no time to waste, therefore, on writing to a formula, and it is no use looking for 'typically Sicilian' tales, or stories that are free from his so-called obsessions. The *novelle* deal with the problems debated in the plays: the nature of identity; reality and illusion; the impossibility of communication; the possibility of a religion of compassion that springs from our common anguish; the ineluctable struggle between form and flux—and our inability to forgo the luxury of ideal images; coming to terms with and living out our aloneness; defining the role of paradox; and the unreasonableness of hope. These are universal problems, implicit in the human situation wherever man finds himself on the social scale. Pirandello refuses to allocate them by class or context, so that it is pointless to speak of middle-class or peasant *novelle*. True, he makes his characters elaborate their dialectic according to context, but he never allows us to believe that the central argument is generated by that context.

I have stressed the importance of dialogue in Pirandello because I feel it to be his especial contribution to the art of the short story. All but a few of the tales are shifting areas of conversation, either between Pirandello and the reader, or between character and character (or character and community). As a consequence, Nature, class, region, profession, and social institution are valued only in so far as they make it possible for him to thrust the sense of the debate tellingly upon us. It is not worthwhile simply to portray the melodrama of adverse fate cruelly defeating man; we must also comprehend and absorb into ourselves the irony beyond the operatic thunder; which means that we must see man as man, and not as a level of society or peculiarly touched by the region that begets him. The conflict in 'The Jar' is not between man and nature, or master and man, but between two artists, each caught in the trap of frustration, each the agent of the other's imprisonment. Only incidentally are we invited to delight in nature in 'The Black Kid',[1] 'Bitter Waters', or 'Cinci', though the passages are wholly satisfying and evocative; our main concern is to be with the symbolic representation they afford of that transcendental farce (Pirandello's term) which we play out.

Pirandello cuts through the picturesque (in whatever disguise it gets into) in order to strip man to those myths by which he organizes his life. For him every story is fundamentally a vision, a journey in search of the unattainable. Frequently, he juxtaposes

[1] Where a title is given in English, it refers to a story in this volume.

people whose quests imply conflict—what resolution can there ever be of the desires of Miss Ethel Holloway and those of Mr. Charles Trockley? Is the dream of Mr. Myshkow capable of fruition in the porcelain world of his wife? Can Dr. Fileno ever be what he himself wants himself to be? These visions are ours, often repressed or disowned (since we are ashamed of our nakedness), but still determinant of the way we aspire to conduct our secret lives. We argue out their refinement, their precise shape, that is, expressing our debate in terms of shared myths. We all own some conviction of a lost paradise and know the longing to regain it; beyond those approximations with whom he mates, man recognizes the perfect mother-mistress; while none of us can do other than re-enact that twin birth to Fate of Love and Death.

When the stories were first collected into the Bemporad series, Pirandello introduced the volumes with an *avvertenza,* in which he asked his readers to forgive him if they saw in, and derived from, the numerous little mirrors reflecting his conception of life and the world which the tales would provide, too much bitterness and too little joy. Pirandello is no pessimist, however, but an ironist, and very much in the tradition of Boccaccio, Ariosto, and Machiavelli, while the presiding *shape* of his work indisputably stems from his assimilation of Dante. He has clarified the general principles governing his work in *L'umorismo,* concluding that humour is the simultaneous comprehension of an ideal or sentiment and of its exact opposite. All too often, art is used to suppress the contrary force—the ordinary artist concentrates on the 'body', and ignores the 'shadow'; the humorist is careful to deal with both body and shadow and, sometimes, is more concerned with the shadow than the body—he remarks all the jokes played by this shadow, the way it grows absurdly long, or grotesquely stunted, almost seeming to be pulling faces at the body, which does not care a jot, and disregards it utterly in making its calculations. We should do well, he suggests, to consider the implications of Von Chamisso's story of Peter Schlemihl. Everything is a fable, everything is true. Over us is forever poised an inscrutable 'if'. That tiny particle (as Pirandello joins with Sterne in asserting) is the arbiter of our entire world. It is quite absurd, but life *is* absurd, as the Father reminds the Producer in *Six Characters in Search of an Author* (*Sei personaggi in cerca d'autore*). Chance rules all. Everything is relative.

The *novelle* of Pirandello may be seen as fairy-tales for modern grown-ups. That they are rooted in the great tradition of Italian story-telling takes away none of their disconcerting up-to-dateness. They belong to our era of disintegration, capturing its inflexions most acutely. The man whose dialectic is revealed in them is man coping with his multiple (and non-existent) identity, acquiescent in the realistic theory that the true events of life are the shades of becoming picked out by the mind, and eliciting his ethic from a compassionate inquiry into that constant dissolution which is the coherence of living. It is noteworthy how frequently he adopts the Dantesque journey, and nowhere more forcefully than in 'A Day Goes By'. Written at the end of his life, when he was preparing to write about a new Adam and a new Eve (in what one can only see as a post-atomic world), it is an allegory of the inner quest of contemporary man.

In all, Pirandello wrote two hundred and thirty-three short stories, if we include 'The Little Hut', which was not reprinted until 1959. (I exclude the two unfinished tales, *Giorno di pioggia* and *L'uomo di tutte le donne,* and *Pianto segreto,* which, although published as a story in the *Marzocco,* was later incorporated in the novel *I vecchi e i giovani.* I also disregard what may have been intended as a tale, *La fanciulla di Kessenich.*) Of these, some ninety-one—as far as I have been able to trace—have already been translated into English. Only one collection of English versions has come out since the war, that made by Lily Duplaix and published in New York in 1959, while more than sixty of the translations are earlier than 1942. Apart from the *novelle* included in the Duplaix volume, only three new stories have since been added to the body of tales in English, none of them dating from later than 1919. Her book, with its twenty new stories (she wrongly credits herself with twenty-one) has been very welcome, therefore, and her new selection of material from the twenties and thirties has done much to extend our experience of Pirandello as a *novelliere*. I am personally grateful that she should have included *Pena di vivere così*, a story of which Pirandello was especially fond, on which he was working at the time of his death.

Like any selection of his tales, however, it is calculated to leave the reader demanding more. Pirandello is a *novelliere* who can be sampled with immense value and enjoyment, but who must finally be read in his entirety, for in every story there is something more, an exciting new discovery put forward, something we cannot afford to miss. Lily Duplaix built on the earlier collections which, though just out of print, could still be found. In making my own selection I have started from scratch and tried to represent Pirandello's work as a short-story writer without distorting its quality or its range. I have also tried to give some idea of its development, and to bring out the links which unite the *novelle* and the plays. I have translated the final texts of the stories, and I submit them in their full form. (In many of the earlier versions severe cuts were introduced, and it was not uncommon for a story to be rewritten completely.) I have attempted to give proper weight to the last period when, it seems to me, he was writing magnificently. There is a new concentration—not that he was noticeably diffuse before—a heightened complexity and lucidity of expression, and a relaxed power to exhibit the whole man alive. Finally, I have sought to illustrate his major preoccupations.

Pirandello himself, largely because of what he saw as Croce's obtuseness in appraising his work, insisted that his art had 'no connexion whatsoever with naturalism'. 'Indeed,' he asserted to Vittorini, 'I feel that I am at the opposite pole from naturalism. I have battered down blind faith in clumsy, tangible reality.' It is particularly interesting, therefore, to study his own very early story 'The Little Hut'. He was probably in his seventeenth year when he wrote it, and unmistakably under the spell of Verga. Yet, it is a remarkable essay, with many hints of a personal style. The tautness may be a little overdone, the assembly of the elements be slightly too careful; the Paolo Veronese look of Màlia is bookish, and *romantically* bookish; while some of the dialogue is equally bookish. But its virtues easily outweigh its deficiencies. The behaviour of the little girl at the beginning of the story is not only finely observed, it is lived through. Papà Camillo's warning to Jeli reaches forward to the maturity of Pirandello as a writer of dialogue. The way in which so much is made to emerge from the very few words exchanged by the lovers; the vigil and prayer of Màlia, neatly straddled by the two uncomprehending vigils of the young girl; the observation of slight detail—the significance of the pipe—the juxtaposition of shut-upness and immensity (an early proof, this, of Pirandello's alertness to compressionism); all give hints of a unique gift. Already Pirandello is challenging the emptiness of form. His solution at seventeen is (not unexpectedly) romantic, but there is more than romanticism to the reactions of Papà Camillo and his destruction of the hut. And it may well be that the memory of that hut survived into the terrible last paragraphs of *Vittoria delle formiche,* which was written some fifty-two years later.

I have included 'The Cooper's Cockerels', partly because it is the only children's story by Pirandello that we have, partly because it is an early proof of how surely he could carry on a tale in dialogue. Here, too, is the Pirandellian thesis that the chance event promotes far-reaching consequences. Again, isn't the cooper's wife a primitive Cesare Vivoli (the anti-hero of his play *Cecè*), fabricating priests and husbands according to her own needs and setting them to act out *her* puppet-show? Is it placing too great a burden on so delightful and galloping a story, to see it as a passionately held vision fought for and achieved? Technically, it is hard to fault: the pace is immaculate; the moods are firmly established and delicately differentiated; and the atmosphere of a significant fairy-tale sustained. We are already in Pirandello's dream-world—it is a marked quality of this story, as indeed of 'The Little Hut', that the characters speak as if in a kind of trance. This quality distinguishes all the mature work of Pirandello, and is of course a principal instrument towards his *invasion* of both reader and spectator. Pirandello, as Corrado Alvaro has pointed out, displaced the literature of determinism and substituted for it something with magic in its bones. His characters use thought as incantation, so justifying his claim that he gave the theatre new frontiers by converting intellect into passion.

'A Dream of Christmas' exhibits a Pirandello too often ignored. He had little time for the Establishment in any form, but (while avoiding the Church as an institution) he remained a religious man. Perhaps one may define him as an ancient Greek pagan with Christian acceptances (notably of the Sermon on the Mount). We can trace an unfaltering line from 'A Dream of Christmas' through *Lazzaro* (his 'religious' myth) to 'All Passion Spent'. (Relevant, I feel, is having in his study a painting of the Crucifixion.) The story underlines Pirandello's resolution to explore life seen as a dream, and by its complex of symbols makes it comparatively certain that he is already obsessed with a need to relive some part at least of Dante's journey. He is positing the demands of the absolute and recognizing his own unworthiness. In technique, he is foreshadowing *Sogno (ma forse no)* and 'The Visit', and several other short stories. He captures exactly the dislocated chronology of the dream—a topic which gripped his imagination, as we know from his making Angelo Baldovino remind us (in *Il piacere dell'onestà*) of Descartes's terrifying observation that, if time in dreams could achieve the same steady flow as clock-time, we should no longer be able to distinguish waking from sleeping. Notice, too, the visionary moonlit scene, of a type which is recurrent throughout his work, and almost always (as here) linked with regeneration and rebirth. (Pirandello is sufficiently Greek to have a sense of the personal relevance of the Persephone legend—made explicit in *All'uscita*—and he appears always to assume the Diana–Persephone equation.) In 'Cinci' the scene contemplated by the *first moon* (it's a different moon, says Cinci, when he reaches another point along the road) is one of blood-sacrifice, and out of it is born the new Cinci. This, I suspect, may have its origin in 'A Dream of Christmas', though the possibility of renewing life for one's loved ones by committing suicide occurred to Pirandello at the time of his ruin in 1903. The suicide-moon-creation nexus is again explored (as blood-curdling farce) in *Niente*.

Much of the force of the story comes from the easy, allusive, and yet heightened dialogue. Once more there is the incantational, inseparable here from the associations of our general Christian heritage. There is no artificial attempt to poeticize, but poetry certainly emerges, possibly because there is more than a memory of the poems *Il paese che un dí sognai* and *Torna Gesú!* (One has always to bear in mind that Pirandello, like Verga in *Cavalleria rusticana,* fuses the Christian resurrection with the old *'Pasqua di Gea'*.)

'Twelve Letters' bites very deep. There are affinities with Schnitzler, and Bourget is a wickedly employed catalyst, but this satire belongs to the Italian tradition. The situation is a network of Pirandellian traps. 'Hell is other people' is the tang of this story. And then, as we are released by and through its sophistication, we realize the tragedy of aloneness which is engaging all these characters. Why are they wearing these masks? Perhaps they're worthless. Nonetheless, they're suffering because society has made them into puppets. A typically Pirandellian reminder—and one we meet again and again in the plays—is the pointed use of the mirror. Tito Rossani sees himself living and at that moment dies. The dialogue is some of Pirandello's most intricate, and a nice counterpoint is maintained between its apparent simplicity (even triviality) and the real worlds which it is laying bare. A fine set-piece—comparable with the final speech in 'The Man with the Flower in his Mouth' or the Irish priest's speech in *Enrico IV*—is Rossani's re-evocation of his walk with Vidoni. If there were nothing else to convince us that Pirandello was aware from very early of the *novella* as theatre, this speech would do so. We can *see* how Adele Montagnani, having to sit and listen to such a speech—and she is compelled to—must reflect in her expression, her movements, and her entire projection the gradations, involution, and associations of what Rossani is saying. We know from the rest of the story that this does in fact occur.

'Fear' resembles 'Twelve Letters' in its use of re-evocation, but this time Pirandello dispenses with satirical farce. The relationships between Andrea and Lillina, and Lillina and Antonio, have been too seriously constructed for them to be conveyed in other than a heavily claustrophobic idiom just lightly flecked with lyricism. The naked appeal by Lillina for sexual fulfilment, when she is caught in the trap of an exploiting society (symbolized for us by her husband and her lover), can only be answered by death. You must never ask to be allowed to live out your reality as you understand it—an admonition Pirandello reiterates in the *Sei personaggi in cerca d'autore* and *Enrico IV*. Sexual reality is the lost world of Pirandellian dreaming. Lillina, the guilty adulteress, is finally innocent, in the same way that Francesca da Rimini is innocent. The symbolism of the story is apt to the limning of her abortive search for the lost world: the kiss on the stairs; candle-light; the turning on the stairs (used comically, but no less poignantly, in 'The Best of Friends'); the trains; the references to time; even the crochet-work. Lillina is a mother, but she is not allowed to be a woman.

'The Best of Friends' is brilliantly comic. An obvious (almost *treacherously* obvious) piece of orthodox Pirandellianism, it tears along with gale-force till suddenly there is a stab of pain which pulls you up short. Gigi Mear doesn't *know* his friend from Padua, and *he* is once more annihilated. Not to worry, though! In this life you simply reconstruct yourself. You came back into Gigi's life as his friend. You'll go out of it again as his melancholy tormentor. Life's hell, so let's all have a good long laugh together. We're already in the world of *Enrico IV*.

The friend from Padua—and how perfect is his outrageous 'mask' name, 'Anthropophagus Goatsbeardhornyfoot'!—is among Pirandello's most vividly realized characters: an ironic wit, compassing his own tragedy, fully aware of himself, sardonically watching himself live, and punished with a clarity of intellect, whose nearness to insanity is manifest in the manic quality of his talk. He has affinities with Ciampa (in *Il berretto a sonagli*) and Angelo Baldovino. He knows the beast in man; he sees right through the lies of our so-called civilization; he is alert to how transforming is the random event; and he is caught in a trap: he needs to love and be loved. Gigi was the far-off, over-idealized simulacrum of affection. Rediscovered, he brings disillusion, as real as the stinking goat that shatters Miss Ethel Holloway.

Typical of Pirandello's method is the economical drawing of pictures in words. They are then so placed in the story that the inevitable patterns of free association develop. A volume of narrative is thus eliminated. Gigi the sluggard, Gigi the conformist (a Count in the State Counting House), and Gigi-in-his-flatlet are remorselessly one. And wasn't it the blow of Gigi-the-diminutive's confession at the end, that Fate was keeping up her sleeve as the crowning humiliation (or joke) for the man who emerged from financial chaos into the farcical shindy of the cross-eyed lady's bedroom?

With 'Bitter Waters' we are unmistakably in the theatre. The construction of the story, the counter-weighting of its areas of dialogue, the various kinds and intensities of time, and its exact sense of pace, are all theatrical. Virtually everything is released in monologue, yet the younger man has an identity that counts, because, embedded in the fat man's lines, are the unavoidable responses of his companion. The messenger *persona* of the fat man —the reporter of past action—is a subtly inflected entity, separate from, but integral with, his other selves, principal among which, of course, is that of creator. Nothing that he recalls has the same emotional tug or the same narrative formulation as anything else that he conjures back into life. The fat man makes everything *grow,* quite naturally, convincingly, into itself.

Fornication, marriage, adultery: all traps, all illusions. We must learn to be philosophers, learn to recognize our sublimity in our own ridiculousness, learn to value our folly, and learn to listen attentively to our own dispute with life. Chance is a tyrant, capable of turning a plaything of a grateful mistress into a nagging, dissatisfied heiress of a wife. Another shuffle, and the lady is transformed from the unattainable adored one into the incurable, ever-present affliction. Paradoxically, the cherub remains, its child-like power holding the vision steady, whatever beastliness the grown-up succumbs to. The balance between sentiment and deflation is the mechanical dynamic of the story, just as the vision of the golden age is its metaphysical drive. The fat man is an exile (and our spokesman), shut out from living by life. We go on striving to attain our vision but its counterfeit, or travesty of it, is all we may hope for. The fat man is left in a grotesque aloneness: a Garden of Eden from which Eve has eloped with the Serpent. It is all extremely funny, and hauntingly moving.

'The Jar' is a parable on the vanity of human wishes. Its two anti-heroes, Zi' Dima and Don Lollò, have caught sight of themselves in the mirror, and both are slightly mad in contrasting ways. Don Lollò is the artist in administration, who is forced to live in a world of fools, knaves, and accomplished shirkers. Zi' Dima is the artist-as-craftsman, anxious to live by the highest standards of his art, yet continually browbeaten by philistines, who don't know anything about art but are quite sure they know what they like. Or is it—and here come the bogeys they're running away from—that Don Lollò is really a bungler and Zi' Dima a hack pot-patcher? Does it matter? However we assess the disputants, the struggle between Zi' Dima and Don Lollò, which is very funny if you can bear to be human, is a dramatic re-enactment of the perpetual conflict between the creative as inspiration and the creative as organization. Zi' Dima stands for mystery, the hazard of chaos; Don Lollò for certainty, empirical enlightenment. These are the crude oppositions, and they are delightfully modulated by the Greek chorus of farm-workers. The drama has a pleasing suppleness of rhythm which issues, naturally enough, in a bacchanalian dance. Since this is a harvest story fertility triumphs, the dionysiac prevails, and administration is left thoughtfully to pick up the pieces.

Little needs to be said about 'The Tragedy of a Character', except perhaps to stress how skilfully Pirandello has converted the intellect into passion. At one level the story is purely didactic, at another it is a reflection of Pirandello's caring about the human dilemma. As Desmond MacCarthy said of *Six Characters in Search of an Author*, the play built upon this *novella*, '. . . in an odd way he has suggested that the fate of many people is not unlike those of the "Characters" in the play; that many of us are in their predicament, namely, like them, real enough people, for whom fate nevertheless has not written the plays in which we might have played a part.'

'A Call to Duty' is rock-firm in its traditionalism, whether like Ernest Newman you recall its affinities with Donizetti's *Il campanello* or, with David Garnett, think of it immediately after mentioning Boccaccio and Apuleius. Pirandello has a new impress to put on an old story. If virtue is neglected by the beast and turns for solace to man (the idealist), is her adultery so corrupt as to merit the destruction of her respectability? Or is it not, rather, the duty of man (the idealist) to defraud the beast into preserving virtue's reputation? Is there not a magnificent justice (and irony) in such a deception? And is it not extremely human that virtue should innocently, by the detail of her announcement, own up to the ripe gratification her body has known as the beast has ravished her back to chastity?

The dialogue, with its controlled use of the broken sentence and language that seems to rise out of a dream or inward tumult, is among Pirandello's finest. Especially applicable to this story is David Garnett's comment on Pirandello's characters and their relationship with his dialogue: 'Pirandello has the gift of making one know them as though they were one's neighbours. Yet he never breaks the thread of his story to describe them: they come alive in action like characters upon the stage.'

How true, in so completely different a context, is this of 'In the Abyss', an astonishingly early and far-ranging exploration of the subconscious. What impresses most about this story—after we have taken in the assuredness with which Pirandello has distinguished the workings of the subconscious—is the way in which he has correlated the inner and outer lives of his characters, plucking them out of the general whirl (the Traldi–Respi confrontation is a minor Tiresias–Oedipus clash in the sight of the chorus), driving down into them, till an image is forced to the surface. The muck at the bottom of Respi's consciousness is a rotted ideal, and he determines to act upon it. But the object of his pursuit has gone. Hers is a simple (naturalistic) going out, but Respi's movement is extinguished as if it occurred in a dream. The whole atmosphere of the story is one of hallucination, a world of contending shadows indicative of the contradictory layers of identity within the characters.

'The Black Kid' is a tightly-reined (almost demure) and gently comic demolition of foolish human beliefs about certainty. Its placidity of tone is deceptive, however. When one has finished reading the story, one is overwhelmed by the 'I' of the subdued narrative. What appeared to be a struggle between the poetry of Miss Ethel Holloway (stupid girl!) and the bureaucratic prose of Mr. Charles Trockley (who likes his poetry to have a healthy respect for rules—and none of that inspiration nonsense!), turns out to be a courteous discussion between Pirandello and us. Must every kid turn into a stinking old billy-goat, must every vision of the idyllic world (when it is young and innocent) decay into the 'realism' of being 'grown-up'? Behind the story lies an early poem, *Quasi cristallo liquido,* in which the profanation of the Temple and the 'araba cantilena' of the goat-herd (seen as the renunciation of sacred ideals) are juxtaposed with his seeking forgetfulness in the sea off Porto Empedocle. He wants to forget 'the sad evil of living'; for today the vulgar triumph, and the cult of eternal beauty—that divine ideal of ours—is dying. The formulation here may be romantic and adolescent; the central notion persisted always in Pirandello, as we shall see when we arrive at the last stories.

Pirandello's answer is the 'yes-and-no' of 'Signora Frola and her Son-in-Law, Signor Ponza'. Reality and truth can only be what you make them. Never be so unkind, though, as not to tread compassionately in the world of another person's dreams. What are facts? What meaning should we concede them? By what right do we grub around for facts, when other people's personal tragedies are involved? Is a working fiction more or less valid than an empty fact? Must each of us make his private world acceptable to the majority? Is the individual doomed to persecution by society and to being bullied into conformity? Is suspicion the farthest that society can reach in the direction of imagination?

There is something of the burlesque in Pirandello's treatment of his story. It is frankly polemical: we are an audience being harangued, cajoled, and entertained. We are having our heads talked off. And all the time things and people are moving at speed. Essentially, there are two intersecting patterns: the frantic rushing around of the chorus and the linked complementary orbits (the 'allow-us-to-explain' circuits) of Signora Frola and Signor Ponza. The tale explodes with motion. It is terrifying, this inane frenzy of ordinary living, swirling about the tragic dignity of the Frola-Ponza universe. It is the sickness of our civilization.

'The Man with the Flower in his Mouth' is, I think, unmatched among Pirandello's short stories, and great by any standards. Seldom can language have been so natural and so precise. Only a writer deeply aware of the processes of thought and image association could achieve such apparent casualness, at the same time as he exposed the desolation of two such divergent characters as the Man and the Other, and the annihilation of a third (the wife), who has not a word to say. It is not easy to pick out where the naturalistic fades into the incantational. Partly as a result of the milieu, partly as a result of the obvious tension informing the very first speech by the man with the flower in his mouth, we are taken straightaway into the brooding territory of loss. We shall not know until the last speech what it is we are mourning, but all the time our grief is personal.

The detail of the woman peering round the corner is autobiographical. Pirandello's wife would come and spy on him as he left the teacher-training college for women at which he lectured. The concept of the preliminary visit by death occurs in *Volare* (1907), while a different treatment of the flower and inevitable death link is to be found in *Di sera, un geranio* (1934), one of the so-called surrealist *novelle,* of which 'The Visit' is a major example.

The man with the flower in his mouth and Nicola Petix in 'Destruction of the Man' are nearly related, but whereas Petix destroys the grotesque hope for the future begotten by others, the Man chooses the alternative commitment, pursuing the logic of illusion past the breaking-point, to a comprehension that even the act of destroying (as, to be sure, *all* action) is futile. Throughout the work of Pirandello this existentialist dualism prevails; some of his characters opt for the illusory form of death in suicide—Diego Bronner in *E due!*, Tommaso Corsi in *Il dovere del medico* and Eleonora Bandi in *Scialle nero* among them; others—Luca Lèuci in *Il marito di mia moglie,* the young woman in *Spunta un giorno,* and Jacob Shwarb in *Una sfida* come to mind—either illogically refrain from killing themselves or someone else, or will their own survival in the moment of attempted suicide.

This is the dispute with life at its most ferocious, the questioning of the vision. The man with the flower in his mouth, having resisted self-destruction, goes on to capture the idyll of the apricot season, and the vision of the other customer's wife and daughters, dressed in blue and white, seated in the shade of a tree in a green field. For a few suspended and enchanted moments he has regained the earthly paradise. Petix is impelled to murder by an overwhelming sense of loss: the filth and animality of life in the tenement, following upon the barrenness of his relationship with his father, are a perpetual reminder of their antithesis, the golden age from which he is excluded. He is one of Pirandello's beggars—like the man we know as Henry IV, the boy in the *Sei personaggi in cerca d'autore,* Lillina in 'Fear', and the eponymous heroine of *Candelora*—who, asking for admittance into the lives of others, into life itself, are demolished, often by being driven mad, frequently by being forced into suicide.

'Destruction of the Man' is an inverted utopian story. It is also representative of a group of tales in which horror or revulsion finds relief in a horrifying action or horrible event. 'Puberty' belongs to this sector of Pirandello's work, as do *La mosca* and *E due!*, while 'Cinci' is clearly not too far removed from it. The form of the *novella,* reminiscent of *Notizie del mondo* (1901), where an old man writes to an old friend now dead, is a dramatic monologue, and the introduction of the various elements and the varying methods by which they are deployed, are strictly governed by the exigencies of theatrical pace. There is an all but cinematic or televisual use of close-up and panorama, and the setting side by side of the general chaos and degradation of post-unification Rome and the waste land of Petix's life foreshadows the work of recent Italian film-makers. Finally, there is his success in implanting the voice of the speaker inside us, so that we cannot avoid participating in the denouement. This is brought off faultlessly, with something of the unbearable understatement of the last lines of 'The Man with the Flower in his Mouth'.

'Puberty' and 'Cinci', separated by six years, are complementary experiences: the latter in part autobiographical, the former another example of his capacity for identifying himself with how a woman is feeling. (The Stepdaughter, Lillina Fabris, and Donata Genzi in *Trovarsi* are major parallels.) Both tales make use of interior dialogue, both use death as the answer to the inquest of the trap, both presuppose that there is somewhere a lost world which we are trying to regain. Some of the slighter touches are the most revelatory and the most poignant: the dropping of the books (with the different-yet-same meaning in both cases); the faltering on both their parts of the desire to probe the mysteries surrounding mother and father; *her* little girl's dress; *his* short trousers; *her* insistence on being called Dreetta; *his* standing under the overflow. Both stories may properly be included among his most successful explorations of the subconscious, and it is well to remark on what images he lays his accent in the secret lives of these adolescents, and with what they identify themselves in their fantasy worlds. Like all Pirandellian characters, they are constructing themselves: Dreetta, with her vision of the Good Old Man who will rescue her and marry her to (a provisional) Prince Charming; Cinci, freeing himself from his clumsy body to unite himself, godlike, with the moon and the sky, repeating, in fact, that unification with anotherness which is so vital to 'The Man with the Flower in his Mouth'.

'All Passion Spent' is a critical story: Pirandello's recognition that his work as a *novelliere* coincided with his work as a dramatist. Its content is an unusual blend of Pirandellian elements, reaching back to 'A Dream of Christmas' (and into his own personal absorption in the Crucifixion), and into everything that made the Stepdaughter. Like *Leonora, addio!* (1910), it exploits our enduring affection for the older, more melodramatic operas. Structurally, this is a journey-vision, borne on a flow of one person's speech, a flow which is never impeded by its having to carry so many different levels of so many people's experience. As we should expect, the inset scenes—the grasping and the loss of hope, separation and death (the double dying for her of her child)—come as natural caesuras, fully co-ordinated with the narrative. The use of the mute chorus is fine stage-craft. (It is, of course, the same chorus of phantoms as fills the tenement where Nicola Petix lives and as constitutes the gathering in *C'è qualcuno che ride,* that hallucinatory story of 1934.)

'All Passion Spent' closes on an impossible dream, a driving back of death, where death has already struck. We have a similar practice in 'The Visit', carried out by completely different means, and stating quite another atmosphere. Basically, it is Pirandello's poetic creation of his own earthly paradise. Anna Wheil is the unattainable lady, Beatrice, and the physical embodiment of longed-for sexual reality. She is a Galatea—and I find it significant that Pirandello should, in an interview with Cavicchioli in 1936, have recalled Nietzsche's saying that the Greeks set up white statues against the black abyss, in order to hide it. I have no space fully to develop my view that this vision is the key to his work, but I should like to say that I believe that Pirandello compounded his own sexual aspirations with an almost tragic assimilation of himself into the mythology, still Greek in what matters, of his native Sicily. Anna Wheil is the same incidence of chance as Jenny Schulz-Lander (the girl whom he loved at Bonn): a crisis in living. To Jenny Schulz-Lander he dedicated his *Pasqua di Gea* with an epigraph from Jaufré Rudel—he could hardly be more explicit. The search for ultimate sexual identity began long before his stay in Germany, of course, and in the early writings it is almost crudely coincident with his fusion of himself and the myths of Gaea, Night, and the Moon.

The creed of arranged marriages militated against attaining sexual totality in wedlock. A natural puritanism made it impossible for Pirandello to seek it carnally elsewhere. It became a dream, therefore. Either you live your life, he used to say, or you write it. Certainly, this quintessence of life was something that he wrote. Like D. H. Lawrence, he was mother-fixated, and the incest-prohibition inevitably created its own exile. His earthy paradise of the remembered desire to possess the mother became the pursuit of the unattainable Lady. This is why the landscape of his dream is filled with images of motherhood and the child's dependence upon the mother. The breasts of Anna Wheil—and the cancer[1] which destroys them is undoubtedly the incest prohibition—are the breasts of the mother. Cinci, it will be remembered, rejecting the blubbery mass of the breast of the woman in the street, evokes his mother's breasts and, by association, the paradise in the country from which

[1] Pirandello may have been drawing upon the legend of Ramon Lull.

he is now shut out. (Is it altogether irrelevant to recall how Pirandello told Antonelli of his being deprived of his mother's milk? As a result of possible danger to her husband from Cola Camizzi—whose name is used as a synonym for evil in another 'breast' story, *L'altro figlio*—she could no longer feed him. He was given a wet-nurse, who one night rolled upon him and came near to suffocating him with her vast breast.) The green light playing upon the breasts of Anna Wheil is not only a memory of the green trees and grass of their day of acceptance (recognition in hope, that is), but also the light of a dream. Finally, it is the moon, Diana–Persephone.

I suspect that, for Pirandello, the unattainable Lady merges into Death the mistress: to love is to die, and to love incestuously is to bring horror into the violence of death. That the Oedipus legend recurs in his work—Dr. Hinkfuss can be no accident of naming—is an unambiguous pointer to his preoccupation with incest leading to destruction. In its primitive form in his writings the desired-but-unattainable is unequivocally identified with death. (We have only to think of the stylized image of Jenny Schulz-Lander in VI of *Pasqua di Gea*—the 'light-bringing' maiden who is his bride, flying before him, leading him to the grave.) There is a parable of sexual revulsion here as well, and one that appears to be related to the coital traumata of marriage arising otherwise than from passion.

'The Tortoise' is another such parable. In such tales as *Scialle nero* and *Prima notte* we have fables of aversion treated as meditations of the love–death twinning. This story is rather an exquisitely intoned threnody on 'the chilly pretence in the bedroom'. (We hardly need to be told that the tortoise is an erotic symbol for Pirandello, belonging to the slightly nonsensical—in the same way as this story is nonsensical—poem *La mia vicina su 'l mattin d'aprile*.) There is strength in this tale, both in the author's duologue with his reader, and in the wonderment at and discovery of life by Mr. Myshkow. There is so much of Pirandello in him, with his child-like candour, and his perturbation at how *old* children are nowadays. He is comically (so gravely) concerned with the vexing problem of our multiple identity. Where *has* one been since one was a child? Has one *really* dreamt all one's dreams with this peculiar body, with its inexorable rhythm of excretion? What is reality and what is illusion? (There's no pedantry in Mr. Myshkow; these are the stumbling demands of an apologetically ordinary man.) Who is this Mrs. Myshkow with whom he's been living? What *is* a wife? He begot these children—yes, but in what way do they connect with him? And love, affection, compassion, tenderness, sensitivity? Life is dream, the dream of a day—a day that goes by.

'A Day Goes By' is pure allegory, an intensification of the whole compass of the real life of Pirandello. Its events are the *meanings* of the things that have happened to him: his movement through life has been from the chaos of error (and Pirandello never ceased to pun on his birthplace), the exile of society, to love in the tomb. His children, it is noticeable, are distinct from the ideal relationship with the beloved. She is the *fidanzata,* the promised bride of *Pasqua di Gea,* and the bed on which they have been united is the grave he foresaw. He is now old, but his child's eyes still scrutinize ironically and with paradoxical hope the stages of his journey and the condition of man. The tale is a direct conversation with the reader, a running commentary on life seen for the wandering and inquiry that it is. Technically, the eeriness of its time-suspended world, and the trance-like precise imprecision of outline of the owner of the restaurant, the clerks in the bank, the light that scurried to the train and away again (with no apparent agent to direct it)—all are brought off with complete success. There is an unflawed sincerity in their control. They *belong,* in fact. We are given the nakedness of the subconscious, human and vulnerable.

The outer world of Pirandello's stories—the appearance of its reality—has a deceptive monotony and a deceptive variety. The monotony is the mask which society exacts from us; the variety is the pathetic series of fragmentary masks in which we strut about the world: the peasant, the clerk, the editor, the landowner, the prostitute, the pseudo-veteran of Garibaldi's campaigns, the member of Parliament, the submissive daughter, the criminal, the usurer.

. . . From this point of view, Pirandello has evolved an imposing range of characters. They are immaculately distinguished, for all the complexities of their interrelationships. But real character resides for him in the unique journey of search and realization, and to this the outer form is largely irrelevant. These people are compellingly attractive and interesting, of course, in their worldly shapes and, though I myself feel this to be absurdly beside the Pirandellian point, can be enjoyed as, say, idiosyncratic doctors, insurance agents in jeopardy, baffled vice-consuls, lawyers with family problems, civil servants, aliens, and sailors. They are answers you put up when you are asked the question, 'What are you doing?' (How right it is that Pirandello should give this question to Signorina Ely Facelli's parrot in *Giustino Roncella nato Boggiòlo*. Back come the replies of a morning, the decent ones called aloud, the more obscene muttered.) If we can say something like this, we can pretend for an instant that we are not isolated by our aloneness, we can shield ourselves from the *infinita vanità del tutto*.

But we can only evade our farcical tragedy for moments at a time.

The literary and philosophical influences on Pirandello are the ones we should expect: Dante, Boccaccio, Ariosto, Machiavelli, Foscolo, Manzoni, Leopardi, Carducci, Verga, Capuana, and De Roberto; Cervantes, Calderon, Shakespeare, Sterne, Ibsen, Flaubert, Hoffman, Zola, and De Maupassant; Vico, Kant, Schopenhauer, and Nietzsche. There is something from Goethe (whom he translated), from Lessing, from Von Chamisso, and from Unamuno. Major influences are exerted by relatively minor writers: Marchesini with his *Le finzioni dell'anima;* Binet and his *Les altérations de la personnalité*; and Theodor Lipps with his *Komik und Humor*. Finally, never completely absent are the pressures of Bergson, Richter, Hegel, Heine, Herbarth, and Friedrich Schlegel, while there is a constant permeation of the thought of the pre-Socratics (especially Gorgias of Lentini) and Plato.

The influences are not the writer, however. Pirandello is himself, one of the most distinctive and characteristic voices of our age; the only great writer, I would suggest, who fully coheres with the relativistic propositions of modern science and modern philosophy. He provides their aesthetic analogue.

A word about the original texts. As I stress in 'The Collections of the Short Stories' (pp. 237–241), we badly need a critical edition. Luigi Pirandello revised his work steadily, so that an early story may be very different in the final edition. He also failed to notice printing errors, and the *novella* may have acquired some unwished-for oddities as the years have gone by.

A regret. I am sorry that I have had to exclude some of the longer stories, such as *Lontano* (of which there exists an unpublished translation by C. K. Scott Moncrieff) and *Pena di vivere così*. Either of these, I felt, would shift the balance of the book dangerously in one direction. With *Pena di vivere così* two other considerations came in: the story was never completely revised—should I translate the first text or the second, where there is a marked disjunction between the parts?—and was always slightly uneasy as a *novella*; the logical thing for the reader to do was to go on to it *after* this volume, and this he could do, since it was included in the Duplaix collection.

The stories are presented in chronological order. Readers anxious to enjoy the mature Pirandello will read the last tales first; for those who wish to follow his development I recommend a straight read-through. Here are the essential data on the *novelle*. The sign *R* means that the story was revised for the Omnibus volumes.

*The Stories*

1884 *Capannetta* (THE LITTLE HUT).
1894 *I galletti del bottaio* (THE COOPER'S COCKERELS).
1896 *Sogno di Natale* (A DREAM OF CHRISTMAS).
1897 *Le dodici lettere* (TWELVE LETTERS).
*La paura* (FEAR).
1902 *Amicissimi* (THE BEST OF FRIENDS).
1905 *Acqua amara* (BITTER WATERS).

1909 *La giara* (THE JAR).
1911 *La tragedia d'un personaggio* (THE TRAGEDY OF A CHARACTER). *R.*
?1911 *Richiamo all'obbligo* (A CALL TO DUTY).
1913 *Nel gorgo* (IN THE ABYSS).
*Il capretto nero* (THE BLACK KID). *R.*
?1915 *La signora Frola e il signor Ponza, suo genero* (SIGNORA FROLA AND HER SON-IN-LAW, SIGNOR PONZA).
?1918 *La morte addosso* (THE MAN WITH THE FLOWER IN HIS MOUTH).
1921 *La distruzione dell'uomo* (DESTRUCTION OF THE MAN). *R.*
1926 *Pubertà* (PUBERTY). *R.*
1932 *Cinci* (CINCI).
1933 *Sgombero* (ALL PASSION SPENT).
1935 *Visita* (THE VISIT).
1936 *La tartaruga* (THE TORTOISE).
*Una giornata* (A DAY GOES BY).

# BIOGRAPHY

Luigi Pirandello was born on 28 June 1867 at Caos, a villa[1] near Girgenti, the modern Agrigento, in Sicily. The house belonged to the Ricci-Gramitto family, and the Pirandellos had retreated there during the cholera epidemic of that year. Luigi's father, Stefano, had served with Garibaldi in 1860 and 1862, and on his return to Girgenti had married, in November 1863, Caterina, the sister of his comrade-in-arms, Rocco Ricci-Gramitto. It was from this uncle that Pirandello gained much of the material which he later used in his Sicilian stories. The elder Pirandello wished his son to have a technical education but, with the connivance of his mother, Luigi was able to study Latin secretly and soon to qualify for admission to the classical stream. At nineteen he fell in love with and became engaged to his cousin Lina. In the same year, 1886, after having worked for three months in the family sulphur business, he persuaded his father to allow him to study letters at the University of Palermo, from where he proceeded, in 1887, to the University of Rome. Here he had the good fortune to work under and gain the friendship of the eminent scholar Monaci, who later, when an irreparable quarrel broke out between Pirandello and the Professor of Latin, counselled and assisted the young man to transfer to Bonn—which he did in October 1889[2]—and there to complete his studies under the distinguished philologist Wendelin Foerster. It was at Bonn that he met and fell in love with Jenny Schulz-Lander, to whom he dedicated his second volume of poems *Pasqua di Gea* (1891).

In 1891 he gained his doctorate with a thesis on the dialect of

[1] The villa, which lies out towards Porto Empedocle (see 'The Black Kid', pp. 132–40), was partly destroyed during the last war. There is now a very interesting museum at the restored villa, with a fine collection of Pirandello material.

[2] He registered at the University on 6 November 1889, according to Mathias Adank (*Luigi Pirandello e i suoi rapporti col mondo tedesco,* Druck: Druckereigenossenschaft Aarau, 1948, p. 10).

Girgenti *(Laute und Lautentwickelung der Mundart von Girgenti),* and after a further period at Bonn, possibly as lector in Italian,[1] during which he fell ill with diphtheria and pneumonia, he returned to Sicily. By 1893 his engagement to Lina was broken off, and in that year he settled in Rome, where he soon became a prominent member of the group of writers and artists who revolved around Luigi Capuana, the novelist and critic and one of Italy's most accomplished and creative naturalistic writers, who, as Pirandello later told Filippo Súrico,[2] was responsible for his seriously beginning to write prose. It was not long before he was considered to be one of the more challenging of the anti-D'Annunzian young authors.

A disciple, but no imitator, of the great verist playwright, short-story writer, and novelist, Giovanni Verga, whose compassionate and clear-headed preoccupation with the agony of man caught in the trap of living he shares, Pirandello impatiently and with fierce irony rejected D'Annunzio's cult of the superman—though not himself uninfluenced by Nietzsche—and the austere purity and unrhetorical dignity of his style are in vigorous contrast with the morbid sensuality, the exoticism, and the (all too often) windy rhetoric of the older writer. D'Annunzio, and frequently magnificently so, is the poet of sensation, while Pirandello is the poet of experience.

His first published work, *Mal giocondo* (1889), was a collection of poems, many of them written when he was fifteen or sixteen, very reminiscent of Foscolo, Leopardi, and Carducci; it was followed by other volumes of poetry, by the publication of his thesis, and by a handful of novels, a flood of short stories, and a number of critical essays.[3] Of his novels, *Il fu Mattia Pascal* (1904) is undoubtedly the most important. A moving and highly original work, it is Pirandello's first major statement of the themes of being and seeming and the nature of personal identity which, under a multitude of aspects, he was to develop with such power and cogency in his plays. From it may be said to stem the entire

[1] Adank (p. 80) suggests that this is doubtful. There is no record at Bonn of his having held such a post.

[2] cf. *Saggi, poesie, scritti varii*, ed. cit., pp. 1246–7.

[3] See the list of works at the end of the book.

*grostesque* movement in Italian drama,[1] a theatre which was to find its natural fulfilment in the plays of Pirandello himself, as it was to deduce its aesthetic from his essay *L'umorismo.*

The year 1894 brought his marriage to Antonietta Portulano, the daughter of his father's partner. Though very much a marriage determined by the commercial interests of the parents, it was none-theless a happy one during the first few years and three children (Stefano, Lietta, and Fausto) were born. Then came financial disaster, with the flooding of the sulphur mines in which Antonietta's dowry had been invested, together with her father-in-law's capital. She succumbed to paresis of the legs and only began to walk again after some six months. Worse, paranoia supervened; she became steadily more and more insane, attacking Pirandello constantly with jealous outbursts (none of them at all founded in reason) and until 1919, when she entered a nursing-home, made his life an unceasing torment. She died in 1959.

This sudden reduction in 1903 from middle-class ease was doubly crucial: Pirandello became dependent upon his earnings as a novelist, reviewer, and short-story writer, where previously he had been free to compose what and when he liked; and the physical tie with his wife was severed. Her revulsion from him, always potential in their relationship because of the intensity of her association with her father, not only confirmed his personal puritanism (and it is important to bear this in mind when appraising his love for Marta Abba in later years), but also brought him to concentrate in his work on the themes of exile and the search for the unattainable woman—the 'immaculate whore', the mother–mistress, the '*faithful* adultress' (as he calls Francesca da Rimini, from whom so much derives in his *opera*).

His first play, *La morsa,*[2] was published in 1898, but it was not until 1915 that he began to write seriously for the theatre. His decision to work more largely in this new medium was due in part

[1] Its first statement was probably Luigi Chiarelli's brilliant (if slightly too sentimental) and satirical comedy *La maschera e il volto* (1916). The poet of the movement and a dramatist of strength is Pirandello's friend and disciple Rosso di San Secondo. Particularly remarkable is his *Marionette, che passione!* (1918).

[2] Derived from 'Fear' (see p. 35 and pp. 36–46).

to the persuasion of Nino Martoglio, the Sicilian playwright; in part to the exhortation of Angelo Musco, the Sicilian actor; but chiefly, I suspect, to his desperate need to find relief from his personal grief, which had become more acute with the capture by the Austrians of his elder son Stefano in November 1915, the illness of Fausto, and the death of his mother in the same year. Though the plays of this period include the remarkable *Liolà* (1916), with its pungent re-evocation of Machiavellian comedy, and *Così è (se vi pare)* (1917)—a savage and tender confrontation of social and authentic man in a theatrically accomplished farce-tragedy—it was not until 1921 that he achieved any real success. The *Sei personaggi in cerca d'autore*—notwithstanding the uproar of the Rome first night, an occasion comparable to the legendary *première* of *Hernani*—rapidly followed by *Enrico IV*, made him famous all over the world, and also made it possible for him to give up academic work. (For poverty had obliged him to devote long hours to lecturing in a teacher-training college for women, a form of drudgery which is amply satirized in his earlier writings.)

From 1923 Pirandello was unceasingly on the move, travelling throughout Europe and to the Americas, either to attend other people's productions of his plays or, for a while, to present his own interpretations of them. Not infrequently, he would stage a postlude of discussion and debate with the audience. (When C. B. Cochran gave him a short season at the New Oxford Theatre in 1925 the discussion seems to have taken place between parts I and II of *Six Characters in Search of an Author*. It was probably during this visit that E. Rowley Smart painted his portrait.) His gifts as a dramatist were greatly enhanced by his being a born producer, as his work with the Teatro d'Arte, based on the Sala Odescalchi at Rome, made abundantly clear. Here Pirandello was trying to create something like a National Theatre. Inevitably, artistic achievement was paralleled by financial collapse. After three years' activity the company was dissolved in 1928.

The next years—indeed, from now till shortly before his death—see Pirandello as a voluntary exile from Italy, spending much of his time in Germany and in France. His love for Marta Abba, his leading lady and the woman by whom so many of his later heroines are inspired, did little to mitigate his sense of annihilation. There is no reason to doubt his own assertion that his relationship with her was that of father and daughter. Certainly, deep as was his affection for her, and strong the bond between them, nothing could modify his sense of aloneness, of the imperative need to spend his last days as a wanderer upon the face of the earth. As he told his daughter in a letter of 30 July 1931, 'A home, a country—these are no longer for me. My spirit is now estranged from everything and no longer finds any point of contact with anything or with anybody.' On 15 May he had written to her, 'Death doesn't frighten me, because I've been ready for it for a long time now, just as I've been ready for everything in life. It's a very bitter serenity, a conquest achieved at the cost of having accepted everything. And I no longer see liberation [anywhere], not even in death. . . .'

Pirandello's encounters with Hollywood—from one of which came the Greta Garbo *As You Desire Me*—had no cheering effect on him. He accepted the cinema, wrote for it, and was a perceptive student of it as an art form. His work lends itself to translation into film and, indeed, for television.[1] (In fact, the first play ever televised in this country was Pirandello's *The Man with the Flower in his Mouth,* put out by the B.B.C. on 14 July 1930.[2]) His repudiation of Hollywood is an abhorrence of the industry, not the proposition supposedly justifying the factories. We gather from Vittorini that he found the abortive discussions with Selznick (over a possible filming of the *Sei personaggi in cerca d'autore*) ample substantiation of his mistrust.

This was in the summer of 1935. The previous year he had been awarded the Nobel Prize for Literature, and on 10 December 1936 he died in Rome. His last wishes were typical of the radiant austerity governing his life. He asked that the utmost simplicity should be observed at his funeral, that he should go naked out of the world, and that he should be cremated. Against the pomp that

[1] I have wondered how much this may be due to his exceptional gifts as a painter. Something of the quality of his writing undoubtedly resides in his ability to put thought into pictures of rugged complexity. For his portrait of Emilia Frateili see *Stand,* vol. 5, no. 3, November 1961, p. 35.

[2] For a photograph of the cast and production team see *Stand,* cit., p. 31.

might have been visited upon him he asked for '*The hearse, the horse, the drive—nothing more.*'

In a way these last wishes provide an answer to a question which must always arise in connexion with Pirandello, coming to fame as he did at the time of the Fascist ascendancy. He joined the party, he became one of Mussolini's Academicians, and in 1935 he gave his Nobel medal to assist the war effort against Ethiopia. We know he detested Mussolini and challenged Fascist officials. His self-exile was in part determined by his need to escape from Fascist Italy. The wishes he promulgated for his own funeral deliberately denied the Fascists an opportunity to use him for their own greater glory. I think all may be resolved by appreciating just how innocent Pirandello was. The son and nephew of *garibaldini,* he felt bound in all patriotism to help in what many honourable people saw as an essential moral reconstruction. (Pirandello's early work is often a horrified picture of the moral collapse after unification had been attained.) He was no politician, however, and could find no organizational correlative for the ever-increasing aesthetic revulsion he experienced. Certainly, his work never coheres with Fascist doctrine. Not seldom does it speak out actively against cherished Fascist concepts and practices. For Pirandello human beings mattered as themselves, for it is finally as themselves that they suffer.

There are few events of the traditional kind in Pirandello's life. Rather does he live according to the precepts of his writing: events are the discoveries of the mind, the stages of becoming, the awarenesses of being for an instant. It was his contention that he had no life outside his writing, and that, like so many of his characters, he could sadly affirm that for himself he was nobody. A significant entry is to be found in his private notebook for 1933–34: 'There is somebody who's living my life. And I know nothing about him.'

# Short Stories

# THE LITTLE HUT

*A Sicilian Sketch*

This story was published in the *Gazzetta del Popolo della Domenica* (Turin) on 1 June 1884, when Pirandello was in his seventeenth year. It is his earliest surviving known prose work. His indebtedness to Giovanni Verga is manifest—that his hero is called Jeli[1] simply underlines that debt. More important, of course, is that the young Pirandello should have to so marked an extent absorbed the implicit teaching of Verga, and, at the same time, begun to speak as himself. *Capannetta* was first reprinted, with a note by Aurelio Navarria in *Narrativa* (IV, 4 December 1959). It is now included in Vol. VI of the *Opere*. (*Saggi, Poesie, Scritti Varii, a cura di Manlio Lo Vecchio-Musti,* Milano-Verona, Mondadori, 1960, pp. 1047–50.



[1] cf. *Jeli il pastore*, by Giovanni Verga.

# THE LITTLE HUT

## *A Sicilian Sketch*

NEVER before had anyone seen such a dawn.

A small girl came out of the little hut. Her dishevelled hair was straggling over her forehead, and she was wearing a faded red kerchief on her head. As she buttoned up her shabby little dress she yawned, still entangled in the net of sleep, and stared straight in front of her. Far into the distance she gazed, her eyes wide-open, just as if she could see nothing at all.

Far, far away, a long fire-red strip wove bizarrely in and out of the vast emerald green expanse of trees, which vanished at last in the distance.

The whole sky was strewn with little yellow clouds that flamed like crocuses.

The girl went on her way, heedless of it all. A little hill rose up on the right. Gradually its slope became gentler and gentler, until suddenly, there beneath her gaze lay displayed an immense flood of water, the sea.

The little girl seemed struck and deeply moved by that scene, and she stood there looking at the boats as they flew over the waves, dyed a pale yellow by the morning sun.

It was completely silent. The almost imperceptible gentle night breeze was still fluttering the air, and making the sea shudder. Slowly, very slowly, the air became perfumed with the delicate smell of earth.

After a short while the little girl turned away. She wandered off through the still uncertain light, reached the top of the cliff and sat down. Absent-mindedly she looked at the green valley, laughing there below her, and began to sing a little song softly to herself. Suddenly, however, as if something had just struck her, she stopped her sing-song, and shouted at the top of her voice, 'Zi' Jeli! Hey, Zi' Jee...!'

And a rough voice answered from the valley, 'Hey-ey!'

'Come up here. The boss wants you!'

Meanwhile, the little girl, her head lowered, was on her way back to the hut. Jeli had come up from down below, still not really awake, with his jacket over his left shoulder and his pipe stuck in his mouth—he always had that pipe clenched between his teeth.

The moment he got inside the hut, he said good morning to Papà Camillo. Malia, the land-agent's elder daughter, gazed intently into his face, her eyes like arrows, so penetrating that they would have pierced through stone.

Jeli returned her look.

Papà Camillo was a stub of a man, as huge in girth as a barrel. Malia this morning had the face of one of Paolo Veronese's women, and in her eyes you could clearly read the blessed simplicity of her heart.

'Listen, Jeli,' said Papà Camillo, 'I want you to get the fruit ready. We've got the gentry coming from the big city. Pick out some good stuff, eh? Because, if you don't—well, as sure as there's a living God . . . !'

'Huh, the usual old guff!' Jeli replied. 'You know very well that you've got no need to try that sort of thing on me! On *me*!'

'Meanwhile,' went on Papà Camillo, taking him by the arm and leading him out of the hut, 'Meanwhile, if you ever get the urge again to. . . . No, I won't say it. You know perfectly well what I'm talking about.'

Jeli just stood there, quite dumbfounded.

Papà Camillo went on down into the valley.

There was no getting the better of him in that argument, so the young man went back up to the hut.

'We're done for now!' said Malia.

'You're a fool!' said Jeli. 'If we can't get what we want by fair means. . . .'

'Oh, Jeli! What are you hinting at, Jeli?'

'*What?* Do you mean to say you don't understand? We'll run away together.'

'Run away together?' said the girl, surprised.

'Or . . .' added Jeli—and he put the shining crescent of the sickle about his neck.

'Oh, my God!' exclaimed Malia, and her shudder seemed to run right through her body.

'Till this evening, then. Seven o'clock. Be ready!' said Jeli, and disappeared.

The girl gave a cry.

It was getting dark.

The appointed hour was approaching and Malia, her face very, very pale and her lips like two dried rose-petals, was seated outside the door. She was watching the waves of darkness engulf the green plain and when, in the distance, the church bell in the village rang out the Ave Maria, she prayed too.

That solemn silence seemed like a divine prayer on the part of Nature.

She'd been waiting there a long time when Jeli came. He'd left his pipe behind this time. He was more passionate and very resolute.

'Is it time already?' asked Malia, trembling.

'A quarter of an hour either way. It's all time gained,' replied Jeli.

'But——'

'Hell's bells! Look, I think it's high time you stopped that *butting* of yours. Haven't you realized, dear heart, that it's a question of——?'

'Oh yes, I realize that. Yes, I know only too well that it's a question of——!' Malia hastened to reply. She still couldn't reconcile herself to what he'd so ill-advisedly resolved to do. In the meantime, a distant whistle told Jeli that the carriage was ready.

'Come on! Let's get moving!' he said. 'Don't look so glum, Maliella! Out there there's a whole world of joy awaiting us.' Malia gave a cry. Jeli took her by the arm, rushed her along the path. The moment he set foot in the dog-cart he said, 'As fast as you can go!'

The two young people clasped one another very tightly and kissed one another for the first time in freedom.

At nine o'clock Papà Camillo came back up from the valley and gave a tremendously loud whistle. The little girl came rushing out, and before she'd got to where he was, he asked her, 'Where's Jeli? Have you seen Jeli?'

'Oh, Papà Camillo! Papà Camillo!' she panted, her voice sounding choked.

'What are you trying to tell me, you skinny little misery?' roared Papà Camillo.

'Jeli's . . . run away . . . with Maliella. . . .'

And a hoarse, savage sound burst from Papà Camillo's throat. He rushed on up the path, flew into the hut, picked up his shotgun, and fired into the air. The little girl looked at him, stunned.

It was a strange spectacle, the mad fury of that man. A frantic laugh burst shatteringly from his lips, and died away in a strangled rattle. He no longer knew what he was doing. Quite beside himself with rage, he set fire to the little hut, as if intent on destroying everything that reminded him of his daughter. Then off he dashed, furiously, shot-gun in hand, along the path. Perhaps he hoped to find the lovers somewhere along it.

The blood-red tongues of fire reached up to the sky through the gloom of the evening.

Smoke rose up from the little black hut. Smoke and a steady crackling—just as if the hut were saying good-bye to the little girl with that persistent crackle, as she stood there staring at it, pale and horrified. You got the impression that her every thought was following that column of smoke, as it mounted up from her modest home. Smoke rose up from the little black hut. Smoke and a steady crackling. And the little girl stood there, not saying a word, her gaze fixed on the sombre ashes.

# THE COOPER'S COCKERELS

*I galletti del bottaio* first appeared in Luigi Capuana's children's paper *Cenerentola,*[1] 23 September 1894. It was not reprinted in any of the subsequent collections of *novelle*—indeed, it is very much *sui generis*—and is now to be found in the appendix of short stories in Vol. II of the *Opere* (*Novelle per un anno,* Vol. II, Milano-Verona, Mondadori, 1957). We are indebted to Manlio Lo Vecchio-Musti for tracking down this *novella.*



[1] *Cinderella*

# THE COOPER'S COCKERELS

THE wife of Marchica the cooper had one overwhelming desire: to be allowed—just *once,* at least!—to have her Christmas dinner alone with her husband. Or dinner on Easter Sunday, for that matter, or on New Year's Day, or at Carnival time. No, whatever the festive occasion, it was his custom to gather round his table hordes of relatives and friends. Very much to his wife's regret. Indeed, very much in spite of her wishes.

This particular year the good woman had reared two fine cockerels in readiness for Christmas, and on Christmas Eve she said, showing them to her husband, 'Look! Don't you think they're fine birds? If you'll give me your word that you won't ask anybody to come and have dinner with us tomorrow, I'll twist their necks for them, and then you'll see what a wonderful cook I am! I'll give you a dainty dish fit for a king!'

The cooper gave his promise, and his wife was happy.

Next day came, and the cooper, dressed in his Sunday best, went to say good-bye to his wife before setting out for Mass.

'Oh, no, dear husband! Just you hold on a moment! You're not setting foot outside this house today! As sure as I'm standing here, if you so much as poke your nose out of doors you'll come in again with somebody in tow that I'll have to feed! One Mass will be quite enough for you. Tonight's!'

'But, I promise you——'

'I'm not listening to any promises! Come on, hand over that hat! It's staying under lock and key today!'

The cooper heaved a sigh and handed his hat over to his wife.

As he sat there in the little kitchen, and gazed admiringly at his wife, while she moved about with even more than usual briskness, her face flushed with the heat thrown up by the fire under the stewpot and her tiny waist nipped in by her new dress with the floral design on it—she was wearing an old tablecloth over it to keep it clean—he thought to himself, 'She's quite right, poor dear woman! It's very pleasant being on our own, just the two of us together, cosy and intimate, without lots of strange faces round the dinner-table. People who keep you in an awful state of suspense, wondering whether you've satisfied all their particular tastes. Ah, she's a dear woman, my wife, a darling! And it's just as if I'm aware of the fact for the first time, today. And, when all's said and done, what *is* it she's asking of me? She finds pleasure in being alone with me, celebrating Christmas with only me for company. Oh, she's a dear! She *is* a dear!'

And deep down inside himself he repeated his promise never again in the future to make his wife unhappy by inviting relatives or friends at Christmas or at any of the other times.

But the Devil, on this occasion, as always, couldn't forbear from poking his tail in. When the woman had been out shopping on Christmas Eve, getting the things she needed for her special dish, she'd forgotten the parsley. The ha'p'orth of parsley.

'Oh, husband dear! Now what shall I do?'

'Give me the ha'penny, I'll go and get it!'

'Oh, no! *You're* not going! I've already told you once, you're not setting foot outside this house today!'

'Oh, don't be such a silly little woman! Do you really think I——? The greengrocer's is only the other side of the—— A couple of yards away.'

'It's no use! You can be as plausible as you like. I'm not listening!'

'Well, in that case, you go!'

'But, don't you see, I *can't*! How can I possibly leave things? Oh, my goodness! Listen! I'll stand here on the doorstep and keep an eye on you. You can go without your hat. Just across the road. A ha'p'orth of parsley!'

'Just you leave it to me! I'll be like greased lightning! I'll be back almost before I'm gone!'

'Mind you are!'

'Don't you worry!'

But no sooner had he got, oh, not half a dozen yards from his own doorstep, than . . . Well, blow me down! He bumped into the old priest from the neighbouring village, where Marchica had once lived for three years.

'Ah, how are you, Father? Bless my soul, it's good to see you! And how *are* you? What are you doing round these parts?'

'Oh, one or two things to see to! One or two things to see to!' replied the old priest smilingly, his eyes disappearing into a mass of wrinkles.

'Well, it really *is* good to see you! How are things with you? How are you keeping? What's the news at Montedoro?'

'Oooh! What sort of news do you expect there to be? Things are all right, my son. The world is old. . . .' And the old priest rubbed his dry, trembling hands together, hands which really *had* been created for the sole task of raising the Host on high.

'Oh, I can see you're in the best of health,' replied the cooper. 'As always, God bless you! Oh yes, I'm all right too, thanks be to God! And I'm never short of work. Yes, Father. . . . I'm just off to buy a ha'p'orth of parsley for my wife. She's very well, too, very well indeed! And she never forgets her old—— No, she never forgets you, Father! She's always saying to me, "Ah, what a good priest he is!" But you know for yourself without me telling you. My wife—well, it's hearth, home, and church with *her*! Oh, she's getting me a dinner and a half today. And just the two of us alone! There we are at the table, me here and her there! But—— Where are *you* eating today, Father? I'm quite sure my wife will be overjoyed to see you again. Will you do me a favour? Now you mustn't say "No"!'

'Willingly, my son, if I can——'

'You must have dinner with us today, in honour of Christmas.'

'I can't, my son——'

'What do you mean, you can't? Oh, so you look down on a poor man's house! I know, the sort of thing a poor man has to offer, a couple of cockerels! While over there. . . .'

'That's not the reason, my son! You know me better than that. I've got to start back in just a moment or so.'

'Go back later!'

'I've left my donkey down at the draper's, he's waiting for me.'

'Let him wait! He'll get a longer rest. No, whatever you say, I'm not letting you get away! You must do me this favour! You will, won't you?'

'Since you force me to accept. Thank you very much, my son.'

'Thank *you,* Father, for the honour. Here's my house, do come and—do come along and step inside. Look, that's the door, the one facing us. Look! There's my wife on the doorstep. I shan't be a moment. A ha'p'orth of parsley!'

The old priest smiled as he looked at the cooper's wife, and greeted her with a wave of his hand, as he walked in the direction of the door.

'He's done it on me again! He's done it on me again!' the cooper's wife was saying through clenched teeth meanwhile. She stood there, clasping and unclasping her fists, simply gnawed away with anger inside. 'Oh, you'll have some explaining to do when you come in, my lad! You'll see!'

'How are you, Father? How are you? This is a great honour, a great pleasure.'

'Your husband literally *forced* me to accept. I just couldn't refuse.'

'Ah, Father!' sighed the cooper's wife, setting her face in an expression of extreme sadness.

'What is troubling you, my daughter?' asked the priest in surprise.

'I'll tell you, Father, I'll tell you! Just wait a moment!' The cooper came in with the parsley, smiling.

'Here's the parsley! See who it is, dear wife? Your good Father! We certainly didn't expect to see *him,* did we? And he's been so kind as to deign to accept our humble invitation. As I've already told him, the sort of thing a poor man can offer—— Still, it's true, isn't it? What *does* it matter? A good heart makes up for all deficiencies.'

'Certainly. Oh yes, indeed.'

'Shall I tell you something, Father? My wife said to me this morning, "Nobody to dinner today!" And, as a matter of fact, I—— But then I caught sight of you, and I'm quite sure—— Well, *you're* an exception. That *is* so, isn't it, dear wife?'

'Oh, no doubt about that! No doubt about that!' his wife

replied, her lips pursed. 'In fact—— Yes, now that I come to think about it, what about the wine? I've forgotten the wine too—— I ask you! Head like a sieve! Run another errand for me, will you, husband dear? You don't mind, do you?'

'Why, of course not! I'll go immediately! Just give me my hat, will you? Hand me my hat!'

'Here's your hat. Don't be long, please! Hurry!'

'Don't you worry!'

The moment the husband had left the house, the woman said to the priest, 'Oh, Father! What a stroke of luck it was that he let himself be persuaded into going for the wine!'

'Why, my daughter, why?'

'Oh, if you only knew, Father! I'd already laid in the wine. I said I didn't have any out of sheer Christian charity. . . .'

'What do you mean?'

'So as to *save* you, Father!'

'Save me?'

'Yes, Father! Do you mean to say you don't know anything about it? You don't know that my husband . . . ?' And she gave an expressive gesture of the hand.

And the poor priest, by way of response, pulled a face a yard long. 'Mad, you say? Mad? But how on earth has——? Poor boy!' And he clasped his hands together. 'How on earth has . . . ?'

'Yes, Father! Yes, Father!' said the woman vigorously. 'I've no more tears left to weep in secret, Father.' And she was crying away as she spoke. 'Oh, what untold floods of tears these eyes have wept! And if you only knew the *kind* of madness that's come upon him. He's only got to catch sight of people's eyes, and immediately he's filled with a burning desire to tear them out. Yes, Father!'

'Oh, Jesus, what an affliction! Sweet Jesus, what an affliction!' stammered the poor priest, his tongue dry within his mouth.

'Oh, Father! I'm speaking for your own good. You can imagine what an honour it would be for me, the pleasure it would give me, having you at table with us today. Look! Take the two cockerels. Or one of them at least. Now, don't refuse! I'll wrap them up in an old newspaper, will that be all right? And you can take them with you. But please, I beg you, *don't* stay here and have dinner with us, that is, if you value your eyesight! Do you know what he does, the poor mad fellow? He invites people into the house, then he shoots the bolts on the door, and when the meal's over he does his best to tear his guests' eyes out! And every time—— Oh, you should see it! Oh, the desperate struggles that go on! Of course, everybody in the village knows about his madness now, and nobody accepts an invitation from him any longer.'

So frightened was the good priest that he could hardly breathe. He stammered, 'And—and I didn't notice it! I didn't notice it!'

When the woman stopped talking he, notwithstanding his advanced age, leapt up from the chair in which he had been sitting, wrapped himself in his cloak, rammed his hat firmly on his head, and well down over his forehead, and said, 'Thank you, my daughter, thank you! Allow me to take my departure immediately. Thank you very much indeed! I owe my life to you!'

'Take the cockerels! Please do me that favour!'

'No, nothing! Of course, I can't take your cockerels, my dear daughter! Oh, poor boy! May the Lord help you, my poor daughter! Good-bye, good-bye! And thank you once again.'

The woman made no effort to prevent his leaving.

'Well, that's settled that!' she exclaimed. She went into the kitchen, took the two cockerels out of the pot, and hid them.

'Now for *us,* my dear lord, master, and husband!'

The cooper came back in with a handsome flask of wine, all out of breath and panting.

He found his wife in the kitchen, crying her eyes out, and with her hair all dishevelled.

'What's happened to you?'

'Oh, if you only knew! Oh, that horrible priest!' lamented the wife, crying her heart out.

'The priest? Where is he? What's happened to you?'

'Now will you learn sense? Are you still going to go on bringing people into my house? Do you see what your worthy priest has done to me? Can you see what he's done?'

'What's he done to you?'

'Oh, dear mother of mine! Oh, dear sainted mother of mine! You certainly never dreamt for one moment that the man to whom you entrusted me would one day leave me so exposed to the outrageous behaviour of wicked people!' And the woman continued inconsolably to cry and cry.

'Good grief, woman, aren't I to be allowed to know what's happened to you?'

'What?'

The wife, having calculated that by now the priest must be a safe distance out of the village—mounted on his donkey, and with fear to spur him on—leapt up from the chair in which she had been sitting and, in tremendous fury, burst out, 'What's happened to me? Your nice, kind priest! Do you know what he did? Your good and worthy priest came skulking into my kitchen and—— Look! Look over there! Look in the pot! See? There's nothing in it now!'

'You mean he's pinched——?' said the cooper, his eyes opening as wide as wide.

'Both the cockerels!'

'Oh, the scoundrel! Are you serious? Is it possible? Oh, the scoundrel! Where is he? Where is he? Which way did he go?'

'I don't know! I didn't see him.'

'Oh, the thieving priest! Oh, the old fox! Let me get at him! I'm going to chase after him! And if I catch up with him—— Let me go!'

'Oh yes, you nasty bully! Take it out on an old man, now!'

'He's pinched my cockerels!'

'Your own silly fault! Pitch into yourself, not him! And let it teach you a lesson! Let it teach you a lesson!'

'No, I'm not going to be satisfied as easy as that. Let me go! Let me go! Let me go, I tell you!'

And having freed himself by sheer brute force from his wife's restraining arms, he began to rush furiously along the main road that led to Montedoro.

After having covered a good stretch of the road beyond the point where it left the village, and being by now all covered with dust and so tired that he couldn't go a step farther, he saw in the distance, far, far away, the old priest, trotting along on his donkey in the middle of a cloud of dust. Then he summoned up all his remaining strength and began shouting, 'Hey, Father! Hey, Father!'

At the far end of the road the priest turned round in his seat to look back, and the donkey went trotting on and on.

And at the other end of the road the cooper was shouting in a loud voice, 'Let me have one of them at least, Father! Give me one of them at least!'

'Goodness gracious, dear man! One of your eyes at least, he says! Good-bye, my dear fellow! Good-bye, my dear fellow!'

And he urged the donkey on with mighty thwacks.

'Just one of them at least! Just one of them at least!' the poor cooper went on shouting, quite exhausted by all his running.

Meanwhile, back in the kitchen, his wife was stripping the flesh from two extremely tasty cockerels, and taking things very easy.

## A DREAM OF CHRISTMAS

First published in *Rassegna settimanale universale* for 27 December 1896, *Sogno di Natale* appeared in volume form only when printed in the Lo Vecchio-Musti appendix to Vol. II of the *Opere*. (*Novelle per un anno,* Vol. II, Milano-Verona, Mondadori, 1957.) It has been issued in English translation[1] in pamphlet form and has been reprinted in three periodicals:

(*a*) *A Dream of Christmas,* Leeds, Pirandello Society, 1959;

(*b*) In the *Listener,* Vol. LXIV, No. 1656, 22 December 1960, p. 1151;

(*c*) In *Harper's Bazaar* (U.S.A.), December 1961, pp. 71–2, 141 and 154;

(*d*) In *English Digest,* December 1961, pp. 11–14.



[1] By Frederick May.

## A DREAM OF CHRISTMAS

My bowed head was resting on my arms, and for some little while now I had had the feeling that. . . . Well, it was just as if a hand were lightly touching my head in a gesture that was part caress, part protectiveness. But my soul was far, far away, wandering through all the places that I had seen since the days of my childhood, and the spirit, the very feel of those places still breathed within me. Not so strongly, however, that it could satisfy the urgent need I experienced then, to live again, if only for an instant, life as I imagined it to be unfolding in them.

There was rejoicing on every hand: in every church, in every home. Up the hill they were gathered round the Yule log. Down the hill, clustered before the Crib. Familiar faces joined with unfamiliar faces in the jollity of supper. Sacred songs, the sound of the bagpipes, the cries of exultant children, and the noisy disputes of the card players. . . . And the streets of the great cities and the little towns, of the villages and of the hamlets up in the Alps or by the sea-shore, all were deserted in the bitterly chill night. And I seemed to myself to be hurrying along those streets, dashing from one house to the next, so as to rejoice in the celebrations of other people, all compactly gathered into their separate worlds. I'd stop for a few moments in each house, then I'd wish them all 'Happy Christmas!' and disappear. . . .

That's how it had happened: all unawares, I'd dropped off to sleep, and I was dreaming. And in my dream, as I hurried along those deserted streets, it seemed to me that suddenly I came upon Jesus. He too was wandering abroad in that night, that very night on which the world still traditionally celebrates His birth. He was moving along almost furtively, very pale and shut up inside Himself, with one hand clasping His cloak and His deep-set, noble, brilliant eyes gazing intently into the void. He seemed filled with an intense grief and prey to an infinite sadness.

I set off along the same path, but gradually His image began to exercise so powerful an attraction over me as to absorb me into itself. And then it seemed to me that He and I made up but one person. Suddenly, abruptly, however, there came a moment when I felt dismay at my own lightness as I roved along those streets—I seemed almost to be flying above them—and instinctively I stopped. Then, on the instant, Jesus disengaged Himself from me and went along on His own, lighter than ever, almost as if He were a feather thrust on its way by a puff of wind. And I, left on the ground like a dark stain upon its face, became His shadow and followed Him.

All of a sudden the streets of the city disappeared. Jesus, like a white phantasm, shining with an inner light, flew up over a tall bramble hedge, which stretched relentlessly in either direction, into the infinite distance, in the middle of a black, unending plain. And when we had reached the other side, above the hedge, He sped easily along, tall and erect, while I scrambled on, sprawled full-length. On and on He drew me, through thorns which pierced me all over, yet without tearing me at all.

From the shaggy, bristling hedge I climbed on up until at last, though in a very short time, I reached the soft sand of a narrow shore. Before me lay the sea, and on its throbbing, black waters, a luminous path, which ran on and on in an ever narrowing band till it became a mere point in the immense arc of the horizon. Jesus started along that path traced out by the reflected light of the moon, and I followed on behind Him, like a small, black boat amidst the flashes of light darting about the surface of the freezing waters.

Suddenly the inner light of Jesus was extinguished. Once again we were traversing the deserted streets of a great city. Now He was stopping every few moments or so to eavesdrop at the doors of the most humble houses, where Christmas, not out of sincere devotion, but because of sheer lack of money, furnished no pretext for guzzling and revelry.

'They're not asleep,' Jesus murmured, and surprising a few hoarse words of hatred and envy uttered within the house, He shrank back within Himself as if assailed by a sharp spasm of pain. Then, the imprint of His nails still vivid in the backs of His pure, clasped hands, He moaned, 'Even for these did I die. . . .'

So we went on, stopping every now and again. We covered a long stretch of road, until we came to a church, and there, in front of it, Jesus turned to me, His shadow on earth, and said, 'Arise and welcome Me within yourself. I wish to go and see inside this church.'

It was a magnificent church, an immense basilica with a nave and two side aisles, rich in splendid marbles, with gold gleaming in the dome, and filled with a great mass of the faithful, all intent upon the service which was being conducted from the High Altar. The altar was gorgeously arrayed and the celebrants were surrounded by a cloud of incense. In the warm light cast from a hundred silver candlesticks the gold flecks in the rich cloth of the chasubles, set against the froth of precious lace upon the Altar, glittered at every gesture.

'And on their account,' said Jesus within me, 'I should be happy, were I really to be born tonight for the first time.'

We came out of the church, and Jesus, coming out from within me and standing in front of me as before, and then placing a hand upon my breast, went on, 'I am seeking a soul in which I may live again. As you see, I am dead as far as this world is concerned. And yet it . . . Yes, it even has the audacity to fling itself into a riot of celebration on the very night of My birth. Perhaps *your* soul would not be too narrow for Me, were it not so cluttered up with all sorts of things that you ought to cast away. From Me you would receive a hundredfold what you would be losing by following Me and abandoning what you so falsely deem needful to you and to yours: this city and its life, your dreams, the creature comforts with which you seek in vain to gladden your foolish suffering in this world. . . . I am seeking a soul in which I may live again. Yours may very well be just like the soul of any other man of goodwill.'

'The city, the life it gives me, Jesus?' I replied, greatly dismayed. 'My home, my dear ones, my dreams?'

'From Me you would receive a hundredfold what you would be losing,' He repeated, taking His hand away from my breast and looking fixedly at me with those deep-set, noble, brilliant eyes of His.

'Oh, I *can't*, Jesus!' I said, after a moment's perplexity, and, utterly ashamed and humiliated, I let my hands fall on to my body.

At the self-same moment, just as if that hand, which at the beginning of my dream I had felt touching my bowed head, had given me a forceful thrust against the hard wood of the little table, I awoke with a start and began rubbing my forehead, for it had gone completely numb. 'This it is, Jesus, this it is that tortures me so! For ever more, without rest and without respite, morning, noon, and night, I must torment my brain with this eternal question.'

# TWELVE LETTERS

*Le dodici lettere* was originally published in *La domenica italiana* on 21 February 1897, and first appeared in volume form in *Quand'ero matto* (Torino, Streglio, 1902). The volume was reprinted by Treves of Milan in 1919 in a '*nuova edizione riveduta*', with some modification of the contents, including the discarding of this story. It was not collected by Pirandello into the *Novelle per un anno* for the Bemporad and Mondadori presentations, but figures now in the Lo Vecchio-Musti appendix to Vol. II of the *Opere*. (*Novelle per un anno,* Vol. II, Milano-Verona, Mondadori, 1957.)

# TWELVE LETTERS

THE moment she'd closed the door behind Signora Baldinotti, Adele Montagnani heaved a sigh of relief, went back into the drawing-room, and looked to see what time it was by the clock on the mantelpiece. Poor, fat, blonde Signora Baldinotti, she'd been so terribly upset! Very quickly, almost as if someone could spy in and observe what she was doing, Adele tidied up her hair a little, front and back, and rearranged the froth of white lace at the neck of her dress. Rossani would be here any minute now.

In anticipation of this visit Adele hadn't slept a wink the whole of the previous night, and all through the morning she'd been prey to a most lively sense of agitation, which had increased greatly in the last hour and been turned into downright anguish by the announcement of the importunate visit of Signora Baldinotti.

By great good luck she'd taken her departure in time. Yes, it really *was* good luck, because the poor lady—among her other deficiencies she was a trifle deaf—was notorious for the length of time she'd stay when she called, and she was totally incapable of realizing when she was (as there came moments when she was indeed) a positive social encumbrance. Neither did she realize just how great an affliction she was being.

Now, freed from this particular danger, Adele could laugh in her usual way at the sorrowful yet quite hilarious confidences the good lady had entrusted to her. Provoked to do so by brief but appropriate questions, or by the occasional exclamation of sympathy or surprise, she'd reveal such secrets and such intimate details of her married life, that it was sheer entertainment just to listen to her. Every time she came, Adele would make a point of enjoying herself for all she was worth at the expense of Signora Baldinotti. From all the confidences of the unhappy woman she derived a great deal of piquant material for conversation with her friends.

She stopped laughing. 'God forgive me!' she said to herself. But immediately she was shaken by another gust of laughter.

Signora Baldinotti flattered herself that she could prevent the multiple and brazen-faced betrayals inflicted on her by her husband (who was eight years younger than she), by decking herself out and generally dolling herself up with the utmost luxury. Such ostentation was, of course, quite unsuitable at her age and with a body like hers, and in highly dubious taste. She herself would confess, 'Do you really think, Signora Montagnani, that I'd dress myself up like this, that I'd spend so much money on myself, if I didn't have a young husband? And, believe me or believe me not, I even—yes, I wait up for him, fully dressed and with my hair done. Yes, Signora Montagnani, until midnight, two o'clock in the morning, three, daybreak. . . . Yes, many a time it's been daybreak when he's come in!' And, as she'd said this, the poor lady's lips and chin had been trembling with emotion and her eyes had been filled with tears.

The clock on the mantelpiece struck four.

Adele drove the thought of the comic figure of Signora Baldinotti out of her mind, and occupied herself once more with thinking about Rossani's imminent visit.

The task she'd undertaken was beginning to appear extremely difficult. But it was by way of returning a service rendered her by a friend, who had undertaken the same task on her behalf, and who'd carried it through to a happy conclusion.

'You'll see, the hardest bit is getting started. I've used my art. You'll certainly not fail to use yours, which is much more refined than mine,' Giulia Garzía had said to her the day before, in bidding her good-bye.

That last expression had greatly tickled Adele's *amour propre.* She'd put a great deal of study and sheer hard work into securing for herself the reputation in society of being a clever and witty woman.

It was a question of getting Rossani to give back the twelve letters that Giulia Garzía had written him in the two years of their so-called love affair. It had been broken off three months ago, after a long series of scenes, which both of them had found quite disgusting. Giulia had rendered her the same service; that is, she'd got back the rather more numerous letters which, in a much shorter space of time, *she'd* written to Tullio Vidoni, who'd taken himself off a brief while before, on the treacherous plea that his heart could no longer stand the strain of betraying an intimate friend—Guido Montagnani.

The two break-ups had occurred at almost exactly the same time, and the two friends had comforted one another in turn; now they were helping one another in turn.

At ten minutes past four Tito Rossani entered Adele's drawing-room, quite resigned to submitting to the thousand little pinpricks of her presumptuous sharpwittedness, exactly as if he were entering a beehive; resigned to that habit Adele Montagnani had when talking to her friends, of sounding as if a French *vous* construction had determined her phrasing. It was quite indiscriminate. Indeed, her whole way of talking was bejewelled with French words and expressions, as if their Italian equivalents were false or vulgar.

'Ah, here you are at last!' she exclaimed.

Rossani bowed, held out his hand and replied, 'On the dot!'

'A fairly elastic dot, if I may say so. But never mind, do sit down. Over here. Over here, by me. You're not afraid to, are you?'

'Courage itself, dear lady. A proper little St. Sebastian. Here I am, by your side, all ready to receive the arrows that it shall please you to bestow upon me!' And sitting down, he tried to catch a glimpse of his own reflection in the mirror over the mantelpiece. There was a set smile on his face, masked rather by his thick, up-swept moustache.

'There's just one tiny little difference, you know! St. Sebastian was terribly handsome. According to all the artists, that is.'

'I know. Please look on me as a St. Sebastian from the neck down.'

'No, we'll include your head as well! I've made quite a nice start, haven't I? Listen, Rossani. . . . I'm going to make love to you. You don't mind, do you? Promise me, though, that you won't start brawling with my husband. . . .'

'Oh, I—— Yes! I see! *Brawl with your*—— Yes, indeed!' observed Tito, laughing and stroking his head with his hand. Like Guido Montagnani he'd gone bald rather early in life. He added, 'It won't be at all easy, you know. . . .'

'Oh, stop it! Do be serious! I'm going to make love to you, even though I do know that you find me completely repulsive. Not that anybody's told me as much, mind you! No, I've worked it out for myself, in my own quiet little way.'

'Ah, dear lady, how very unobservant you've been! So many brilliant gifts! How sad that perspicacity should not be among them!'

'What a sweet man you are! Perhaps you're right, you know! But, well, suppose you *are* right? I shouldn't really be wronging you. Likes and dislikes, *loving* people and *hating* people; it's something you feel, not something you sit down and discuss cold-bloodedly. Even if we admit that you *don't* hate the sight of me. Well, go on, own up! You're *frightened* of me, aren't you? Of course you are, and you can't deny it! You had to have a proper invitation, didn't you, before you'd come and see me? Still, we mustn't start getting biased, must we? I know . . . I know why you haven't been to see me since—— And, if you don't mind my saying so, it was very wicked of you! No, don't interrupt! People have noticed that you haven't been coming to see me. They've started making comments. You've done yourself—— Rossani, I'm very sorry to have to say this, but your reputation has suffered very greatly as a result. Why, we all thought you such a dashing, witty sort of a man.'

'Did you indeed?' said Tito. 'So I've got that sort of a reputation, too, have I? I hadn't the faintest idea. Borrowed plumes, dear lady, quite unmerited! Shall I prove that to you? Well, without any further beating about the bush, let me ask you why you did me the honour of writing me the note I received this morning, and what it is I can do for you?'

Adele was somewhat disconcerted by the serious note in his voice and by the urgent tone of his reply. She responded by trying to retreat a little, in order to mount a stronger counter-attack.

'So you don't believe me when I say that I intend to make love to you? You don't want to, do you?'

'You think that? My dear Signora—— My dear *lady,* I shouldn't dream of doubting your word! So I'll begin by asking you to——'

'Swear undying love?'

'No, God forbid! It would be a sin against Nature!'

'Well, in that case. . . . I'm sorry if I—— But why? Look, this is in confidence, m'm? After all, we are having a little flirtation, *n'est-ce pas*? But you mustn't think that *I'm* jealous too. As I was saying, why—— Oh, I don't know how to put it! Look! Why are you acting so harshly, so resentfully—and that's putting it mildly! —towards *somebody we both know*, if you really believe that undying love is a sin against Nature?'

'I don't see what you're driving at!'

'Oh, don't pretend! You're not that thick-witted! Don't force me to tell you her name! You know perfectly well who it is! My most intimate friend. Almost a sister to me. . . .'

'Oh, indeed? *Still?*' said Rossani, his affectation of ingenuous surprise shot through with malice.

'What do you mean, "still"?' Adele demanded, thoroughly annoyed. 'Let me tell you something, my dear. We women aren't the least bit fickle in our affection for one another! We're not like—— At least, I suppose . . .'

Tito burst in with, 'I don't believe you!' his tone lively in the extreme. 'It's no use your going on, I don't believe you! Anyway, if what you say is true, I feel terribly sorry for you! As far as I'm concerned, I give you my solemn assurance that I don't usually harbour the slightest feeling of rancour against anyone. Especially afterwards.'

'Oh come, Rossani, don't be so dishonest!' Adele interrupted him in her turn. 'Look! I'm speaking quite frankly to you, straight from my heart! And you, you're busy covering up, defending yourself against me! Do be honest with me! If what you say is true, why . . . ?'

'Why what? Look, let's get one thing straight, at least, my dear *friend*. I consider myself extremely fortunate in being freed from my chains! God knows, they were heavy enough, in all conscience! So why on earth should I be feeling embittered? I mean—— Well, if I did feel any bitterness, it would all be directed against myself. If it were, well—*possible*. I was quite incredibly stupid! Do you feel like laughing? Do you know why I kept on dragging my chains around like that? Because I was afraid of injuring . . . Yes! Afraid I might *kill* her most intimate friend! Sounds quite incredible, doesn't it? Look, there's something you must know. It might help to explain why I—— But you know all this! That dear lady made my life unmitigated hell with one jealous scene after another! Oh, the ferocity of the woman! On the flimsiest of pretexts she'd——!'

'It looks to me as if she had very good reason to!'

'I don't feel the slightest bit sorry, let me tell you!'

'There! What did I say? Oh, you men!' Adele Montagnani burst out, 'Oh, Bourget, how divinely right you are! Wait till I——! Just you wait there, Rossani!' She leapt to her feet and went into the adjoining room (a small room that she used as a study), her elbows moving as if she were intent on flying, and took out of her elegant English-style bookcase Bourget's *Physiologie de l'amour moderne.* She then rushed back into the room and stood there, riffling through the pages of the book. 'Oh, where does it come? Where *does* it come? Where does he——? Ah, here it is! Of course, I'd put the marker in! *Par amour propre simple.* Here you are! Read that! Just the bit in italics. The aphorism. You don't need to read the rest!'

Tito had got up, so as to look at himself in the mirror, and gave himself a smile. He took the book and read the passage to himself. Then he gave a slight shake of his head and said unhurriedly, 'Nothing to do with my case.'

'What do you mean, "nothing to do with . . ."? *Ce que certains hommes pardonnent le moins à une femme, c'est qu'elle se console d'avoir étée trahie par eux.*'

'Nothing to do with my case,' Rossani repeated and sat down again. 'Look, dear lady, if there really *is* anybody I can never forgive, it's myself. Me! And if your intimate friend has found such easy consolation for my betrayal of her, then so much the better. Or so much the worse for her! *M'm!* So you too know that your friend has found consolation? In that case, my admiration for you is quite unbounded. Ah, a truly rare spirit!'

'*Who* is?'

'You, dear lady.'

'Thank you, but I don't understand what you're talking about. I'm sorry to be so tiresome, but I *was* trying to ask you why, if you feel the way you say you do, you're so unwilling to give back the letters she wrote you.'

'Oh!' exclaimed Rossani, 'so you know about the letters too? Good God! She's been a bit prodigal, hasn't she, this intimate friend of yours? Dashing around all over the place, telling everybody about this wonderful present she's given me! A dozen highly-perfumed, exquisitely elegant little pieces of cardboard! Go on, own up! She *is* a bit prodigal, isn't she? Do you think she's planning a gorgeous little private edition of them? Sale restricted to well-bred pornographers only? You know the sort of thing: *Some Love-Letters by a Lady of Quality*. If that's what she's got in mind, I'll set up as a publisher myself, even if it does mean robbing my modest private collection of manuscripts. I've been saving them up for my old age. They'll help to pass the time.'

'Oh, Rossani, what a brute you are! How can you say such dreadful things? Who else has been talking to you about Giulia's letters? I mean, who could possibly know enough about——?'

'You'll never guess, dear lady,' said Rossani, his face settling into a serious expression. He went very pale, but a nervous little smile still trembled on his lips. 'It's someone you'd never even suspect. If you had, you certainly wouldn't be talking to me like this. Guessed who it is?'

Adele's expression became troubled. Her forehead wrinkled, as if her sight had suddenly become clouded. She whispered a name.

'Tullio Vidoni?'

Rossani nodded in reply. There was just a hint in his eyes of the sneering smile that was playing on his unmoving lips.

And, in point of fact, only Vidoni—yes, only Vidoni—could possibly have known about the letters. Vidoni, to whom Adele had talked about them without even asking him to keep the whole thing secret, so completely at that time did she trust him. Why, there was nothing she didn't tell him! Ah, now she understood how it was that Giulia had been able to get back *her* letters from him so easily! He'd been in a tremendous hurry, then, to give his new mistress the letters he'd received from his old one. God only knows how they must have laughed over all her outpourings of love and sorrow!

Adele twisted her hands in her lap, almost breaking her finger-bones in the process. All the time she kept on smiling at Rossani, her face deathly pale and her teeth clenched.

'Oh, it was really extraordinarily funny,' the latter resumed, hesitantly, 'Comical! If you like, I'll tell you all about it, it's not a very long story.'

'Yes! Yes! Tell me all about it!' Adele hastened to say, her voice and manner indicating very vividly the anguish she was suffering, the anger, contempt, and sheer hatred with which her body was torn. 'Tell me what happened!' she urged him.

'It was yesterday. Yesterday afternoon. I was walking along the Corso, with Vidoni. I hadn't the slightest suspicion that he had already taken my—well, let's put it like this; that he was my successor. We both noticed, and both pretended we hadn't noticed, the lady in question. She was a little way ahead of us, having just passed us in her carriage. I must confess that I *did* observe a slight put-outness in my friend's manner, and a kind of sudden pallor come over his face. But, I repeat, I hadn't the slightest suspicion that he stood in need of my sympathy. After all, he knew everything there was to know concerning the dear lady. All about my charming and short-lived idyll with her, as well as the whole mythology—let's call it that, shall we?—of her inexhaustible love-life in Milan, before her husband came to Rome to take his seat in the Senate, poor devil! But that's enough on that subject! "Oh, so she's back?" I said, half to myself, though, to tell the truth, I *was* hoping that Vidoni might be able to give me some news about her. I knew that he'd just got back from Milan himself, and that he must have seen quite a lot of her there.'

'Well? Oh, do go on! Do go on! What did he——?' Adele interrupted, finding Rossani's long drawn-out narrative all but intolerable.

'Oh, I—— Oh, I *see*! Forgive me for asking this, but I suppose *you'd* spotted what was happening long before I did, h'm? You saw that he was falling desperately in love with Signora Garzia?'

'I? Why, no. That is—well, you know Tullio Vidoni as well as I do. The most ridiculous man who ever trod the face of the earth! As you know, he's an acute case of *Dongiovannitis*. He makes love to every woman he sets eyes on. Good Heavens, surely nobody takes the man *seriously*?'

'Oh no, of course not! But *he* does, you know! He takes himself terribly seriously! Good God, yes! And he's certainly fallen for your most intimate friend! Oh yes, he's got it badly! At least, if what he did to me's anything to go by!'

'Didn't you say he'd talked to you about the letters?'

'Patience is a virtue! Just you listen and you'll hear all about it. When I said, "Oh, so she's back?" he told me that Signora Garzia had been back in Rome for the past three days, and that he'd travelled down from Milan with her. Then he manoeuvred me into talking about her. Well, I hadn't the slightest suspicion as far as he was concerned, and a great deal of suspicion as far as other men were concerned, so I—— Yes, let me confess my sins! I was weak minded enough to talk and talk and talk, and not very charitably, either, as you may readily imagine. Nothing to do with the aphorism of that divine Bourget of yours, though, let me tell you! Well, there I was talking away, when I noticed that my dear friend's face was gradually getting more and more sombre. "Nasty pain, old chap?" I said, jokingly. Whereupon he exploded, and in rather lively terms had the nerve to reproach me with what I'd been saying, and for the manner in which I'd been saying it. I just stood there, looking like the village idiot. Gaping at him! I couldn't believe that he was serious in what he was saying. So he said his little piece all over again, adopting even more picturesque terms. I got a trifle annoyed at this, and gave him the answer he was asking for. Well, one thing led to another. Quite a violent little argument it developed into. All in very gentlemanly undertones, of course. Well, to cut a long story short, I gave him a fully-detailed account of my own affair with the dear lady and left him standing there, in the middle of the road, staring after me.'

Adele was terribly agitated by this time. She hid her face in her hands and sobbed. 'Oh, God! Oh, God!' Then she looked at Rossani, her face twisted with anguish and her eyes glistening with hate. 'What's going to happen now?' she asked him. 'Tell me the truth, Rossani! Have you run yourself into any danger? You know that Tullio Vidoni's——'

'No, I'm not in any danger, dear lady! Besides, I've never allowed myself to be deterred by my adversary's prowess in the shooting-gallery or in the fencing *salle*. If I'm going to fight, I'm going to fight. Regardless.'

'Oh God, no, Rossani! He's a crack shot! And you'll see, he'll take advantage of his skill, the coward!' cried Adele. 'No! No! Listen! If you—— If you could only teach him a lesson! Oh, in that case, I'd urge you with all my heart to go ahead! Yes, teach him a lesson that he'd remember to his dying day!'

'Let's hope it *will* be!' exclaimed Rossani.

'But it *won't*! Can't you see?' resumed Adele. 'I'm terribly afraid for you. And then, just imagine how puffed up with pride he'll be, when he returns safe and sound, victorious, to his beloved mistress! No! *No!*'

'Well it's—— I mean, now that . . .' said Rossani, shrugging his shoulders.

'You don't mean——? So it's all settled, is it? You're going to fight a duel? Oh, Rossani, no! For *her* sake? A worthless creature like that! No! No! Do let me go on with what I'm saying! She came here to see me, the day before yesterday. She actually *kissed me*! Just think of it! With that stereotyped smile glued on her painted lips! Oh, the viper! Oh, my God! Do you know what she did? She even went so far as to ask me to do something for her. To try and get back her letters for her. From you. While she—— Oh, it's utterly monstrous, Rossani! Don't *you* think it's monstrous? Monstrous! And to think that it'll be you who'll have to pay for it all! Oh, no! No, for pity's sake! Listen! Listen . . . ! Do it for *my* sake!' Adele put her arm round his neck, almost burying her face in his breast. 'Do it for *my* sake!' she begged him.

Tito, at a loss as to how to disengage himself, tried to stop that flow of supplicatory words:

'If I fight him . . . If I fight him, I shall do so for my own sake. For my own sake, and for no one else's, believe me, dear lady! And I've got the proof of that here in my pocket! Here, in these letters of hers! The truth positively shines out of them!'

'Oh!' cried Adele, 'So you've got them with you now? Give

them to me!' She moved her hand in the direction of his inside jacket pocket, driven to do so by an uncontrollable impulse of hateful joy.

Tito rose to his feet. Severely, he said,

'Oh no, dear lady! Even if I no longer have the slightest affection for that woman, it's still in my own interest to behave like a gentleman! Now more so than ever! I'm sorry, but . . . Not to you! I can't give *you* the letters! I'll see she gets them back some other way.'

When he said this, Adele, throbbing with passion, burst into noisy laughter. On and on her laughter went, and you got the feeling that she was straining every nerve to keep it going. She flung her head back on to the raised end of the sofa. Tito stood there looking at her, thoroughly disconcerted.

'Oh, wonderful! What a wonderful man you are!' she exclaimed, sitting up, her words punctuated by her laughter.

'You're quite right! Give me your hand, Rossani! Give me your hand! Didn't you see what I was driving at? This is precisely what I *wanted* you to do! I *wanted* you *not* to give them to me. Now you *will* play fair, won't you? Word of honour? You *will* let her have her letters back? You're very sweet, Rossani! Thank you. You really *are* a perfect gentleman.'

Tito Rossani went away awkwardly, quite nonplussed, almost astounded by a dull vexation. Ah, what a fool he was! What a fool! So that Montagnani woman had been fooling around with him, had she? She'd played a huge joke on him, acting out that melodramatic little jealousy scene, had she? And what an actress! All right? He'd get his own back, though! He wasn't giving those letters back! Not on any account!

Which was very poor consolation for Adele, who'd dearly have loved to get her hands on those letters, and then to . . .

'Oh, what a fool the man is!' she said very quietly with a lively gesture of contempt for Rossani, who'd already turned his back on Adele's drawing-room.

She buried her face in the sofa and burst into sobs, biting the raised end of the sofa, so that no one should hear her.

# FEAR

*La paura* was presented originally in *La domenica italiana* for 1 August 1897. It was gathered into none of the volumes of *novelle* arranged by Pirandello, and is now among the *racconti aggiunti* in Vol. II of the *Opere* (*Novelle per un anno,* Vol. II, Milano-Verona, Mondadori, 1957). Pirandello expanded and dramatized the story a year after its publication. It appeared in *Ariel* for 20 March 1898, bearing the title *L'epilogo,*[1] and was reprinted in *Noi e il mondo* for 1 March 1914, under its definitive title, *La morsa.*[2] It is now included in Vol. V. of the *Opere.* (*Maschere Nude*, Vol. II, *prefazione di Silvio D'Amico; cronologia della vita e delle opere di Manlio Lo Vecchio-Musti,* Milano-Verona, Mondadori, 1958).



[1] *The Epilogue* (or *The End of It All*).

[2] *The Vice.* The available English translation is by Frederick May, Leeds, Pirandello Society, 1962.

# FEAR

'OH!' she said, giving a start of surprise and drawing back from the window. She had her crochet-work in her hand, and she now put it down on a small table, and went over and closed the door on the left, which led into the other rooms. Her movements were rapid but cautious. She then stood waiting, half-hidden in the folds of the curtain across the other door, which gave on to the hall.

'Back already?' she said quietly, happily, her arms raised towards him. Such a graceful, tiny little woman. Such a Herculean man, Antonio Serra. Her face was bent forward immediately to receive the usual furtive kiss. He avoided her embrace, his manner thoroughly disturbed.

'Aren't you alone?' Lillina Fabris asked, recomposing herself immediately. 'Where have you left Andrea?'

'I came on ahead. Last night!' Serra answered roughly, then added, as if to mitigate his rudeness, 'Oh, I made some sort of excuse for leaving. It was the truth, incidentally. I had to be back here this morning to attend to some business.'

'You didn't say a word to *me* about it,' she gently reproached him. 'You might have let me know. What's happened?'

Serra looked into her eyes—almost hatefully. Then, in a low but tense voice, he burst out, 'What's——? I'm afraid your husband suspects us.'

She stood stock-still, just as if a thunderbolt had landed at her feet. Then, fear and surprise in her voice, she said, '*Andrea?* How do you know? Have you given yourself away somehow?'

'No. It's something we've *both* done. If he really *has* found out!' he hastened to reply. 'The night we went away.'

'Here?'

'Yes. As he was going downstairs, do you remember . . . ? Andrea was going down in front of me, carrying his suitcase. You were by the door, holding a candle so as to give us a little light.

And as I went past you I—— Oh, my God! The mad things we do sometimes!'

Lillina Fabris clasped both hands to her face. Then she waved them questioningly, 'He saw us?'

'I got the impression that he turned as he was going down,' he replied in arid, gloomy tones. '*You* noticed nothing?'

'*I?* No, nothing! But where's Andrea? Where is he?'

It was just as if Serra hadn't heard the anguished question of his tiny mistress, the greatness of whose soul, and the greatness of whose love, he'd never for one moment comprehended. Sombrely he went on, 'Tell me. Had I already started to go downstairs when he called out to you?'

'And said good-bye to me?' she exclaimed. 'When he waved to me! It was when he turned down there on the landing, then?'

'No, before that! Before that!'

'But if he *had* seen us——'

'He'd only have caught a glimpse at most! The merest glimpse!'

'And he let you come back ahead of him?' she replied with growing anguish. 'You're quite sure he didn't leave when you did?'

'Absolutely. I'm absolutely sure about that. And the next train doesn't get in until eleven.' He looked at his watch, and his face grew dark again. 'He's just about due in now. And meanwhile, we—— All this uncertainty—as if we were dangling over a precipice!'

'Sh! Sh! Please!' she begged him. 'Control yourself! Tell me all about it. What has he done? I want to know everything.'

'What do you expect me to tell you? When one's in this sort of state, even the most innocent words seem like allusions to—— Every glance becomes a hint.'

'Control yourself! Control yourself!' she repeated.

'Oh yes! Control myself! Control myself! It's all very well for you!' And Serra started walking up and down the room, wringing his hands. Then he stopped and said, 'It was here. Do you remember? Before we left. He and I were discussing this confounded case we had to go up to town about. He got quite angry.'

'Yes. *Well?*'

'As soon as we got outside the door, Andrea stopped talking. He walked on, with his head bent. I looked at him; he seemed agitated. He was frowning. "He's found out!" I thought to myself. I didn't say a word. I was afraid that my voice might be wobbly and give me away. I started trembling like a leaf. But all of a sudden he said, quite simply and naturally, "Sad, isn't it? Starting off on a journey in the evening. Leaving home in the evening." And his words rang out clearly in the cool, calm evening air.'

'Just like that?'

'Yes. It seemed a sad thing to him. For those who were left behind as well. Then he said something that sent me into a cold sweat. "Saying good-bye by candle-light. On a stairway. . . ." '

'Oh, he said that? *How* did he say it?' she exclaimed, somewhat shattered.

'In the same tone of voice,' replied Serra. 'Quite naturally. I don't know. . . . He said it on purpose! He spoke to me about the children, whom he'd left in bed, asleep. But not with that simple loving affection that reassures you. And he spoke about you.'

'About me?'

'Yes. But he was looking at me as he spoke.'

'What did he say?' she asked, her whole body in an agony of suspense.

'That you love your children very dearly.'

'Nothing else?'

'In the train he started discussing again the case we were going to deal with. He asked me about Gorri, the lawyer. Whether I knew him.'

'Sh!' she said quickly, interrupting him.

The maid came in. She wanted to know whether it was time for her to go and fetch the children. (They'd been sent that morning to spend the day with their grandparents—*his* mother and father.) The master *was* due back today, wasn't he? The cabs had already left for the station.

Lillina was undecided. She told the maid to wait a little while longer and, meanwhile, to finish laying the table and to make sure everything was ready in the other room. Once they were on their own again, they looked at one another in dismay. He repeated, 'He'll be here any minute now.'

Angrily she seized his arm, gripping it fiercely. 'Have you really got nothing to tell me? You couldn't find out *anything* for certain? It sounds so utterly fantastic! *Andrea!* Who's usually so hot-tempered! With his heart so full of suspicion! To be able to pretend like that, with you! It's quite——!'

'It's true, nevertheless!' he said, clapping his hands together. 'Could my uneasiness have made me *so* imperceptive? Does it seem feasible? You see—more than once I thought I got a glimpse of some hidden meaning in what he was saying. The next moment I'd steady my nerve by telling myself, "It's only because you're afraid." '

'Afraid? *You?*'

'Yes, me! Because he's in the right, you know!' declared Serra, all the grossness of his character coming through the words, which were spoken with all the spontaneity of a man convinced of something that seems only natural. 'Every single moment of the time I was studying him, spying on him. How he looked at me, how he spoke to me. You know he doesn't usually have very much to say for himself, and yet you should have heard him during these last three days! Time and again, however, he'd shut himself up for long spells in a restless kind of silence; but every time he'd emerge and take up again the thread of what he'd been saying about the case. I'd ask myself, "Was he *really* thinking about this? Or about something altogether different? Perhaps he's only talking now so as to conceal his suspicions from me." Once I even got the impression that he hadn't wanted to shake hands with me. You see, he must have been perfectly well aware that I was holding out my hand. He pretended to be absent-minded. . . . He certainly *did* behave rather strangely the day after we left. He'd only gone a couple of steps when he called me back. "He's changed his mind," I thought immediately. And, as a matter of fact, he *did* say, "Oh, forgive me. I was forgetting to shake hands. It doesn't matter, though!" At other times he'd talk to me about you, about his home, all without any apparent innuendo. Just like that. It seemed to me, however, that he avoided looking me in the eye. Often he'd repeat something three or four times, without the slightest rhyme or reason, as if he were thinking about something else. And right in the middle of talking about something completely different, he'd suddenly contrive—I don't know how—to start off very abruptly talking to me again about you or about the children. Looking me straight in the eye, holding my gaze, asking me questions. *Deliberately?* God only knows! Did he hope to catch me unawares? He'd laugh. But if you looked into his eyes, there was ugliness in his humour.'

'And what did *you* do?' she asked, hanging on his words.

'Oh, I kept on the alert all the time.'

Lillina Fabris shook her head angrily, contemptuously. 'He must have been aware of your mistrust!'

'If he already had his suspicions!' he said, shrugging his huge shoulders.

'It will have confirmed them!' she snapped back. 'And then what? Nothing more?'

'Yes. The first night we were in the hotel.' Serra went on, thoroughly downcast now, 'He'd asked for a double room. We'd been in bed for some little while; he noticed that I wasn't asleep. That is—— No, he didn't *notice* it—we were in the dark! He *guessed* it! Look! Just imagine what it was like! I didn't move. There, at night, in the same room with him and suspecting that he knew. . . . Just imagine it! I strained my eyes in the darkness, waiting, waiting. To defend myself, perhaps, if he should—— At the slightest movement on his part I'd have been out of that bed and then I'd have—— Well, you *do* realize, don't you——? If it had been a question of his life or mine, much better for *him* to get killed! Suddenly, in the silence, I heard him speak. And these are his very words; "You're not asleep." '

'And what did you do?'

'Nothing. I didn't reply. I pretended to be asleep. After a while he repeated what he'd said, "You're not asleep." Then I called out to him. "Did you say something?" I asked. "Yes," he replied, "I wanted to know if you were asleep." But it wasn't true. He *hadn't* been asking a question when he'd said, "You're not asleep." No, he'd said it in the certainty that I wasn't asleep. Do you understand? In the certainty that I *couldn't* sleep! Or, at least, that's how it looked to me.'

'Nothing else?' she asked once more.

'Nothing else. I haven't shut my eyes for two whole nights!'

'And afterwards. Did he behave as usual towards you?'

'Yes. Just as usual.'

She stood there a moment or so, deep in thought, her eyes staring fixedly into nothingness. Then she said slowly, almost as if talking to herself, 'All this pretending—*Andrea*! If he *had* seen us. . . .'

'Yet he *did* turn; as he was going downstairs,' objected Serra.

'But he couldn't possibly have noticed anything! How could he and not have——?'

'Well, if he were in any doubt . . .' he said.

'Oh, you don't know him as I do! Even if he still had his doubts. Andrea. To control himself like that; not giving a thing away! What can you possibly know about him? Nothing! Suppose we admit that he may have seen us as you passed me and bent towards me. If he'd conceived the slightest suspicion that you'd kissed me he'd have come dashing back upstairs! Of course he would! Just think how he'd have treated us! No! Listen to me! It's quite impossible! You were afraid, that's all! *You*, Antonio. *Afraid!* No, no! There's not the slightest possibility that he's started thinking things about us! He's got no reason to suspect us. You always treated me with considerable familiarity in front of him.'

Though somewhat cheered in his mind by the sudden belief in their safety conceived by his mistress, Serra was still determined to insist on being racked with doubt in order to be even more greatly reassured by her.

'Yes. . . . But suspicion can flash into existence in an instant. And then—— Well, you know how it is. A thousand and one hardly-remembered incidents, things of which you took no notice at the time, suddenly appear in a new light. The vaguest of hints becomes proof conclusive. Doubt becomes certainty. That's why I'm afraid.'

'We must be careful,' she replied.

In his disappointment Serra felt somewhat annoyed with his mistress.

'*Now?* I've said so all along.'

Angrily, contemptuously, she looked at him.

'Are you reproaching me now?'

'I'm not reproaching you with anything,' he replied, more annoyed than ever. 'Isn't it true, though? Haven't I said over and over again, "Look, Lillina, we must be careful."? But you——'

'Yes. Yes. . . .' she agreed, as if sick to death of the whole thing.

'I don't know what perverse pleasure there is in letting yourself get caught,' he went on, 'for nothing at all, a moment's trifling imprudence, like that of three evenings ago. It was you.'

'Yes, I'm always the one who's——'

'If it weren't for you . . .'

'Yes,' she said, getting up, a sneering smile on her lips. 'You're *afraid*!'

'But do you think we've any reason to be cheerful, you and I? *You* especially!' He started walking up and down the room again. Every now and again he'd stop and stay something, almost muttering the words to himself.

'*Afraid!* Do you really believe that I'm not thinking of you too? *Afraid!* If you think that—— We were too sure of ourselves! That's what it was! And now, as I look back, I can see just how imprudent and mad we really were! It comes out and hits you! Why, I find myself wondering how on earth it is that he hasn't suspected anything long before this!'

Her lover's accusation struck home. She pressed her hands to her cheeks. 'Yes, you're quite right,' she agreed. 'You're quite right. We've gone too far in the way we've deceived him.' For a long time they remained there in silence. Then, lowering her hands from her face, she went on: 'And now you reproach me with it? It's only natural that you should. Yes, I've deceived a man who trusted me more than he trusted himself. Yes, indeed, it *is* my fault.'

'That wasn't what I meant!' he said dully, continuing to walk up and down.

'But it is! I know it is!' she replied feverishly, moving towards him. 'And you might as well add that I ran away from home with him. And that I more or less forced him into running away with me. *Because I loved him!* And then I betrayed him with you! You're quite right to condemn me now! Absolutely right! But listen to me! I ran away with him because I loved him. Not just so as to get all the peace and quiet I get here; all the ease and comfort, a new home. I had a home of my own. I shouldn't have run away with him if—— But he, you see, he had to make his excuses to the world somehow for the foolish action he'd committed. A steady, serious-minded man like him! Ah, well! The damage was done. And now amends had to be made, everything had to be set to rights again, and quickly too! But how? By throwing himself completely into his work. By giving me a fine house again to live in. A life simply oozing with leisure. So he worked like a galley-slave. He never thought of anything but work, asking for nothing from me except praise for his industry, praise for his uprightness. And, of course, my gratitude. Yes, because I might not have been so lucky. He was a good man, an *honourable* man. He'd made me rich. As rich as I'd been before—*richer!* This . . . *to me!* . . . to me, who waited impatiently every evening for him to come home, happy to see him back! He came home tired, completely worn-out. Pleased with his day's work. And already thinking about what there was to do the following day. Well, at last *I* got tired *too,* tired of almost having to force this man to make love to me! Of forcing him to respond to my love! There are times when the esteem, the trust, the friendship of her husband seem like insults to a woman's nature! To her womanhood itself! And *you've* reaped the benefit of all this! You, who are now reproaching me with my love for you, and with my treachery, now that there's danger! And you're afraid. I can see it in your eyes. *You're afraid!* But what have *you* got to lose? Nothing! While *I*——'

'And *you* tell *me* to keep calm!' said Serra coldly. 'But if I am afraid it's on your account. On account of your children.'

'No! Don't you dare talk about them!' she cried, deeply wounded, her eyes flashing with hate. 'Poor innocent little creatures!' she added, bursting into tears.

Serra looked at her for a little while. Then, more irritated than upset, he said, 'Now, if you're going to cry, I shall leave you.'

'Yes, wait till now! Wait till now to do it!' she sobbed. 'Yes, off you go! Now's the moment! Now that there's nothing more for you to do here!'

'That's not fair!' he replied, emphasizing each word, 'I've loved you as you've loved me. And you know it! I've told you to be careful. Was it wrong of me to do so? It was more for your sake than mine. Yes, because *I* should lose nothing if anything happened; you said so yourself. Come on, Lillina, come on! Pull yourself together! It's too late to start recriminations now. Andrea, we'll take it, knows nothing. That's what you believe, and that's how it shall be! I myself, now I come to think about it, find it difficult to conceive of his being able to control himself to such an extent. Andrea's noticed nothing. And so, buck up! Cheer up! Nothing's finished. We'll be——'

'Oh, no!' she interrupted proudly, 'it's no longer possible! How can you want to go on, *now*? No! The best thing for us—much the best thing for us to do, is to end it all now.'

'As you will,' said Serra simply.

'So that's your love for me!' she exclaimed indignantly. Serra moved towards her, almost threateningly.

'Are you trying to drive me out of my mind?'

'No, it's best to end everything now. Once and for all!' she replied, 'regardless of what may or may not be going to happen. Everything's over between us two. What's more, Antonio, it would be best for him to know everything. Yes, it would be much the best thing! Much the best thing! What sort of life am I going to have from now on? Can you imagine what it'll be like? I no longer have the right to love anyone. Not even my own children! If I bend down to kiss them, the shadow of what I've done seems to be there, darkening and disfiguring their innocent little faces. No! No! Would he kill me? I should kill myself if he didn't do it!'

'Now you're just not sane!' he said, his voice calm and hard.

'But I should!' Lillina insisted. 'I've always said I should! It's too much—too much for me to bear. There's nothing left for me to live for now!' Then, making an effort to pull herself together, she added, 'Now, go! Go! Don't let him find you here!'

'What? Do I *have* to go?' asked a perplexed Serra, 'and leave you? I came on purpose to—— Wouldn't it be better if I . . . ?'

'No,' she interrupted, 'He mustn't find you here. Come back, though, after he's got in. He won't be long now. We've still got to wear our masks when we're together. Come back soon. Try and look very calm, unperturbed. Not like this! Talk to me in front of him, make a point of frequently asking me what I think. You see what I'm driving at, don't you? I'll back you up.'

'All right. All right.'

'Quickly. But, just in case——'

'Just in case . . . ?'

She stood there for a moment, deep in thought. Then, shrugging her shoulders, she said, 'Nothing! So much——'

'What is it?' asked Serra in confusion.

'Nothing! Nothing! Good-bye!'

'But, in that case—we really——' he tried to get the words out.

'Oh, do go!' she interrupted contemptuously.

And off Serra went, promising, 'See you soon!'

She remained there, in the middle of the room, her gaze oblique, her eyes staring, as if her mind were filled with horrible thoughts that were coming vividly to life before her. Then she shook her head, and gave a sigh of utter weariness and desolation that was instinct with her inner anguish. She rubbed her forehead harshly with her hand, but failed completely to chase away the thought that was obsessing her. She wandered restlessly about the room a little, then stopped in front of a swivel-mirror at the back, by the door. The reflection of her own face in the mirror distracted her and she moved away. Then she went over to the little work-table and sat there with her head bowed over it and buried in her hands. She remained like this for a little while. Then she lifted her head and murmured, 'But surely he'd have come back upstairs! Made some excuse! He'd have found me there, standing by the window,

# THE BEST OF FRIENDS

GIGI MEAR was waiting on the Lungo Tevere de'Mellini for the Porta Pia tram, which would drop him in the Via Pastrengo—as it did every day—right in front of the Treasury, where he worked.

That morning he was well wrapped up in an Inverness cape—you don't do anything rash when you're over forty, and the north wind's on the prowl. His scarf was carefully wrapped round his neck and pulled well up, so that his nose was barely showing. He was wearing a pair of large English gloves. A well-fed, smooth-faced, rubicund man, Gigi Mear: a Count by birth. Unfortunately he no longer possessed either a county to lord it over, or the cash to count in his counting house. As a child—such is the blissful unconsciousness of the stern realities of life we enjoy when young—he'd informed his father of the noble resolution he'd arrived at: to become a clerk in the government office in which he was now employed, since, in all innocence, he believed that the *Corte dei Conti*—the Treasury, that is—was a Court for Counts, to which all Counts naturally enjoyed the right of entrance.

It's notorious, of course, that trams never come when you're waiting for them. They much prefer to get stuck half-way along the route, either because there's been a failure in the current or, it may be, because they've decided they'd rather have a collision with a cart or run some poor devil over. Still, all things considered, excellent gadgets, trams.

The north wind was certainly having a good old blow that morning—cold, cutting blasts—and Gigi Mear stamped his feet and looked down at the grey-looking river, where even the water seemed to be feeling the cold. Poor thing, it was as if it had been caught out in the open with only its shirt on, stretched out there between the stiff, colourless walls of the newly built embankment.

All in God's good time, the tram came clanging up. *Ding-ding!*

*Ding-ding!* Gigi Mear was just getting into position to clamber aboard when, from the direction of the new Ponte Cavour, there came a tremendous shout of, 'My dear Gigi! Gigi, old chap!'

Gigi Mear looked round and caught sight of a gentleman rushing towards him and gesticulating like a semaphore. The tram drew away and, in recompense, Gigi Mear had the consolation of finding himself in the arms of a man he didn't know, but who was obviously the dearest of long-lost friends—that is, if the violence of his greeting was anything to go by. Gigi Mear felt him kiss him vigorously on the scarf: *Phloff! Phloff!*

'I recognized you the moment I set eyes on you, my dear Gigi! The moment I set eyes on you! But what's this I see? Declining into the sere and yellow already! Tut-tut, your hair's as white as snow! Aren't you ashamed of yourself? Let me give you another kiss. You don't mind, do you, Gigi, old fellow? As a token of respect for your venerable and hoary old locks! I saw you standing here; I thought at first you must be waiting for *me*. Then, when I saw you put out your hand to get on that infernal contraption, I thought to myself, "It's downright treachery, that's what it is! Nothing short of downright treachery." '

'Oh, yes!' said Mear, with a forced smile, 'I was on my way to the office.'

'Do me the kindness of not talking about such obscene subjects —not for the moment!'

'What?'

'You heard! Do what I tell you, and don't argue!'

'Now, look here! You'll say "Please". And *politely*, too, if you want *me* to do anything. You know, you're a rum sort of character, and no mistake!'

'Yes, I know. You *weren't* waiting for me, though, were you? Why, of course you weren't! Everything about you just shrieks it at me. You weren't waiting for me.'

'No, to tell you the honest truth.'

'I arrived last night. Your brother asked me to give you his love. You know, he—— Oh, this'll make you laugh! He wanted to give me a note of introduction to you! *"What?"* I said. "To old Gigi? Let me tell you something: I knew him long before you did! In a manner of speaking, that is. Good God, we were boys together! Many's the time we've cracked one another's skulls! Good Lord, yes! We went up to the University at the same time, too." Inseparable. *Padua*. Greatest university of the lot of them! Do you remember, Gigi, old boy? That huge bell—the one you never used to hear! You never heard it once! There you'd lie, sleeping like a log! Well, that's how we'll put it, shall we? Though it was really more like a *hog*! Huh! The way you positively *wallowed* in sleep! Oh well, we'll say no more on that subject! There was *once,* though, when you heard it! Just the once! You thought it was the fire-alarm! Happy days! Your brother's very well, you know, thank God! We've joined forces in connexion with a business deal. That's why I'm here. Hey, what's the matter with you? You're looking a bit funereal. Committed matrimony?'

'No, my dear chap, no!' exclaimed Gigi Mear, shaking himself.

'On the point of?'

'Are you out of your mind? At gone forty? Oh no, not on your sweet life!'

'Forty, did you say? Sure you don't really mean *fifty,* Gigi old chap? Fifty years. Fifty times they've rung in the new and rung out the old as far as you're concerned! Oh, but of course! You make a speciality of never hearing bells! You don't hear bells, and you don't notice how the years are rushing past you. I was forgetting that. *Fifty!* Yes, cross my heart. As far as you're concerned, my dear fellow, they've rung the old bells fifty glorious times! *Altogether now!* Let's heave a sigh, shall we? This thing's beginning to get serious. You were born, now, wait a moment. . . . In April 1851, weren't you? Or *weren't* you? April 12th.'

'*May* 12th, if you don't mind. And in the year eighteen hundred and fifty-*two*, if you *don't* mind!' Mear corrected him, stressing the syllables. He was thoroughly piqued. 'Or are you now claiming that you know more about it than I do myself? The 12th of May 1852. All of which being which, I am, at this precise moment, forty-nine and some months.'

'And no wife! Jolly good going. *I've* got one, you know. Oh, it's an absolute tragedy! It'll make you split your sides laughing! It's agreed, I take it, that you're inviting me to lunch with you? Where do you do your guzzling these days? Still at Old Barba's?'

'Oh!' exclaimed Gigi Mear, growing more and more astonished, 'so you know all about old Barba's as well? I suppose *you've* been there too?'

'Me? To Barba's? How on earth could I possibly have managed that, seeing that I live in Padua? Oh, they've told me over and over again about all the mighty deeds that you—and all the others who eat there—get up to at that old—what's the word for it? Pub? Chop-house? With the emphasis on the *chop*! Ha! Ha! Restaurant?'

'Pub, sort of. But, look here, if you're going to have lunch with me, I'd better let my housekeeper know.'

'Young?'

'Oh no, my dear fellow; old, ever so old! By the way, I don't go to Barba's any longer. I've given up doing mighty deeds. Yes, I came to the conclusion that I'd had enough of that sort of thing. It must be three years ago now. When you reach a certain age——'

'Once you get past forty!'

'Once you get past forty, you've got to have the guts to turn your back on a way of life which, if you go on with it, will lead you straight over the edge of the precipice. I've no objection to going downhill. Not the slightest. But gently. Very gently. Very, very gently: no tumbling head-over-heels! Here we are! This is where I live! Do come on up! I've found myself a very pleasant flatlet. I'll show you just how very comfortable I've made things for myself.'

'Gently. Very, very gently. Very comfortable. Very pleasant *flatlet*,' his friend started to declaim as he climbed upstairs behind Gigi Mear. 'Flatlet, indeed! A hulking great creature like you, reduced to using incy-wincy diminutives! Poor Gigi, and you such a superlative hunk of manhood! What *have* they been doing to you? Putting salt on your tail? You'll have me crying my eyes out in a minute!'

'It's all very well for *you* to——' said Mear as they waited on the landing for the old woman to come and open the door. 'You've got to use a little soft-soap with this horrible life of ours. You've got to caress it, caress it with incy-wincy diminutives, or it does for you. I've got no desire to land in the grave yet awhile—back on four feet, and for ever this time!'

'Oh, so you believe man's a biped, do you,' the other burst out at this point. 'Don't you dare utter such heresies, Gigi, old fellow! God only knows—well, *I* know too!—the efforts I sometimes have to make to keep myself up on just the two paws. Believe me, dear friend of my bosom, if we were to leave it to old Mother Nature, we'd all, from sheer inclination, be quadrupeds, the whole lot of us! Much the best thing, too! Much more comfortable, and the *poise*. . . . My dear! Always thoroughly well-balanced! The number of times I've had to stop myself from throwing myself on the ground and trotting along on four paws! *Pussy, pussy, pussy!* Oh, this damned civilization of ours is ruining us! If I was a quadruped I'd make a wonderful wild beast! If I was a quadruped I'd give you a nifty couple of kicks in the guts for the beastly things you've been saying. I shouldn't have any wife, I shouldn't have any debts, and I shouldn't have any nasty nagging thoughts. You'll have me crying my eyes out in a minute! Is that what you're trying to do? I'm going!'

Gigi Mear was quite shattered by the comic way this 'friend' of his was talking, this 'friend' who'd dropped out of the sky just like that. He looked at him, racking his memory to try and work out what the blazes his name was and how the blazes it was that he knew him; where in Padua he'd got to know him—both as a boy and as a student, it seemed. And he held a kind of march-past in his head of all the intimate friends of those days, but it was all in vain that he scanned their ranks. Not one of them answered to the features of this man. And he didn't dare ask for any sort of clarification. The intimacy that the man revealed was such and so great that he was afraid of offending him. He decided in his own mind, therefore, to gain his end by low cunning.

The old woman was a long time coming. She hadn't expected her boss to be back so soon. Gigi Mear rang the bell again, and at last she came shuffling along.

'It's me, old girl,' Mear said to her, 'I'm back! And I've brought a friend with me. Lay lunch for two today, and don't be too long about it! Watch your step with my friend here! He's got one of the most peculiar names in the world, and there's no fooling about with him!'

'Anthropophagus Goatsbeardhornyfoot!' exclaimed the other, pulling a horrible face—which left the old woman completely at a loss as to whether to smile or to cross herself. 'And there's not a living soul that doesn't screech to a halt when he hears this name of mine, old girl. Mention it to any bank manager and he wrinkles his nose as if he's smelt a nasty smell. As for the money-lenders, they go sick of the palsy! My wife's been the only exception: she was jolly glad to take it. It was only my name I let her take, though! She didn't get *me*! Oh, dear no! She didn't get me! I'm far too handsome a young fellow, God rot me with a hey nonny no! Get cracking, Gigi, old scout! Since you've got this weakness for domestic bliss, show me the appalling slum in which you manage to pig it! As for you, old ducks: fodder for the beasties!'

Mear, discomfited at the failure of his stratagem, took him round the five small rooms of the flat. They were all furnished with loving care, the loving care of a man who has no desire to seek anything outside his own home, once he's made up his mind to settle for such a snail's existence. A tiny sitting-room, bedroom, minute bathroom, dining-room, and a little study.

In the sitting-room his amazement and self-torment grew and grew when he heard his friend talking about the most intimate details, the most closely-guarded family secrets, as he looked at the photographs displayed on the mantelpiece.

'Oh, Gigi, old chap! I wish *I* had a brother-in-law like this one of yours! If you only knew what a rogue mine is!'

'I suppose he ill-treats your sister?'

'Worse! He ill-treats *me*! And it would be the easiest thing in the world for him to help me in my little disasters! Still!'

'I'm terribly sorry, but . . .' said Mear, 'I simply can't remember your brother-in-law's name.'

'Oh, don't bother to try! Anyway, you *can't* remember it! You don't know him! He's been in Padua barely two years. Do you know what he did to me? Well, *your* brother. . . . Oh, *he's* been extraordinarily kind to me! Your brother promised to help me if that swine would agree to back my promissory notes; and would you believe it? He refused to sign! So your brother who, when all's said and done, is—well, great friend though he is—he's not one of the family. Oh, he got so indignant about it all, that he took the whole affair into his own hands. It's true, of course, that our little bit of business is an absolute cert; but if I were to tell you the reason why my brother-in-law refused, you'd hardly credit it! I'm still a handsome young man—you can't deny it. A captivating sort of chap in a big way, and no bones about it! No need for false modesty! All right! My brother-in-law's sister got the perfectly nauseating idea into her head to fall in love with me, poor girl! Excellent taste, too little discretion in the exercise of it. I ask you, do you think I'm the sort of chap to——? Oh, phooey! She poisoned herself!'

'Is she dead?' asked Mear, pulled up short.

'No. Vomited a bit and then got better. But, as you'll readily appreciate, I couldn't set foot again in my brother-in-law's house after that tragedy. Good God, man, are we going to eat or aren't we? My eyes grow dim for want of nourishment! Hungry as a wolf, that's me!'

Later on, when they were seated at table, Gigi Mear started to find the affectionate expansiveness of his friend most oppressive. (He was positively loading him down with wicked words, and it was only by a miracle that he wasn't banging away at him too.) So he began asking him for news of Padua and about this and that, hoping to trap him into letting slip his own name—just by chance, just like that. And if he didn't manage *that* . . . Well, he hoped, in his exasperation—which was growing stronger every minute—that he'd somehow contrive, by talking of other things, to distract himself from his fixation to get at the bottom of things.

'Tell me, now. That fellow—*Valverde*—yes, that's his name. The Manager of the Bank of Italy. Got a very beautiful wife. And that simply superb monster of a sister. Squints into the bargain, unless I'm very much mistaken. Are they still living in Padua?'

At his question, his friend gave a huge roar of laughter—laughed fit to burst.

'What's up,' asked Mear, his curiosity aroused. '*Doesn't* she squint?'

'Oh, do stop! Do stop talking, please!' the other begged him. He just couldn't stop laughing. He was simply convulsed with laughter. 'I'll say she squints! And her nose! Good God Almighty, it's so big, you can see right up into her brains! That's the lady!'

'*Who* is? Which one d'you . . . ?'

'My wife!'

Gigi Mear was absolutely shattered. He could hardly manage to stammer out his feeble words of excuse. But the other man began to laugh even louder and even longer than previously. Finally he quietened down, knitted his brows, and gave a huge sigh.

'My dear fellow,' he said, 'there's a great deal of mute inglorious heroism in this life of ours that the world knows nothing at all about, and that even the most unbridled poetic imagination could never so much as conceive!'

'Yes! Yes!' sighed Mear, 'you're quite right! I see what you——'

'You don't see a damn thing!' said the other, instantly slapping him down. 'You surely don't think I was alluding to myself? What, me a hero? At the very outside I might rank as a *victim*. But I'm not even that. No, all the heroism's been put in by my sister-in-law, Lucio Valverde's wife. Let me tell you something—— God, what a man! Blind, barmy, and as stupid as they make them.'

'Who, me?'

'No, me! Me! For having been unclever enough to kid myself into believing that Lucio Valverde's wife was so deeply in love with me that she'd even go to the length of deceiving her husband! And in all conscience, you can believe me, Gigi, my dear chap, he *deserved* to be betrayed! Huh; Ha-ha! Ha-ha! What happened, though? Huh! Disinterested spirit of self-sacrifice, tra-la! Listen! Off went Valverde; or rather, off he pretended to go, as usual. All a put-up job, of course, with *her* in it up to the neck. Then she lets me into the house. The tragic moment of being discovered together by jealous husband arrives. She pops me into the bedroom of her cross-eyed sister-in-law, who welcomes me in an appropriately chaste and trembling fashion, with all the air of . . . She too was ready to sacrifice herself. . . . Tra-la! . . . On the altar of her brother's honour and peace of mind. I hardly had time to shout, "Now, take it easy, dear lady! How on earth can Lucio possibly seriously—— Ha! Ha!—believe that" I didn't get a chance to finish. Lucio burst into the room, furious with rage, and the rest you can easily imagine for yourself.'

'Do you mean to say . . . ?' exclaimed Gigi, 'With *your* brains——?'

'And all my promissory notes, as well!' shouted the other. 'My unredeemed notes, on which Valverde was granting me renewals on account of my supposed enjoyment of his wife's good graces! Now he'd have protested them *ipso facto*! Get me? And he'd have ruined me. Filthy low-down blackmailing skunk! Please, I beg you, don't let's say another word on the subject! When all's said and done, and seeing and giving due weight to the fact that I haven't got a penny of my own, and that I'm never likely to have, and seeing and giving all proper weight to the fact that I haven't got the faintest intention of marrying anybody——'

'What did you say?' Gigi Mear interrupted at this point. 'But you *are* married!'

'Who, me? Oh no, not on your life! Honest! *She* married *me*! *She* was the only one who got married in that little carry-on! As far as I was concerned, I told her what I thought about it all *before* the fatal day. Cards on the table and no hard feelings afterwards—that's my motto. "You, dear spinster, want my name, do you? Go ahead and take it! I don't mind admitting I haven't the faintest idea what to do with it! Nothing *else,* though! That'll do you, eh?"'

'And so,' ventured Gigi Mear, inwardly rejoicing, 'there's nothing more to it. Her name was originally Valverde, and now it's . . .'

'Unfortunately!' puffed the other, getting up from the table.

'Oh no, *look*!' exclaimed Gigi Mear, unable to stand it any longer and taking his courage in both his hands. 'You've made me spend a very delightful morning. I've received you like a brother. Now you must do me a favour.'

'You wouldn't like the loan of my wife by any chance, would you?'

'No, thank you. I want you to tell me what your name is.'

'What my . . . ? What *my* name is?' asked his friend, looking as if he'd dropped down from the clouds. He pointed with his index finger at his own chest, as though he couldn't believe in his own existence. 'And what do you mean by *that*? Don't you *know* what my name is? Can't you remember?'

'No!' confessed a thoroughly humiliated Mear. 'Forgive me, call me the most forgetful man on the face of the earth, but I could really and truly put my hand on my heart and swear I've never met you in my whole life.'

'Oh, you could, could you? H'm, excellent! Jolly nice!' replied the other. 'My dear Gigi, here's my hand, old fellow. Thank you from the bottom of my heart for the lunch and for your company. Now I'm off, and I'm not telling you what my name is! So there!'

'By God, you *shall* tell me!' burst out Gigi Mear, leaping to his feet. 'I've been racking my brains for a whole morning! I'm not letting you out of here until you tell me!'

'Kill me!' replied his implacable friend. 'Chop me into little pieces. *I still* shan't tell you.'

'Oh, come now! Be a good chap!' replied Mear, changing tack. 'I've never had such an experience as this in my whole life before. Look, this loss of memory—and I swear it's made a most painful impression on me . . . You at this moment represent a walking nightmare as far as I'm concerned. For pity's sake, tell me what your name is!'

'Go and fish!'

'I beg you, on my bended knees. Well, almost! My forgetfulness hasn't prevented me from giving you a place at my table. What's more, even if I *have* never set eyes on you in my life before, even if you *have* never previously been a friend of mine, you've become one now, and a very dear one at that! Believe me! I feel for you a brotherly love and all the bonds of—— I *admire* you. I'd like to have you always by my side. So. . . . Tell me who you are!'

'It's no use, you know,' the other said, with an air of finality. 'You're not getting round me like that. Be reasonable. Do you really want to deprive me now of this unexpected source of enjoyment? Of leaving you gibbering with curiosity because, old Nosey Parker, you aren't able to find out who you've been entertaining to lunch? Get along with you! No! You're asking too much! It's perfectly obvious that you don't remember me from Adam. If you don't want me to harbour all sorts of nasty rancorous feelings about your unworthy forgetfulness, let me go. Here and now. Leaving things just as they are.'

'In that case, get out immediately, please, I beg you!' exclaimed Gigi Mear in exasperation, 'I can't bear the sight of you any longer!'

'Yes, I'm going. But first a little kiss, Gigi, old scout. I'm going back to Padua tomorrow.'

'I'm not giving you a kiss,' yelled Mear, 'unless you tell me——'

'Oh, no! Now that's enough of that carry-on! No! That'll do! Good-bye, then!' the other said, cutting things short.

Off he went, laughing. And he turned as he went down the stairs, and gave him another farewell wave of the hand.

# BITTER WATERS

*Acqua amara* was first published in *Il XX di Genova,* No. 27, 1905.[1] It was reprinted in *La vita nuda,* the collection of Pirandello's *novelle* published by Treves of Milan in 1910 (2nd edition 1917). When the stories were collected together for the Bemporad *Novelle per un anno* presentation, this tale was included in Vol. II, *La vita nuda,* Firenze, 1922. The volume passed through a number of reprints (with Bemporad and Mondadori), and the story is currently to be found in the Biblioteca Moderna Mondadori text of *La vita nuda* and Vol. I of the *Opere*. (*Novelle per un anno,* Vol. I, *con una prefazione di Corrado Alvaro,* Milano-Verona, Mondadori, 1956.)



[1] MLV–M.

# BITTER WATERS

THERE were very few people about that morning, in the grounds surrounding the Pump Room and Baths. It was very near the end of the season for taking the cure.

Two men were seated on small benches under the lofty plane trees: a fat man and a thin young man. The young man was very pale, yellow even, and so thin that it made your heart bleed to see him. He was wearing a new light-coloured suit, the folds of which —still fresh from the presser's iron—hung upon him like a concertina, so over-large for him was it. The fat man was a coarse, huge man of about fifty. He was wearing a grubby and badly wrinkled linen suit. So colossally fat was he that he seemed on the point of bursting out of his clothes; indeed, across the tighter-fitting areas his suit was ironed by his fatness to a taut smoothness. On his close-cropped head he sported a battered old panama.

Both were holding glasses in their hands, glasses that were still full of the tepid, thick, alkaline water which they had just taken from the fountain.

The fat man's face put you in mind of a well-fed and thoroughly self-satisfied Abbot. Every now and again he closed his eyes, which were glazed with sleepiness. (He was probably deafened by the shattering snores which had blasted from his nose during the night.) The thin young man obviously felt the stinging morning air strike cold, for he was shivering a little.

Neither seemed able to pluck up courage enough to drink his glass of water. In fact, it seemed as if each was waiting for the other. Finally, having taken their first sip, they looked at one another, and both their faces were twisted in the same expression of nausea.

'Liver, eh?' the fat man suddenly asked the young man in a low tone, shaking himself. 'Hepatic colic, m'm? You're a married man, by the look of you. Are you?'

'No. Why do you ask?' asked the young man in his turn, accompanying his words with a horrible grimace which took in his whole face, and which was intended to be a smile.

'Well, you just *look* like one. Something about the way you . . . ?' sighed the other. 'But if you *aren't* a married man, then just you stop worrying. You'll get better.'

The young man gave another grimace of a smile.

'Are *you* suffering from liver-trouble too?' he asked sharply.

'Oh, no! No! I've managed to lose *my* wife!' the fat man made haste to reply, seriously. 'I used to suffer from it, but, thanks be to God, I'm now freed from my wife and a cured man as a consequence. I've been coming here for the past . . . thirteen years it'll be now. Out of gratitude. I don't want to seem nosey, but when did you get here?'

'Yesterday evening. Six o'clock,' said the young man.

'That explains things!' exclaimed the other, half-closing his eyes and wagging his massive head. 'If you'd got here in the morning, you'd know who I was.'

'I'd . . . know who you were?'

'Why, of course you would. Just as everybody else here knows me. I'm famous! Look! Up in the Piazza dell'Arena, in all the hotels, in all the boarding-houses, at the Caffè Pedoca itself. In all the chemists' shops. For the past thirteen years, season after season. Nobody ever talks about anything else except me! I know all about it and I get a terrific kick out of it. I come here on purpose. Where are you staying? At Rori's? Good man. You can be absolutely certain that at lunchtime today at Rori's they'll trot out my story for your entertainment. If you don't mind, I'll get my version in first! I'll tell you the whole thing exactly as it happened. All right?'

Saying this he got up laboriously and went over to the bench on which the younger man was seated. The thin young man made room for him, his bony yellow face twisted in a grimace of pleasure.

'Well, first of all, just to get things sorted out properly, they call me The Doctor's Wife's Husband here. My real name's Cambiè, and my christian name's Bernardo. Or, as the wags put it, Bernardo the Great—because I'm the size I am. Drink up! I'll have a drop too!'

They drank. Once again their faces twisted into those grimaces of disgust. They were trying hard to smile, of course. They exchanged glances of commiseration. Cambiè resumed:

'You're very young. And you really look pretty knocked up! These gut-twisting confidences I'm going to share with you will do you a great deal more good than this foul water here! It's bitter all right but, by way of compensation, it doesn't do you a scrap of good, believe me! They expect us to swallow it—in every sense of the expression—and we drink it because it's nasty! If it tasted nice——! No, I must stop running it down! You're here for the cure, and I mustn't do anything to shake your faith.

'Well, then. . . . So that you'll be able to understand just how I felt about things, I must tell you that I had an utter abomination of marriage when I was a young man. I only had to hear the sound of the word and I got an awful griping in my guts, if you'll forgive the expression. I really felt like—— Oh, yes! I only had to see a wedding procession, or hear that a friend was getting married, and my belly was all of a heave. But what are we to do, we wretched mortals? A tiny spot on the sun, and there's an absolute deluge of cataclysms. A king gets up with fur on his tongue one morning, and off we go on an endless round of war and extermination. A volcano gets a sob in the throat, and it's earthquakes, catastrophes, and carnage all round!

"Well, when I was about your age, we were living in Naples at the time, there was a terrible cholera epidemic. It was something like twenty years ago now; I'm sure you must have heard of it. My father, who was a poverty-stricken clerk, with the usual good luck which persecuted him throughout his whole life, managed to find himself in Naples when the epidemic arrived. I was thirty at the time. *I'd* managed to find myself a pretty good job, and I was living in a snug little bachelor flat not very far from my parents' home. I'd set up my own establishment, and was keeping a girl. You know, it was just as if she'd dropped straight out of Heaven into my arms!

'Carlotta—that was her name. She was the daughter of a—

nothing bad, you know! It takes all professions to get the world's work done—daughter of a money-lender. A spoilt priest into the bargain!

'She'd run away from home on account of an awful series of rows she'd been having with her mother, who was an old bitch, and her younger brother, who was a thoroughgoing scoundrel. But I won't bore you with all the sordid details; she looked all right to me, the one good thing in a family of—— At the time, of course. . . . But—well, you'll know without my telling you—I was in love with the girl and you don't do any really profound thinking when you're in *that* state!

'Sorry if I'm—— You're not religious by any chance, are you? So so. Maybe a little less than more? Like me. My mother, on the other hand, my dear fellow, was as religious as they make them. Poor woman, she suffered a great deal on account of that little tie-up of mine! As far as she was concerned, it was absolutely sinful. You see, she knew that the girl hadn't been anybody else's before she was mine. When the cholera broke out, she was terrified by it all. Particularly by the rate at which people were dying off. She was absolutely convinced that we were all doomed to die. Me above all, because, according to her, I was in a state of mortal sin. And, just so as to appease the Divine Wrath, she demanded that I should marry the girl at once. In church at least. And *only* in church if I felt that strongly about matrimony. Yes, that was the little sacrifice she demanded of me!

'Believe me, I should never have agreed to do it if Carlotta hadn't suddenly fallen ill. I had to save her soul at least—I'd promised my mother I would. I rushed off to get a priest and married the girl. Then, what happened? Was it the Hand of God? Some sort of miracle? On the point of death . . . And then, she got better!

'My mother, out of a spirit of charity, you might even call it self-sacrifice, insisted on being present at the ceremony, though she was scared stiff all the time. And insisted, too, on staying on with the sick girl.

'It was just as if the cholera had come to Naples on purpose to spite me, to punish me for my mortal sin. And that it would be passing on now that Carlotta was getting better! Oh, yes! She was getting better, so carefully, so zealously had my mother set about nursing her back to health. As soon as she'd got her safely back from the jaws of death it began to dawn on her that that little flat of mine was altogether lacking in the comforts necessary for the convalescent girl. She insisted on taking her into her own home. Despite my vigorous opposition.

'As you'll readily appreciate, Carlotta didn't set foot outside that door again until she was very thoroughly my lawfully wedded wife! That was accomplished very soon afterwards. As soon as the epidemic eased off.

'Ah well, let's try another sip, shall we?'

'By great good luck, Carlotta's whole family died during the epidemic. Mother, father, brothers, and sisters. Good luck and bad luck. For *me*! You see, she was the sole surviving member of her family, so she inherited everything, thirty-eight to forty thousand lire. The fruits of the noble profession practised by her father.

'I'd landed myself with a wife, and a wife with money of her own! You can imagine what that meant, can't you? She changed just like that, from one day to the next.

'Now listen. It's not beyond the bounds of possibility that I'm a bit of a philo—*philosopher*. The idea strikes you as a pretty rum one, I suspect. But let me say what I was going to say.

'Are you one of those people who believe that there are only two genders, masculine and feminine?

'You're wrong if you do!

'Wives are a gender all on their own! So are husbands!

'And, as far as those genders are concerned, it's the woman that always wins in the state of Holy Matrimony, and no two ways about it! She sweeps down upon him, she's through his defences in an instant, and then she starts mopping-up operations! She takes over so much that belongs to the masculine gender that, of sheer necessity, the poor man starts losing his masculinity. And, believe me, he loses a whale of a lot of his masculinity!

'If it were ever to be my misfortune to have to compose a

grammar-book—one that thought about things along my lines—I'd make it a rule that *wife* should always be considered as masculine, and, as a direct consequence, *husband* as feminine.

'You laugh, do you? But, my dear fellow, as far as my wife's concerned, a husband ceases to be a man! So much so that she stops bothering about doing anything to please him. "What's the point of doing anything for your benefit?" she thinks to herself, "You know all about me already!"

'And yet, you know, if the husband is daft enough to get something of the old feeling, and to make the mistake of protesting about it when he sees her lying there in bed, her face all smeared with muck, her hair in curlers, and generally looking like a devil up from Hell . . . Well, as sure as eggs is eggs, she's quite capable of answering back with, "Silly man, can't you see. I'm doing it for *your* sake!"

' "For *my* sake?"

' "Why, of course I am! So as not to let you down in public. You wouldn't like people to say, 'Oh, just look at the ghastly creature that poor man's had wished on him as a wife!' Now would you?"

'And the husband; I do assure you—— Well, he's stopped being a man. He doesn't say a word! While all the time he ought to be on his hind legs, shouting, "I'm the one that's going to do the criticizing, my dear. I'm the one that's going to tell you what an awful fright you look? Look at you now! Lying in bed beside me, looking like a——! Oh yes, you let *me* have the benefit of all your horrible smearing and plastering! *My* house, *my* bed see you at your most revolting, so that the rest of the world, seeing you pass on your elegant way, shall exclaim, 'Oh, look at the lovely wife that dreadful man's got!' So they're supposed to envy me, too, are they? Thank you, my dear, thank you very much! This envy of me is—oh, so very naturally!—is translated into desire for you! *Thank you!* You wish to be desired, do you, so that I may be envied? Oh, how good and kind you are! But I'm even more good and kind than you are, because I married you!"

'Of course, the dialogue could be carried on still further. You see, there's the possibility that the wife might even have the brazen impudence to ask her husband if—now that she's all dressed and titivated up ready to go out—to ask her husband whether he thinks she looks all right!

'The husband *ought* to reply, "But my dear——! Well, tastes differ so very much, you know! Speaking for myself, and only for myself, mind you; well, as I've already told you, I don't like the way you've done your hair. Who are you trying to please? You really must tell me, so that I shall know how to answer your question! Nobody? *Really* nobody? Oh, well, in that case, what a lucky little woman you are! If it's merely a question of pleasing *nobody,* why not try and please your husband? At least he's *somebody*!"

'My dear fellow, if he gave her an answer like that, the wife would look at the husband almost pityingly. Then she'd shrug her shoulders, as if to say, "What's it got to do with you anyway?"

'And she'd be right, you know. Women can't do without it. The power to attract men is something they all desire, *instinctively.* They simply *need* to be desired. *Women!*

'Now, as you'll readily appreciate, a husband can't possibly go on desiring the wife he's got hanging around him day and night. What I mean is, he can't possibly desire her as she herself would like to be desired.

'Yes, you see; just as the wife stops seeing the man in her husband, so the husband stops seeing the woman in his wife.

'The man puts up with it . . . because men are naturally more philosophical. The woman, on the other hand, feels herself insulted, and, as a consequence, her husband soon becomes an utter bore, and quite often totally unbearable as far as she's concerned.

'And so, she must be free to do as she pleases! But her husband? *Oh, no!*

'But, believe me, whatever he does, it'll never satisfy her, because her husband can never—simply because he *is* her husband—can never give her the love she—— That *special* kind of love she needs. Perhaps more than love, it's a—well, an atmosphere of *admiration.* She'd like to feel that she was completely surrounded by it. Go on, off you go! Admire her in the privacy of her own home—when she's got a splitting headache—when she's slopping about the house in her slippers and without her corsets on. Let's take a look at her today. Let's suppose she's got the belly-ache. Tomorrow it'll be the toothache. That atmosphere of admiration will be breathed forth only from the eyes of the men who don't know her when she's like that. The men whom she, with all the refinements of her art, has done her damnedest to attract. *And* succeeded! Their gaze falls upon her and they're delightfully intoxicated by what they see! If she's an honest and virtuous wife, that'll be quite sufficient for her. I'm talking now about the virtuous ones, you understand, the absolutely pure and spotless ones. There's no real point in talking about the other kind!

'Just let me indulge in one more little reflection! We men have got into the habit of saying that woman is an incomprehensible being. My dear fellow, quite the contrary! Woman is just like us. But she can neither say that she is nor let the world see that she is, because she knows that, in the first place, society would refuse to let her do so, calling a sin in her what it deems only natural in man, and secondly because she knows that she'd stop attracting the men if she *did* tell them or let them see that she was just like them! There you are, there's your enigma all neatly explained! Any man who's had the misfortune, like me, to stumble on a wife who doesn't care a damn what she says, will know only too well what I mean!

'Let's have another little drink! Oh, come on! It's not as horrible as all that!'

'Carlotta wasn't like that to start with. She got like it immediately after we were married. That's to say, as soon as she felt thoroughly settled in and had started noticing that I'd—quite naturally—begun to see in her, not just a source of pleasure, but also that ugly thing called duty.

'It was my duty to respect her, now wasn't it? She was my wife! Well, you know, I've got a suspicion that she didn't really want to be respected. Who knows? Perhaps the sight of me suddenly switching from being the bold bad lover to being the exemplary husband was too much for her poor tattered nerves!

'Life became utter Hell for the pair of us! She was always sulky, touchy, restless. I took it all patiently, submissively, partly out of fear, a little bit because I'd come to realize that I'd committed the stupidest of all stupid actions, and that I'd soon have plenty of consequences to lament. I followed her around like a puppy. Oh, I sank even lower! But, try as I would, I could never get so much as an inkling of what it was my wife wanted. And I'd have been willing to wager that nobody else could have guessed either! D'you know what it *was* she wanted? She wished she'd been born a man! My wife wanted to be a man! So she took it out on me because she'd been born a woman. "Oh, to be a man," she'd say, "even if I were blind in one eye!"

'One day I asked her, "Tell me something, what would you have done if you'd been born a man?"

' "I'd have become a crook!"

' "Good girl!" I said.

' "There wouldn't have been any of this wife stuff for me!" said she. "You wouldn't have caught me getting married!"

' "Thank you, dear!"

' "Oh yes, you can rest assured on that point!"

' "But you'd have had your bit of fun with the women, wouldn't you? You do believe, I suppose, that there's some fun to be had with women?"

'My wife looked at me. Deep down into my eyes she looked. "You're asking me?" she said. "I suppose *you* don't know? I should never have taken a wife, so as not to have made some poor woman my prisoner!"

' "Oh!" I exclaimed, "So you feel you're a prisoner?"

'To which she replied, "*Feel,* did you say? What am I *but*? I've always been a prisoner, haven't I, from the moment I was born? You're the only man I've ever known. When have I ever got any enjoyment out of life?"

' "Have you ever felt the desire to know other men?"

' "Why, of course I have! In precisely the same way as you. After all, you'd had your fling with a fair number of women before you met me! And God only knows how many since!"

'So, my dear fellow, let me urge you to bear this thought in mind. A woman's desires are exactly the same as a man's. Let's suppose, for example, that you see a beautiful woman walking along. You follow her with your eyes. In your imagination you see every little bit of her. In your thoughts you've got her in your arms and you're making love to her. You naturally don't say a word to your wife about it! There she is, walking along beside you. Meanwhile, she's caught sight of a handsome man. She follows *him* with her eyes. In her imagination she sees every little bit of him. In her thoughts she's in his arms and they're making love together. Naturally, she doesn't say a word to you about it.

'There's nothing extraordinary in all this. But, believe me, there's nothing very jolly about imagining all this to be going on inside your own wife. Oh, yes! It's all very obvious; a commonplace, everyday occurrence! Your wife, though—her body's your prisoner. And her spirit? *Oh, no!* And you can't be too sure about the body, either! Tell me. We men, we know, don't we, that if the opportunity came our way, we shouldn't, for one moment, be able to resist it? H'm? Of course we do! Well, just imagine; it's exactly the same for the women! They fall, they fall. Oh, it's a joy to behold them! Easy as winking. Just like us, if the opportunity presents itself! That's to say, if they find a man who's determined enough, a man on whose discretion they can rely. My wife made all this very, very clear to me when she was talking to me about—you'll appreciate—*my other women!*

'Which brings me to my own case.

'It was only natural, of course, that after a year of marriage, I should run into trouble with my liver.

'For six years, one after the other, I tried every cure under the sun. All of them were absolutely useless. And my poor body was tormented and rent asunder. Oh, I became a total wreck! So much so that even the other liver-sufferers felt something like compassion for me.

'I was destined to find the remedy here.

'I came here with my wife, and first of all we stayed at Rori's, where you're staying now. As soon as I got here I ordered them to call a doctor, so that I could ask him to visit me and prescribe the number of glasses of this stuff that I ought to drink. Or tell me whether I'd do better to go in for douches or baths in sulphur-water.

'The young man who presented himself to me was a handsome

fellow, tall, dark, robust-looking, military appearance, and dressed all in black. I found out afterwards, as a matter of fact, that he *had* been in the army. A military doctor. Surgeon lieutenant, they called them in those days. At Rovigo he'd got himself involved with a girl, the daughter of a printer. She'd presented him with a baby. A little girl it was. Her father had put the screws on and forced him to marry her. He'd resigned his commission—he'd had to—and then he'd started practising here. Eight months after this heroic sacrifice on his part both his wife and daughter had died, within a very short time of one another. Three years, more or less, had passed since that double misfortune, and he was still wearing black, and looking exactly like a very handsome raven.

'As you'll readily appreciate, he was immensely popular! That heroic sacrifice of his—for Love he had yielded up his career! And fortune had so scurvily rewarded him for his nobility! And then the double misfortune, the marks of which were carved, one might say, into the very lines of his body! Oh, he was the living embodiment of romantic heroism! All the women here, if you'd given them half a chance, would have provided him with consolation, just like that! He knew all about it, of course, and treated them with utter contempt.

'Well, he came and saw me. Gave me a good going-over. Tapped and prodded me thoroughly. And repeated more or less what umpteen other doctors had already told me. Finishing up by writing out the course of treatment: three half-glasses of this stuff, provided by the medical pimps who run this place, for the first few days. Then three full glasses. A bath one day, douche the next. He was just about to leave when, so he pretended, he caught sight of my wife for the first time.

' "Your wife, too?" he asked, looking at her coldly.

' "No, no!" my wife replied immediately, pulling a long, long face and with her eyebrows raised so far that they almost reached the line where her hair began.

' "All the same," he insisted, "May I . . . ?"

'He went over to where she was standing and very delicately raised her chin with one hand, while with the index finger of the other he just slightly turned back her left eyelid.

' "A touch of anaemia," he said.

'My wife looked at me. She was very pale and wan, just as if that snap diagnosis had instantaneously anaemiatized her. Then, with a nervous little smile on her lips, she gave a slight shrug of her shoulders and said, "I really feel quite all right."

'The doctor bowed. Very seriously he said, "It's much better that way."

'And, the acme of dignity, off he went.'

'It might have been the water. It might have been the baths or the douches. Or, more probably—so I'm inclined to think myself—the wonderful air one enjoys here, the gentle calmness of the Tuscan countryside. Well, whatever it was, the fact is I started feeling better at once. So much so that I decided to stay on here for a month or two. I thought I'd like to have a bit more freedom of movement, so I rented a little flat near the Hotel; a short way down the hill, at Coli's. It's got a lovely little balcony overlooking the garden, from which you can see the whole valley, with the two little lakes of Chiusi and Montepulciano.

'*Then* . . . ! I don't know whether you've guessed what I'm going to say? Well, my wife started feeling ill.

'She didn't call it anaemia, because that was what the doctor had suggested it was. She said she felt a certain tiredness round the heart. It was just as if there was a heavy weight on her chest which was stopping her from breathing properly.

'Whereupon I, with all the ingenuousness I could muster, said, "Would you like the doctor to look you over, too?"

'At that, she got thoroughly up on her high horse. Just as I'd foreseen, of course, and said no, she *wouldn't*!

'You won't need to be told, I'm sure, that she got steadily worse from day to day. In direct proportion, as a matter of fact, to the obstinacy with which she said, no, she didn't want to see the doctor! I just hardened my heart and never referred to the subject. So it was finally she herself who—— You see, she couldn't stand it any longer! No, one day she said to me, "All right, I'll see the doctor. But not that man of yours! Most definitely not! No! I'll see the other one." There were a couple of them practising here in those days. It was Dr. Berri she wanted to come and see her. He was a shaggy lump of a man, about a hundred and three. Practically blind and practically retired. He's retired altogether now. Into the next world!

'"Oh, come, come, come, come!" I exclaimed. "Nobody ever calls in Dr. Berri these days! Besides, it would be an altogether undeserved slap in the face for Dr. Loero, who's shown us every courtesy and been a perfect paragon of medical attentiveness."

'And, to tell the truth, every day, here at the Baths, the moment Dr. Loero saw me get out of my carriage with my wife, over he'd come to greet us, bearing himself in that proud, military, and punctiliously correct way of his. Full of concern for me, he'd congratulate me on my rapid improvement. He'd come over to the fountain with me. Then he'd walk up and down the paths with me, round the grounds. Never failing to treat my wife with proper respect. But in those first days, you understand, he didn't really pay very much attention to her, and she, as you'll also understand, suffered in silence. Getting madder and madder.

'For the last week, though, they'd been busy skirmishing about the age-old question. Men and Women! You know the way it goes! Man is a tyrant and a bully, Woman is his victim. Society is fundamentally unjust... et cetera... et cetera!

'Believe me, my dear fellow, I never want to hear another word on that drivelling subject. The whole seven years we were married my wife and I talked of nothing else.

'I must confess, however, that I had a thoroughly enjoyable time that week, listening to Dr. Loero repeating my own arguments in the most self-possessed manner in the world, and liberally seasoning them with the salt and pepper of scientific authority. When *I* put them forward, my wife would hurl every kind of insult at me. When Dr. Loero, on the other hand, put them forward, she had to bite upon the bit of social decorum. But the nasty poison was lurking there all the same. She couldn't spit it out, but the words she spoke tasted of it!

'I was hoping that this would help her to get over her heart trouble. Not on your life! As I've already told you, it got steadily worse from day to day. Significant, don't you think? A sure sign that she was trying to convince her opponent by means of a different kind of argument! Now, just take a brief look at the sort of role it falls to the poor old husband to play on occasion! I knew for a certainty that she wanted Dr. Loero to come and examine her, and that it was all a fabulous piece of play-acting, the antipathy which he displayed towards her. It was play-acting, too, that business about preferring to be examined by that asthmatic and infantile old dotard, Dr. Berri. And that heart trouble of hers was the biggest bit of play-acting of the lot. But I still had to go on pretending that I really and truly believed in all three things. And I had to sweat my guts out persuading her to do what she, at the bottom of her heart, had already made up her mind to do.

'My dear fellow, when my wife, with her bust uncorseted—as you'll readily appreciate—lay down there on the bed, and when he—the doctor—looked into her eyes, as he bent over to place his ear upon her breast, I could see that she was almost swooning, on the verge of collapse. I saw in her eyes and in her whole face that terrifying experience. You feel disturbed in a way you—you're trembling all over. Oh, you know perfectly well what I mean, don't you? I knew her through and through. There was no possibility of my being mistaken.

'That might have been as far as it went, mightn't it? Your wife's still a thoroughly honest woman after an examination of that sort. Pure and chaste and totally undeserving of all moral correction. A medical examination, carried out under the husband's very eyes. . . . Nothing you can say, is there? Well and good! What I'd like to ask, though, is, What need was there for him to come and shout the truth out in my face? After all, I knew it already, deep down within me. I'd seen it with my own eyes. I'd all but touched it with my own hands.

'Oh, well! Don't let's get downhearted! Cheer up! Let's try another drop of this stuff! Down the hatch!

'I was standing there one evening, out on the balcony, gazing at the magnificent spectacle of the valley, stretching away into the distance. There in the moonlight.

'My wife had already gone to bed.

'I suppose you're just like everybody else. You see me merely as a fat man, and quite incapable of being moved by the wonderful sights of nature. Believe me, I'm a very sensitive, very tender-hearted soul. There's a cherubic infant soul tucked away inside this body of mine; with lovely fair hair, a tiny, sweet little face, and sky-blue eyes. It's a cherubic little soul that reminds you of one of those sweet little English girls, particularly when it looks out of the windows of these huge ox-eyes of mine, and gets all soft-hearted and sentimental as it catches sight of the moon, and hears the bell-like sound of the crickets as they chirp away, scattered throughout the countryside.

'Men by day in the town, crickets by night in the country. Never a moment's rest do they allow themselves! Wonderful life they lead, crickets!'

' "What are you doing, cricket?"

' "I'm singing!"

' "Why are you singing?"

'He doesn't even know himself why he's singing. He just sings. And all the stars twinkle in the sky. You look up at them. Wonderful life they lead, too, the stars! What are they up to, up there? Nothing. They're gazing into the void, too, and it seems just as if they were shuddering all the time. And if you only knew the sheer delight I get out of listening to the owl who, in the midst of all this sweet serenity, starts sobbing his anguished heart out, there in the distance. There he is, weeping away, so moved is he by all this loveliness.

'But don't let's wander from the subject. As I've just told you, there I was, looking out over the valley, and feeling very moved by what I saw. I was beginning by this time to feel a little chilly. It was gone eleven. I was just about to go to bed, when all of a sudden I heard a prolonged and loud banging on the front door. Who on earth could it possibly be at this time of night?

'*Dr. Loero.*

'And in a fine state, my dear fellow! The very stones themselves would have been moved to compassion!

'He was as tight as a newt! Absolutely sozzled!

'A group of doctors, five or six of them in all, had come from

Florence, Perugia, and Rome to take the cure, and he and the chemist had thought it would be a good idea to give a dinner in honour of their learned colleagues up at the little cottage hospital. The Green Cross it's called. It's behind the collegiate church, quite near to Rori's.

'You can just imagine what a dinner up at the hospital's like! A gay occasion in the fullest sense of the word! To Hell with the cure! They'd been knocking it back till they were as drunk as—— No, don't let's insult the newts any more, because, since truth will out, newts don't indulge in that particular pastime!

'What had made the idea flash into his wine-fuddled brain to come along and make my life a misery? There I was, as I've just told you. There I was that evening, completely wrapped up in the magic spell of that moonlight.

'He was swaying about all over the place, and I had to support him all the way from the front door to the balcony. When we got there, he flung his arms round me and held me very tight, telling me that he loved me ever so dearly, just like a brother. All evening, he said, he'd been talking about me with his colleagues. About the ghastly state of ruin my liver and my stomach were in. And so very dear to his heart were my liver, my stomach, and me. So very dear to his heart were they that, as he'd happened to be passing my door, he'd felt that he just couldn't neglect to pay me a short visit. Because he was very much afraid that he wouldn't be able to go to the Baths next morning because—— Hee! Hee! Never let it be said, of course! But, well . . . Well, he'd had just a tiny little drop too much to drink! As you may imagine, I thanked him very much for his kindness, and urged him to go off home, since it was so very late. Not on your life! Nothing doing! He demanded a chair, so that he could sit out there on the balcony. Then he started talking to me about my wife! He told me he liked her very much, and he wanted me to go in and wake her up, because dear darling Signora Carlotta was a bit of all right as far as he was concerned! Oh, she certainly was a bit of all right as far as he was concerned! She certainly was! Oh, she certainly was! She was a beautiful filly, very susceptible and very restless, who lashed out with her heels, and kicked you in order to get you to caress her. . . . Oh, loving kicks they were! On and on he went in this manner, giggling away, and trying to wink slily at me. Only his eye-work was a bit wonky.

'But—— Well, *you* tell me, what could I possibly do to him, when he was in that state? Can you give a man a thrashing when he can't stand on his feet? My wife, who'd woken up by now, called out from bed three or four times. She was in a hell of a temper! I must own that I could certainly feel coming into my hands the desire to give him a good hiding. But Heaven only knows what effect a hard wallop would have had on that poor young man! In the beatific unconsciousness which the wine had bestowed upon him, he'd lost all notion of social obligations or the demands of civilization. There he was, happily shouting the truth in my face! I grabbed hold of him and pulled him up from the chair—I couldn't help giving him a bit of a shaking as I lifted him —but, since he was on the verge of toppling over every inch of the way, and I had to be very careful about his state of health until I'd got him as far as the door; well, when I finally succeeded in getting him there—yes, quite right—I gave him a little shove that sent him trundling down the street.

'When I went into the bedroom, I found my wife nearly out of her mind. . . . She was absolutely frantic. She'd got out of bed, and now she let rip at me, calling me all the bloody cowards in creation. The insults just came raining down. She told me that if I'd been anything like a man I'd have trampled that scoundrel underfoot and then thrown him off the balcony! She added that I was only a puppet—a mere cardboard puppet! That there wasn't a drop of real blood in my veins. That nothing could bring the blush of shame to my face. That I was quite incapable of defending the honour of my wife. And that I was only too capable of bowing and scraping and doffing my hat to the first man who came along and——

'I didn't let her finish. I raised my fist. I shouted that she'd better watch out. The blow I ought to have landed on him, if only he hadn't been drunk, I'd be planting somewhere on her, if she didn't shut up! Did she shut up? Did she hell! From utter fury she passed to making nasty, taunting remarks. Oh yes, nothing easier, as far as I was concerned, than coming the big, bad bully with her! Beating up a woman was just typical of me! Especially after I'd welcomed into my house, and then, with all proper respect, shown out of my house, a man who'd come and insulted me in my own home! Why, oh why, hadn't I come in and woken her up immediately? Come to that, why hadn't I shown him into the bedroom and begged him to pop into bed with her?

'"You'll challenge him to a duel!" she shouted finally, quite beside herself with rage, "You'll challenge him tomorrow, and God help you if you don't!"

'There are some things that—well, when he hears a woman say them, I think even the meanest of men will rebel! By this time, I was already undressed and in bed. I told her once and for all to shut up her silly nonsense, and to let me get to sleep in peace. I wasn't challenging anybody. I wouldn't give her that much satisfaction!

'But during the night, you know, I thought the whole thing over very carefully. I knew nothing, I still know nothing, about this Code of Honour business. I certainly didn't know whether a gentleman was supposed to take any notice of the insults and the provocation of a man who was too drunk to know what he was saying. Or whether they were adequate reasons for challenging him to a duel. Well, next morning I was just about to go off and consult a retired major whom I'd got to know at the Baths, when this self-same major arrived, in the company of another gentleman living in the town. He'd come on behalf of Dr. Loero to demand satisfaction from me. Yes, because of the way in which I'd shown him the door the previous night! It appeared that, when I'd given him that final shove, he'd fallen and damaged his nose.

'"But he was as drunk as they come!" I shouted at the two gentlemen.

'So much the worse for me, they suggested. I should have treated him with a little more consideration. *I* was the one who should have done all this, you understand! And to think that it was only by a miracle that my wife hadn't eaten me alive, simply because I hadn't thrown him off the balcony!

"Still, that'll be enough on that topic! Let me get on! I shan't be long now! I accepted the challenge, but my wife just laughed contemptuously at me and without waiting for the outcome of the duel, started packing her trunks, so as to lose no time. She was all for leaving at once. And she knew it was to be a *very serious* duel.

'As for me . . . Well, since I was at the ball, I intended to dance. He'd made the choice of weapons—pistols. Excellent! I made the decision concerning distance—at fifteen paces. On the eve of the duel I wrote a letter—— It makes me nearly die laughing every time I re-read it. You've no idea the sort of daft nonsense you get into your head on an occasion of that kind! Still . . . ! After all, they're pretty shattering moments, those!

'I'd never been used to handling arms. I give you my solemn oath; when I fired, I instinctively shut my eyes. The duel took place in the beech-wood. The first two shots went wide. The third —no, the third went wide too. The *fourth*—my God, what a thick head that doctor had! The bullet took aim for me and went straight for the middle of his forehead. It failed to penetrate the bone, but slid up under the skin, along the top of his scalp, and came out round the back by the nape of the neck.

'In the excitement of the moment it looked very much as if he was dead. We all rushed over to where he was lying, me included. But then one of my seconds advised me to put as much distance between myself and here as I possibly could. To get into the carriage and make my escape along the Chiusi road.

'So, my escape I made.

'Next day I found out what had happened. And I found out something else, too, something which filled me with joy and regret at the same time. Joy as far as I was concerned. Regret as far as my adversary was concerned. After all, poor man, he didn't deserve *this* cruel blow. Not when he'd just got a bullet in his forehead!

'When he'd opened his eyes in the Green Cross Hospital, Dr. Loero had been confronted by a magnificent sight. *My wife.* Who'd dashed to his bedside to comfort him in his hour of pain!

'He recovered from his *wound* in a fortnight. But, my dear fellow, he *never* recovered from my wife!

'Shall we go and get another glass?'

# THE JAR

*La giara,* in many ways the best known of Pirandello's short stories, was first published in the *Corriere della sera* for 20 October 1909. In 1912 it appeared as one of the collection *Terzetti,* put out by Treves of Milan. There were new editions of the volume in 1913 and 1915. In 1928 it provided the title-story for Vol. XI of the Bemporad series of the *Novelle per un anno*. After this Florentine presentation the volume was reprinted by Mondadori. It now forms part of the Biblioteca Moderna Mondadori. The definitive text of the story is in Vol. II of the *Opere*. (*Novelle per un anno,* Vol. II, Milano-Verona, Mondadori, 1957.) Pirandello dramatized the story in 1917, rendering it into Sicilian for presentation by Angelo Musco. The Italian text was published by Bemporad of Florence in 1925 in Vol. XII of the *Maschere nude*. In 1924 it received its first performance as a ballet, to music by Alfredo Casella. The available English translation of the play is Frederick May's (published by Heinemann).

# THE JAR

THERE was a wonderful olive harvest as well that year. The mature trees, which had been groaning under the weight of olives the previous year, were all as heavily laden again, despite the mists which had attacked them at blossom-time.

Zirafa had a good acreage of them on his farm, Le Quote, at Primosole and, foreseeing that the five old glazed earthenware jars which he had in the cellar wouldn't be sufficient to contain the new harvest, he'd ordered (and in good time, too) a sixth from Santo Stefano di Camastra, where they made them. Tall as a man's chest it was, with a big fat belly, and most majestic-looking—admirably equipped to rank as a Mother Superior over the other five.

Needless to say, he'd had a row with the jar-maker over this jar. But then, who *didn't* Lollò Zirafa have rows with? Over every slightest trifle—even over a tiny slab of stone that had fallen off the boundary wall, even over a handful of straw! He'd yell at them to saddle his mule, so that he could rush into town and take out all sorts of summonses and things. And so, by sheer dint of using up vast quantities of legal documents (with heavy stamp-duty on the lot of them), meeting lawyers' fees, quoting this and quoting that, and always having in the end to pay everyone's costs, he'd just about half-ruined himself.

People said that his legal adviser had grown so tired of seeing him turning up in his office two or three times a week that, in order to get him from under his feet, he'd made him a present of a little book, which was just like a missal to look at. It was the *Civil Code*. So that he could drive *himself* round the bend rummaging through it on his own, to try and find out whether there was any judicial foundation for the lawsuits he was wanting to bring.

Whereas previously those with whom he had a difference of opinion would take the rise out of him by yelling after him 'Saddle my mule!' Now, instead, it was, 'Out with your *A.B.C.*, man!'

And Don Lollò would reply, 'I certainly *shall* get it out! And I'll blast you all off the face of the earth, you sons-of-bitches!'

That new jar, for which he'd paid four lovely, bouncing, chinking *onze,* had been lodged temporarily in the press-room—for convenience, while they were waiting for room to be found for it in the cellar. No one had ever seen such a jar. It really *hurt* you to see it there, lodged in that cavern stinking with must and that harsh crude smell which lurks in places that are deprived of light and air.

Two days earlier the knocking-down of the olives had begun, and Don Lollò was nearly going out of his mind with sheer rage because, what with the knockers-down to look after, and mule-drivers, who kept turning up with mules loaded with manure to deposit on the slope by the field where he was going to sow beans next year—well, he just didn't know how to split himself into enough selves to go round, and who to see to first. So he went about swearing like a trooper, threatening with direful extermination first this one, then that, if so much as one olive, *one single olive,* got overlooked; almost as if he'd counted them all beforehand, one by one, while they were still on the trees. Then off he'd go and threaten the others with all sorts of dreadful things if every heap of manure wasn't exactly the same size as the others. Wearing his battered old white hat, and in his shirt-sleeves, with his chest bare, his face ruddy to the point of apoplexy, and all dripping with sweat, he'd rush hither and thither, with his wolf-like eyes roaming all over the place, and angrily rubbing his cheeks—those cheeks on which his ferocious and indomitable beard virtually sprouted afresh as the razor cut away the old growth.

Now, at the end of the third day, three of the peasants who'd been knocking-down, on going into the press-room to put their ladders and poles, had been struck all of a heap by the sight of the new jar—cracked in two, just as if someone, with a neat cut, had taken the jar in all its fullness and removed the whole of the front bulge.

'Just look at that! Just look at that!'

'Who can possibly have done it?'

'Oh, God help us! Who's going to tell Don Lollò? Oh, what a pity! The new jar!'

The first of them, more terrified than the rest, proposed that they should shut the door immediately and go off ever so quietly, leaving their ladders and poles leaning up against the wall outside. The second, however, said, 'Are you mad? Try *that* one on *Don Lollò*? He's quite capable of believing that we broke it! No! We all stand fast here, every single one of us!'

He went out of the press-room and, making a megaphone with his hands, called, 'Don Lollò! Oh, Don Lollòòòò!'

There he was, at the bottom of the slope, with the men who were unloading the manure. As usual, he was gesticulating away furiously, and every so often banging his white hat on to his head with both hands. Sometimes he banged it on again so hard that he couldn't shift it, either at the nape of his neck or over his forehead. Already the last flames of sunset were being extinguished in the sky, and, cutting through the peace and quiet that was descending on the countryside—as the shadows of evening with its sweet coolness closed in—there came, *hurled* at you, those gestures on the part of that man who was always in a fury.

'Don Lollò! Oh, Don Lollòòòò!'

When he came on up and saw the damage, it looked just as if he was going to go out of his mind. He hurled himself first at the three men who'd made the discovery. One of them he grabbed by the throat and pinned against the wall, shouting, 'By the Blood of the Virgin Mary, you'll pay for it!'

When he in his turn had been grabbed by the other two, their earthy, bestial faces twisted with emotion, he turned all his mad rage against himself. He tore off his hat and flung it on the ground; he slapped himself hard on both cheeks, stamped his feet and bawled away like a man mourning the death of a relative. 'Oh, my new jar! Four *onze* worth of lovely jar! I hadn't even christened it!'

He wanted to know who'd broken it! Was it conceivable that it had got broken all by itself? Somebody *must* have broken it, either out of envy or out of sheer human wickedness! But when? And how? There wasn't any sign of violence! Had it by any chance been broken when it had arrived from the jar-maker's? Of course it hadn't! It had rung like a bell when it'd come!

As soon as the peasants saw that his immediate anger was abating, they started urging him to calm down. The jar could be mended. After all, it wasn't very *badly* damaged. Only one piece had got broken off. A good jar-mender would be able to put it together again so that it came up just like new. There was Zi' Dima Licasi, for instance. Just the man for the job! He'd discovered a miraculous cement, the secret of which he guarded most jealously. A cement you couldn't even bash apart with a hammer, once it had set. Look! If Don Lollò would like him to, Zi' Dima Licasi could come along tomorrow morning—at the crack of dawn—and before you could say two twos are four the jar would be mended and better than ever.

Don Lollò said 'No' to all their exhortations. It was quite useless. There wasn't any way he could see of making good the damage. In the end, however, he let them talk him round. So next morning, punctually at the crack of dawn, Zi' Dima Licasi presented himself at Primosole, with his tool-kit slung over his shoulder.

He was a misshapen old man, with swollen, knotty joints, just like an ancient Saracen olive log. Every word had to be dragged out of him. His deformed body positively bristled with stand-offishness. Or was it really *sadness*? Or was it disappointment that no one was able to appreciate at their proper value—or even to *comprehend*—his merits as an inventor? Zi' Dima Licasi hadn't yet patented his discovery because he wanted deeds to speak louder than words on a bit of paper. So he had to keep a sharp look-out, fore and aft, as it were, to make sure that no one stole his secret from him.

'Show me this cement of yours,' were Don Lollò's first words to him after he'd looked him mistrustfully up and down for several minutes.

Zi' Dima, the acme of dignity, shook his head.

'You'll see how good it is when the job's done.'

'Will it end up all right?'

Zi' Dima put his tool-kit on the ground. He fished out a rolled up and very well-worn cotton kerchief. Very slowly he started to unroll it, while they all stood around him, consumed with curiosity, their whole attention riveted upon him. When, finally, a pair of spectacles appeared, with the bridge and sides broken and tied up with string, *he* gave a sigh and all the rest of them burst into hearty laughter. Zi' Dima took no notice. He wiped his fingers before handling the spectacles and then fitted them carefully on to his nose and over his ears. Then very, very solemnly he began his examination of the jar—which by now had been brought out into the threshing-yard. Finally he said, 'It'll be all right.'

Zirafa started laying down his conditions. 'I don't trust it with cement alone. I want rivets as well.'

'I'm off,' replied Zi' Dima, and, without even pausing to argue the point, he got up and slung his tool-kit over his shoulder again.

Don Lollò grabbed him by one arm. 'Where are you off to? Is this the way you treat people, you high-and-mighty old swine? Huh! Look at him! As full of airs and graces as if he was Lord Tomnoddy himself! Ger, you old hunk of cat's meat! You stupid old donkey! I've got to use that jar for putting oil in! It'll ooze through! You don't mean to say you think you can mend a crack a mile long—*look at it!*—just with cement! I want rivets as well. Cement and rivets. Those are my orders!'

Zi' Dima closed his eyes, pursed his lips and shook his head. They were all the same! He was always being deprived of the opportunity of doing a good clean job, conscientiously carried out according to the rules of his craft. He was always being deprived, too, of an opportunity of demonstrating the virtues of his cement.

'If that jar,' he said, 'doesn't ring like a bell again——'

'I'm not listening to a word you say,' interrupted Don Lollò. '*Rivets!* I'm paying you to use cement and rivets. How much do I have to give you?'

'If, with my cement alone——'

'Oh, God rot me! What a stubborn brute the man is!' exclaimed Don Lollò. 'Am I talking sense or *aren't* I? I tell you, *I want rivets.* We'll settle things when the job's done. I haven't got any more time to waste on you!'

And off he went to look after his workmen.

Zi' Dima started on his job, simply bristling with anger and contempt. And his anger and contempt grew with every hole that he drilled in the main body of the jar and in the broken-off bit—

this was to make it possible for the steel wire used in the riveting to be threaded through. He accompanied the *frou-frou* of the bit with a running commentary of grunts, which gradually got louder and louder. And his face took on an ever more bilious hue and his eyes became ever sharper and more flaming with annoyance. The first stage of the operation completed, he flung the drill angrily back into the tool-bag. He stuck the broken-off piece back into position in the jar, to see if the holes were the right distance apart and to see if they corresponded with one another, then, with his wire-cutters, he cut off as many pieces of steel wire as he'd need to insert rivets, and called over one of the peasants who were knocking-down to help him.

'Cheer up, Zi' Dima!' said this fellow, seeing his face twisted with anger.

Zi' Dima raised his hand in an angry gesture. He opened the old tin which contained his cement, and, holding it up to heaven, brandished it in the air, as if offering it up to God—seeing that men had no desire to recognize its virtues. Then with his finger he began to spread it along the edge of the broken-off piece and the edge of the jar where it had come away. He took the wire-cutters and the pieces of wire he'd prepared in advance and tucked himself away inside the open belly of the jar, instructing the peasant to stick the broken-off piece in position, just as he himself had done only a few moments earlier. Before he started putting in the rivets, he said to the farm-hand, from inside the jar, 'Go on, tug away! Tug away with all your might! *See?* You can't get them apart, can you? So to hell with anyone who doesn't believe me! Bang away! Bang away! Does it, or does it not, ring like a bell? Even with me inside it! Run along! Run along and tell your boss all about it!'

And Zi' Dima began to pass the pieces of wire through the pairs of holes that lay next to one another, one this side, the other that side of the mend. Then with his wire-cutters he twisted the ends together. It took him an hour to do the lot of them. The sweat was pouring off him, there inside the jar. As he worked, he lamented his wretched fate. And the peasant on the outside spent *his* time comforting him.

'Now help me to get out!' said Zi' Dima at the end of it all.

But, no matter how large in the belly it was, that jar was very tight in the neck. Zi' Dima had been so angry that he hadn't checked up on *that* detail. Now, try as he would, he couldn't find any way of getting out again. And the peasant, instead of helping him—look at him, the idle lout, doubled up with laughter!—there was Zi' Dima, *imprisoned*! Imprisoned in the jar which he himself had mended, and which now—there was no possibility of half-measures—would have to be broken all over again! And broken for good this time!

Hearing all the laughter and shouting, Don Lollò came up. Zi' Dima, inside the jar, was like a demented tomcat.

'Let me out!' he was howling. 'God Almighty, I want to get out! At once! Help!'

At first Don Lollò just stood there like a man dazed. He simply couldn't believe his eyes. 'But, how on——? In there? Has he riveted himself up in there?'

He went up to the jar and yelled at the old man, '*Help?* What sort of help can *I* give you, you obstinate old dodder? It was your job to take your own measurements before you got in, wasn't it? Now, come on. Try getting an arm out first—that's the way. Now your head—come on! Come on! No, gently—— What the——! Down with it! Now, wait a minute! Like *that*! No! Down with it! Down with it! How the devil did you manage to——? Hey, what about the jar now? Now, keep calm! Keep calm! Keep calm!' he started advising all and sundry around him—just as if *they* and not he were likely to begin getting all worked up. 'Oh, my brains are boiling! Now, keep calm! This is a completely new case. Where's my mule?'

He rapped on the jar with his knuckles. It really *did* ring like a bell.

'Lovely! Come up like new! Hang on a minute!' he said to the prisoner. '*You,* go and saddle me my mule!' he said to the farm-hand. Then, rubbing his head vigorously with both hands, he went on muttering away to himself. 'Just look at the sort of thing that happens to me! This isn't a jar—it's the devil incarnate! Keep still! *You in there,* keep still!'

And he rushed over to steady the jar, in which an infuriated Zi' Dima was bashing about like an animal in a trap.

'It's a completely new case, my dear fellow! I must get my lawyer to sort it out for me. I don't trust my own judgement. Where's my mule? Get me my mule! I'm going now! I'll be back immediately! Just be patient! It's in your own interest. . . . Meanwhile, *keep quiet*! Keep calm! I must look after my own interests. And first of all, just so as to preserve my rights, I'll do my duty. Here you are! I'm paying you for your work. I'm paying you a day's wages. Five lire? That do you?'

'I don't want anything!' yelled Zi' Dima. 'I want to get out of here!'

'You'll get out all right! But meanwhile. I'm paying you. Here you are—five lire!'

He took the money out of his waistcoat pocket and threw it into the jar. Then he asked, solicitously, 'Have you had your breakfast? Bread and something to go with it, eh? Right away! You don't want it? Throw it to the dogs, then! It's enough for me to know that I've given it to you!'

He ordered them to give him the food, leapt into the saddle, and he went to town at a gallop. Everyone who saw him as he galloped along gesticulating, thought he must be off to shut himself up in the lunatic asylum, so extraordinarily was he behaving.

As luck would have it, he didn't have to wait long before the lawyer was free to see him. But, when he'd laid the case before him, he *did* have to wait a long time before the lawyer had finished laughing. Thoroughly annoyed by the lawyer's laughter, he said, 'Forgive the question, but what's there to laugh at? It's not your lordship's backside that's getting burnt! The jar's *mine*!'

But the other man just went on laughing. He insisted on his telling him the story all over again. On his telling him exactly what had happened. So that he could have another good laugh. Inside it, eh? He'd riveted himself up inside it, had he? And what was it Don Lollò thought he was entitled to? Did he think he was entitled to—k-k-keep him in there? Ha! Ha! Ha! Ho! Ho! Ho! Keep him in there, so as not to lose the jar?

'Oh, so I'm supposed just to write it off, am I?' asked Don

Lollò, clenching his fists. 'What about all the harm he's done me? What about all the derision I'm going to have to put up with?'

'But do you know what they call this?' the lawyer finally managed to ask him. 'They call this sort of thing kidnapping!'

'Kidnapping? Who's kidnapping him?' exclaimed Don Lollò. 'He kidnapped *himself*! Off his own bat! What fault is it of mine?'

The lawyer then explained to him that there were two sides to the case. On the one hand he—Don Lollò—had immediately to set the prisoner free, in order not to be answerable to a charge of kidnapping. On the other hand, the jar-mender was answerable for the harm he'd caused with his stupidity and uppitiness.

'Ah!' Don Lollò breathed again. 'By paying me for the jar?'

'Gently!' observed the lawyer. 'Not as if it were new, mind!'

'Why not?'

'Oh, good grief, man, because it was broken!'

'Broken? Oh, no! It's mended now. It's *better* than mended! He says so himself! And now, if I break it again, I shan't be able to get it mended again. One jar lost, Mr. Lawyer!'

The lawyer assured him that that would be taken into account, by making him pay whatever the jar was worth in the state in which it now was.

'So!' he advised him, 'I should get him to give you an estimate of its worth before you go any further.'

'I kiss your hand!' said Don Lollò and off he went at a hell of a lick.

When he got back, towards evening, he found the peasants having a high old time round the inhabited jar. Even the watchdog was taking part in the fun and games, jumping about all over the place and barking. Zi' Dima had not only calmed down, but had also come round to enjoying his bizarre adventure, and he was laughing away with that sick gaiety that characterizes the unfortunate of this world.

Zirafa shoved them all to one side and stuck his neck over the top and peered into the jar.

'Hey! All right in there?'

'Absolutely all right! Beautifully cool,' replied Zi' Dima. 'I'm better off here than in my own home.'

'Glad to hear it. Meanwhile, allow me to inform you that that jar cost me four *onze* new. How much do you think it would cost now?'

'With me inside?' asked Zi' Dima.

The farm-hands laughed.

'Shut up!' shouted Zirafa. 'Two propositions—take your choice. Either your cement's good for nothing or it's good for something. If it's good for nothing, then you're a downright twister. If it's good for something, then the jar, just as it is now, must have some sort of value. What value? *You* say! Give me an estimate!'

Zi' Dima paused for a moment, reflecting. Then he said, 'Here's my answer. If you'd let me mend it with cement alone, as I wanted to, first of all I shouldn't be stuck inside here, and the jar would have more or less the same value as it had originally. All mucked-up as it is now, with these filthy rivets stuck in it, which I had necessarily to do from the inside, what value could it possibly have? A third of what it was worth in the first place—more or less.'

'A third?' asked Zirafa. 'One *onza,* thirty three?'

'Maybe less. Certainly not more.'

'Well, then,' said Don Lollò, 'I'll take your word for it. Hand over the *onza* and thirty three.'

'What?' said Zi' Dima, as if he didn't understand what he'd said.

'I'll break the jar and let you out,' replied Don Lollò, 'and you, so my lawyer says, must pay me whatever you value it at. One *onza* and thirty three.'

'Me *pay*?' sniggered Zi' Dima. 'Your lordship will have his little joke! I'd sooner stay in here till I make food for the worms!'

And, pulling his tar-encrusted pipe out of his pocket with some difficulty, he lit it and started smoking, puffing the smoke out through the neck of the jar.

Don Lollò was utterly taken aback. This other possibility, that Zi' Dima would no longer wish to quit the jar, neither he nor the lawyer had foreseen. How was this new difficulty to be resolved? He was on the verge of again ordering them instantly to saddle his mule, when it occurred to him that it was already evening.

'Oh, indeed?' he said. 'So you wish to take up permanent residence in my jar? You lot—you're all my witnesses! He doesn't want to come out again, so as not to have to pay for it. I'm ready to break the jar! Meanwhile, since he wishes to remain in there, tomorrow I'll sue him for trespassing on my property, and for wilfully preventing me from using the jar!'

Zi' Dima puffed another mouthful of smoke out of the jar, then he placidly replied, 'No, sir. I'm not trying to stop you from doing anything. Not me. Do you think I'm in here for my own amusement? You get me out of here, and I'll be off willingly. As for paying you anything—— Not on your sweet life, your lordship!'

In an access of rage, Don Lollò lifted his foot to launch a kick at the jar. He refrained, however. He seized hold of it instead with both hands and shook it vigorously, trembling all over.

'See? Wonderful stuff, my cement!' said Zi' Dima to him.

'Jailbird!' roared Zirafa. 'Who's done the harm, you or me? And have I got to pay for it? You can starve to death in there! We'll see who wins this little battle!'

And off he went, quite forgetting the five lire which that morning he'd thrown into the jar. To start off with, Zi' Dima thought it would be a good idea to have a party with the farm-hands who, having been kept late because of that strange accident, were going to spend the night in the country, out in the open, on the threshing-yard. One of them went off to the pub nearby to lay in stocks. Most appropriately, there was a moon—so bright that it seemed as if day had come again.

Don Lollò went to bed, but in the middle of the night he was awakened by an infernal din. He went out on to the balcony of the farm-house and, by the light of the moon, he saw out in the threshing-yard hordes and hordes of devils. They were the drunk farm-hands who'd linked hands and who were dancing round the jar, inside which Zi' Dima was singing away at the top of his voice.

This time Don Lollò couldn't restrain himself. He hurled himself at the jar like a mad bull, and before they had time to stop him he'd given it a huge shove and sent it rolling down the slope. The jar rolled on and on, accompanied by the laughter of the drunks, and ended up by splitting open against an olive-tree.

Zi' Dima had won.

# THE TRAGEDY OF A CHARACTER

*La tragedia d'un personaggio,* which first appeared in print in the *Corriere della sera* for 19 October 1911, was collected into the volume *La trappola* (Milano, Treves, 1915), and subsequently into Vol. IV *(L'uomo solo)* of the *Novelle per un anno* (Firenze, Bemporad, 1922). After a second Bemporad edition in 1929 the book was reprinted by Mondadori in 1934, and now forms part of the Biblioteca Moderna Mondadori. The definitive text of the story is in Vol. I of the *Opere*. (*Novelle per un anno,* Vol. I, *con una prefazione di Corrado Alvaro,* Milano-Verona, Mondadori, 1956.)

# THE TRAGEDY OF A CHARACTER

It's a long-standing habit of mine to give audience, every Sunday morning, to the characters of my future stories.

Five hours I give them—eight till one.

Almost invariably I find myself in bad company. It just seems to happen somehow.

I don't know why, but these receptions of mine seem, as a rule, to be attended by the most discontented people in the world, people it's really absolute misery to have to deal with: either they're afflicted by some strange disease or other, or else they've got themselves entangled in the most specious of fates.

I hear them all out with forbearance. Politely, I ask them all questions. I make a note of the name and other particulars of each one. I record all their feelings and aspirations. I must add, however—and this is my misfortune—that I'm not easily satisfied. Forbearance, politeness—— Oh, yes! But I don't like to be fooled. Besides, I want always to penetrate, by means of long and subtle inquiry, to the very depths of their souls.

Now, it quite often happens that, when I put some of my questions, more than one of them starts getting suspicious, starts jibbing, and then becomes furiously recalcitrant, because, perhaps, he's got the impression that I find particular pleasure in shattering his self-composure, that seriousness with which he introduced himself to me.

Patiently, very gently, I exert every effort to get them to see, to convince them conclusively, that my questions are in no way superfluous, but derive from my eagerness to make use of them in one way or another.

Everything turns, therefore, on whether we can be what we want to be. Where that power is lacking, our desire must of necessity appear ridiculous and quite futile.

They just refuse to recognize that this is how things are.

And then I feel compassionate towards them, for I'm fundamentally very kind-hearted. But can you *really* feel compassion for certain kinds of misfortune, unless you can laugh at them, too?

Well, the characters from my stories go about the world telling everybody that I'm a cruel writer—completely heartless. It would need a very sympathetic critic to make people see how great is the compassion that lies behind that laughter.

But where today are there any sympathetic critics?

It would be a good thing, I think, to let the reader know that some of the characters who come to these receptions of mine push their way in front of the others, thrusting themselves upon me with such overbearing petulance that, yes, there are times when I find myself forced quite brusquely to extricate myself from among them.

Then some of them bitterly repent their display of bad temper, and start singing my praises for having mended such and such a defect in this character here, or some other defect in such and such another character. I merely smile and tell them very quietly that now they must expiate their original sin, and wait till I have the time and the means to return to them.

Among those who remain at the back of the room, waiting, rather overcome by it all, some sigh, some retreat a little into the shadow, while some grow tired of waiting and go away and knock at the door of some other writer.

Not infrequently, it's fallen to my lot to discover in the stories of quite a few of my colleagues certain characters who'd originally offered themselves to me. It's even so happened that I've recognized among them certain others who, not content with the way I'd treated them, had decided to try and cut a better figure elsewhere.

I don't complain, for I usually have two or three new characters a week coming and offering themselves to me. And often the press is so great that I have to try and pay attention to more than one at a time. And so it goes on, unless things get to such a pitch that my spirit becomes so divided and disturbed that it revolts against this double or treble creation, and cries out in exasperation that it must be either one at a time, very quietly and very peacefully, or into Limbo with all three!

I shall always remember how very meekly a poor little old man, who had come to my house from far away, awaited his turn. He was a certain Maestro Icilio Saporini, who'd gone off to America in 1849, upon the fall of the Roman Republic—he'd been exiled for having set to music some patriotic hymn or other—and who now, at the age of almost eighty, had returned, some forty-five years later, to die in Italy. Extraordinarily punctilious in his observance of all the refinements of etiquette, and with a small gnat-like voice, he let all have precedence. And then, at last, one day when I was convalescing after a long illness, I saw him come into my room, very humbly, with a slight, timid smile on his lips.

'If I might—— If you wouldn't mind . . . ?'

Why, of course, my dear little old man! He'd chosen a most opportune moment. And I made him die immediately in a short story called *Old Music.*

Last Sunday I went into my study for my reception a little later than usual.

A long novel, which had been sent me as a present and which had been lying about for more than a month, waiting to be read, had kept me awake until three in the morning, on account of the many considerations which one of its characters had suggested to me—the one living character among so many empty shadows.

It told the story of a poor man, a certain Dr. Fileno, who believed that he had discovered a most effective remedy for every sort of ill, an infallible prescription for bringing consolation to himself and to all men in any calamity, public or private.

In point of fact, it wasn't so much a remedy or a prescription as a *method,* this discovery of Dr. Fileno's. It consisted of reading history books from morning till night and in seeing the present as part of history, too. That's to say, as if it were already far distant in time and deposited in the archives of the past.

Adopting this method, he had freed himself from all pain and irritation and found peace without needing to die; an austere, serene peace, suffused with that particular sadness without regret which would still be conserved by all the graveyards on the face of the earth, even if the whole of mankind were dead.

Dr. Fileno never for one moment dreamt of drawing from the past guiding principles for the present. He knew that it would be a waste of time, and a foolish waste of time at that, because history is an ideal composition of elements gathered together according to the particular temperament, antipathies, sympathies, aspirations, and opinions of the historian, and that it's quite impossible, therefore, to make this ideal composition be of service to life, which moves steadily on with all its elements still uncomposed and scattered about all over the place. Similarly, he never for one moment dreamt of drawing from the present standards for the future, or provision against it. Quite the reverse. He did just the opposite: he placed himself ideally in the future in order to look at the present, and he saw it as if it were the past.

For instance, one of his daughters had died a few days before. A friend had gone to visit him to condole with him on this misfortune. Well, he had found him already as consoled as if his daughter had been dead for well over a hundred years.

He had, without more ado, pushed his grief, all burning as it still was, far back in time, pushed it back and encompassed it in the past. But you really needed to *see* him, to observe from what lofty heights and with how great a dignity he spoke of it.

Briefly then, by adopting the method he'd discovered, Dr. Fileno had turned himself into an inverted telescope. He opened it out, but not to set himself at looking at the future, where he knew there would be nothing for him to see. . . . No, he prevailed upon his spirit to be content with setting itself to look through the larger lens towards the smaller, which was focused on the present, so that immediately everything seemed small and far away. And he had been engaged for several years on the writing of a book which would most certainly be quite epoch-making when it came out. He called it *A Philosophy of Remoteness*.

During my reading of the novel it had become more and more obvious to me that the author, being completely absorbed in artificially tying up the threads of one of the most commonplace of plots, hadn't had the remotest idea how to assume complete awareness of this character who, alone of all the characters in the novel, contained within himself the germ of a true and living creation; who had succeeded, to a certain extent, in taking the author by the hand and in hacking out a life for himself. For a long time he'd succeeded in being himself, standing out in vigorous relief against the other characters whose fates, the commonest of fates, were depicted and narrated in that novel. Then, all of a sudden, enfeebled and twisted out of all recognition, he had allowed himself to be bent and adapted to the exigencies of a false and completely silly ending.

I remained for a long time speculating fancifully in the silence of the night, with the picture of that character before my eyes. What a pity! There was so much material in him—enough to create a masterpiece! If only the author hadn't so unworthily misunderstood and neglected him! If only he'd made him the central figure in his narrative, perhaps all those other elements—those highly artificial elements—of which he'd made use, would have been transformed, too, and sprung immediately to life. And a great sorrow and an immense contempt filled me on account of that life which had remained so miserably unfulfilled.

Well, that morning, entering my study late, I found an unusual state of confusion. Dr. Fileno had already forced his way into the midst of my waiting characters. He'd so put their backs up, and made them so thoroughly angry, that they'd jumped on him, and now some of them were trying to drag him to the back of the room, while others were trying to throw him out altogether.

'Come, come, ladies and gentlemen,' I cried. 'What a way to carry on! Dr. Fileno, I have already wasted far too much time on you. What do you want with me? You don't belong to me. Please go away and leave me in peace so that I may attend to my own characters.'

Such an intense and desperate expression of anguish came over the face of Dr. Fileno that immediately all the others—*my* characters, who were still standing there holding him back—grew pale and shrank away, suddenly feeling very humble.

'Don't send me away! For pity's sake, don't send me away! Only give me five minutes of your time—if these ladies and gentlemen will be so kind as to allow me to. And for pity's sake, do let me try and convince you that——'

Perplexed, and yet moved to compassion, I asked him, 'Try and convince me of *what*? I'm already completely convinced, my dear Doctor, that you deserved to fall into better hands. But what do you expect me to do about it? I've already grieved a great deal at your fate. That must do for you!'

'That must do for me? Oh no, for God's sake!' burst out Dr. Fileno, a shudder of indignation running through his whole body. 'You talk like that because I'm not one of *your* characters. Believe me, your not-caring, your disdain, would be much less cruel to me than this passive commiseration which, if you'll pardon my saying so, is unworthy of an artist. No one can know better than you that we are living beings—more alive than those who breathe and wear clothes. Less real, perhaps, but more alive. One is born into life in so many ways, my dear sir, and you know very well that nature avails herself of the instrument of human fantasy in order to pursue her work of creation. And the man who's born as a result of this creative activity, which has its seat in the spirit of man, is destined by nature to a life greatly superior to that of anyone born of the mortal womb of woman. The man who is born a character, the man who has the good fortune to be born a living character, may snap his fingers at death even. He will never die! Man will die. The writer, the natural instrument of creation, will die. What is created by him will never die. And in order to live eternally he has not the slightest need of extraordinary gifts or of accomplishing prodigies. Tell me, who was Sancho Panza? Tell me, who was Don Abbondio? And yet, they live eternally because, living seeds, they had the good fortune to find a fruitful womb, a fantasy which knew how to raise and nourish them, so that they might live throughout all eternity!'

'My dear Doctor, that's all very well,' I said to him. 'But I still don't see what it is you want with *me*.'

'No? You can't see what I want?' Dr. Fileno replied. 'Have I made an awful mistake? Have I, by some mad chance, arrived on the moon? Forgive my asking, but what kind of a writer *are* you? Quite seriously, though, can't you really comprehend the horror of my tragedy? To have the inestimable privilege of being born a character—in this day and age—I mean *today*, when material life is so bristling with all sorts of vile difficulties that throw obstacles in our way, that deform and impoverish every aspect of existence; to have the privilege of being born a living character, of being destined, therefore, for all my insignificance, to immortality, and—— *Yes!* Then to have fallen into *his* hands, to be condemned to perish iniquitously, to suffocate in that world of artifice where I can't breathe, can't move an inch, because it's all make-believe, false, full of sophistical quibbles, the product of chance! Mere words and paper! Paper and words! A man who finds himself enmeshed in conditions of life to which he can't or doesn't know how to adapt himself, can escape from them, can run away! But a poor character can do no such thing. There he is—*fixed*! Nailed to a never-ending martyrdom! Give me air! Give me life! But, look here. *Fileno . . . !* I was given the name *Fileno*! Quite seriously, do you really think I can call myself *Fileno*? The fool! The utter fool! He didn't even know how to name me! *Fileno! Me!* And then—— *Yes! I!* I, indeed—the author of *A Philosophy of Remoteness*—*I* had to finish up in that unworthy way, simply so as to resolve his stupid turmoil of fortuitous happenings. I had to *marry* her, didn't I? I had to take that goose Graziella as my second wife —instead of her marrying Negroni the solicitor! No, please listen to me a little longer! These are crimes, my dear sir, crimes which should be paid for with tears of blood. Now, instead, what will happen? Nothing. Silence. Or, maybe, a slashing critique in two or three of the lesser dailies. Perhaps some critic or other will exclaim, "That poor Dr. Fileno! What a pity! A really good character, that chap!" And that will be that. Condemned to death! *I*, who wrote *A Philosophy of Remoteness*. . . . Which that idiot didn't even have sense enough to get me to print at my own expense! No, it's no use. If he hadn't been a fool, how could he possibly have made me take that goose Graziella as my second wife? Oh, don't make me think about it! Let's get on! Let's get on with *our* work! *Redeem me!* At once! Immediately! *You* must make me live, because *you've* understood so completely what a wealth of life there is within me!'

At this proposal, hurled at me furiously as a conclusion to his long outburst, I remained awhile gazing at the face of Dr. Fileno. 'Have you got some sort of scruples about doing it?' he asked me agitatedly, his face darkening. '*Have* you? But it's quite legitimate, it's quite legitimate, you do realize that? It's your inviolable right to take me up again, to give me the life that that idiot didn't know how to give me. It's your right and mine! You *do* understand that, *don't* you?'

'It probably *is* your right, my dear Doctor,' I replied. 'It probably would also be quite legitimate for me, as you believe. But I don't do these things. And it's useless your insisting. I don't *do* these things. Try taking yourself somewhere else.'

'But where do you expect me to go, if you . . . ?'

'I don't know! Just—*try*! You probably won't have much difficulty in finding someone who's convinced of the legitimacy of this "right" of yours. There's another thing, too. Listen to me a moment, Dr. Fileno. Are you, or are you not, the author of *A Philosophy of Remoteness*?'

'What do you mean, "are you or are you not"?' burst out Dr. Fileno, falling back a pace and clasping his hands to his breast. 'Do you dare to doubt my word? I understand! It's all the fault of my murderer. Very briefly, scarcely saying anything at all, he gave an idea in passing of my theories, not supposing, even remotely, that there was all that advantage to be gained from my inverted telescope.'

I held out my hands to stop him and smilingly said, 'Yes. . . . Yes. . . . But, forgive me, what about *you*?'

'Me? What do you mean, "what about *me*"?'

'You're busy complaining about your author. But have you really known how to derive full advantage from your theory, my dear Doctor? Well, there's just this one thing I wanted to say to you. Do let me say it. If you really and truly believe in the validity of your philosophy, as I do, why don't you apply it a little to your own case? At the present moment you're trying to find, from among our number, an author who will consecrate you to immortality. But look at what all the most considerable critics say of us poor trashy writers of today. We *are,* and at the same time we are *not*, my dear Doctor. Look, suppose you put us, together with all the most notable deeds, the most burning questions, the most admirable works of our day, under your inverted telescope. My dear Doctor, I'm very much afraid that you would no longer see anything or anybody. Go away, therefore. Console yourself with the—or rather, *resign* yourself. And let me attend to these poor characters of mine, who are probably very wicked, who are probably very captious, but who are, at least, most unlikely to be possessed of your extravagant ambition.'

## A CALL TO DUTY

*Richiamo all'obbligo* was probably written in 1911. It was first published in the collection of stories entitled *Terzetti* (Milano, Treves, 1912). The volume enjoyed a second edition in 1913 and a third in 1915. The story was included next in Vol. XI *(La giara)* of the *Novelle per un anno* (Firenze, Bemporad, 1928). Reprinted by Mondadori in 1934, the volume now forms part of the Biblioteca Moderna Mondadori. The definitive text is in Vol. II of the *Opere*. (*Novelle per un anno,* Vol. II, Milano-Verona, Mondadori, 1957.)

# A CALL TO DUTY

Paolino Lovico flung himself down on a stool in front of Pulejo's, the chemist's shop in the Piazza Marina. He felt like death. He took a look into the shop, glared in the direction of the counter, dabbed away at the sweat that was streaming down from under his hair and all over his face, which was flushed purple with the heat, and asked Saro Pulejo, 'Has he looked in yet?'

'Gigi? No. He shouldn't be long, though. Why?'

'Why? Because I need his help! Because—— You're asking a hell of a lot of questions!'

He left his handkerchief where it was, spread out over his head, rested his elbows on his knees, and sat there, staring at the ground, his chin resting on his hands. His face was gloomy and his brows knitted.

Everybody knew him, there in the Piazza Marina. A friend came by. 'Hello there, Paolí!'

Lovico raised his eyes and lowered them again instantly, muttering, 'Oh, leave me alone!'

Another friend, 'What's up, Paolí?'

This time Lovico tore the handkerchief from off his head and changed his position. Now he was sitting with his face almost turned to the wall.

'Aren't you feeling well, Paolí?' Saro Pulejo then asked him from behind the counter.

'Oh, Good God Almighty!' burst out Paolino Lovico, hurling himself into the shop. 'What the hell have my troubles got to do with *you*? Who's asking *you* anything? Aren't you feeling well? *Are* you feeling well? What's up? What *isn't* up? Oh, leave me alone!'

'Hello-hello-hello!' said Saro. 'Been bitten by a tarantula, old chap? You asked for Gigi, so I thought you——'

'I suppose I'm the only soul on the face of the earth?' shouted Lovico, waving his arms in the air, his eyes flashing. 'Couldn't it be my dog that's ill? One of my prize chickens suffering from whooping-cough? God Almighty, and anything else that's suitable that I can't think of just at the moment, mind your own blasted business!'

'Ah, here comes Gigi now!' said Saro, laughing.

Gigi Pulejo came hurrying in, and went straight across to the box on the wall to see if there were any messages for him in his pigeon-hole. 'How's tricks, Paolí?'

'Are you in a hurry?' Paolino Lovico asked him, frowning, without replying to his greeting.

'Yes, very much so!' sighed Dr. Pulejo, throwing his hat onto the back of his head and fanning his forehead with his handkerchief. 'Terrible days, these, my dear fellow.'

'What did I say?' laughed Paolino Lovico, angrily, scornfully, his fists dancing about in front of him. 'What's the epidemic this time? Cholera? Bubonic plague? Some nasty horrible cankerous thing that's going to carry off the whole lot of you? You've got to listen to me! Hey, Saro, haven't you got anything you need to pound in that mortar of yours?'

'No, nothing. Why?'

'In that case, we'll go somewhere else!' replied Lovico, grabbing hold of Gigi Pulejo by his arm and dragging him out of the shop, 'I can't talk to you here!'

'Is this going to be a long talk?' asked the Doctor as they walked along.

'*Very* long!'

'I'm terribly sorry, old chap, but I haven't got the time!'

'You haven't got the time? D'you know what I'll do? I'll throw myself under a tram, and break a leg! And I'll force you to dance attendance on me for the best part of the day! Where have you got to go?'

'First of all, just round here. Via Butera.'

'I'll come with you,' said Lovico. 'You go up and see your patient, and I'll wait downstairs for you. Then we'll resume our chat.'

'God Almighty, what the hell's up with you?' asked Dr. Pulejo, stopping and taking a look at him.

And as the Doctor stood there and watched him, Paolino Lovico flung his arms wide apart, flexed his knees, relaxed his whole untidy little body, and replied, 'Gigi, old chap, I'm a dead man!'

And his eyes filled with tears.

'Go on! Tell me all about it!' the Doctor urged him. 'Now, come on! What's happened?'

Paolino took a few more steps, then stopped again and, holding Gigi Pulejo by the sleeve, launched mysteriously into his tale with, 'Now, look, I'm talking to you like a brother! Otherwise, nothing doing! A doctor's like a father-confessor, isn't he?'

He placed his hand on his belly and, giving him a meaningful look, said, 'As secret as the grave-oh, *h'm*?'

Then, opening his eyes very wide, and holding his thumb and forefinger together, as if to lend greater weight to the words he was about to utter, he said, stressing the syllables, 'Petella keeps two homes.'

'Petella?' asked a thoroughly bewildered Gigi Pulejo. 'Who's Petella?'

'Good God, man! *Petella! Captain* Petella!' exclaimed Lovico, 'Petella who works for the General Steamship Company!'

'I don't know him,' said Dr. Pulejo.

'You don't know him? So much the better! Still, as secret as the grave-oh, nonetheless! Two homes,' he repeated in the same gloomy serious voice. 'One here, and one in Naples.'

'Well?'

'Oh, so it seems the merest trifle to you, does it?' asked Paolino Lovico, losing all his self-composure in the rage that was devouring him. 'A married man! Who takes blackguardly advantage of his profession as a sailor to set up another home in another part of the country! So that's the merest trifle according to you, is it? My God, this is the sort of thing you expect the Turks to get up to!'

'Oh, yes? It's scandalous to the *n*th degree! Who's saying it isn't? But what's it got to do with you? Where do *you* come in?'

'Oh, so you want to know what it's got to do with me, do you? You want to know where *I* come in?'

'I don't want to seem nosey, but is she a relative of yours, Petella's wife?'

'No, she isn't!' shouted Paolino Lovico, his eyes bloodshot. 'She's a poor woman who's suffering! Going through absolute hell! An honest, respectable woman! Do you understand? Who has been betrayed in the most infamous manner! Do you understand? *By her own husband!* Do you *have* to be a relative in order to feel your blood boil at such a state of affairs?'

'Well, you'll forgive my saying so, but I can't see what *I* can do about it,' said Gigi Pulejo, shrugging his shoulders.

'Of course you can't! And you never *will* if you don't give me a chance to finish what I'm saying! Oh, hell and damnation! Oh, everything's hell! The weather's hell! Life's hell!' puffed Lovico. 'Feel how hot it is? It's killing me, this heat! That dear kind Captain Petella! That dear, *dear,* kind Captain Petella isn't satisfied with betraying his wife and keeping another home in Naples! Oh, no! He's got three or four children by that woman down there. And only *one* up here by his wife! He's refused to have any more! But, as you'll readily appreciate, those other children of his down there aren't legitimate! If he has any more by that woman in Naples he can throw them on one side! Just as if they didn't matter at all! Whereas, up here, when it's a question of his wife—— Well, it's quite a different matter! You can't get rid of a *legitimate* child! Well then, seeing that's how things are, what does he cook up, the murdering swine? Oh, you know, this little business has been going on for the last couple of years! What he cooks up is this. During the few days he's ashore here he seizes on the slightest pretext to pick a quarrel with his wife. Then, when night-time comes, he shuts himself up in his room and sleeps by himself. Next day, off he goes again. And to hell with what anybody thinks about him! Things have been going on like this for the last couple of years!'

'Oh, poor lady!' exclaimed Gigi, and though the commiseration in his voice was genuine, he couldn't quite succeed in removing the smile from his words. 'But—— Well, I still don't understand what it's got to do with me.'

'Listen, my dear chap, my dear Gigi,' Lovico resumed in a different tone of voice, clinging on to his arm, 'for the past four months I've been coaching the boy—Petella's son, that is—in Latin. He's ten, and in the first form.'

'Oh!' said the Doctor.

'If you only knew with what compassion that unfortunate woman has inspired me!' went on Lovico. 'Oh, the tears she's wept! The tears she's wept, the poor, dear woman! How *good* she is! She's still beautiful, you know! I'd understand it if she were ugly . . . ! But she's *beautiful*! To see her treated like that—betrayed, despised, just chucked in the corner like a useless piece of old rag! I'd like to meet the woman who *could* have stood up to it! Who *wouldn't* have rebelled against it! Who is there among us that would dare to condemn her? She's an honest woman, my dear Gigi! She simply *must* be saved! It's absolutely imperative! Do you hear me? She's in a terrible plight at the moment—the situation's *desperate*!'

Gigi Pulejo stopped and looked severely at Lovico.

'Oh no, my dear chap!' he said to him. 'I don't do that sort of thing. I haven't got the slightest desire to try conclusions with the Law! *Not me!*'

'Oh, you stupid fool!' burst out Paolino Lovico. 'Now what daft notion have you got into your head? What are you busy imagining I want you to do? What sort of person do you take me for? Do you think I'm an *immoral* man? A ruffianly scoundrel? Do you think I'm asking for your help with an—— Oh, it fills me with revulsion, sheer horror, just to think of it!'

'Then what the devil *do* you want with me? I can't see what you're driving at!' shouted Dr. Pulejo, losing all patience with him.

'I want what's right and proper!' shouted Paolino Lovico in reply. 'Morality, *that's* what I want! I want Petella to be a good husband, and not to slam the bedroom door in his wife's face when he comes ashore here!'

Gigi Pulejo burst into noisy laughter. 'And what do—do you think *I* . . . what do you think I can do? Poor—poor Pet—! Ha! Ha! Ha! Take the stupid donkey to water and—Ho! Ho!—make him *drink*? Ha! Ha! Ha!'

'You laugh, do you, you hulking beast, you! You *laugh*?'

bellowed the trembling Paolino Lovico, brandishing his fists in Pulejo's face. 'You've got a tragedy staring you straight in the eyes *and you laugh*! Here's a low-down scug refusing to do his duty, *and* you laugh! You see before you a woman whose honour is threatened—whose very life is threatened—*and you laugh, do you?* To say nothing of my own situation! I'm a dead man! I'll go and throw myself in the sea, if you don't help me! *Now* do you understand?'

'But what sort of help can *I* possibly give you?' asked Pulejo, still unable to stop himself laughing.

'Do you know what's going to happen?' he asked him gloomily. 'Petella gets in this evening. Tomorrow he leaves again for the Levant. He's off to Smyrna. He'll be away about a month. There's no time to be lost. Either we act promptly, or—*all is lost*! For pity's sake, my dear Gigi, save me! Save that poor, suffering martyr! You *must* know *some* way of managing it! You *must* know *some* remedy. Don't laugh, my God! Or I'll strangle you! No, go on! Laugh away! Laugh if you feel like it! Laugh at my despair! But *do* give me your *help*! Do find me a remedy for—— Some means of—— Some sort of medicine——'

Gigi Pulejo had now reached the house in the Via Butera where he was due to make his call. He made a mighty effort to stop laughing and asked, 'What it all boils down to is this, isn't it? You'd like *me* to prevent the Captain from finding an excuse for starting a row with his wife this evening. M'm?'

'Precisely!'

'For morality's sake, um?'

'For morality's sake! Are you still fooling about?'

'No! No! I'm quite serious now. Listen! I'll go on up. You go back to the shop—Saro's—and wait for me there. I'll be along in no time.'

'What do you intend to do?'

'Leave it to me!' said the Doctor, reassuringly. 'Go along to Saro's and wait for me there!'

'Do be quick, won't you?' shouted Lovico after him, his hands clasped in supplication.

* * *

At sunset, Paolino Lovico was down at the pier to watch the arrival of Captain Petella and his ship the *Segesta*. He felt he simply *had* to be there—to watch from a distance, at least. He didn't really know why. He had to see how he was looking and hurl a string of oaths after him.

He'd been hoping, after his onslaught on Dr. Pulejo, and the help he'd succeeded in getting from him, that the intense state of excitement to which he'd been prey since that morning would now subside—at least for a little while. Not on your life! After he'd delivered a certain mysterious little packet of cream cakes to Signora Petella—the Captain was extremely partial to sweet things—he'd come on down here, and his overwhelming feeling of excitement had grown steadily stronger and stronger. He'd have preferred to put off going to bed as long as possible. But he soon got tired of roaming about the town, his nagging sense of worry exacerbated by his fear of starting a row with one or other of his innumerable acquaintances who might be so ill-advised as to come up and say something to him.

It was all because he had the misfortune to be—well, *transparent* is the only word for it. Oh, it certainly was a blight! And this 'transparency' of his had proved a source of endless amusement—ah, *most* hilarious!—to all of them, those hypocrites sheathed in lies! It was as if his clarity of vision—the way he could look open-eyed on all human passions, even the saddest, the most anguished—had the effect of inspiring laughter in all those who either hadn't experienced them or, so used were they to masking them, no longer *recognized* them when they occurred in a poor man like himself, who had the misfortune of being unable to hide and control his passions.

Back home he went, and retreated to his lair. He threw himself on to his bed, without bothering to undress.

How pale she'd been, how pale she'd been, poor darling, when he'd handed her the packet of cakes! So pale, and with those dismayed-looking eyes of hers, clouded with anguish. She didn't really look beautiful any more. . . .

'Look cheerful, my dear!' he urged her with a sob in his throat, 'and make yourself look very nice, for pity's sake. Put on that

Japanese silk blouse, the one that suits you so well. But, above all, I do beg you, don't let him find you looking like this—you look like a funeral! Cheer up! Go on! Cheer up! Have you got everything all laid on? The best of everything! Remember, don't let him have the slightest cause for complaint! Be brave, darling! Good-bye! Till tomorrow! Let's hope everything goes off all right. For pity's sake, don't forget to hang a handkerchief out of the window, as a signal; on the bit of cord outside your bedroom window. Tomorrow morning, my first thought will be to come along and see. Oh, do make sure I find that signal, my dear! Do make sure I find it!'

Before leaving the house, he'd taken out his blue pencil and scattered 'ten out of ten' and 'ten—a really excellent piece of work' all over the exercise-book in which that stupid lout of a Petella boy did his translations. He was supposed to be *working* at his Latin, and he was in a bit of a flap because of his father's homecoming.

'Just you show that to Daddy, Nonò. You know how pleased Daddy will be! Just you go on like that, my dear boy, just you go on like that, and in a few years' time you'll know Latin better than one of the geese in the Capitol. You remember *them,* don't you, Nonò? The ones that put the Gauls to flight, you know, eh? Three cheers for Papyrius! Let's be happy, lad! We must all be bright and cheerful this evening, Nonò! Daddy's coming! Happy and good! Clean and well-behaved! Let me see your finger-nails. Are they clean? Good boy! Mind you don't get them dirty now! Three cheers for Papyrius! Nonò, three cheers for Papyrius!'

The cakes now. Suppose that fool of a Pulejo had been pulling his leg? No, no! Quite impossible. He'd made it very clear to him just how serious the situation was. It would have been treachery of the foulest kind for his friend to deceive him. However . . . However . . . However . . . Suppose the remedy wasn't as effective as he'd assured him it was?

The *nonchalance* of that man—his *contempt* even—for his own wife! Oh, it made his blood start boiling all over again, just as if it were a direct affront to him personally. It certainly *was*! How on earth was it that that woman, with whom he, Paolino Lovico, was quite satisfied—no, not merely satisfied—whom he thought eminently *desirable* should be held of no account by that scoundrel? It almost looked as if he, Paolino Lovico, was content with someone else's leavings, a woman who didn't count at all as far as another man was concerned. Oh, he supposed that lady down in Naples was a better proposition! What, lovelier than his wife? He'd like to see her. He'd like to put them side by side, the one beside the other, and then show them to him and shout in his ugly mug, 'Oh, so you prefer the other one, do you? But that's only because you're a nasty beast with no taste, and no discernment! As if your wife isn't worth more than that woman a hundred thousand times over! Look at her! Look at her! How can you have the heart not to touch her? You don't understand what real refinement is. You don't understand *delicate* beauty. You can't appreciate the lovely sorrowing quality of melancholy grace! You're an animal, you're a huge wallowing hog, and you can't understand these things. So you despise them. And then what do you try and put in their place? A nasty slut of a female in the place of a decent, respectable woman, an honest woman!

Oh, what a night he had! Not a wink of sleep.

When at last it looked as if dawn was about to break, he couldn't stand it any longer.

Signora Petella didn't share her husband's bed. She slept in a separate room. She could then, perfectly easily, even though it was night-time, have hung the handkerchief to the little cord by the window, so as to put him out of his misery as soon as possible. She must have realized that he wouldn't sleep a wink all night long, and that the moment dawn came he'd be along to see.

That was what he was thinking as he rushed over to the Petella house. Flattered by his own burning desire that it should be there, he was so confident that he *would* find that signal by the window, that not finding it was like death to him. It really was. He felt his knees buckling under him. Nothing! Nothing! And how funereal those barred shutters looked!

A savage desire suddenly assailed him—to go upstairs, to hurl himself into Petella's bedroom and to strangle him on his bed! Then, all at once, he felt completely at the end of his tether, done up, an empty sack—just as if he had in fact gone upstairs and committed that crime. He tried to cheer himself up by telling himself that it was probably still too early, probably asking too much. Expecting her to get up in the middle of the night to hang out that signal for him to find in the morning. Perhaps she hadn't been *able* to—who knows?

Now, come, come! There was no need to despair yet awhile. He'd have liked to have waited. But not there! Waiting there, every minute would seem an eternity. His legs, however,—he couldn't feel his legs any longer!

By great good luck, he found a wretched little café open, only a few yards along the first alley he turned into. It was a favourite haunt of workmen who came along early in the morning from the dockyard nearby. He went in and slumped down on to a wooden bench.

There wasn't a soul in the place. He couldn't even see the proprietor. He could hear him, however, busying himself about the place, and chatting away to somebody in the dark cavern of a back room. They were probably just lighting the stove.

When, shortly afterwards, a huge rough-looking man in his shirt-sleeves put in an appearance, and asked him what he wanted, Paolino Lovico turned and looked at him in utter and ferocious astonishment. Then he said, 'A handkerch—— That is—— I mean coffee! Strong! Please make it lovely and strong!'

It was brought to him immediately. I'll say it was! Half of it he slopped all over himself, half he spurted out as he leapt to his feet. Good Lord! The stuff was boiling!

'What's up, sir?'

'Aaaaaah!' groaned Lovico, his eyes staring and his mouth gaping.

'What about a drop of water? A sip of water?' the café proprietor suggested. 'Here, try a drop of water!'

'And what about my trousers?' moaned Paolino, looking down at them.

He fished his handkerchief out of his pocket, dipped a corner in the glass of water and started rubbing the stain vigorously. Now his thigh felt horribly cold.

He spread out the sodden handkerchief, looked at it, and went pale. He threw a twenty *centesimi* piece on the tray and made his escape. But he'd hardly turned the corner again, when he—*wheroomph*! He found himself face to face with Captain Petella!

'Hello-hello-hello! You here?'

'Yes—I. I——' stammered Paolino Lovico. (There wasn't a drop of blood left in his veins.) 'I—I got up early. And——'

'You thought you'd take a stroll in the cool of the morning, eh?' Petella finished his sentence for him. 'Lucky man! No responsibilities. No worries. A free man! A bachelor!'

Lovico looked deep into the other man's eyes, trying to discover whether—— But, well, you only had to consider the fact that the horrible beast was out and about at that early hour, and that he had that nasty, stormy look about his face. Oh, the miserable wretch! Oh, no doubt about it! He must have had a row with his wife again last night! 'I'll kill him!' thought Lovico to himself. 'On my word of honour, I'll kill him!' Meanwhile, however, he was saying, a slight smile on his lips, 'But I see that you too . . .'

'Me?' growled Petella. 'What about me?'

'Why. So early in the morning!'

'Oh, you're wondering why you see me out and about as early as this? Oh, I had a terrible night, my dear Lovico! Maybe it was the heat. I don't know.'

'You didn't—— You didn't—— You didn't *sleep* well?'

'I didn't sleep at all!' shouted Petella in exasperation. 'You see, when I can't sleep—when I don't get to sleep—I get as mad as hell!'

'And what—forgive the question—what fault is it of other people?' Lovico stammered away, trembling all over, yet still managing to smile, 'What fault is it of other people? Sorry if I——'

'Other people?' asked an astounded Petella. 'What have other people got to do with it?'

'Well. You said you got as mad as hell. Who do you get mad with? Who do you take it out on if it's hot?'

'I take it out on myself, I take it out on the weather, I take it out on everybody!' burst in Petella. 'I want air. I'm used to the sea and I can't bear the land, my dear Lovico, especially in the summer! I just can't bear it! The house, the walls, all that worry, worry, worry. *Women!*'

'I'll kill—— On my word of honour, I'll kill him!' muttered Lovico, to himself, trembling away. And with his usual little smile, he went on aloud, 'Oh, you can't stand women either?'

'Huh, shall I tell you something? As far as I'm concerned, and well, it's really—— You travel about; you're away so long. I don't say *now,* now that I'm old. But when you're young and lusty—— Ah, *women*! There's one good quality I've always had, you know! When I want a woman, I *want* a woman. When I don't, I don't. There's never been any doubt about who's been the boss!'

'What, *never*?' Then, to himself, 'I'll kill him!'

'No, never. When I've *wanted* them, of course! The other way on with you, eh? They twist you round their little finger, eh? A pretty little smile, a tiny little wiggle, a modest little look. Just a teeny-weeny bit shamefaced. Go on, own up! Eh? Tell me the truth?'

Lovico stopped and looked him straight in the face.

'So you want the truth, do you? If *I* had a wife——'

Petella burst out laughing.

'We're not talking about *wives,* at the moment! What have wives got to do with it? Women! Women!'

'And aren't *wives* women? What are they?'

'Yes, they probably *are* women. On occasion!' exclaimed Petella. 'You haven't got one yet, my dear Lovico, and for the sake of your health, I hope you never *do* get one. You see, *wives*——'

And as he said this, he tucked Paolino's arm under his own, and went on talking and talking. Lovico was trembling all over. He looked into Petella's face, he looked into those puffy eyes of his, with the blue rings round them, and thought. . . . Perhaps . . . Yes, perhaps they were like that because he'd been unable to sleep. One moment, from one or two things that the Captain was saying, he got the impression that—— Well, that he could deduce that that poor woman was saved. The next moment, on the other hand, as a result of something else he said, he was plunged back into doubt and desperation. His torment lasted an eternity because the horrible beast had a desire to walk and walk and walk, and dragged him all the way along the sea front. At last, he turned to go back home.

'I'm not leaving him,' thought Lovico to himself. 'I'll go up into the house with him and if he hasn't done his duty, this is the last day on earth for all three of us!'

He became utterly absorbed in this murderous thought. He was filled with overwhelming rage and violence. He was so taut with nervous energy that he felt his limbs somehow dissolving, almost falling into pieces. Then, after he and the Captain had turned the corner, he raised his eyes to look at the window of Petella's house, and suddenly saw, hanging from the cord . . . Oh, God! Oh, God! Oh, God! . . . One . . . Two . . . Three . . . Four . . . *Five* handkerchiefs!

He wrinkled his nose, he opened his mouth, his head whirled and swam, and he gasped a great 'Ah!' in a paroxysm of joy which was almost choking him.

'What's up?' shouted Petella, holding him up.

And Lovico said, 'Oh, my dear Captain! Thank you very much, my dear Captain! Thank you! Ah! It's been perfectly delightful. This—this lovely stroll. But I'm tired, dead-beat. I'm dropping, I really *am*. I'm dropping! Thank you! Thank you from the bottom of my heart, my dear Captain! See you again soon! Have a pleasant trip, *eh*? See you again soon! Thank you! Thang you!'

And hardly had Petella got inside his big front door than off he set, down the road, running along, jubilant, exultant, grinning all over his face, his eyes shining with riotous merriment, and displaying the five fingers of his hand to everyone he met.

## IN THE ABYSS

*Il gorgo* (as it then was) appeared originally in *Aprutium* for July–August 1913. Still under this title, it was incorporated in *Le due maschere* (Firenze, Quattrini, 1914). It retained its original title for the 'new, revised edition' of the volume put out by Treves of Milan in 1920 under the name *Tu ridi*. As *Nel gorgo* it was included in Vol. VIII of the Bemporad series of *Novelle per un anno* (*Dal naso al cielo,* Firenze, 1925). The volume was reprinted by Bemporad and by Mondadori, and is now part of the Biblioteca Moderna Mondadori. The definitive text is in Vol. I of the *Opere*. (*Novelle per un anno,* Vol. I, *con una prefazione di Corrado Alvaro,* Milano-Verona, Mondadori, 1956.)

# IN THE ABYSS

At the Rackets Club they talked of nothing else the whole evening.

The first man to give them the news was Respi—Nicolino Respi—who was terribly grieved by it. As usual, however, despite the emotion he felt, he was quite unable to prevent his lips from curling in that nervous little smile which—even in the most serious discussions and in the most difficult moments of play—made his small, pale, jaundiced face, with its sharp features, so completely and so characteristically *his*.

His friends clustered around him in consternation.

'Has he *really* gone out of his mind?'

'Oh, no! Only for a joke.'

Traldi, who was buried deep in the settee, with the entire weight of his enormous pachydermatous body driving him farther in, gave a series of heaves in an attempt to prop himself into a more upright position. The effort made his bovine bloodshot eyes open wide and pop out of their sockets. He asked, 'Forgive the question, old man, but have you . . . *Oooh! Oooh!* Have you—I mean, did he give *you* that look, too?'

'Did he . . . ? Give *me* . . . that . . . look? What do you mean?' asked Nicolino Respi in return, utterly astonished, and turning questioningly to his friends. 'I arrived only this morning from Milan, to find this wonderful item of news waiting for me. I don't know a thing. I still can't understand how it is that Romeo Daddi—My God, Romeo Daddi of *all* people! The most even-tempered, serene, level-headed one of the lot of us . . . !'

'Have they locked him up?'

'Of course they have! Didn't I say so? Three o'clock this afternoon. In the Monte Mario Asylum!'

'Poor Daddi!'

'How's Donna Bicetta taking it? But, how on——! Did *she* . . . ? I mean, was it Donna Bicetta who sent for them?'

'No, of course it wasn't? No, as a matter of fact, *she* wouldn't hear of it? No, her father dashed down from Florence the day before yesterday.'

'Oh, so that's why . . . !'

'Precisely. He made her take the decision, to—— For *his* sake as well. But tell me how it all happened. Traldi, why did you ask me whether Daddi'd given *me* that look as well?'

Carlo Traldi had blissfully buried himself again in the settee with his head thrown back, and his purple, sweaty double-chin exposed to full view. Wriggling his little slender frog's legs, which his exorbitantly huge belly forced him perpetually to keep obscenely apart, and continually and no less obscenely moistening his lips, he replied abstractedly, 'Oh yes, so I did. Because I thought that *that* was why you said he'd gone mad.'

'What do you mean, *that* was why?'

'Why, of course! That's how his madness revealed itself to him. He looked at everybody in a particular way, my dear fellow. Oh, don't make me talk, you chaps, *you* tell him how poor Daddi looked.'

Whereupon his friends told Nicolino Respi that Daddi, after he'd got back from his holiday in the country, had appeared to all of them like someone completely dazed. It was as if he were somehow *outside* himself. He'd look at you with an empty smile on his lips, his eyes dull and glazed. He wasn't *really* looking at you, as was obvious when anyone called him. Then that astounded look had disappeared and been transformed into an acute and strange kind of staring. First of all, he'd stared at things from a distance, obliquely. Then, gradually, as if attracted by certain signs which he thought he could observe in one or other of his most intimate friends—especially in those who most assiduously frequented his house—highly *natural* signs, for everyone was thrown into a state of utter consternation by that sudden and extraordinary change. It was so completely in contrast with the usual serenity of his character. Gradually, he'd come to watch them attentively from close to, and in the last days he'd become downright unbearable. He'd suddenly plonk himself in front of now one, now another of them, place his hands on the man's shoulders, look into his eyes—deep, deep down into them he'd look.

'God Almighty, it gave you the shudders!' Traldi exclaimed at that point, dragging himself up again, in an attempt to get his body into a slightly more upright position.

'But—— Why?' asked Respi, nervously.

'Listen to what I'm going to tell you, if you want to know why!' Traldi exclaimed in reply. 'Ugh! So you want to know why we all got the shudders, do you? My dear fellow, I'd like to have seen *you* getting to grips with that look of his! I suppose you change your shirt every day. You're quite sure your feet are clean, and that your socks haven't got holes in them. But are you quite sure you haven't got anything mucky inside, on your conscience, down in your subconscious?'

'Oh, my God, I'd say——'

'Bunkum! You're not being honest with yourself!'

'And you are?'

'Yes, I am! That's one thing I am sure about! And believe me, it happens to all of us. We all discover, in some lucid interval, that, to a greater or lesser degree, we're swine! Almost every night—for quite some time now—when I put out the candle, before dropping off to sleep...'

'You're getting old, my dear chap, you're getting old!' all his friends yelled at him in chorus.

'Maybe I am getting old,' admitted Traldi. 'So much the worse! It's no fun foreseeing that in the end I'll be firmly fixed in such an opinion of myself. An old swine, that's what I'll be in my own eyes. Anyway, wait a minute! Now that I've told you this, let's try a little experiment shall we? Shut up, you lot! Quiet!'

And Carlo Traldi got laboriously to his feet. He placed his hands on Nicolino Respi's shoulders and shouted in his face, 'Look into my eyes! Deep down into my eyes! No, don't laugh, my dear fellow! Look into my eyes! Deep down into my eyes! Wait! And you lot wait, too! Shut up!'

They all became silent. They were held in suspense, intent on that strange experiment.

Traldi, his huge oval, bloodshot eyes popping out of their sockets, stared acutely into the eyes of Nicolino Respi, and it seemed as if that malignant, shining gaze, which got gradually more and more acute and intense, was rummaging in his conscience, in his sub-conscious. . . . Discovering, there in the most intimate hiding-places, the most wicked and atrocious things. Little by little, Nicolino Respi began to grow pale and—although lower on his face his lips, with their usual little smile still playing upon them, seemed to be saying, 'Oh rubbish! I'm only taking part in your little joke because——'; his eyes started to cloud over. He found he couldn't meet Traldi's gaze all the time, till finally, amidst the silence of his friends Traldi, in a strange voice, without lowering his staring gaze, without slackening one jot the intensity of his gaze, said victoriously, 'There you are, you see? There you are!'

'Oh, rubbish!' burst out Respi, unable to stand it any longer, and shaking himself vigorously.

'The same to you, with nobs on! We understand one another all right!' shouted Traldi. 'You're a worse swine than I am!' And he burst out laughing. The others laughed too, with a sense of unexpected relief. Traldi resumed, 'Now this has been a joke. Only for a joke can one of us set himself to look at another of us like that. Because you and I alike still have that little machine known as civilization in good working order inside us; so we let the whole bang shoot of all our actions, all our thoughts, all our feelings sit there, hidden, at the bottom of our consciousness. But, now suppose that someone, whose little civilization machine's broken down, comes along and looks at you as I looked at you just now, no longer as a joke, but in all seriousness, and without your expecting it removes from the bottom of your consciousness all that assembly of thoughts, actions, and feelings which you've got inside you. . . . Then tell me that you wouldn't get the shudders!'

Saying which, Carlo Traldi moved furiously towards the door. Then he turned back and added, 'And do you know what he was murmuring under his breath. . . . ? Poor Daddi, I mean! Go on, you lot; you tell him what he was murmuring! I must fly!'

' "What an abyss. . . . What an abyss. . . ." '

'Just like that?'

'Yes. "What an abyss. . . . What an abyss. . . ." '

After Traldi left the group broke up and Nicolino Respi was

left, feeling thoroughly disturbed, in the company of just two friends, who went on talking for a little while about the terrible misfortune which had overtaken poor Daddi.

About two months before he'd gone to visit him at his villa near Perugia. He'd found him as calm and serene as ever, together with his wife and a friend of hers, Gabriella Vanzi—an old school-friend, who'd recently married a naval officer, who was then on a cruise. He'd spent three days at the villa, and not once—not once—had Romeo Daddi looked at him in the way that Traldi had described.

If he *had* looked at him like that...

A wave of dismay swept over Nicolino Respi. He felt suddenly giddy, and for support he took the arm of one of those two friends of his, making it look like a confidential gesture. His face was very pale, but the smile was still on his lips.

What had happened? What was that they were saying? Torture? What kind of torture? Oh, the torture Daddi had inflicted on his wife....

'Afterwards, eh?' the words escaped from his lips.

They both turned and looked at him. 'What do you mean, afterwards?'

'Oh. . . . No, what I meant was afterwards—when his . . . Well, when his little machine broke down.'

'Oh, it must have been! It certainly couldn't have been before!'

'My God, they were a miracle of conjugal harmony and domestic bliss! It's obvious that something must have happened while they were on holiday in the country!'

'Why, yes! At the very least some sort of suspicion must have been aroused in him.'

'Oh, don't be so utterly——! Concerning his wife?' burst out Nicolino Respi. 'That, if anything, might have been the *result* of his madness, certainly not its cause! Only a madman——'

'Agreed! Agreed!' his friends cried. 'A wife like Donna Bicetta!'

'No one could possibly suspect her! But—— Besides...!'

Nicolino Respi could no longer bear to stand there listening to the pair of them. He felt as if he were stifling. He needed air. He needed to walk about in the open air. On his own. He made some excuse and got away.

A terrible, tormenting doubt had insinuated itself into his mind and brought turmoil with it.

No one could know better than he that Donna Bicetta was completely above suspicion. For more than a year he'd persisted in declaring his love for her, besieged her with his courtship, without ever once obtaining anything more than a very gentle and compassionate smile in recompense for all his wasted labour. With that serenity which comes from being very sure of yourself, without either feeling insulted or rebelling against his onslaught, she'd made it perfectly plain to him that any kind of persistence on his part would be quite in vain, because she was just as much in love as he was—perhaps more than he was—but with her husband. Since she was in love with her husband, if he really loved her, he'd realize that her love could never grow less. If he didn't realize that, then he didn't really love her. So . . . ?

Sometimes, in certain solitary bathing spots, the sea water is so limpid, so clear, and so transparent that, however great your desire to immerse yourself in it, to enjoy its delicious refreshing coolness, you feel an almost sacred restraint inhibiting you from bringing turmoil into it.

Nicolino Respi always had the same feeling of limpidity and restraint when approaching the soul of Donna Bicetta Daddi. This woman loved life, with such a tranquil, attentive, and gentle love! Only once—it was during those three days spent in her villa near Perugia—had he, overcome by his burning desire, done violence to that restraint, had he brought turmoil into that limpidity, and he had been sternly repulsed.

Now his terrible tormenting doubt was this: that perhaps the turmoil he'd caused in those three days hadn't quietened down again after he'd left. Perhaps it had grown so great that her husband had become aware of it. Certainly, on his arrival at the villa, Romeo Daddi had been perfectly calm, and within a few days of his departure he'd gone out of his mind.

Well then, was it on *his* account? Had she, then, been left profoundly disturbed, quite overcome by his amorous aggression?

Why, of course! Yes. Why doubt it?

All night long Nicolino Respi argued the question backwards and forwards in his own mind. He twisted from one frenzied extreme to the other. One moment he was torn by remorse away from a malign and impetuous sense of joy; the next he was torn by this joy away from his remorse.

The following morning, as soon as he thought he might properly do so, he rushed round to Donna Bicetta Daddi's house. He simply had to see her. He simply had to clear things up at once. Somehow resolve those doubts of his. Perhaps she wouldn't see him. But, in any case, he wanted to present himself at her house, ready to confront and submit to the consequences of that situation.

Donna Bicetta Daddi wasn't at home.

For the past hour, without in the least wishing to, without knowing she was doing it, she'd been inflicting the most cruel of martyrdoms on her friend Gabriella Vanzi, the woman who'd been her guest for three months at her villa.

She'd gone to see her, so that together they might try and work out—not the reason, alas! No, what had driven him to—what had caused that misfortune of his. Try and pinpoint the moment in three days during their stay in the country—the last days of their time there—when it had first revealed itself. And, though she'd ransacked her memory, she hadn't succeeded in discovering anything.

For the past hour she'd been stubbornly calling back those last days, reconstructing them minute by minute. 'Do you remember this? Do you remember that morning he went down into the garden without taking his linen hat, and called up for it to be thrown down to him from the window. Then he came back up, laughing, with that bunch of roses. Do you remember—he wanted me to wear a couple of them? Then he went with me to the gate and helped me into the car, and told me he'd like me to bring him back those books from Perugia. Wait a moment! One was—— Oh, I don't know. Something to do with seeds—do you remember? Do you remember?'

So thoroughly upset was she by the grief the re-evocation of so many minute and valueless details was inflicting on her, that she didn't observe the steadily growing anguish and agitation of her friend.

Already she'd re-evoked without the slightest indication of being upset the three days spent in the villa by Nicolino Respi, and she hadn't for one moment paused to consider whether her husband had found provocation for his madness in the innocent courtship of that man. It wasn't even remotely possible. It had been very much a laughing matter for the three of them, that courtship of his after Respi's departure for Milan. How could she possibly imagine that——? Besides, after his departure, hadn't her husband remained quite serene, quite tranquil for . . . ? Well, it was more than a fortnight.

No, never! Never the remotest hint of suspicion! Never once, in seven whole years of marriage! How, where, would he ever have found cause for suspicion? And yet look, all of a sudden, there amidst the peace and quiet of the Umbrian countryside, without anything at all happening——

'Oh, Gabriella! Gabriella, my dear! I'm going out of my mind now! Believe me, I'm going mad too!'

Suddenly, as she was recovering from that crisis of desperation, Donna Bicetta Daddi, raising her weeping eyes to look at her friend's face, discovered that it had become very set and gone deathly pale. She looked just like a corpse. She was trying to get control over a paroxysm of unbearable anguish. She was panting. Her nostrils were flaring. And she was watching her with evil in her eyes. Oh, God! Almost the same look in her eyes as that with which, in those last days, her husband had stood there looking at her.

She felt her blood freezing. She felt terror crowding in upon her.

'Why—— You as well? Why?' She stammered, trembling all over. 'Why are *you* looking at me like that?'

Gabriella Vanzi made a hideous effort to force the expression on her face, which she'd assumed quite unknown to herself, to dissolve into a benign smile of compassion. 'Me . . . ? Was I looking? No, I was thinking. Yes, look—— I meant to ask you. Yes, I know—you're so sure of yourself—is there nothing that you—absolutely nothing—nothing you've got to reproach yourself with?'

Donna Bicetta was startled out of her wits. With her hands clasped to her cheeks, and her eyes wide and staring, she cried, 'What? *You're* saying it to me now! His very words as well! How . . . ? How *can* you?'

Gabriella Vanzi's face took on a false expression and her eyes glazed over, 'How can *I* . . . ?'

'Yes, you! Oh, my God! And now you're getting all dismayed, just like him! What does it all mean? What does it all mean?'

She felt herself gradually sinking deeper and deeper. She was still whimpering 'What does it all mean?' when she found her friend in her arms, and clinging tightly to her breast.

'Bice. Bice. Do you suspect me? You came here—because you suspected me, didn't you?'

'No! No! I give you my solemn oath, Gabriella. Now, however. . . . Only now——'

'You do now, don't you? Yes, you do! But you're wrong, you're wrong, Bice! Because you can't understand.'

'What's happened? Gabriella! Now, come on! Tell me! What's happened?'

'You can't understand. You can't understand. I know why—I know the reason why your husband's gone mad!'

'The reason why . . . ? *Which* reason?'

'I know the reason why he—— Because it's in me. It's in me too. This reason for going mad. Because of what happened to both of us!'

'To *both* of you?'

'Yes! Yes! To me and your husband.'

'Well?'

'No! No! It's not what you're thinking! You can't possibly understand. Without any attempt at deceiving anybody—without thinking about it—without wanting it to happen. . . . In an instant; something *horrible*! And nobody can blame himself for it. You see how I'm talking to you about it? How I *can* talk to you about it? Because I'm not to blame! And neither is he! But just because that's how things are. Listen! *Listen!* And when you've found out everything, maybe *you'll* go mad as well, in the same way as *I'm* just about to go mad! In the same way as *he's* gone mad! Listen!

You've been busy reliving that day when you went into Perugia from the villa, in the car, haven't you? The day he gave you those two roses and asked you to bring him back those books.'

'Yes.'

'Well. It was that morning!'

'*What* was?'

'Everything that happened. Everything and nothing. . . . Let me tell you, for pity's sake! It was terribly hot, do you remember? After seeing you off, he and I walked back through the garden. The sun was simply scorching and the chirping of the crickets was quite deafening. We went back into the house and sat down in the drawing-room, over by the dining-room door. The blinds were drawn, the shutters were pulled to. It was almost dark in there. There was a feeling of coolness. Everything was still. I'm giving you my impression of it now—the only one I could possibly have. The one I remember. The one I shall always remember. Maybe he had the same memory of it himself. He must have done, otherwise I'd never be able to explain anything to myself! It was that stillness, that coolness, coming after all that sunshine and the deafening noise of the crickets. In an instant—— Without thinking about it, I swear! Never, never. . . . Neither he nor I. . . . Oh yes, of that I'm positive——! As if there were some irresistible attraction implicit within that astonished emptiness, within the delicious coolness of that semi-darkness. . . . Bice, Bice. . . . It happened just like that. . . . I swear it! In an instant!'

With a sudden movement, Donna Bicetta Daddi leapt to her feet—impelled to do so by a sudden access of hatred, anger, and contempt.

'Oh, so that's why?' she hissed between her teeth, drawing away like a cat.

'No, that's not why!' cried Gabriella, stretching her arms towards her in a gesture of despair and supplication. 'That's not why? That's not why, Bice! Your husband went mad on your account, on *your* account, not because of me!'

'He went mad on my account? What do you mean? Out of remorse?'

'No! What do you mean, remorse? There's no occasion for

remorse, when you haven't willed the sin. . . . You can't understand! Just as I shouldn't have been able to understand things if, in thinking about what's happened to your husband, I hadn't thought about my own! Yes, yes, I can now understand your husband's madness, because I think of my own husband, who'd go mad in the same way, if what happened to your husband with me ever happened to him! Without remorse! Without remorse! And precisely because it is without remorse . . . ! Do you realize? This is the horrible thing about it! Oh, I don't know how to make you understand! *I* understand it, I repeat, only if I think of my own husband and see myself, like this, without remorse for a sin I had no desire to commit. You see how I can talk to you about it, without blushing? Because I don't know, Bice, I really don't know anything about your husband—physically—just as he most certainly doesn't, *can't* know anything about me. It was like an abyss. Do you understand me? Like an abyss which suddenly opened up between us. There we were, all unsuspecting, and it seized hold of us and overthrew us in an instant. Then, just as suddenly, it closed again, leaving not the slightest trace behind it! Immediately afterwards the consciousness of each one of us was once again quite limpid and undisturbed. We didn't think any more about it, about what had happened between us. Not even for an instant. Our disturbance had been purely momentary. We left the room, he through one door, I through the other. But the moment we were alone—nothing. It was just as if nothing whatever had happened. Not only when we were with you—when you returned home shortly afterwards—but even when we two were alone together. We could look into one another's eyes and talk to one another, just as before, *exactly* as before, because no longer was there in us—I swear it!—the slightest vestige of what, for an instant, *had been*. Nothing. Nothing. Not even the shadow of a memory. Not even the shadow of desire. Nothing! Everything was over and done with. It had disappeared. The secret of an instant was buried for ever. Well, this is what's driven your husband mad—not the sin itself, which neither of us thought of committing! No, it's this: his being able to imagine what can happen—that an honest woman who's in love with her own husband can, in an instant, without wanting to, as a result of a sudden ambush of the senses, because of a mysterious conspiracy of time and place, fall into the arms of another man. And, a moment later, everything's over—for ever. The abyss has closed again. The secret's buried. There's no remorse. No turmoil. No effort's needed to lie in front of others. To one another. He waited a day, two days, three. . . . He didn't feel any further stirring there inside himself, either in your presence, or in mine. He could see that I'd gone back to being what I was before—just what I was before—both with you and with him. He saw, shortly afterwards—do you remember?—my husband arrive at the villa. He saw how I welcomed him—with what concern, with what love. And then the abyss, in which our secret was buried deep, for ever, without leaving the slightest trace, began gradually to exercise a fatal attraction for him. Till finally it overthrew his reason. He thought of you. He began to wonder whether perhaps you too . . . ?'

'Whether I too?'

'Oh, Bice, I'm sure it's never happened to you! I can quite well believe it! Yes, Bice, my dear! But I . . . He and I, we know from experience what can happen! And we know that, since it was possible in our case without our wanting it, it can quite well be possible for anyone at all! He'll probably have thought of how there've been times when, coming back home, he'll have found you alone in the drawing-room with a friend of his. And he'll have thought of how, in an instant, there could quite well have happened to you and to that friend of his, what happened to me and to him. In exactly the same way. He'll have thought of how you'd have been able to shut up inside yourself, without there being any trace of it, to hide without lying, the same secret that *I* shut up inside myself and hid from my husband without lying. And the moment this thought entered his mind a subtle, acute, burning sensation would begin to gnaw away at his brain, as he saw you, so detached, so happy, so loving, with him. Just as I was with my husband. With my husband whom I love, I swear, more than I love myself, more than I love anything in the world! He started thinking, "And yet, this woman, who's behaving like this towards her husband, was in my arms for a moment? So, perhaps, my wife too, in a moment. . . . Who knows? Who can *ever* know?" And he went out of his mind. Oh, hush, Bice! Hush! For pity's sake!'

Gabriella Vanzi got up. She was trembling and terribly pale.

She'd heard the front door open, out there in the little hall. Her husband was coming back in.

Donna Bicetta Daddi, seeing her friend suddenly transformed like this, suddenly in control of herself again—her face had become pink, her eyes were now limpid, and there was a smile on her lips, as she went to meet her husband—was left standing there, almost annihilated.

Nothing. Yes, it was quite true what Gabriella had said. . . . No more turmoil, no remorse, no trace of——

And Donna Bicetta understood perfectly why her husband, Romeo Daddi, had gone out of his mind.

## THE BLACK KID

*Il capretto nero* was first published in the *Corriere della sera* for 31 December 1913. It was gathered into the volume *Un cavallo nella luna,* put out by Treves of Milan in 1918, and in 1925 was one of the stories included in Vol. IX *(Donna Mimma)* of the Bemporad series of *Novelle per un anno.* After this Florentine presentation, the book was reprinted by Mondadori. It is now part of the Biblioteca Moderna Mondadori, while the definitive text of the story is to be found in Vol. II of the *Opere.* (*Novelle per un anno,* Vol. II, Milano-Verona, Mondadori, 1957.)

# THE BLACK KID

Mr. Charles Trockley's quite right, of course. Oh, indubitably. As a matter of fact, I'm even prepared to admit that Mr. Charles Trockley can never be wrong, because being in the right and being Mr. Charles Trockley are one and the same thing. Every movement Mr. Charles Trockley makes, every look, every gesture, is so precise and correct that you're all forced to recognize that, whatever the circumstances, whatever the question put forward for his consideration, whatever the incident that befalls him, it's quite impossible for Mr. Charles Trockley to be in the wrong.

Let me give you an example of what I mean. He and I were born in the same year, in the same month, and on almost the same day—he in England, and I in Sicily. Today, June the 15th, he completes his forty-eighth year. I shall be forty-eight on the 28th. All right! How old shall we be, he on the 15th and I on the 28th of June next year? There's no confusing Mr. Trockley. He doesn't hesitate for an instant. Firmly, positively, he maintains that, on the 15th and 28th of June next year, he and I shall be a year older—that's to say, we shall be forty-nine.

Can Mr. Trockley ever conceivably be wrong?

Time doesn't go by in the same way for everybody. I could quite well suffer in one single day, in one single hour, more damage than he'd have inflicted on him in *ten* years spent the way *he* spends his life, that life of rigorously disciplined well-being. As a consequence of the deplorable state of disorder reigning in my spirit, I might, during this coming year, live through more than a whole lifetime. My body, weaker and less well-cared-for than his, has already, as a result of these forty-eight years, suffered much more wear and tear than Mr. Trockley's will have done after *seventy*. And if you want proof of this, just look at him: though his hair's silvery white, there's not the slightest sign of a wrinkle on his boiled-lobster face, and he can still fence of a morning with an agility that's positively youthful.

Well, so what? As far as Mr. Charles Trockley's concerned, all these philosophical considerations, whether of fact or fantasy, are quite otiose and far removed from any notion of right or reason. His reason tells Mr. Charles Trockley that, when we've done all our arithmetic, he and I shall be a year older on the 15th and 28th of June next year—that's to say, we shall be forty-nine.

Now, having established all this, listen to what happened recently to Mr. Charles Trockley, and see if you can prove that he was in the wrong in acting as he did.

Last April, following the usual itinerary laid down by Baedeker for travellers in Italy, Miss Ethel Holloway, the very young and the very vivacious daughter of Sir W. H. Holloway, an extremely wealthy and highly influential English baronet, arrived at Girgenti in Sicily, intent on visiting the wonderful remains of that ancient Doric city. She was simply delighted with the enchanting countryside, for in that month the hillsides were a glorious mass of white almond blossom, and the warm breezes blew in over the sea from Africa. So she decided to spend a few days at the huge *Hôtel des Temples,* which is not in the steeply sloping and wretched little town of today, but out in the open country—in a very agreeable spot.

Mr. Charles Trockley has been British Vice-Consul at Girgenti for the past twenty-two years, and every day at sunset for the past twenty-two years he's taken a stroll—and how springy and measured his step is—from the city high up on the hill to the ruins of the Akragantine temples. Airy and majestic, they stand on a sheer-faced embankment which halts the downward slope of the nearby Akrea Hill, on which at one time there stood that ancient city, rich in marble statuary, which Pindar exalted as fairest among mortal cities.

Ancient writers tell us that the Akragantines used every day to eat as if they were doomed to die the following day, and to build their houses as if they were destined to live forever. They have very little to eat now, so great is the wretchedness of the town and of the surrounding countryside. What's more, after so many wars and after the town's having been set on fire seven times and sacked as often, there's no trace left of the houses belonging to the ancient city. In their place there stands a wood of almond trees and saracen olives, known as the Old Town Wood, on account of its site. And the hoary, ash-grey olive trees march on in their rows, right into the shadow of the columns of the majestic temples, and they look just like ambassadors suing for peace for those deserted hills. Under the brow of the embankment the River Akragas flows —when it *can* flow, that is—the river which Pindar glorified as 'rich in herds'. The occasional herd of goats still crosses through the stony bed of the river and climbs up the steep slope of the rocky cliff. Then they stretch themselves out and graze on the meagre pasturage to be found in the solemn shade of the ancient Temple of Harmony, which is still intact. The goatherd, as animal-like and somnolent as an Arab, copies their example and sprawls on the ruined steps of the forecourt; then he draws a few plaintive notes from his reed pipe.

Mr. Charles Trockley has always looked on this intrusion of the goats into the temple as a horrible profanation. Time and time again he's lodged a formal protest with the custodians of the ancient monuments, without getting any other answer than a philosophical and indulgent smile and a shrug of the shoulders. Occasionally I accompany him on his daily stroll, and Mr. Charles Trockley has been simply shuddering with indignation, as he's complained away to me about those smiles and those shrugs of the shoulder. It quite often happens that Mr. Trockley, either in the Temple of Harmony, or in the temple higher up, dedicated to Hera Lacinia, or in the other one, popularly known as the Temple of the Giants, bumps into parties of his compatriots who've come to visit the ruins. And he points out to them, with the same indignation, which neither time nor habit has mellowed or weakened, the profanation inflicted by those goats lying about all over the place and grazing in the shade of the columns. But, to tell you the honest truth, not all the English visitors share Mr. Trockley's indignation. For many of them, indeed, the fact that the goats are taking their ease in the temples, which have been left there like that, in their solitude, in the midst of all this vast expanse of deserted countryside, is not altogether without an element of poetry. More than one of them, in fact—to the utter dismay of the scandalized Mr. Trockley—even goes to far as to make it quite plain that *he* finds the sight highly admirable and a joy for ever.

The very young and extremely vivacious Miss Ethel Holloway surpassed them all in finding the sight she saw that April day highly admirable and a joy for ever. As a matter of fact, just as the indignant Vice-Consul was about to give her some incredibly valuable archaeological information, which neither Baedeker nor any other guide-book has yet stored up as treasure within its pages, Miss Ethel Holloway committed the social indiscretion of suddenly turning her back on him, in order to chase after a graceful black kid that had been born only a few days before. There he was, skipping about all over the place, in the midst of all those reclining goats, just as if in the air around him there were dancing myriads of rainbow-glinting midges. Then he'd suddenly stand perfectly still, and look for all the world as if he were startled by his own daring and gawky leaping about, because he was still at the stage where the slightest noise, the faintest breath of wind, or the tiniest patch of shadow, made him shudder and tremble all over with timidity, still so full of uncertainty for him was the spectacle of life.

I was with Mr. Trockley that day, and if I found myself deeply in sympathy with the joy that little Miss Holloway was feeling—for she'd fallen in love just like that with the black kid, and wanted to buy him, no matter what it cost—I was also extremely grieved because of the great deal of suffering being inflicted on poor Mr. Charles Trockley.

'You want to *buy* the kid?'

'Yes! Yes! I want to buy him! *Now!* Straightaway!'

And little Miss Holloway too was trembling all over, just like that dear little animal. I don't suppose she dreamt for one moment that she couldn't possibly have inflicted a graver insult on Mr. Trockley. How ferociously he hated those goats, and how long-standing his hate was!

In vain did Mr. Trockley try to dissuade her, try to get her to consider all the ghastly snags she'd encounter if she made such a purchase. He was forced to give way in the end, however, and out of respect for her father, to go over to the goatherd and enter into negotiations for the acquisition of the black kid.

Having handed over the money needed to complete the purchase, Miss Ethel Holloway told Mr. Trockley that she would be entrusting her kid to the manager at the *Hôtel des Temples,* and that, as soon as she got back to London, she would telegraph, and ask them to send her the darling creature with all possible speed. *She'd* meet all the expenses, of course. And she went back in her carriage to the hotel, with the kid bleating and squirming in her arms.

I watched her as she drove off, framed against the sun that was setting in the midst of a wonderful lacework of fantastic clouds. Drifting over the sea, that shone beneath them like a boundless mirror of burnished gold, they were alight with the sun's rays. I watched her drive away in her black carriage, that fair-haired young girl, so graceful, so fervently happy, bathed in a halo of refulgent light. It seemed just like a dream to me. Then I realized how things were: since she'd been able, so far from her native land, so far, too, from the accustomed sights and affection of her life, immediately to conceive so passionate a desire, so vital an affection for a little black kid, she couldn't possibly have even a crumb of that solid reason, which, with so much gravity, regulates the actions, the thoughts, the steps, and the words of Mr. Charles Trockley.

What, then, did little Miss Ethel Holloway have in the place of reason?

Nothing but stupidity, maintained Mr. Charles Trockley with scarcely restrained fury, almost doing himself an injury. . . . And he a man with everything always so thoroughly under control.

The reason for his fury lies in the events which followed on the purchase of that black kid.

Miss Ethel Holloway left Girgenti next day. From Sicily she was due to go on to Greece; from Greece to Egypt; from Egypt on to India.

It's an absolute miracle, of course, that having reached London safe and sound towards the end of November, after eight months abroad and after the many adventures which must inevitably have befallen her on so extended a trip, she should still have remembered the black kid she'd bought one far-off day amidst the ruins of the Akragantine temples of Sicily.

As soon as she reached home, she wrote to Mr. Charles Trockley, as agreed, and asked him to get them to send her the kid.

The *Hôtel des Temples* shuts every year in the middle of June and reopens at the beginning of November. When the manager of the hotel, to whom Miss Ethel Holloway had entrusted the kid, went off in the middle of June, he in his turn handed him into the safe-keeping of the hotel porter, without bothering to leave any very precise instructions. As a matter of fact, he'd made it perfectly obvious that he was more than a little fed up with all the trouble that little creature had caused him—and was *going on* causing him. Every day the porter was expecting Mr. Trockley, the Vice-Consul, to turn up—well, that's what the manager had led him to believe would happen—take over the kid, and dispatch it to England. Then, seeing that nobody did in fact turn up, he thought it would be a good idea to shed responsibility for the kid, by handing him over to the same goatherd who'd sold him in the first place to Miss Ethel Holloway, promising him the animal as a gift if, as seemed only too likely, she didn't really care to have him back, or —should the Vice-Consul finally come and ask for the beast—some sort of recompense for looking after him and feeding him.

When, after almost eight months, Miss Ethel Holloway's letter arrived from London, the manager of the *Hôtel des Temples* (to say nothing of the porter and the goatherd) found himself overwhelmed with confusion. The manager was all of a dither because he'd entrusted the kid to the porter; the porter, because *he'd* entrusted him to the goatherd; and the latter, because he in his turn had given him into the safe-keeping of another goatherd, with the same promises that had been made to him by the porter. The trouble was, nobody had the faintest idea where this second goatherd was to be found. The search for him lasted over a month. At last, one fine day, Mr. Charles Trockley was suddenly confronted in his Vice Consulate in Girgenti by a horrible, huge, horned and fetid beast, with a coat of faded red hair, from which lumps had been torn away, and which was encrusted with mud and dung. From his throat there issued raucous, deep, tremulous bleating noises. With his head lowered menacingly, he seemed to be demanding what it was they wanted with him. They'd dragged him along to this place, which was so remote from his customary haunts! And just look at him! Look at the state life had reduced him to!

Well, as usual, Mr. Charles Trockley wasn't for one moment thrown off balance by such an apparition. He didn't hesitate for an instant. He totted up the time that had gone by, from the 1st of April to the end of December, and concluded, quite reasonably, that the graceful black kid of the earlier date could quite well be this huge unclean beast of today. And without the faintest hesitation he replied to Miss Holloway's letter, saying that he was sending him from Porto Empedocle by the first merchant vessel homeward bound for England. He attached a card with Miss Ethel Holloway's address to the neck of that horrible animal, and gave orders for him to be taken down to the docks. Here, at grave risk to his own dignity, he himself dragged the restive beast behind him at the end of a rope along the quay, followed by a mob of urchins. He put him on board the steamer, that was due to depart very shortly, and returned to Girgenti, quite sure in his own mind that he'd scrupulously fulfilled the duty he'd undertaken, not so much out of consideration for the deplorable frivolity of Miss Ethel Holloway, as out of a proper respect for her father.

Yesterday Mr. Charles Trockley came to seek me out at home, in such a state of mind and body that I immediately and in utter consternation, rushed forward to support him. I got him to sit down and asked them to bring him a glass of water.

'Good Heavens, Mr. Trockley, what's happened to you?'

Still quite speechless, Mr. Trockley took a letter from his pocket and handed it to me.

It was from Sir W. H. Holloway, Baronet of the United Kingdom, and it contained a lively flow of invective of the most insolent kind, directed at Mr. Trockley, for having dared to insult his daughter, Miss Ethel Holloway, by sending her that foul and frightful beast.

This, *this* was poor Mr. Trockley's reward for all the trouble he'd taken.

But what had that more than ordinarily stupid girl, Miss Ethel Holloway, been expecting? Did she really expect that, almost eleven months after she'd bought it, there'd arrive at her house in London that same black kid which had been bounding about among the columns of the ancient Greek temple in Sicily? That tiny creature, glistening in the sunshine and trembling with timidity? *Really*—could anyone be *so* stupid? Mr. Charles Trockley was nearly driving himself mad trying to fathom it out.

Seeing him sitting there before me in that state, I comforted him as best I could. I agreed with him that Miss Ethel Holloway was—oh, she really *was*!—not only capricious in the extreme, but unreasonable beyond expression.

'Stupid, stupid, *stupid* girl!'

'No, let's say, rather, that she's *unreasonable,* my dear Mr. Trockley, my dear friend. But—— Well, look.' I permitted myself the liberty of adding, timidly, 'When she left here last April, she carried away in her mind's eye—and deep within her heart—the delightful picture of that black kid. Now, let's be fair to her: she couldn't possibly be expected to welcome with open arms—— Yes, I know! It's completely unreasonable of her! That's obvious!—the "rightness"—the "reasonableness"—with which you suddenly confronted her, Mr. Trockley, the "rightness" and the "reasonableness" summed up in that monstrous huge goat you sent her.'

'Well, so what?' asked Mr. Trockley, rising and fixing me with a hostile stare. 'What ought I to have done—*according to you*?'

'I shouldn't like you to think, my dear Mr. Trockley,' I hastened in my embarrassment to reply, 'I shouldn't like you to think that I was as unreasonable as that dear young lady from your far-away native land. If *I'd* been in your place, however, Mr. Trockley, do you know what *I'd* have done? I'd either have replied to Miss Ethel Holloway that her delightful black kid had pined away and died because he was missing her kisses and caresses, or else I'd have bought another black kid, ever so tiny, and with a lovely shiny coat—similar in every respect to the one she bought last April—and I'd have sent him to her, for I'd have been quite, quite sure in my own mind that Miss Ethel Holloway would never for one moment have dreamt that her kid couldn't possibly have remained just like that. As you'll readily appreciate, by putting forward such a suggestion, I in no way modify what I said earlier. I still agree with you that Miss Ethel Holloway is the most unreasonable creature in the world, and that you, my dear friend, have, as always, behaved perfectly reasonably. My dear Mr. Trockley, you are, as ever, completely in the right.'

# SIGNORA FROLA AND HER SON-IN-LAW, SIGNOR PONZA

*La signora Frola e il signor Ponza, suo genero* has been provisionally dated 1915 by Manlio Lo Vecchio-Musti. It was first published in the collection of stories, *E domani, lunedì . . .*, Milano, Treves, 1917. Subsequently it was included in the final (and posthumous) volume of the *Novelle per un anno*—Vol. XV, *Una giornata,* Milano-Verona, Mondadori, 1937. The volume now forms part of the Biblioteca Moderna Mondadori, while the definitive text of the story is to be found in Vol. II of the *Opere*. (*Novelle per un anno,* Vol. II, Milano-Verona, Mondadori, 1957.)

# SIGNORA FROLA AND HER SON-IN-LAW, SIGNOR PONZA

WELL, I ask you! Just imagine what it's like! It really *is* enough to drive you out of your mind. I mean, to be completely unable to find out which of these two people is mad—this Signora Frola we're talking about, or Signor Ponza, her son-in-law. It's the sort of thing that could only happen in a place like Valdana. Valdana's an unlucky town, with a fatal attraction for all sorts of queer folk who come rushing in from all over the country.

Either she's mad or he's mad. There's no room for compromise in matters of this sort. Of sheer necessity, one of them must be mad. Because—well, it's a matter of nothing more or less than . . . No! It'll be much better if I do things properly and begin at the beginning.

I give you my solemn oath, I'm seriously disturbed about the sheer mental anguish that's been afflicting the inhabitants of Valdana during these last three months. What's more, let me tell you, I'm not over-concerned about Signora Frola and her son-in-law, Signor Ponza. Because even if it's true that they've been the victims of a terrible disaster, it's nonetheless also true that at least one of the precious pair has had the good luck to go mad, and that the other one's helped him (or her) live out that madness—and, moreover, has gone on helping him (or her) to do so—and to such good effect, in point of fact, that, I repeat, nobody's able to find out which of them is really the mad one. They certainly couldn't wish for finer consolation that that! But, I ask you—to keep a whole town on tenterhooks like this! It's a living nightmare. Well, it's no joke; now, is it? To deprive people of all foundation for any kind of judgement, so that they can no longer distinguish between fantasy and reality. It's sheer agony. You live in a state of perpetual bewilderment. Everyone sees those two people before them, day in, day out. They look them in the face. They know that one of them's mad. They study them. They eye them up and down. They watch them very carefully. And they're not a jot the wiser. I mean, to be completely unable to discover which of them it is. In which of them is sanity a reality? In which of them is it merely fantasy? Naturally, the pernicious suspicion springs up in everyone's mind that the reality's just as bad as the fantasy, and that every reality can quite well be fantasy and vice versa. It's no joke, now, is it? If I were in the Prefect's shoes, I'd tell Signora Frola to leave Valdana and take her son-in-law, Signor Ponza, with her—if only to save the rest of the inhabitants from damning their souls eternally.

Still, let's do things properly and begin at the beginning. This Signor Ponza arrived in Valdana three months ago, as Secretary at the Prefecture. He took a flat in that big new building at the far end of the town, the place they call 'The Beehive'. Yes, there! On the top floor, a little flat.

It's got three windows looking out over the countryside—gloomy windows, they are, set high-up. That side of the building, which faces north and looks out over all those dismal orchards, has for some unfathomable reason, although the building's a new one, come to look terribly gloomy. Then there are three windows on the inside, looking on to the courtyard, round which there runs a gallery, with an iron balustrade, divided off into sections by railings. Right up at the top, hanging from the balustrade, there are masses of little baskets, all ready to be let down on a rope when the need arises.

At the same time, however, and to everyone's amazement, Signor Ponza took another flat in the centre of the town. (To give you the precise details, at 15 Via dei Santi.) A small, furnished flat: three rooms and a kitchen. He said he wanted it for his mother-in-law, Signora Frola. The good lady did in fact arrive some five or six days later, and Signor Ponza went—all by himself—to meet her at the station, took her along to the flat and left her there—all by herself.

Now. . . . Well, bless my soul! It's perfectly understandable for a young woman, when she marries, to leave her mother's home and go off and live with her husband and even, perhaps, to go off and live in some other town. But when a poor mother, unable any longer to stand having to live so far away from her daughter, leaves the town where she's living, leaves her own house and follows her and then, although both she and her daughter are strangers here, goes and lives in another part of the town. Well, I ask you. That's *not* so understandable, now *is* it? Unless, of course, you're prepared to admit that the incompatibility between mother-in-law and son-in-law is so strong in their case, that living together is rendered quite impossible, even in these circumstances.

Quite naturally, this was what they all thought in Valdana at first. And, no doubt about it, the one who suffered in everybody's opinion as a result was Signor Ponza. As far as Signora Frola was concerned, even some people were willing to go so far as to concede that—well, perhaps she was a little to blame, too, either because she'd been a trifle lacking in forbearance, or proved somehow obstinate or intolerant—they all took into consideration the mother love which drew her to where her daughter was, even though she was condemned to live apart from her.

It must be admitted that the personal appearances of the pair of them played an important part in determining the attitude of people towards them: their consideration for Signora Frola, and the concept of Signor Ponza that they'd all formed—that had immediately been imprinted on their minds—that he was *hard,* downright cruel, even. Squat, with no neck worth talking about, as swarthy as a negro, with thick bristly hair growing well down over a very narrow forehead, with bushy, aggressive eyebrows that joined in the middle, heavy, glistening moustache like a police superintendent and in his sombre, staring eyes, which had scarcely any white, a violent, exasperated intensity, hardly kept under control (and it was difficult to tell whether it arose from black misery or from contempt aroused in him by the sight of other people)—Signor Ponza was certainly not designed by nature to win people's affection or confidence. Signora Frola, on the other hand, was a charming little old lady; frail, pale, with distinguished features and an air of melancholy, but it was a vague, gentle melancholy that didn't weigh her spirits down and didn't prevent her from being affable with everybody.

Now, Signora Frola gave immediate proof to the townsfolk of this affability of hers—it came so very naturally to her—and immediately (as a result) their aversion for Signor Ponza grew stronger within people's hearts. For her disposition appeared clear to everyone: mild, submissive, tolerant, but also full of indulgent compassion for the wrong her son-in-law was doing her. It's grown stronger, too, because people have found out that Signor Ponza's not satisfied with relegating that poor mother to another house, but pushes cruelty so far as to forbid her even to see her daughter.

But, you know, it's not cruelty, it's not cruelty, Signora Frola instantly protests when she calls on the ladies of Valdana, clasping her tiny little hands in front of her, deeply afflicted that they can think such a thing of her son-in-law. And she hastens to sing his praises, and to say all the good that's possible and imaginable about him. How loving he is, how very attentive, not only towards her daughter, but towards her as well. . . . Yes! Yes! Towards *her* as well! Solicitous and disinterested. Oh, no, for pity's sake! He's not cruel! There's just this: he wants her all for himself, does Signor Ponza, that darling little wife of his, even to such an extent that her love for her mother (which she must have, and he concedes this—how could he do otherwise?), well, he wants it to reach her, not directly, but through him, by way of him. There, that's how things are! Yes, it can look like cruelty, but it *isn't*. It's something different, something quite, quite different that she (Signora Frola, that is) understands very well, and she's terribly sorry she can't explain it to them. It's his *nature*. Yes, that's it! But—no! Oh, dear! It's a kind of disease, maybe. Yes, let's call it that, if you like! My goodness, you've only got to look into his eyes! Perhaps they make a bad impression at first, those eyes of his, but they reveal everything to anyone who, like her, knows how to read what they've got to say. It's as if they spoke of a fullness of love, all locked up. Yes. So as to keep out everybody and everything. In that fullness of love his wife must live without ever coming out. And no one else must ever be allowed to enter into it, not even her mother. Jealousy? Yes, perhaps. But that would be a very crude way of defining this total exclusiveness of love. Selfishness? But a selfishness which gives itself utterly and completely, like a whole world of tenderness and devotion, to a woman he loves. After all, it would be she who would be selfish if she tried to force her way into this closed world of love, when she knows that her daughter lives happily in it, and that he adores her so. That ought to be enough for a mother, oughtn't it? Besides, it's not in the least true that she doesn't see her daughter. She sees her two or three times a day. She goes into the courtyard of that house, she rings the bell, and her daughter immediately comes out on to the balcony up there.

'How are you, Tildina?'

'Very well indeed, Mamma. What about you?'

'I mustn't grumble, my dear. Let down the basket—quickly!'

Then into the basket goes a little note—just a few words—with news of the day's doings. There, that's quite enough for her. This sort of life's been going on for the past four years now, and Signora Frola's got used to it. Yes, she's resigned to it. It hardly hurts at all now.

It's easy to understand how this resignation on Signora Frola's part, and the way she's turned her martyrdom into a habit, as she put it, redound to the discredit of Signor Ponza, her son-in-law, the more so because she makes every effort, goes off into a long rigmarole, in an attempt to excuse his conduct.

It was with very real indignation, therefore—and, I'll go so far as to say, with very real *fear*—that the ladies of Valdana, who had had the pleasure of Signora Frola's first visit, received the announcement the following day of another unexpected caller—Signor Ponza, this time. He begged them to grant him just two minutes of their time, to hear a 'statement he felt it his duty to make', if it wouldn't be disturbing them.

Signor Ponza appears, red in the face and almost apoplectic-looking, his eyes harder and more gloomy than ever, handkerchief in hand—that handkerchief almost shouting aloud its whiteness, just like his cuffs and his white shirt set, as they are, against his swarthy complexion and his dark hair and clothes. He's continually wiping away the sweat that dribbles down in drops from his low forehead and from his prickly purple cheeks, not so much because of the heat but because of the extreme and obvious violence of the effort that he's making to control himself, and with which even his huge hands, with their long fingernails, are trembling. In this drawing-room and in that, then, he appears before those ladies, who gaze at him almost in terror. First of all he asks whether Signora Frola, his mother-in-law, came and called on them the day before. Then, with a great effort, his distress and agitation growing more and more pronounced as he goes on, he asks if she's talked to them about her daughter, and if she's said that he absolutely forbids her to see her daughter and to go up and visit her in her flat.

Seeing him so worked up, the ladies, as you'll readily imagine, hasten to reply to that, Yes, it's true that Signora Frola has told them about his forbidding her to see her daughter, but she's also said all the good that's possible and imaginable about him, even to the extent of excusing his conduct, *and*, what's more, of denying that even the slightest hint of blame for that prohibition is attaching to him.

The trouble is that, instead of being quietened down, Signor Ponza get more worked up than ever at this reply from the ladies. His eyes become harder, more staring, more sombre. The huge drops of sweat become more frequent, and, finally, making an even more violent effort to control himself, he actually starts on the 'statement he feels it his duty to make'.

Quite simply, it's this. Signora Frola, poor dear, although it doesn't show in the slightest, is mad.

Yes, she's been mad for the past four years. And her madness, in fact, takes the form of her believing that he refuses to let her see her daughter. Which daughter? She's dead—her daughter's been dead for the past four years. And it was precisely as a result of her grief over her daughter's death that Signora Frola went out of her mind. Yes, she had the good luck to go mad. I say good luck, because madness has been a way of escape for her from her desperate grief. Naturally, she could only escape from it in this way; that is, by believing that it isn't true that her daughter's dead, and that instead it's her son-in-law who's refusing to let her see her any more.

Out of sheer charity towards an unhappy woman, Signor Ponza has been humouring her for the past four years in this piteous folly of hers, at the price of great and heavy sacrifices. He has kept two homes, at a cost in excess of his resources, one for himself and one for her. And he obliges his second wife, who—fortunately—most charitably agrees to do so, to humour her in this folly too. But charity, duty . . . Well, you know, there are limits. There's his position as a public servant to be considered, too. Because of that, Signor Ponza can't allow people here in the town to believe of him that he'd be guilty of this cruel and outlandish thing—either from jealousy or from some other cause—of forbidding a mother to see her own daughter.

Having made this statement, Signor Ponza bows to the utterly bewildered ladies and off he goes. But this bewilderment on the part of the ladies hasn't even time to wear off a little before, lo and behold! Here's Signora Frola back again, with her vague air of melancholy, begging them to forgive her if, on her account, those good ladies have been given an awful fright by the visit of Signor Ponza, her son-in-law.

And Signora Frola, with the utmost simplicity and all the naturalness in the world, declares in her turn—but, for pity's sake, please treat this as highly confidential, because Signor Ponza is a public servant, and it was precisely because of that that she abstained the first time from saying anything, because—— Oh, yes! It might seriously damage his career. Signor Ponza, poor dear—— Oh, he's an excellent, a really excellent, secretary at the Prefecture. Faultless. So well-bred, so scrupulous in everything he does. In all his thoughts. Full to overflowing with good qualities. Signor Ponza, poor dear—in this one respect only, isn't—— Well, *yes*! Well, he's no longer in control of his reason. He's the one that's mad, poor dear boy, and his madness consists entirely in this one thing, in his believing that his wife's been dead for the past four years, and in his going about saying that she's the one that's mad—Signora Frola, that is—because she believes that her daughter's still alive. No, he certainly doesn't do it to justify somehow in everybody's eyes that almost maniacal jealousy of his and the cruel way he refuses to let her see her daughter. No, he believes—he really seriously believes—poor dear boy, that his wife's dead and that the woman he has living with him now is his second wife. It's a most pathetic case. Because, really, with the excessive passion of his love, he did at first come very near destroying, very near *killing* his delicate young wife with the violence of his passion. So they had to take her away in secret, and shut her up, all unknown to him, in a nursing home. Well, quite naturally, his mind was already seriously unbalanced as a consequence—his love had become a frenzy—and the poor man went mad. He really believed that his wife was dead. He got the idea so firmly fixed in his mind that nothing could drive it out. They couldn't even get him to cast it off when, just about a year later, his young wife, now completely well and blooming again, was brought back to him. He thought she was some other woman. And so convinced of this was he, that we had to have a make-believe second wedding with the connivance of everybody—friends and relatives. That fully restored his mental balance.

Now Signora Frola thinks she has good reason to suspect that her son-in-law recovered his wits quite a long while ago, and that he's pretending now, only pretending to believe that his present wife's his second wife, so as to keep her all to himself, without her coming into contact with outside people, because perhaps, from time to time, there still flashes into his mind the fear that she may again be secretly taken away from him. Oh yes, indeed! If this weren't the case, how could you possibly explain all the consideration he shows her, all the solicitude he lavishes upon her—his mother-in-law, that is—if he really believes that it's his *second* wife he's got living with him? He wouldn't feel any obligation to show so much consideration for a woman who, in point of fact, would no longer actually be his mother-in-law, would he? This, mind you, is what Signora Frola says, not so much to reinforce her demonstration of the fact that he's the one that's mad . . . No, it's more to prove to herself that her suspicions are well-founded.

'And meanwhile,' she says, with a sigh that, on her lips, turns into a sweet and extremely sad smile, 'meanwhile my poor daughter has to pretend to be some other woman, and not herself. And I'm forced to pretend to be mad too, because I believe that my daughter's still alive. It doesn't cost me a great deal, thanks be to God, because my daughter's up there in her flat, healthy and full of life. I can see her, I can talk to her. But I'm condemned to live away from her, and even to see her and talk to her only from a distance, in order that he may believe—or pretend to believe—that my daughter's . . . Oh, God forbid! . . . That my daughter's dead, and that this woman who's living with him is his second wife. But I repeat, what does it matter if, by doing all this, we're able to give them both back their peace of mind? I know that my daughter's happy, and that he adores her. I can see her. I can talk to her. And I resign myself, out of my love for her and for him, to living like this, and even to allowing myself to be considered a madwoman. Well, dear Signora—— Never mind. . . .'

I ask you! Don't you think that those of us who live in Valdana have got good reason to stand about gaping at one another open-mouthed; staring into one another's eyes like a lot of half-wits? Which of the pair shall we believe? Which is mad? In which one of them is sanity merely a fantasy?

Signor Ponza's wife could tell us. But you won't be able to rely on what she says if, when she's in his presence she says she's his second wife, any more than you'll be able to rely on what she says if, in the presence of Signora Frola, she confirms that she's her daughter. You'd have to take her on one side and make her tell you, and you alone, the truth. You can't do it. Signor Ponza, whether or not he's the one that's mad, is certainly extremely jealous, and doesn't let anyone see his wife. He keeps her up there, under lock and key—it's just like a prison. And this fact undoubtedly tells in favour of Signora Frola. But Signor Ponza says he's forced to do it, and that his wife herself in point of fact insists on his doing it, out of fear that Signora Frola might unexpectedly walk in on her. It may all be an excuse, of course. It's also a fact that Signor Ponza doesn't keep one single servant in the house. He says he does it in order to save money, seeing that he's obliged to pay rent for two flats. And he even puts up with the nuisance of doing the day-to-day shopping himself. And his wife, who according to him is not Signora Frola's daughter, puts up with the annoyance of doing all her own housework, even the roughest part of it, depriving herself of the help of a servant, out of sheer compassion for a poor old woman who was her husband's mother-in-law.

Everyone thinks it's a bit thick; but it's also true that this state of affairs, even if it can't be explained in terms of compassion, can be put down to his jealousy.

Meanwhile, the Prefect of Valdana has expressed himself as quite satisfied with Signor Ponza's statement. But it's quite certain that Signor Ponza's appearance, and to a great extent his conduct, don't dispose you in his favour—at least, as far as the ladies of Valdana are concerned. To a woman, they're much more inclined to believe Signora Frola.

She, in fact, comes along with great eagerness to show them the affectionate little notes that her daughter lets down to her in the little basket and, over and above these, lots and lots of other private documents. Signor Ponza, however, destroys their value as evidence by saying that they've been issued to her to lend colour to the pitiful deception.

One thing's certain, anyway—that they both show for one another a wonderful spirit of self-sacrifice—it's most touching. And each has for the presumed madness of the other the most exquisitely compassionate consideration. They both of them argue their case with the most wonderful clarity and logic. So much so, that it would never have entered anybody's head in Valdana to say that either of them was mad, if they hadn't said so themselves, Signor Ponza about Signora Frola, and Signora Frola about Signor Ponza.

Signora Frola often goes and sees her son-in-law at the Prefecture, to ask his advice about something or other, or else she waits for him at the porter's lodge, so that she can get him to accompany her on a shopping expedition. He, for his part, goes every evening (and very frequently in his spare time, too) to call on Signora Frola in her little furnished flat. Then, every so often, they bump into one another quite by chance in the street, and immediately, with the utmost cordiality, they walk along together. He steps politely to the outside and, if she's tired, offers her his arm, and so they go on their way together, amidst the angry frowns, the utter astonishment, and the total consternation of the people who study them, stare at them, watch their every movement—without being a scrap the wiser. They still can't—it doesn't matter how hard they try—they still can't fathom which of the two is the mad one: in which of them sanity is a reality, in which of them it is merely fantasy.

# THE MAN WITH THE FLOWER IN HIS MOUTH

*La morte addosso* was first published, as *Caffè notturno,*[1] in the *Rassegna italiana* for 15 August 1918. It became *La morte addosso*[2] when collected into Vol. VI *(In silenzio)* of the Bemporad *Novelle per un anno,* Firenze, 1923. It has remained in this volume through subsequent Mondadori reprints, and is currently available in the Biblioteca Moderna Mondadori and in Vol. I of the *Opere.* (*Novelle per un anno,* Vol. I, *con una prefazione di Corrado Alvaro,* Milano-Verona, Mondadori, 1956.) Pirandello dramatized the play under the title *L'uomo dal fiore in bocca.*[3] It was staged first on 21 February 1923, and published in Vol. XX of the Bemporad edition of the *Maschere nude,* Firenze, 1926. I find this last title so perfectly apt, that I have decided to use it for the present translation.



[1] *All-Night Café.*

[2] Possibly best rendered as: *'Perhaps they too have death upon them. . . .'*

[3] Vol. IV of the *Opere.* (*Maschere nude,* Vol. I, *prefazione di Silvio D'Amico; cronologia della vita e delle opere di Manlio Lo Vecchio-Musti,* Milano-Verona, Mondadori, 1958.) Available English translations are: (*a*) by Eric Bentley in *One Act,* ed. Samuel Moon, New York, Grove Press, 1961; (*b*) by Frederick May—as a pamphlet, Leeds, Pirandello Society, 1959.

# THE MAN WITH THE FLOWER IN HIS MOUTH

'AH! Well, I mean—— That is—you seem a good-natured sort of man. Have you missed your train?'

'By a minute! I get to the station. And there it is, going out before my very eyes!'

'You might have run after it!'

'True enough. It's ridiculous, I know. Good Heavens, I'd have managed it all right, if I hadn't been cluttered up with all those parcels. Parcels and packets of all sorts and sizes! I was loaded worse than a packhorse! Oh, these women! Nothing but errands, errands! They're never-ending! Do you know, it took me fully three minutes after I got out of the taxi, to loop all those parcels on to my fingers! Two parcels to every finger!'

'You must have looked a fine sight! Do you know what I'd have done? I'd have left them all in the taxi!'

'And what about my wife? Oh, yes! And what about my daughters? And all their bosom friends!'

'Weeping and wailing and gnashing of teeth, eh? I'd have enjoyed myself no end!'

'That's because you—well, I suppose it's because you don't know what women get like when they're on holiday in the country!'

'Oh yes, I do know. I said that just now, precisely because I do know. They all say they won't need a thing.'

'Is that all they say? They're quite capable of maintaining even that they go into the country in order to save money! Then, no sooner have they got to some place at the back of beyond—— The uglier the place is, the more wretched and filthy it is, the more frenziedly they insist on livening it up by decking themselves out in all their frills and fal-lals! Oh, women, my dear fellow! But, when all's said and done, that's the way God made them! "My dear, if you *should* be running into town, I really need such-and-such a thing—and some of that other stuff too. . . . Oh, yes! You might also—if it's not too much trouble. . . ." Charming, isn't it, the way they say, "If it's not too much trouble"? "And then, since you're there anyway, on your way back . . ." "But, my dear, how do you expect me to get through all that business for you in three hours?" "What was that you said? Why, by taking a taxi!" The awful thing is that, only intending to spend three hours in town, I came away without the keys to my house here.'

'Oh, wonderful! So . . . ?'

'So I left that small mountain of parcels and packets in the cloak-room at the station. Then I went along to a restaurant and had some dinner. Finally, so as to give my temper a chance to cool down a little, I went to a theatre. The heat was killing! When I came out, I said to myself, "Well, what shall I do now? It's twelve o'clock already. I can get the first train back at four. Barely three hours left for sleep. It's not worth the expense." So I came here. This café doesn't shut, does it?'

'No, it doesn't shut. So you've left all those parcels in the cloak-room at the station?'

'Why do you ask me that? Don't you think they're safe there? They were all well tied up.'

'No, that wasn't what I meant. H'm! Well tied up. Yes, I can imagine. Tied up with that special art which shop assistants put into the wrapping up of purchases. What wonderful hands they have! They pick up a fine large sheet of double-thickness paper, all pink and shiny. It's a joy to behold in itself! It's so smooth that you almost feel that you'd like to put it up to your face. Just to feel its cool caressing touch. Well, they spread it out on the counter—and then, in the most self-possessed manner in the world, they put your piece of cloth, all neatly folded, exactly in the middle of it. First of all, with the back of their hand, they bring up one edge of the paper from underneath. Then they bring the other down from on top to meet the first, and so deftly, so gracefully, make the narrowest of folds—one they don't really need—put in, as it were, for sheer love of the art. Then, first at one end, then at the other, they fold the corners in to make two triangles. The points are turned under. They reach out a hand for the string. Pull out just the length they'll need. And tie up your parcel so quickly, that you haven't even time to admire their dexterity, before they're presenting you with it. With a little loop all ready for you to put your finger through.'

'H'm! H'm! It's easy to see that you've paid a great deal of attention to shop assistants.'

'I? My dear fellow, I spend whole days at a time watching them. I am capable of standing quite still for a whole hour, looking into a shop through the window. By so doing I am able to forget myself. To myself I seem to be—I should really very much like to be—that silk material over there; that strip of braid; the red or blue ribbon that the girls in the haberdashery department—— After they've measured it out on the yard-stick, have you noticed what they do? They twist it in a figure-eight round the thumb and little finger of their left hand before they wrap it up. I watch the customers, men and women alike, as they come out from the shop with their parcels dangling from their fingers, or in their hands, or under their arms. I follow them with my eyes. Until I lose sight of them, imagining—— Oh, how many things I imagine! You can have no conception! But it helps me. Doing that helps me.'

'*Helps* you? Forgive my asking. But *what* helps you?'

'Attaching myself like that. With my imagination, I mean, to life. Like a creeper to the bars of an iron railing. Ah, never letting my imagination rest for a single moment. Holding on—holding on with it to the lives of others. But not to the lives of people I know! No! No! I couldn't do that! If I do try, a feeling of utter weariness comes over me. Oh, if only you knew! A feeling of absolute nausea! I hold on to the lives of strangers, upon whom my imagination can work freely but not capriciously. On the contrary, it takes into account even the slightest characteristic, the slightest appearance of reality to be observed in this person or in that. And if you only knew how my imagination works; how hard it works! If you could only realize just how far I succeed in putting myself inside these people! I see the house of such-and-such a person, or such-and-such another. I live in it. I feel myself completely at home in it. I even get to the point of noticing—do you know that faint smell which lurks in a house? Every single house has its own particular smell. It's there in your house; in mine. But in our own house, of course, we're no longer aware of it, because it is the breath of our very life itself. Do I make myself clear? Ah, yes. I see you agree with me.'

'Yes, I agree, because, I mean, you must experience a great deal of pleasure, imagining all these things.'

'Pleasure? I?'

'Yes. I imagine . . .'

'Tell me something. Have you ever been to see a good doctor?'

'Who, me? No! Why do you ask? There's nothing the matter with me!'

'Oh, don't start getting agitated! I only ask because I want to know whether you've ever seen the rooms in those good doctors' houses where the patients sit and wait for their turn to go in.'

'Oh, yes. As a matter of fact, it did so happen once that I had to go with one of my daughters. She was having a bit of trouble with her nerves.'

'Good. Please don't think I'm trying to be inquisitive. What I mean is, those rooms—— Have you ever looked at them really attentively? A black, old-fashioned, horsehair sofa. Those stuffed chairs, which all too often don't match one another. Those little armchairs; second-hand stuff, picked up quite at random, just put in there for the patients. It doesn't really belong to the house at all! The doctor has quite another sort of room for himself and for his wife's friends. A fine, handsome, sumptuously furnished drawing-room. Can't you just imagine how it would shriek to high heaven if you were to bring one of the chairs—stuffed or otherwise—out of that drawing-room, and set it down in the patients' waiting-room? This sort of furniture is good enough for in here. It's not showy but it's honest-to-goodness, solid, hard-wearing stuff. What I should like to know is whether you looked attentively at the chair or armchair in which you sat, waiting. That time you went with your daughter.'

'Did I . . . ? Well, to tell you the truth, no!'

'Of course not. Because you weren't ill. But quite often not even the sick notice, all wrapped up as they are in the illness from which they're suffering. Yet, how often do some of them sit there intently watching their fingers tracing meaningless patterns on the polished

you kick them, the closer they stick to your heels. Obstinate creatures! You can't possibly imagine what that woman is suffering on my account. She doesn't eat, she doesn't sleep any longer. Night and day she follows me around, like this, at a distance. And she might at least brush her clothes every now and again! And that old shoe of a hat she wears! She no longer looks like a woman. She looks more like a rag-doll! And her hair—well, the white dust has settled there at her temples. *For ever.* And she's only just thirty-four. She makes me so terribly angry! Oh, you'd never believe how angry! There come times when I round on her. Hurl myself at her. And shout in her face, "Idiot!" shaking her furiously. She just takes it all. She stands there, looking at me with such an expression in her eyes . . . such an expression in her eyes, that I feel a savage desire to choke the life out of her coming into my fingers. And from her, not a flicker! She just waits for me to get a little way off, and then she starts following me again at a distance. There! Look! She's stuck her head round the corner again!'

'Poor woman!'

'What do you mean, "poor woman"? Do you realize what she'd like me to do? She'd like me to stay at home. Quietly and peacefully. She'd like to coddle me with all her most loving and heartfelt care. She'd like me to enjoy the perfect order of all the rooms, the polish on all the furniture, that mirror-like silence that there was at first in my house. Measured out by the tick-tock of the grandfather clock in the dining-room. That's what she'd like! Now, I ask you—in order to make you understand the absurdity—— No, why do I say absurdity? The macabre ferocity of what she wants! I ask you! Do you think it at all possible that the houses of Avezzano, the houses of Messina, knowing about the earthquake that was, in a short time from then, to send them crashing down in ruins, would have found it possible to stay where they were? So peacefully there in the light of the moon, ordered in their nice straight lines along the roads, flanking the squares, obedient to the master-plan of the Municipal Housing Committee. My God, houses though they were, for all their bricks and mortar, they'd have found some way of escaping! Just imagine the people of

Avezzano, the people of Messina, undressing themselves quite unconcernedly to go to bed. Neatly folding their clothes, putting their shoes outside the door, and burying themselves under the bed-clothes. Enjoying the cool freshness of their clean sheets. And all this in the knowledge that within a few hours they'd be dead. Does it seem possible to you?'

'But perhaps your wife——'

'Please. Do let me say what——! If death, my dear fellow, were like one of those strange, loathsome insects that somebody—all unexpectedly—finds walking up his sleeve. You're going along the street, another passer-by suddenly stops you, and cautiously, with his thumb and forefinger outstretched, says to you, "Excuse me, but may I . . . ? You, my dear sir, have death upon you." And with his outstretched thumb and forefinger he picks it off you, and throws it away. Oh, that would be magnificent! But death is not like one of those strange, loathsome insects. So many people who pass by, coolly, unconcernedly—quite unpreoccupied with one another—perhaps they too have death upon them. . . . No one sees it. . . . And they go on thinking calmly and peacefully about what they will do tomorrow. Or the day after. Now I . . . Look here. . . . Come over here! Over here; under this light. Come on! I want to show you something. Look, *here*. Under my moustache. Here. Can you see a purplish spot? Do you know what its name is? Ah, it's one of the prettiest names—prettier than a picture! *Epithelioma,* they call it. . . . You say it! Then you'll hear how lovely it sounds! *Epithelioma*. . . . Death, do you understand? It has passed this way. It has planted this flower in my mouth, saying "Keep it, my friend! I shall come this way again in nine or ten months' time." Now tell me whether—with this flower in my mouth—I can stay at home peacefully and quietly. As that unfortunate woman would like me to. I scream at her, "Oh yes, I see! You'd like me to kiss you?" "Yes, kiss me!" But do you know what she did the other week? She took a pin and made a scratch. Here, on her lip. Then she took my head in her hands, and wanted to kiss me—to kiss me on the mouth. Because, so she says, she wants to die with me! She's mad. I can't stay at home. I need to stand in front of the shop windows, gazing in, admiring the dexterity of the shop assistants. Because, you understand, if there is one single moment of emptiness within me—— You do understand, don't you? I might even kill all the life in someone I don't know. Just as if it were nothing at all. . . . Take out a revolver and kill someone who, like you, has had the bad luck to miss his train. . . . No! No! Don't be afraid, my dear fellow! I'm only joking! I'm going now. If it ever came to that, it'd be myself I'd kill, rather than—— But these days there are some fine apricots to be had—how do *you* eat them? Skin and all, am I right? You split them in half. Then you squeeze the halves between your thumb and forefinger, till they lengthen out, and look just like two juicy lips. Oh, how lovely! My best wishes to your wife and daughters in the country. I can just picture them. . . . Dressed in blue and white. Seated in the shade of a tree. In a beautiful green field. . . . Do me a favour—— Tomorrow morning, when you get back. I imagine that the village where you're staying is some little way from the station. It'll be dawn; you can make the rest of your journey on foot. The first tuft of grass by the roadside—count the number of blades for me. The number of those blades will be the number of days that I have yet to live. But I beg you—please choose a fine large tuft. Good-night!'

## DESTRUCTION OF THE MAN

*La distruzione dell'uomo* was first published in the Christmas number of *Novella* for 1921. It was collected into Vol. V of the *Novelle per un anno* (*La mosca,* Firenze, Bemporad, 1923), reprinted by Mondadori in 1932, and now, as part of the volume, is incorporated in the Biblioteca Moderna Mondadori. The definitive text is in Vol. I of the *Opere*. (*Novelle per un anno,* Vol. I, *con una prefazione di Corrado Alvaro,* Milano-Verona, Mondadori, 1956.)

# DESTRUCTION OF THE MAN

ALL I should like to know is whether the Examining Magistrate[1] sincerely believes that he's found one single reason which is in itself sufficient to explain—in some measure, at least—why the defendant committed (and I use his own term) *premeditated* murder? Should murder be proved, of course, it would be a *double* murder charge that would have to go to the jury, for the murdered woman was about to bring to a happy conclusion her final month of pregnancy.

We know that Nicola Petix has retreated behind a barrier of impenetrable silence. Not only did he refuse to answer any of the questions put to him by the Police, after he was arrested; not only did he preserve silence when brought up before the Examining Magistrate, who tried time and again, using one approach after another, to get him to speak; not only did he refuse to answer *his* questions, but he also declined to give any assistance to the counsel assigned by the court to undertake his defence, since he had indicated his unwillingness himself to instruct counsel.

It seems to me that some explanation should be provided for so stubborn a silence.

They say that, while he's been in prison on remand, Petix has shown all the callous indifference and unmindfulness of a cat which has just slaughtered a mouse or a bird, and which is now happily sunning itself.

It's perfectly obvious, however, that such a rumour is quite obnoxious to the Examining Magistrate, if he's seeking to establish premeditation, and intends to provide evidence to support that contention. You see, to accept such a notion would be to accept the implication that Petix carried out his crime *with all the unawareness of the nature of what he was doing that is characteristic of an animal*. Animals are incapable of premeditation. If they lie in wait for their prey, their lurking in ambush is an instinctive and natural

[1] We're talking about the crime alleged to have been committed by Petix.

aspect of their completely natural urge to hunt. It doesn't turn them into thieves or murderers. As far as the owner of the chicken's concerned, the fox is a chicken-thief; but, as far as the fox himself is concerned, he's not a thief—he's hungry; and when he's hungry, he grabs hold of a chicken and eats it. And after he's eaten it . . . good-bye! He doesn't give it another thought.

Now, Petix isn't an animal. We must, therefore, see whether this indifference of his is real. Because, if it *is* real, then we must also take this indifference into account, in the same way as his stubborn silence. To my manner of thinking, it's the completely natural consequence of that silence. Both seem confirmed by his explicit rejection of defending counsel.

I have no desire, however, to anticipate the jury's verdict, nor, for the moment, do I wish to put forward my own view of the case.

Let me return to what I was discussing with the Examining Magistrate.

If the Examining Magistrate believes that Petix should be punished with all the vigour that the Law provides, because, as far as he's concerned, he's neither a violent lunatic, and so properly comparable to a savage beast, nor a madman who, for no reason whatsoever, killed a woman only a few weeks before she was due to give birth to a child. What can possibly be the motive for this crime? This *premeditated murder*?

A secret passion for the woman? No. I think that possibility is easily ruled out. If the young barrister they've given him to defend him will very kindly show the jury the photograph of the poor dead woman for a moment. Signora Porrella was forty-seven years of age and must, at the time of her death—whatever else she may have looked like—have borne not the slightest resemblance to a woman.

I remember seeing her myself only a few days before the crime. Towards the end of October, it must have been. Walking along the street, arm in arm with her husband. It was early evening. Her husband, you will recall, is a man of fifty. Slightly shorter than his wife. Still, not without his proper share of middle-aged spread, Signor Porrella. And proud of it. Out for a stroll, along the Viale

Nomentano, despite the wind, which was whirling the dead leaves about in warm, noisy gusts.

On my word of honour—yes, I do assure you, there was something provocative about the sight of those two, out walking on a day like that, with all that wind, amidst all those dead, swirling leaves. Two tiny figures dwarfed by the naked plane trees, that seemed to brandish the harsh intricacy of their branches in that stormy sky.

They walked in step. Their feet hit the ground in the same way. Seriously. As if they had a task to perform. A duty laid upon them.

Perhaps they thought that that walk of theirs was absolutely essential, now that her pregnancy was in its final stages. Prescribed by the doctor; recommended by all her friends and neighbours.

Rather annoying for them, maybe. Yes! But they saw it as perfectly natural that that wind should blow up like that, and that it should get stronger every minute, furiously hurling those curled-up leaves hither and thither, without ever succeeding in sweeping them out of the way. Neither did they see anything strange in those naked plane trees there—they'd put forth their leaves in due season, and in due season they'd shed them. Naked they would now remain till the coming spring. Nothing unusual, either, about that stray dog. And the fact that, at every gust of wind which assailed his nostrils with fascinating smells, he would stop at almost every single one of those plane trees, exasperatedly cock a leg against the trunk, and then merely squirt out a few miserable drops; after having frenziedly chased round and round himself in search of his own backside.

I give you my solemn assurance that not only I, but every single person walking along that street that day, thought it quite incredible that that man—such a small man—could possibly feel as satisfied as he looked. I mean, taking his wife out for a stroll in that condition. What was even more incredible was that his wife should let him take her. She seemed most obstinately determined to be cruel to herself, and the more resigned to making that intolerable effort she appeared, the more cruel to herself she seemed. What it must have cost her! She was staggering with every step, panting away, and her eyes were glazed and staring in a spasm of—well, it wasn't because of that far-from-human effort she was being called upon to make. No, it was because she was terribly afraid that she wouldn't succeed in bringing to full term that obscene encumbrance in her slumping belly. It's true, of course, that from time to time she would lower her ashen lids over her eyes. But it wasn't so much from shame that she lowered them, as from the feeling of irritation she got, seeing herself compelled to sense other people's *projecting* shame at her. Everyone who looked at her, and saw her in that condition. At her age. A shapeless and worn-out old hag, still being used for something that—— Well, they ought to have stopped that sort of thing long ago. As a matter of fact, walking along there, arm in arm with her husband, she could quite easily have given his arm a tiny squeeze and given a jolt to his little world of self-satisfaction. All too often and all too obviously, he would disappear into that world, wallowing in the knowledge that he—fifty, bald, and diminutive—was the author of that huge affliction she was trundling around. She didn't give him a jolt, because she was, yes, she was rather pleased that he should have the nerve to show her off like this. That he should feel so self-satisfied, while she felt so ashamed of it all.

In my mind's eye I can still see her, suddenly caught from behind by a more than usually violent gust of wind. She'd stop short on those thick, stumpy legs of hers, which the wind, thrusting her frock hard against them, threw into obscene relief, while simultaneously bellying her out in front like a balloon. With her only free hand, she didn't know what to deal with first. Should she push down that balloon in front, before it . . . ? Well, any minute now the whole world would see what she had on underneath! Or should she clutch at the brim of her old mauve velvet hat, with its melancholy black feathers, in which the wind had stirred up a desperate and foolish desire to fly?

Let's get to the point, however.

I would urge you, should you ever have the time, to go along to the Via Alessandria, and take a look at the huge, rambling old house, in which Signor and Signora Porrella lived. Nicola Petix lived there too, in two small rooms on the floor below.

There are thousands of houses just like it, all hideous in the same way. It's as if they'd been branded with the hall-mark of the highest common vulgarity of the time in which they'd been thrown up in such furious haste—in the expectation (later recognized to be erroneous) that there'd be an abundant and immediate flood of his Majesty's subjects rushing to Rome upon the declaration of that city as the third capital of the Kingdom.

So many private fortunes, not only of the newly rich, but of many men of illustrious and ancient families, even. And all the loans made by banks to speculative builders, who seemed, year after year, to be in the grip of an almost fanatical frenzy, were swallowed up in an enormous wave of bankruptcy. People still remember it very vividly.

And so we saw houses going up where formerly there had been the extensive grounds of patrician houses, magnificent villas, and, on the other side of the river, orchards and meadows. Houses, houses, houses. Isolated units, scattered along hardly defined streets, miles from anywhere. So many of them were destined suddenly to be left unfinished—newly constructed ruins—run up as far as the fourth floor, then left to rot, roofless and with the window-openings still gaping emptily. Higher up, the remnants of the scaffolding, just abandoned when work stopped, stuck into holes in the raw, unfinished walls. Flooring left uncompleted, and now all blackened and rotted by the rain. There were other isolated buildings, too, buildings that were already completed, doomed now to remain deserted. Whole streets of them. Whole areas of them. Streets and areas through which not a soul passed. And in the silence of month succeeding month the grass began to sprout again along the edges of the pavement, up against the walls. And then, slender, tenderness itself, shuddering at every breath of wind, it resumed its sway over the whole stone-faced street.

A number of these houses, which had been equipped with all modern conveniences with the aim of attracting the better-off sort of tenant, were later thrown open to an invasion of working-class people—principally in order to make *something* out of them. As you'll readily imagine, these people very quickly made havoc of what they found. So much so that, when, as the years went by, there really *did* develop a housing shortage in Rome, the new owners thought it best, all things considered, to do nothing about their property. Yes, a housing shortage—prematurely feared in the first place, and cautiously remedied later. Because of that awful shaking-up earlier, people were terribly afraid now of putting up any new buildings. As I've already said, the new owners—who'd acquired the property from the banks that had financed the bankrupt builders—having worked out what they'd have to spend on putting things to rights and getting their houses into a fit state to rent them to tenants who would be willing to pay a higher rent, thought it best to leave things as they were. To go on happily in the same old way, with the steps all chipped away, the walls obscenely spattered with filth, the shutters hanging askew on their broken hinges, the window-panes smashed, and the windows themselves garlanded with filthy, patched rags, stretched out on lines to dry.

Every now and again, however, a lower middle-class family (or a better-class one that had come down in the world) would seek refuge in one of these large, miserable houses. It's become more common nowadays: a clerk and his family; a schoolteacher and his—coming to live among the tenants I've just referred to, all busy finishing off the work of destruction of the walls, doors, and floors. They'd come because they hadn't been able to find anywhere else, or because they were desperately poor, or because they just wanted to economize on rent. It was a case of conquering your disgust at all that filth and—even worse—having to mix with. . . . Oh, my God! Yes, he's my neighbour, all right! True enough! I don't deny it! But—— Well, he's got so little fondness for cleanliness and the ordinary decencies of civilized living, that you've no desire to get too near him. Moreover, I'm not denying that the feeling's mutual. As a matter of fact, all newcomers are looked at in a pretty surly way at first. It's only gradually, and only if they've shown willing that they . . . Yes, if they've wanted people to look more favourably on them, they've had to resign themselves to a number of liberties which have been taken rather than granted.

Now, when the crime occurred, the Porrellas had been living in the house in the Via Alessandria for the past fifteen years, more or less, and Nicola Petix for about ten. But, while *they* had for some time enjoyed the favour of all the most long-established inmates, Petix on the other hand, had always attracted the strongest antipathy, on account of the contempt with which he looked on everybody, from the inefficient caretaker up. Never a word for anyone. Not even a nod, by way of greeting.

Still, as I said a little while ago, let's get to the point. A fact's like a sack, though—when it's empty it won't stand up.

As the Examining Magistrate will very soon become aware when, as it seems he intends to do, he tries to make his 'sack' stand up, without first of all filling it with all those reasons and experiences which most certainly determined its existence, and of which he has, it may well be, not the faintest idea.

Petix's father was an engineer who had emigrated to America many years before and who died there. He'd amassed a pretty large sum of money over there, working at his profession, and left it all to another son, two years older than Petix, and an engineer himself, on condition that he paid his younger brother a few hundred lire every month for the rest of his life. It was more a kind of alms bestowed upon him than anything the young man was rightfully entitled to, because he'd already 'gobbled-up', as his father's will put it, 'all that was legitimately his, in a life of shameful idleness'.

Before we go any further let me ask that we consider this 'idleness' not only from the point of view of the father, but also, for a moment or so, from his. To tell the truth, Petix was up at a number of universities for many, many years, moving on from one group of subjects to another. From Medicine to Law, from Law to Mathematics, from Mathematics to Letters and Philosophy. It's true, of course, that he never sat any examinations, but only because he never for one moment dreamt of being a doctor or a lawyer, a mathematician, or a man of letters. Bluntly, Petix has never wanted to be anything, but that doesn't mean to say that he's spent his time in idleness, or that that idleness has been shameful. He's spent his time in contemplation, studying in his own way the things that happen in life and the customs of man.

And the fruit of this contemplation has been infinite boredom—a completely insupportable boredom, not only with me, but also with life itself.

Do we do a thing merely in order to do a thing? Either we must remain completely absorbed in the thing that's to be done—be inside it, like a blind man, without ever looking out—or else we must assign some sort of purpose to it. What purpose? Merely that of doing it? Good God, why, yes, of course! That's the way life's lived. This thing today, something else tomorrow. It might even be the same thing every day. According to your inclination, or what you're capable of; according to your intentions or according to your feeling and instincts. It's the way life's lived.

The trouble arises when you want to see from the outside what the purpose is of all those inclinations, capacities, intentions, feelings, and instincts that you've obeyed inside yourself, simply because you've got them and can feel them. And precisely because you do try and find it outside yourself, you don't find it at all. . . . Just as you'll always find nothingness outside yourself.

Nicola Petix very soon arrived at a knowledge of this nothingness, which must, of course, be the quintessence of *all* philosophy.

Being forced every day to see the hundred or so tenants of that large, filthy, gloomy house—people who lived merely in order to live, without knowing anything about living, other than that tiny fragment which they seemed condemned to live out every day. Every day the same old things. Well, very soon he began to get terribly irritated by it all. A frenzied intolerance swept over him. Every day he got more and more enraged by it.

Particularly unbearable were the sight and din of the countless small children who swarmed all over the courtyard and up and down the stairs. He couldn't even put his head out of the window and look out into the courtyard, without seeing four or five of them in a row, squatting down to pot, chewing away all the time at a rotten apple or a crust of bread. Or, there on the cobbled path, where half the cobbles had come loose, and where water (if it was in fact water) stood about in stagnant pools, three little boys down on their hands and knees, studying a little girl who was having a pee, and trying to see how she managed it and where it came out. She didn't care in the slightest. There she was—solemn, ignorant, and with one eye bandaged. And the way they'd spit at one another! And all that kicking and scratching! Tearing one another's hair! And all the shrieking that led to! Their mothers would join in as well, yelling from every window of the whole five floors in the house. Oh, look! Right in the middle of it all, there's the little schoolmarm, with that run-down-looking little face of hers, and her hair tumbling onto her shoulders and down her back, coming through the courtyard carrying a large bouquet of flowers, which she's just been given by her fiancé, who's there, smiling, beside her.

Petix felt very tempted to rush over to his chest of drawers, take out his revolver and shoot that little schoolmistress—such and so great were the indignation and fury that those flowers and that smile on her fiancé's face provoked in him! The flattering hopes of love, in the middle of that sickening obscenity, that filthy proliferation of children. And soon she too would be busy increasing their number.

I would now ask you to remember that every day for the past ten years Nicola Petix, living there in that house, had been a member of the audience for Signora Porrella's unfailing sequence of pregnancies. She would reach the seventh or eighth month, having gone through all the refinements of vomiting, suffering, and trepidation, and then miscarry. And every time she'd nearly die. In the nineteen years she'd been married, that carcase of a woman had had fifteen miscarriages.

The most terrifying thing as far as Nicola Petix was concerned was this: he'd never been able to understand what it was in those two people that made them want a child so stubbornly and with such blind ferocity. Tearing away at themselves like that!

Perhaps it was because, eighteen years ago, at the time of her first pregnancy, the woman had prepared a layette for the baby she was expecting. There wasn't a thing she hadn't thought of: swaddling clothes, bonnets, little shirts, bibs, long day-dresses with pom-poms on the strings, woollen bootees—still waiting to be used, and now all yellow and dried-up, stiff and starched, like so many tiny corpses.

For the past ten years there'd been a kind of implied wager

between the women of the tenement, who spent their time spawning brats at an incredible rate, and Nicola Petix, who loathed with every fibre of his being their filthy proliferation of children. *They* were busy maintaining that *this time* Signora Porrella would have her baby, while he said, 'No, she won't even bring it off this time.' And the more care they lavished on the belly of that woman as it grew from month to month, the more attentive they were, the more anxious for her well-being, the more they recommended her to do this, that, and the other, the more he felt his vexation, his frenzy, his fury growing within him, as he saw her getting larger and larger with each succeeding month. In the last days of every one of her pregnancies—so over-excited was his imagination—he would gradually come to see the whole of that vast house as an enormous belly, caught in the desperate travail of the gestation of the man who was destined to be born. It was no longer a question for him of Signora Porrella's imminent confinement. Oh, yes! That would mean defeat for him. It was a question of the man, the man whom all those women were willing to be born from the belly of that woman: such a man as can be born from the brute necessity of the two sexes when they're coupled!

Well, it was that man whom Petix wanted to destroy, once he was sure that that sixteenth pregnancy of hers was going to come at last to a successful conclusion. *That* man. Not one man among many, but one man in whom all men were summed up. And he was going to revenge himself on that one man for all the others, the hundreds and hundreds he had to watch swarming around, little brutes who lived merely in order to live, without knowing anything about living, except for that tiny fragment which they seemed condemned every day to get through. Every day the same old thing.

It all happened a few days after that occasion when I chanced to see Signor and Signora Porrella walking along the Viale Nomentano amidst the swirling gusts of dead leaves. Walking in step. Their feet hitting the ground in the same way. Seriously. As if they had a task to perform. A duty laid upon them.

The goal of their daily walk was a large stone on the other side of the Barrier, where the lane, after turning again once you're past

Sant' Agnese—you remember, it narrows a bit, and then drops down towards the valley of the Aniene. Every day, seated on that stone, they'd rest for about half an hour from their long, slow walk. Signor Porrella would look over at the gloomy bridge, thinking no doubt that the ancient Romans had passed that way. Signora Porrella would follow with her eyes the movements of some old woman rummaging for edible greenstuff among the grass on the slope that runs along the riverside. The river makes a brief appearance here, after emerging from under the bridge. Or else she'd study her hands, slowly twisting her rings round her stubby fingers.

Even that day they were quite determined to reach their usual objective, despite the fact that the river, as a result of the recent heavy rain, was in flood and had broken its banks, so that it was encroaching threateningly on the slope leading down to it. As a matter of fact, it had almost risen as far as that stone of theirs. Despite the fact, too, that they could see in the distance their fellow-tenant, Nicola Petix, seated on their stone, just as if he were waiting for them. He was all hunched-up and drawn into himself like some huge owl.

They stopped for a moment or so when they caught sight of him, rather bewildered. Should they go and sit somewhere else or should they turn back? But the very fact that he just *sat* there, seeming somehow to warn them—radiating distrust and hostility —well, it made them decide to go on and to go up to him. Because it seemed to them irrational to allow the unlooked-for presence of that man. And the fact that it seemed obvious that he'd come there especially to meet them. Well, it couldn't mean anything terribly serious, as far as they were concerned. Not so serious as to make them give up their usual little rest. After all, the pregnant woman had special need of that rest.

Petix said nothing. Everything happened in an instant. Almost *quietly*. As the woman came up to the stone to sit down, he seized her by the arm and with one tug dragged her to the edge of the flooding river. Then he gave her a shove that sent her flying into the river, where she was drowned.

# PUBERTY

*Pubertà* is one of the very few stories written by Pirandello during the nineteen-twenties, a decade when he was greatly preoccupied with work for and in the theatre. It was first published in the *Corriere della sera* for 11 April 1926. Two years later it was included in Vol. XII *(Il viaggio)* of the *Novelle per un anno* (Firenze, Bemporad). Reprinted by Mondadori in 1934, the volume now forms part of the Biblioteca Moderna Mondadori. The definitive text is in Vol. II of the *Opere*. (*Novelle per un anno,* Milano-Verona, Mondadori, 1957.)

# PUBERTY

SHE was far too big to wear that sailor-suit now. Grandma should have realized.

Of course, it wasn't easy to find a way of dressing her that didn't make her look either like a little girl or like the young woman she hadn't quite grown into. She'd seen the Granchi girl yesterday. Oh, what a horrible sight she'd looked! Weighed down by a huge hairy grey skirt that almost reached to her ankles! She couldn't move her legs about under it! Didn't know what to do with them!

Still, look at her! With all that bosom stuffed inside that baby-sized blouse of hers!

She gave a huge, puffing sigh and shook her head in vexation.

There were times during the day when her awareness of the exuberant fragrance of her own body became so acute that the blood rushed to her head. The smell of her thick, black, rather curly, rather dry hair, as she loosened it to wash it; the smell that breathed out from under her bare arms, when she lifted them to support that suffocating mass of hair; the smell of powder saturated with sweat—all filled her with a madness that was instinct more with a sick feeling of revulsion, than with any feeling of being intoxicated by the many, many secret and burdensome things that her unexpected and violent growing-up had suddenly revealed to her.

Things that, sometimes of an evening, while she was undressing to go to bed, if she allowed her thoughts to dwell upon them, or their image for a moment to leap up before her eyes, her rage and disgust grew so great that she suddenly felt like throwing her shoes at the white lacquered cupboard with its three mirrors, where she could see her whole body, just like that, half-naked, with one leg crossed a little obscenely over the other. She felt like biting herself, scratching herself—or just starting to cry, never to stop again. Then she'd be seized with a frantic desire to laugh, and she'd be convulsed with hysterical laughter through her tears. And if she thought of drying those tears, then, why off she'd go again, crying her eyes out! Perhaps she was just being a silly fool! Heaven only knows why such a natural thing should appear so strange to her!

With that same proptness which makes all women realize from a single glance that someone's started thinking about them in a particular kind of way, she'd already got to that stage where, if, as she was walking along the street, a man looked at her, she immediately lowered her eyes.

She still didn't know exactly what went on in a man's mind when he thought in that way about a woman. She was disturbed, and as she walked on, with her eyes lowered, she felt an irritating shudder run through her, for she found she was imagining to herself, in her uncertainty—without wanting to do so—that there was some intimate secret in her body. Oddly enough, it was just as if she knew all about it.

And now, even without actually seeing, she could feel when she was being looked at.

And she nearly drove herself out of her mind, desperately trying to guess what it was that men looked at in a woman for preference. But this, perhaps, was something she'd already guessed.

The moment she got indoors, and was on her own, she'd let her school-books or her gloves drop from her hand, deliberately, so that she'd have to bend over and pick them up again. And in bending over, she'd squint down her dress at her breasts. She'd hardly finish having a peep at them and getting the sensation of how heavy they were, before she'd grab hold of the big knot of the black silk kerchief under the collar of the sailor-blouse and immediately tug it up! Up! Up! Right up to her eyes she'd pull it, utterly disgusted with herself.

The next moment, she'd be gathering into both hands, one on either side, the material of that blouse. Then she'd smooth it downwards, so that it clung to her erect breasts. After that she'd move over to the mirror. She'd stand there, feeling pretty smug about the promising curve of her hips as well.

'Oh, you're a most seductive young lady, that you are!'

And she'd burst out laughing.

* * *

She heard the nattering voice of her grandmother, calling her down into the hall of the little villa, telling her to come and have her English lesson.

Just to annoy her, her grandmother usually called her *Dreina* and not *Dreetta,* as she herself wanted to be called. All right: she'd only go down when at last her grandmother took it into her head to call her Dreetta, and not Dreina.

'Dreetta! Dreetta!'

'Coming, Grandma!'

'Oh, Good Lord in Heaven! You're keeping your teacher waiting!'

'I'm sorry. I didn't hear you before.'

In the summer, of an afternoon, by order of her grandmother, all the windows in the little villa were kept hermetically shut. Dreetta, of course, would have liked them all to be flung wide open. She liked it tremendously, therefore, when the all-powerful and overbearing sun still managed to find some way of penetrating into that wilful shadow—it was almost pitch-black in the house!

Light trembled and squirmed in all the rooms, like little outbursts of childish laughter in periods of severely ordered silence.

Dreetta herself was very often like that, a trembling, squirming mass. Time and time again it was as if she were completely wrapped up in and ravished by real lightning flashes of madness. Immediately afterwards she'd cloud over again, because of her secret suspicion that these flashes of madness came to her from her mother, whom she'd never known, and about whom no one had ever told her anything. About her father she only knew that he'd died young; she didn't know from what cause. There was a mystery, and perhaps it was a really nasty and atrocious one, about her birth and the premature death of her parents. You only had to look at her grandmother to realize that. Her grandmother, with that cartilaginous face of hers, and those turbid eyes, whose huge eyelids seemed to weigh heavily upon them—on one a little more than on the other. Always dressed in black, and humpbacked, she kept that mystery firmly locked within her breast, holding it firmly in with both hands. One hand clenched into a fist, the other, which was deformed with arthritis, resting on top of it;

both hands tightly there, under her throat. But Dreetta had no desire to find out anything at all about it. She thought she already knew what it was, because of the way in which so many people looked at her without mentioning her name, and because of the glance they then exchanged with one another, as they exclaimed almost involuntarily, 'Oh, that's . . . daughter. . . .' And they paused before the word 'daughter', failing to put in the possessive. She pretending not to hear. Besides, she'd got Uncle Zeno now, and her aunt and all her cousins. They came over and took her out almost every day, and provided her with all sorts of entertainment. Her uncle had wanted to take her into his home, seeing that Aunt Tilla, his wife, loved her almost as dearly as she loved her own daughters. But, so long as Grandma was alive, she had to stay with her.

Dreetta was quite sure that her grandmother, with that fist always resting there under her chin, was never going to die. And this was one of the things that most frequently sent her off into one of those lightning flashes of madness.

Those cousins of hers had a high old time showing her the room she'd have when she came to live with them; telling her how they were going to decorate it; what pictures they were going to put on the walls; and inventing all sorts of wonderful stories about how the four of them would live together. They'd be together for always, of course. She loved every minute of it; always said 'yes' to everything; and threw herself with great zest into the inventing of stories. But, at the bottom of her heart, she didn't indulge even the faintest illusion that that dream would ever come true.

If ever she was going to be in a position to free herself, her freedom would have to come about as the result of pure chance, something quite unforeseeable, something that happened just like that. A chance encounter in the street, for instance. That was the reason why, when she went out walking with her uncle and her cousins, or went to school or came back from school, she was always somehow—ablaze. Just as if she were intoxicated. She'd be trembling with anxiety and quite unable to lend an ear to what they were saying to her. Intently looking over here and over there, with her eyes shining brightly and a nervous smile on her lips, as if she really and truly felt somehow exposed to that unforeseeable, chance happening which was simply bound to gather her up and suddenly ravish her away. She was ready for it. Wasn't there some old English or American gentleman who'd take such a fancy to her, that he'd come along and ask her uncle . . .? And before he got any farther with this request, she imagined her uncle misunderstanding and saying, 'You want to marry the girl?' 'What? Why, of course not!' No, he'd come along and ask her uncle if he might be allowed to adopt her, and take her away with him. Far, far away, away from the living nightmare of life with Grandma, and from the so ostentatiously pitiful kindness of her aunt—to London, to America, where he'd marry her to a nephew or to the son of a friend.

This fantastic notion of an old English or American gentleman had come into her head to save her from having to admit that freedom—well, immediate freedom, at least—might come to her through marriage. It all derived from those turbid sensations that impetuously cluttered up her spirit with shame and with contempt for the precocious exuberances of her body, and from the way in which men looked at her in the street. As a result of those things the idea had come to birth in her, it was something that was possible, but something to blush about. Oh, get away with you! *Yes!* Get married, at her age! In order not to blush at the thought, she interposed—as if to ward off the thought—the highly unlikely possibility of a chance adoption by an old English or American gentleman. He had to be English or American because—— Oh, yes! She was really serious about this! She would only marry an Englishman or an American, a man who'd been washed by the Seven Seas of the World, and in whose eyes, yes, in whose eyes there was at least some fragment of the blue, blue sky.

That's why she was studying English.

Curious, wasn't it, that, resolutely keeping the idea of marriage at such a distance (so as not to blush at it), she shouldn't till now have seen in the person of Mr. Walston, her teacher of English, an Englishman who could marry her and, what's more, who was right on her doorstep!

And immediately she was aflame, just as if Mr. Walston were standing there expressly for this purpose. She felt herself shudder from head to foot, noting at the same time that he too was blushing. And yet she knew perfectly well that it was Mr. Walston's nature to blush at nothing at all. Time and time again she'd laughed at it, as at something quite ridiculous in a man of such powerful physique—though he looked an absolute babe in arms.

He looked even more enormous, standing there by the graceful little gilt table in the drawing-room, in front of the window. It was where he usually gave her her lesson. He was dressed in a light grey summer suit, with a light blue shirt and brown shoes. He was smiling. It was a meaningless smile, which revealed in the aperture of his large mouth those few teeth that were left to him as a result of a disease of the gums. He was smiling, without even being aware of the fact that he'd blushed when he'd got up as his little pupil had come into the room, so utterly remote from his own thoughts was anything remotely resembling the thought she'd had about him. She asked him to sit down, and, having done so, he picked up the English grammar from the table, looked over his glasses at his pupil with those tender blue eyes of his, as if to urge her not to interrupt his reading—as she usually did—with those unrestrainable bursts of laughter at the way he pronounced certain words, and began to read, crossing one leg over the other as he did so.

Now it so happened that, being the huge man that he was, as he crossed his legs over one another, he bared almost the whole of his calf, as his trouser-leg rode up past the top of white silk sock, which was held up by the taut elastic of his old pink suspenders. Dreetta caught a glimpse of it, and immediately felt a terrible sick sense of revulsion. And yet her revulsion drew her back to look at it again and again. She observed that the flesh of that calf was a dead white colour and that on that skin there curled a few reddish metallic little hairs. In the half-shadow the whole drawing-room seemed to be very still, waiting for something. As if to urge more and more upon Dreetta's awareness the contrast between the strange exasperated anxiety of that revulsion of hers, which was almost like a shattering shameful contact, and the extraneous placidity and way of thinking of that huge Englishman reading away there, with his calf bare, like some old husband, already quite deaf to the sensibilities of his wife.

'Present Tense:[1] I do not go, *io non vado*; thou dost not go, *tu non vai*; he does not go, *egli non va*.'

All of a sudden Mr. Walston's ears were deafened by a cry, and, raising his eyes from the book, he saw his pupil shudder as if some terrible sensation had suddenly passed through her flesh. She hurled herself out of the drawing-room, howling frantically and with her face buried in her hands. Jarred and deafened, with his face all aflame, he was still standing there, looking about him in bewilderment, trying to gather his wits together again, when suddenly the old grandmother popped up in front of him. There she was, almost dancing with rage, completely convulsed with anger and contempt, shouting incomprehensible words at him. The last thing the poor man could have imagined at that moment was that the meaningless smile of dismay on his large flaming-red face could have been mistaken for a smile of impudence. It was, however.

He found himself picked up by the front of his jacket by a man-servant, who'd rushed up at the cries, and hurled, with a great deal of banging and shoving, out through the door and into the garden. He hardly had time to raise his head when he heard a shriek that came to him from up above, 'Catch me, Mr. Walston!'

He half saw a body dangling from the eaves of the villa. It was Dreetta, with her hair all dishevelled, and her eyes flashing with madness, clenching her teeth with terror, and desperately wriggling about, as if trying to get back to safety, after having repented her original intention. Then there came a jagged, tearing laugh, that remained poised in the air for an instant, like a strange kind of wake to the horrible thud made by that body as it hit the ground at his feet, and smashed into fragments.

[1] This speech is given as it appears in the original, with the exception of 'Present Tense' for which Pirandello had erroneously written 'Present Time'.

# CINCI

*Cinci,* one of the last of Pirandello's stories, was originally published in *La lettura* for June 1932. It was subsequently collected into Vol. XIV of the *Novelle per un anno* (*Berecche e la guerra,* Milano-Verona, Mondadori, 1934), and now is included in the Biblioteca Moderna Mondadori volume of the same name. The definitive text is in Vol. II of the *Opere.* (*Novelle per un anno,* Vol. II, Milano-Verona, Mondadori, 1957.)

# CINCI

THE dog squatted there patiently on its hind legs, in front of the closed door, waiting for someone to open it and let him in. The nearest he came to protesting was to let out an occasional low whine, as he lifted a paw and scratched himself.

He was a dog, so he knew there was nothing more he could do.

When Cinci got back from afternoon school, with his textbooks and his exercise books all strapped together and tucked under his arm, he found the dog stuck there outside the door. It irritated him to see it waiting there, patiently like that, so he gave it a kick. Then he gave the door a good kicking, too, even though he knew it was locked and there was nobody at home. Finally, if only because he felt they were the worst of his burdens, he flung his bundle of books furiously against the door—just to get rid of them—as if he had some daft idea that they'd pass straight through the woodwork and land up in the house. Contrary to any such expectation, however, the door flung them straight back at his chest with the same force with which he'd hurled them originally. Cinci was quite surprised: it was as if this were some wonderful game that the door was suggesting they might play. So he threw the bundle back at the door. Then, since there were already three of them playing this game—Cinci, the bundle of books, and the door—the dog thought he'd join in as well. Every time Cinci slung the books at the door and every time they bounced back, he'd leap in the air, barking away. Several passers-by stopped to watch. A few of them smiled, almost ashamed of themselves, of course, because of the utter silliness of the game and because of the equal silliness of the dog, who was having such a riotous time. Others waxed highly indignant, because of the way those poor books were being treated. Books cost money, you know. People oughtn't to be allowed to treat them like that, with so little regard. Cinci brought the show to an end, dropped his bundle of books on the ground, and slumped to a sitting position by sliding his backbone down the wall. It had been his intention to sit on the books, but the bundle slid from under him and he landed on the ground with a sudden jolt. He gave a wry, comic grin and looked around, while the dog bounded back and eyed him speculatively.

All the devilment that passed through Cinci's mind was—well, you could almost see it written all over that untidy thatch of straw-coloured hair of his, and in those sharp green eyes, which seemed almost to be wriggling with life. He was at the awkward age, all gawky and sallow. He'd left his handkerchief at home when he'd gone back to school that afternoon. Now, as a consequence, he'd every so often give a snuffle, as he sat there on the ground. He drew his enormous knees up until they almost reached his chin. His huge legs were bare, because he was still wearing short trousers —and shouldn't have been. When he ran, his legs splayed out sideways. There wasn't a pair of shoes that could stand up to the treatment he meted out to them; the ones he had on then were right through already. He was bored stiff. He folded his arms round his knees, gave a huge, puffing sigh, and then dragged his spine up the wall again until he was standing upright once more. The dog got up too, and it was just as if he was asking, 'Well, where are we off to now?' Yes, where were we going? Out into the country, to have a snack? Knock off the odd fig or apple? It was an idea. He hadn't quite made up his mind, though.

The paved road ended at their house, and the cinder-path took over, and if you went on and on through their suburb you landed in the country. What a wonderful sensation it must be—if you were riding in a carriage, that is—when the horses' hooves and the carriage-wheels passed from the hard surface of the stridently noisy paving, to the soft, silent cinder-road. It's probably like what happens when the teacher who's been busy shouting your head off—oh, you've made him so angry!—starts talking to you gently, kindly, with a sort of resigned melancholy. You find it so much more agreeable, because it puts a safe distance between you and the punishment you were afraid you were in for. Yes, it would be a good idea to go into the country, to get away, out along the narrow stretch of road flanked by the last houses of this stinking suburb, down to where the road widened out into the little square that marked the end of the town. The new hospital was down there now, the walls of which were so freshly white-washed that when the sun was shining on them you had to shut your eyes, or you got blinded. In the last few days they'd been busy bringing down all the patients from the old hospital—ambulances and stretchers galore there'd been. It had been as good as a procession, as they all filed along. The ambulances in front, with all their curtains fluttering away at the windows, and then, for the more seriously ill patients, those lovely hammock-trolley things, bouncing along on their springs, like a lot of spiders' webs. It was pretty late now, though, and the sun was just about to set, so there wouldn't be the occasional convalescent patient up at one or other of the huge windows, wearing his grey nightshirt and his white nightcap, and sadly looking at the little old church opposite, as it stood there among a cluster of houses as old as itself and the odd tree or two. Once you'd left that little square, the road became a country-lane and went on up the side of the little hill.

Cinci stopped and gave another huge puffing sigh. Ought he to go? Really? He set off again in a resentful sort of way, because he was beginning to feel boiling away in his guts all the horrible feelings that kept welling up inside him because of so many things that he couldn't explain to himself. His mother, now: how did she live and what did she live on? Never at home, still stubbornly insisting on sending him to that damned school. Yes, that *damned* school—miles away from home it was! Every day he went there—and you had to run like hell for at least three-quarters of an hour to get there in time, from where they lived, out there on the outskirts, that is. Then another three-quarters of an hour sprint to get back home at midday; then another three-quarters of an hour to get back again, after he'd managed to bolt down a couple of mouthfuls—how the hell was he supposed to do it in the time? And his mother busy telling him that he wasted all his time playing with the dog, that he was an idle layabout. And, oh bloody hell! Always throwing the same old muck in his face: he didn't study, he always looked dirty, and if she sent him out to buy something at the shop, they always fobbed him off with any old rubbish.

Where was Fox?

There he was, trotting along behind him, poor little beast. Huh, at least he knew what he had to do: just follow his master. To do something. That's what all the frenzy of life's about—not knowing *what* to do. She could leave him the key, couldn't she—his mother, he meant—when she went off, as she did every day, to sew in gentlemen's houses? (That's what she told him she did.) Oh, no! She said he wasn't to be trusted, and that if she wasn't back by the time he got in from school, she couldn't possibly be long, and that he was to wait. Where? Outside the door, like a lemon? There'd been times when he'd waited for two whole hours, out in the cold—out in the rain, even. As a matter of fact, on *that* particular occasion, he'd deliberately not taken shelter, but had gone and stood under the overflow, so that when she came in she'd find him all sopping wet. Finally she'd appeared, all out of breath, her face flushed, and carrying a borrowed umbrella, her eyes bright, unable to meet his, and so nervy that she couldn't even find the key in her purse.

'Are you soaked? Shan't be a moment now. I had to stay late.'

Cinci frowned. There were certain things he preferred not to think about. He'd never known his father. They'd told him he was dead, that he'd died even before he was born. But they didn't tell him who he'd been. And now he no longer had any desire to know, or to ask any more questions. He might even have been that cripple, the one who was paralysed down one side, but who still managed to drag himself along to the pub, stout fellow. Fox used to rush up to him and bark at him. It was probably the crutch he didn't like. And look at those women standing around in a huddle—all that belly and not one of them pregnant. No, maybe one of them was. The one with her skirt hoicked up a good six inches at the front and sweeping the street behind. And that other one with the baby in her arms, fishing out a breast to—— *Ugh!* What a horrible blubbery mass of flesh! His mother was beautiful, and still very young, and when he'd been a baby, she'd given him milk from her breast, just like that. And perhaps it had been in a house in the country, or out in the sun, in the yard where they did the threshing. Cinci had a vague recollection of a house in the country.

Perhaps it was there—always supposing he hadn't dreamt it—that he'd lived when he was a tiny child. Or perhaps he'd seen it somewhere when he was small. Heaven only knows where, though. Certainly now when, from a distance, he saw houses in the country, he felt that same sort of melancholy which you feel *must* come into those houses when it begins to get evening. When the lamps are lit—the sort you fill with paraffin and carry about in your hand from one room to another—and you see the light disappearing from one window and reappearing at another.

He'd reached the little square by this time. And now he could see the whole vast expanse of the sky. The last rays of the setting sun had disappeared and, over the now darkened hill, the sky was the tenderest of clear blues. The shadow of evening was already upon the earth, and the great white wall of the hospital was muted to a dull grey. The occasional old woman hurried along to the little church, late for Vespers. Cinci suddenly felt a desire to go in himself. Fox stood and looked at him. He knew perfectly well that he wasn't allowed into churches. In the church doorway the old woman who was late was panting and moaning away as she struggled with the leather curtain. It was far too heavy for her to cope with. Cinci helped her to hold it to one side but, instead of thanking him, she only gave him a nasty look. She'd realized only too clearly, of course, that he hadn't gone into that church for devotional reasons. The little church was freezing; cold as a cave. On the main altar two candles burned fitfully, while scattered here and there about the church there were a few dismayed-looking little oil-lamps. The dust of ages lay thick on everything in that little old church and, there in the crude dampness, the very dust itself had a smell of decay about it. And it was for all the world as if the shadow-filled silence were lying in ambush for the slightest noise, so that it could go crashing off into echo upon echo upon echo. Cinci felt a terrible temptation to let out a mighty yell, just to start all those echoes bounding about the place. The pious old dears had already filed into their pews. No, it wouldn't be a good idea to give a yell. But why not throw that bundle of books on to the ground? Well, they were awfully heavy, and they might quite well have dropped from his arm by sheer accident. . . . Why not? He hurled them to the ground, and instantly, the moment they hit the ground, the echoes came raining down upon him, thundering in his ears, crushing him beneath their weight—almost contemptuously. Cinci had often (and with very great relish) tried this experiment of raising echoes. He liked to feel the echo pouncing on a noise and crushing it to the ground, just like a dog that's been irked by something while he's asleep. There was no need for him to tempt the patience of those scandalized and pious old bodies any further, so he mooched out of the church, where he found Fox all ready to follow him, and off he set again along the road leading to the little hill. He felt the need to lay his hands on some fruit somewhere—something he could get his teeth into. Over the low wall he went, and hurled himself among the trees. He felt an enormous sense of tormented longing. But whether it was simply because of that frenzy which was biting into his guts, the frenzy to do something, he just couldn't say.

It was a country road, steep and lonely, strewn with pebbles that got caught by the hooves of passing donkeys, got sent rolling for a little way, and then—where they stopped, there they stayed. Look, there was one of them! He gave it a kick with the toe of his shoe. Go on, stone, enjoy yourself! Oh, it flies through the air with the greatest of ease . . . ! Grass was growing by the roadside and, at the foot of the low walls, long plumed stalks of oats which were very pleasant to chew on—when you'd stripped off the little plumes. They came off like a bouquet when you ran them through your fingers. Then you threw them at somebody, and the number of them that stuck on her (assuming she was a woman), was the number of husbands she was going to have—or, if it was a man, the number of wives. Cinci thought he'd try it out on Fox. Seven wives! No less than seven wives was his ration! It didn't really count, though, because they all stuck on Fox's black coat, the whole lot of them. And Fox, the silly old stupid, just stood there with his eyes shut! He didn't get the joke! There he was, with seven wives on his back.

Cinci didn't feel like going any farther. He was tired and he was bored. He swerved to the left and sat down on the low wall beside the road. And as he sat there he began to study the new moon, whose pale gold crescent was just beginning to gleam brightly through the green light that filled the sky in those last moments of sunset. He saw the moon and yet somehow he didn't see it—it was like so many things that were wandering through his mind, one thing merging into another, and every single one of them receding farther and farther away from that young body of his as it sat there, so motionless that he was no longer aware of it. If he'd caught sight then of his own hand on his knee, it would have seemed like a stranger's to him—just as his own leg would have done, as it dangled there, with his dirty, broken-down shoe at the end of it. He was no longer in his body. He was in all those things which he saw and didn't see: the sky that grew darker as the day died; the moon that was getting brighter and brighter; he was there in those gloomy clumps of trees, which stood so sharply in the empty air, and in the earth over there—the fresh, black, recently hoed earth, from which there still breathed that smell of damp, rotting vegetation, so characteristic of the sultry tedium of the end of October, when the days are still very warm and sunny.

While he was sitting there, completely absorbed, an extraordinary and unidentifiable *something* suddenly ran through his body, distracting him. Instinctively he raised his hand to his ear. A shrill little laugh came from behind the wall. A boy of about his own age, a well-built peasant lad, had been hiding behind it, on the field side. He too had plucked and stripped a long blade of oats for himself. He'd made a little noose at the top of it, and then, very, very quietly, he'd raised his arm and tried to hitch the noose over Cinci's ear. This annoyed Cinci, but the moment he turned round, the boy immediately gestured to him to shush, and held the blade of oats along the wall, towards where the head of a lizard was popping out from between a couple of stones. He'd been trying for the last hour to snare that lizard with his noose. Cinci leant backwards and down, anxiously trying to see what happened. Without realizing what it was doing, the little creature had popped its head into the noose which had been put there in the hope that it would be just so obliging. There was a long way to go yet, however. You had to wait till it stuck its head out a little farther. And it might well be that, instead of doing so, it would withdraw, especially if the hand which was holding the blade of oats trembled and so gave it warning of the ambush. At that very moment it might be on the point of darting out like an arrow, in order to escape from that refuge which had become a prison. Yes! Oh, yes! But you had to stand by, ready to give the jerk that would put the noose round its neck, just at the right moment. It was the work of an instant! There, he'd got it! The lizard was squirming like a fish at the end of that blade of oats. Cinci couldn't resist! He jumped down from the wall. But the other boy, afraid, perhaps, that he was planning to take over the little creature, whirled his arm round several times in the air, and smashed the lizard ferociously down again and again on a huge slab of stone that lay there among the weeds.

'No!' screamed Cinci, but it was too late. The lizard lay motionless on the slab of stone, with the white of its belly gleaming in the light of the moon. Cinci flew into a rage. Yes, he too had wanted that poor little creature to get caught, because he himself had for the moment been overpowered by that instinct to hunt which lurks insidiously in every single one of us. But to kill it like that, without even taking a close look at it; without looking into those eyes—those sharp, almost frantically sharp little eyes; without studying the steady rhythm of its sides as it breathed, and the whole trembling mass of its tiny green body. No, that had been stupid and utterly shameful! Cinci hurled himself at the boy, and punched him in the chest with all his might, sending him sprawling on the ground. He landed a little farther away than he might have done, because he'd been a bit off-balance when Cinci had hit him, and he'd tried and tried to prevent himself from falling. But, no sooner had he hit the ground, than he leapt up again, livid with fury, dug a clod of earth out of the ground and hurled it in Cinci's face. Cinci stood there for a moment, blinded by the dirt. The damp taste in his mouth only gave him a worse sense of outrage. He became like an animal in his fury. Now he grabbed a clod of earth, and hurled it back. The fight immediately became desperate. It was a duel now. The other boy was quicker on his feet, however, and a much more skilled fighter. He never missed.

He moved in steadily, getting closer and closer, keeping up a bombardment with those clods of earth, which, even if they didn't actually injure Cinci still hit him pretty hard, as they rained down on him. It was like a hailstorm as they disintegrated with a thud on his chest or in his face. The dirt got in his hair, and in his eyes—even into his shoes. Choked with dirt, and completely at a loss to know how to defend himself or shield his body, Cinci, now quite beside himself with rage, leapt in the air, stretched out his arm, and snatched a stone from the top of the wall. He was vaguely aware that something scurried away—Fox, probably. He hurled the stone, and all of a sudden—— How did it happen? Everything had been spinning round before. Sort of upside-down. Dancing in front of his eyes. Those clumps of trees. The moon, like a sliver of light in the sky. And now, nothing was moving any more. Almost as if Time itself, and everything else in the world too, were standing still in amazement and stupefaction at the sight of that boy stretched out there, face downwards on the ground.

Cinci, still panting, and with his heart in his mouth, gazed at it all in utter terror. His back against the wall, he gazed at the incredible, silent stillness of the countryside, with the moon high above. He gazed at that boy, lying there with his face half-hidden in the ground, and he felt growing within him, as a formidable reality, the sensation of an eternal solitude, from which he must immediately run away. It wasn't him! He hadn't wanted it to happen! He didn't know anything about it! And then, just as if he really hadn't done it, just as if he were simply going over to him out of curiosity, he took a step forward. Then another, and leant over him to have a look. The boy's head was bashed in, and his mouth was black where blood had dripped through it and on to the ground. You could see part of one of his legs, where his trousers had ridden up above the top of his cotton sock. He was dead, just as if he'd always been dead. Everything lay there, as if it were in a dream. He really must wake up, if he was to get away in time. Over there—just as if it were in a dream—that lizard, lying on its back on the stone, belly upwards to the moon, and with the blade of oats still hanging round its neck. Off he went, with his bundle of books under his arm once again, and Fox trotting along behind him. He didn't know anything about it either.

Gradually, as he went down the slope and moved farther and farther away from the spot, he got more and more the—yes, a strange feeling of being safe. So he didn't even bother to hurry. He reached the little square—it was quite deserted by this time. The moon was shining there too. It was another moon, though. One that didn't know anything at all about—things. It was busy lighting up the white façade of the hospital. He'd reached the road for their part of the suburb by this time, just like before. He reached home. His mother still hadn't got back. So he wouldn't even have to tell her where he'd been. He'd been there all the time, waiting for her. And this statement, which immediately became true as far as his mother was concerned, immediately became true as far as he himself was concerned. Yes, as a matter of fact, there he was, with his shoulders resting against the wall by the door.

It would be quite sufficient for all concerned, if he let her find him like that.

## ALL PASSION SPENT

*Sgombero*[1] remained unpublished until Manlio Lo Vecchio-Musti included it in the appendix to Vol. II of the *Opere*. (*Novelle per un anno,* Vol. II, Milano-Verona, Mondadori, 1957.) He dates it 1933. It seems that Pirandello originally intended to include it in Vol. XIV of the *Novelle per un anno*. He discarded it, however, in the final preparation of that volume *(Berecche e la guerra),* and omitted it from the contents list of Vol. XV *(Una giornata)*. Vol. XV was published posthumously. I think myself that Pirandello decided not to publish *Sgombero* as a story, meaning to complete it as a play and to present it in that form. It has, in fact, been presented in play-form both in Italian[2] and in English.[3]

*100*

[1] A difficult title to translate. *Sgomb(e)ro* means: clear, free, empty, untenanted (as an adjective), or: clearing, emptying, freeing, removing (as a noun).

[2] At Taormina, 2 February 1951, by Paola Borboni.

[3] Translated by Frederick May, under the title *The Rest Is Silence*—the title was chosen to avoid confusion with Miss Sackville-West's novel—and published by the Pirandello Society, Leeds, 1958 (2nd ed., 1961). It was played at Bradford Civic Playhouse, 6 May 1956.

# ALL PASSION SPENT

A SQUALID ground-floor room in a tenement house. The body of an old man is lying on a rickety, shabbily-covered bed. The body lies stiffly, but it has not yet been composed in the traditional way that the dead are laid out. The balls of the eyes are staring in dismay at the world—they seem almost transparent under the delicately thin eyelids, thin as onion-skins: the beard is the unkempt beard of a sick man. The dead man's arms are outside the bedclothes, and his hands are clasped across his breast. The head of the bed is against the wall, and there is a Crucifix attached to the headboard. Beside the bed is a night-table on which are several medicine glasses, a bottle, and an iron candlestick. Centre back is a small door; it is half-open. Beyond it there is an old-fashioned and well-worn chest of drawers, from which the veneer is flaking; on top of it there is a number of crudely-made bits of fittings. Kneeling on the floor by the right-hand side of the bed is the dead man's wife, an old woman. Her body from the waist up and her head have tumbled across the bed and are buried in the bedclothes; her arms are flung full-length across the bed. She is dressed in black, and is wearing a violet-coloured kerchief on her head. She shows no sign of life. Standing by the half-open door is a little girl, about eight or nine years old. She is the daughter of one of the neighbours. She is standing there, with her eyes wide and staring, and with one finger in her mouth, looking at the body in utter dismay and bewilderment. In the shadow-filled passage, which you can see through the half-open door, you catch a glimpse of men and women who live thereabouts; they're peeping in, but don't dare to venture inside the door. In the wall right there is a window which looks out onto a courtyard. And when you look at the window, you see that there are faces there too. You get glimpses of them as they peer curiously in through the window-panes, trying to see what's going on. Against the wall left is a decrepit double wardrobe of stained wood. There are a little table and some padded chairs.

Lora's voice is heard out in the passage, 'Let me get by! Mind out of the way!'

She comes in. She is only just over twenty. There is something ambiguous about her. Her manner is abrupt, brusque.

She is carrying a paper package, containing a large wax candle and, loose in her hand, some brightly coloured fruit—oranges and apples.

As soon as she's in the room she says to the girl,

'Oh, so they've let you come in, have they, dear? So as you'll remember, when you're a big girl, the first time you ever saw a dead man. Would you like to touch him as well— Just with your finger. . . . No? In that case run along! Off you go!'

She takes hold of her and pushes her through the door, saying at the same time to the people standing in the passage,

'There's a lovely funeral up at the top of the road. I saw it as I came by. There was a coach and four horses. Coachman in full rig-out, flunkeys in white wigs. Oh, it was lovely! Go on, run along and have a look! Go on! You're like a lot of flies, aren't you? You love a good muck-heap!'

And she draws the door to. She moves over towards the middle of the room and, shrugging her shoulders, exclaims,

'Yes! Yes! It's like the hippopotamus. That time you saw the hippopotamus at the Zoo. And you realized that God created the hippopotamus too! So what was there left for you to be surprised at? The hippopotamus is a fact. Just like the man who gets hold of little girls and then kills them. He's a fact too. And then there's the whore. She's a fact too. It's her job in life to be a whore. And there's the man who throws you out on to the streets. And then there's the flies. *Flies!*'

She sets the candle and the fruit down on the chest of drawers. Then her eyes wander across the room till they settle on the other group of people that's looking in through the window to see what she's doing. Irritated, she runs over to the window.

'God, look! They're even over here, with their noses glued to the window-pane!'

The moment she opens the window they make their escape. She sticks her head out through the window and shouts after them:

'Yes, it's me! It's me all right! Yes, it's me! I know. I'm a slut, aren't I? I'll corrupt everybody, won't I? But can you tell me why you're so much better than me, eh? I suppose it's because you stay at home and sell the stuff wholesale! Sell it by the length! While I hawk the stuff round the streets and sell it by the yard! What do you expect? You can still have a good time, seeing how you like the feel of the stuff. That's it—thumb and finger—feel it! I don't feel anything at all now. As far as I'm concerned it's all bankrupt. Just bankrupt stock! Go on, get up those stairs! Go on, up you go! You never know—you might be the next one to slide down . . . down . . . down. . . . Cheer up, love! We came in here this morning, arm in arm. Together, death and dishonour! Yes, dears! *Dis—hon—our!* My! My! Just look at her face! Coo! Dear, dear! Wait a minute, love! I'll throw you an apple!'

She takes a red apple from off the chest of drawers and draws her arm back, in readiness to throw the apple to the girl whom, a short while before, she had pushed out of the room.

'Running away? Don't you want it? Oh, in that case I'll eat it myself.'

She sinks her teeth in the apple and closes the window. Immediately she has done so she puts her fingers to her nose and pinches it.

'Pooh! Pooh! This place stinks to high heaven of soap and water! It's like a wash-house!'

She looks at her father's body stretched out on the bed.

'Yes, I'm having something to eat! Yes, I'm having something to eat! And you hope it chokes me! I haven't had a bite to eat since yesterday morning! Those hands of yours—look at them now! They won't do any moving now, will they? They've given me some hard knocks in their time, haven't they? And you even spat in my face! And grabbed me by the hair! And kicked me all around the room, you were so flaming mad! "What are you trying to do, girl?" I already knew more about things than you can learn from a holy picture stuck up over the bed! And now those hands of yours are like this. Crossed on your chest. And as cold as ice.'

She goes over and shakes her mother by the shoulder. 'Get up,

Mamma! You haven't had anything to eat since yesterday morning either! You must eat something!'

Suddenly the doubt assails her that they've diddled her in giving her her change. She starts working out what she's spent.

'Four and eight. Twelve. And five. That makes seventeen. Wait a minute! What else did I buy? Oh, yes. There's the fruit I got from that old fool! He was selling little birds in bunches. All tied together by string threaded through holes in their beaks. He just flung the fruit at me, the swine. Didn't even notice I was carrying a candle.'

She gives a little jump as she remembers.

'Oh, yes! The candle!'

She goes and fetches it from off the chest of drawers and unwraps it.

'Just so as people can't say we didn't light one for you.'

She takes the iron candlestick from off the night-table.

'Let's hope it'll stand up in this thing.'

She fixes the candle into the holder.

'Coo! Look, might have been made to measure!'

There is a box of matches on the night-table. She lights the candle and sets it down on the table.

'Just burn away. And drip, drip, drip. Lovely life! Like virgins. They just burn away and drip!

'Can't you see? No. Neither can the wooden saints, stuck up there over the altar! But we can see them. All lit up. And down on our knees we go. It all comes down to faith—the whole business of candle-making depends on the faithful being faithful! And now we're all busy believing that you're busy enjoying it all up there! But you can't let us see you are, can you? Poor devil! Get up, Mum! Oh! We'd better get him dressed before he starts going stiff on us! Yes! Go on, cry away! Cry your eyes out! You look as though you're dead yourself, sprawled out there like that! Now we'd better get on with this quick! It was lucky for us they were expecting him to die! They want to have everything out of here before it starts getting dark. And at four o'clock they'll be coming from the Chapel of Mercy. That won't even leave time for the candle to burn right down.'

She looks at the lighted candle, then raises her eyes to the Crucifix hanging on the wall.

'Oh! Better put him with his hands round the Crucifix!'

She goes over to the other side of the bed, pulls a chair up, gets onto it and takes down the Crucifix. She holds it in her hands for a moment or so.

'Oh, Christ! And the poor make haste to come unto You. . . . You did it on purpose! Which of us would have the nerve to come complaining to You about how life's treating us? Come moaning to You about how everybody's doing this to him and doing that to him? You, who, though You were without sin, suffered them to nail You upon the Cross. With Your arms flung wide open. You, the Christ! You, the hope that we enjoy when we get to Heaven! Yes! You. The flame that burns from this tuppenny candle.'

She leaps off the chair and puts the Crucifix between the fingers of the dead man, saying to her mother,

'Now, look! You'd better get moving! His fingers are quite stiff already. You won't be able to dress him now. You'll have to slit his jacket down the back and slip it on both arms separately. Do it in two bits. Aren't you going to budge? Don't you want to? Are you going to stick there until they come and grab you by the arm and sling you out of the door? Oh, well! All right! Now you watch me!'

She grabs hold of the chair and sits down on it.

'I'm going to settle down and wait too! I'll stick here till the dustman comes with his broom and shovel and chucks me on the dustcart. Blessed are they that even think of moving. Happy lot. Even if they only think of moving from one side of the room to the other. Even if all they can manage to do is to think of lifting a bite of something up to their lips! Still, when all's said and done, if you really get down to rock bottom, you're right, you know! When you've got nothing left that you want to do everything gets done by itself. They come in; they grab hold of you by the arm and shove you up on to your feet. You start toppling over. . . . Oh, don't worry, though! If they don't want you for anything, they don't give you time to topple over and bang yourself. They give you a kick up the backside. Or else they give you a hefty shove. And out into the street you go—*sprawling*. All your old rags, the bed, body and all. The chest of drawers. All out in the middle of the street. Roll up! Roll up! Come along and take anything you fancy! And there you are, sprawling in the gutter. You. Looking just like you're looking now sprawling on that bed. And everybody standing around gawking at you. Up comes a policeman, "Move along there! No sleeping in the street!" "Then where can I sleep?" "Come on, get moving! Move along there!" You stay where you are. You don't move along. You're not afraid. Then, if you're really stubborn about it—— Then somebody takes it into his head to make you move. You've still got the right—since you haven't got a home—to have some place whereon to lay your head. Yes—you can rest it on the ground. On the kerbstone. Just like a puppet that's been stuck there—so! On one of the steps leading up to the church; on a park bench. Up rush the little boys and girls! Yes, it's Granny! "What did you say, darling? Puffer-trains? I don't know what you mean, dear. Oh, you want me to play puffer-trains with you. Mummy doesn't want me to. Well then, you'd better go and look at the fish in the pond. Yes, they're goldfish. . . ." Uh—huh! Praise be to God! Then you settle down. Hold out your hand like this, and a passer-by throws you a ha'penny and a crust of bread. But, not for me! Oh, no! Nothing like that for me! Pooh!' She spits. 'That's what I think of that for a notion! If it was me, I wouldn't stick out my hand and beg. . . . Oh, no! I'd stick it out so as I could scratch! And steal! And kill! And then—— Oh, yes! Then I'd end up in gaol. Board and lodging free!'

Enraged, she gets up and goes over and says to her father,

'I'm taking this opportunity of getting my own back on you for all the wallops you gave me! You can't hear me now, so I can really let you have it! You didn't even try to understand, did you? You never even so much as tried to understand how—without knowing you've done so, and when you least think you're likely to be; how it happens that you're taken by a man. Even while you're crying your eyes out in utter despair. . . . Because your body—— Suddenly he's touched you—there wasn't any special meaning in that touch—but your body suddenly feels an all-pervading sweet tenderness and you're tingling with life, even in the very midst of all your despair and desperation. With a rush you find yourself blazing into a living torch of joy. Everything around you is consumed. You no longer see anything at all. You're in a blind, intoxicated, desperate frenzy! You're lost in a world of delight such as you'd never dreamt was possible! That's how it happened. That's how it happened. Here—in this room. You left me here with him. Your nephew. His wife had been having an affair with another man. He was sitting here; on the very bed you're lying on now, crying his heart out. I took his head, like this, so as to try and comfort him. He started to rave about how—— Oh, dear! Then he buried his head between my breasts. Felt my breasts. Oh, yes! Yes! How can a woman help feeling joy when a man does that? I didn't make myself the kind of woman that finds such a deep delight in holding a man's head to her breast! It was God that made me what I am! The blood started to race faster in our veins. Passion seized us both. And then, afterwards. . . . Just like you, he lay stretched out there on the bed, like a dead man. Filled with terror and dismay at having taken my body. And then the miserable bastard went back home to his wife—all nice and consoled! And do you know what he said? He said that he'd learnt from what I'd done that there's no such thing as a chaste and virtuous woman! They're all the same, he said. In fact, they're no better than men. They're all made of the same flesh and blood, all lusting after the flesh. And so, said he, there's no reason why—if men are allowed to do it as often as they like—there's no reason why we should write a woman off as a dead loss if she does it once. "After all, you had your fun too, didn't you?" Miserable bastard! And what about the baby? But it's a bit different for me. . . . Oh yes, Dad! You're dead now and I forgive you. But if I'm damned like I am, it's all your fault! You all gang up together, you men, to condemn a woman! You're all the same! You cease to be the woman's father, or her brothers. No, as a matter of fact, instead of pleading for her, you're the most ferocious against her! And the most ferocious of them all was you! You flung me out into the street like a bitch. But listen! I wiped the tears away from my eyes. I wiped the spit off my face. And I offered myself to the first man that came along! The *street* . . . ! And all the rage I felt! The passionate longing I felt to throw in your face the shame that you hadn't wanted to keep hidden from the world! But then there was the baby. . . . The baby. It's not true what they say! It's true afterwards—after it's—but not before. It's absolutely terrifying, feeling it inside you! And then, when he's born. . . . Yes, it's true after he's born. This tiny little creature, nuzzling his way in, trying to find you. I came here and left him with you when he was eight months old. One night, I came and left him here, behind the door, in the box with all his baby clothes. They ought still to be here, those things of his. Or have you sold them? Thank you, God, for taking him to Yourself when he was so tiny! Come on! Come on! Let's get him dressed!'

She goes over and opens the wardrobe. She takes out a brown suit that's hanging on a clothes-hanger, and turns to her mother and says,

'He used to sing him to sleep, didn't he? Every night he used to sing him to sleep, with that song—how did it go . . . ? The one you used to sing to me when I was a little girl. Somebody came and told me—— It was one night when it was raining—came and told me how he'd heard him from the courtyard, singing to the baby. And then. . . . Then he wanted to—to—— Do you understand? After telling me *that*!'

She looks at her father's suit, which she's still holding. She examines it carefully.

'Oh, this suit's still in good condition! You might almost . . . Yes. . . . In any case, if he's already appeared before God up in Heaven . . . why should he worry about the people that are coming to collect him in a few minutes? Why should he worry about what sort of suit he's got on to meet *them*? And you, sprawled out there like that! You'll be pretty hard up. There's some other stuff here; you might try and get something for it from the old-clothes man! Are you listening? We'd better make it up into a bundle! There's probably some stuff in the chest of drawers. . . .'

She goes over to the chest of drawers, opens the top drawer and rummages inside—nothing but rags. She opens the next drawer—

nothing at all. She opens the third drawer—inside are all the baby's clothes.

'Oh, this is where they are!'

She looks at them. She sinks down onto the ground. She takes out one of the garments. A rolled-up swaddling band, a little vest, a baby's bib. Then, last of all, she takes out a baby's bonnet. She clenches her fist and puts it into the hood of the bonnet, and, just as if she were cradling a baby in her arms, she begins to hum, in a faraway kind of voice, the old song that her mother used to sing. And while she sings, gradually the room gets darker and darker until, with all other lights completely extinguished, nothing is to be seen but the flame of the candle.

Silence.

# THE VISIT

*Visita* belongs to the group of stories written at the end of Pirandello's career. There is a remarkable resurgence of his powers as a writer in this medium during the nineteen-thirties, and in 1935 and 1936 he produced some of his finest *novelle*. *Visita* was first published in the *Corriere della sera* for 16 June 1935 and subsequently included in the last (and posthumous) volume of the *Novelle per un anno* (Vol. XV, *Una giornata,* Milano-Verona, Mondadori, 1937.) *Una giornata* now forms part of the Biblioteca Moderna Mondadori. The definitive text of *Visita* is in Vol. II of the *Opere*. (*Novelle per un anno,* Vol. II, Milano-Verona, Mondadori, 1957.)

# THE VISIT

If I'd told him once, I must have told him a hundred times not to let people into the house without first coming to tell me. It was a lady. A fine excuse!

'Did she say her name was Wheil?'

'Yes, sir, *Vile*. At least, that's what it sounded like.'

'Mrs. Wheil died yesterday, in Florence.'

'She says there's something she has to remind you about.'

Now I must confess that I no longer know whether I dreamt all this, or whether this exchange of words between myself and my manservant did in fact take place. He's let innumerable people into my house without first coming to tell me, but that he should, on this particular occasion, have gone so far as to let in a dead woman. . . . Well, it seems quite incredible to me. It's all the more incredible, because I had in fact seen her in a dream. Mrs. Wheil, I mean. And still looking so very young and beautiful. I'd only just woken up when I read the news of her death in Florence in the newspaper. I remember falling asleep again, and I saw her in a dream, all smiling and covered with confusion. You see, she hadn't known how to set about covering herself up. She was wrapped in a white cloud, the kind you get on a spring day, and it was gradually becoming more and more wispy, until finally it was so transparent that you could see the whole rosy nakedness of her body. It was especially wilful in revealing that very part of her body which modesty demanded should remain hidden. (She kept on tugging at it with her hand—but how on earth can you draw together such an immaterial thing as a fold of cloud?)

My study is so situated that it's got garden on both sides. There are five huge windows, three down one side, two down the other.

The former, which are larger than the others, are bow-windows, the latter glass-doored, and opening on to a lake of sunshine out there on the balcony, which has a south aspect. All five of them have blue silk curtains which never stop fluttering. But the light in the room is green, because of the trees that grow out there.

There's a large upholstered settee with its back to the middle window. This is green, too, but a lighter shade—*sea*-green. And it's perfectly delightful just to abandon yourself to the joy of that room—I almost said *immerse yourself in it*—what with all that green and blue, all that light and air.

When I enter the room I'm still carrying in my hand the newspaper containing the news of Mrs. Wheil's death yesterday, in Florence. There can be not the slightest possible doubt about my having read it. Here it is—in print. But here too, sitting on the settee, waiting for me, is Mrs. Wheil. Yes, the lovely Anna Wheil in person. It's possible, of course—oh, yes!—that this is not in fact true. I shouldn't be in the least surprised, for I've been accustomed for some time to seeing such apparitions. Or perhaps it's the other way round—— I mean, there's very little to choose between the two propositions. That's to say, the news of her death, that's printed here in the newspaper, isn't true.

Here she is, dressed as she was three years ago, in a white organdie summer dress, very simple, almost little-girlish, though very low-cut and revealing a great deal of her breasts. (I see: *that's* why there was that cloud in my dream.) On her head is a large straw hat, with broad black silk ribbons, which are tied in a knot under her chin. Her eyes are lowered a little in sheer self-defence against the dazzling light that's pouring in through the two vast windows immediately facing her. But later—and this is very strange—she deliberately leans her head back, so as to let me see the full beauty of the wonderful, gentle sweep of her throat, the loveliness of her neck, as it rises from the warm pure whiteness of her breast, and passes on to the exquisitely pure curve of her chin.

It's as she strikes this attitude (and there can be no doubt that she wanted to strike it), that everything becomes very clear. The 'something' that Anna Wheil has to remind me about is all summed up there—in the gentle sweep of that throat, in the pure whiteness of that breast. And it all came to me in an instant, one of those instants of time that is transformed into an eternity, and that annihilates everything—even life, even death—plunging it into the suspended world of a divine intoxication. In this world, there suddenly leap out of the realm of mystery, once and for all, the *essential* things of life, quite unambiguous, and brilliantly highlit.

I hardly know her. (Since she's dead, I ought to say, 'I hardly *knew* her'; but she's here now, as if caught in the absolute state of an eternal present, so I can say, 'I hardly *know* her.') I only saw her the once, at a garden-party in the grounds of a villa belonging to friends we had in common. She'd come wearing this white organdie dress.

That morning, in our friends' garden, the younger and more beautiful of the women had been radiant and alive with passion—that passion which surges to life in every woman when she knows the joy of feeling herself desired. They'd let themselves be swept into the whirl of the dance, and then, with a smile that was calculated to kindle desire to fever pitch, they'd gazed so intently at their partners' lips as irresistibly to tempt them to kiss them. It was spring, of course, with all its moments of rapture, and the glorious warmth of the first real sunshine of the year—oh, how intoxicating it is!—when the air is still redolent with a vague ferment of subtle perfumes, and the splendour of the fresh green world that spreads like a lake through the meadows and glistens with exciting vivacity on all the trees around. Strange luminous threads of sound enfold us; sudden bursts of light dazzle our senses. Moments of flight that are like lightning flashes; and a wonderful giddiness that invades our happy senses. Then the sweetness of life no longer seems true, so completely is it made up of everything and nothing; no truer, and no more to be taken into account, when later you come to remember all that was said and done. Later—when the shadows have fallen again and that sun is extinguished. Yes, I know you kissed me. Yes, I know I promised you I'd—— But it was only—well, you could hardly call it a *kiss*. . . . Just on my hair. As we were dancing. And the promise I—

well, it was—yes, it was only a joke. I'll say I didn't notice that you were kissing me. I'll tell him, 'You must be out of your mind if you think I meant what I said. Or that I'm going to keep that promise!'

We can be quite sure that nothing of all this happened to the lovely Mrs. Anna Wheil, whose own particular kind of attractiveness seemed to everyone so serene, so remote, that nothing even faintly resembling carnal desire would have dared to raise its head in her presence. I'd be willing to wager, however, that she looked on the immense respect they all showed her with an ambiguous and pungent smile glinting in her eye, though not because she didn't feel that she deserved it. No, quite the contrary, it was because no one let her see that he desired her as a woman, simply because of all that respect he still felt compelled to show her. Her smile was, perhaps, one of envy or jealousy; or, it may be, of contempt, or melancholy touched with irony. It might even have expressed all these things at one and the same time.

This was something I suddenly perceived. I'd been watching her for some little time, while all the dances and games had been going on—she'd taken part in them too—and it came to me in a flash. Later on she'd even taken part in mad races over the lawns with the children—perhaps to give her a chance to work things out of her system. I was with our hostess at the time, and she'd decided she must introduce me to her. There she was, still bending down, putting the children's clothes to rights, and tidying their dishevelled hair. Getting up suddenly like this to return my 'How d'you do?' Mrs. Anna Wheil, quite forgetting how very low-cut it was, didn't think for the moment of rearranging the top of her organdie dress. So I just couldn't help getting a glimpse of rather more of her breasts than in all propriety I ought to have done. It was only an instant. She immediately raised her hand to pull her dress back into place. But from the way in which she looked at me, as she made that would-be surreptitious gesture, I realized that she wasn't in the least displeased with me for my involuntary and almost inevitable indiscretion. That joyous light in her eye glinted with quite a different kind of radiance from previously. It was radiant with an almost mad ecstasy of gratitude, because in my eyes there shone, without the faintest hint of that 'respect', so pure a gratitude for what I had glimpsed, that all sensation of concupiscence was completely excluded. Shiningly manifest was what I saw as the supreme reward—that joy which the love of a woman like her, so completely lovely as she was, with all the treasures of a divine nakedness with such modest haste covered up, could bring a man who had learned how to be worthy of her.

All this my eyes, still radiant with that flash of admiration, told her very plainly. And in that instant I became the only Man for her, the only real man, among all those who were in that garden; at the same time she appeared to me as the only Woman, the only real woman among all those other women. We couldn't bear to be separated from one another during all the rest of the time that that party went on. But apart from this tacit understanding, which lasted only an instant, but forever, there was nothing more between us. No exchange of words, except the usual commonplaces—about how lovely the garden was, what a jolly party it was, how charmingly hospitable our friends-in-common were. But, even talking like this, of things casual and quite remote from us, there remained in her eyes that glint of happy laughter, which seemed to bubble up like living water from the secret depths of that understanding of ours, and to rejoice—without heeding the stones and grass through which it now scurried. One of these stones was a husband, into whom we bumped shortly after, as we turned the corner in one of the paths. She introduced me to him. I raised my eyes for an instant and looked into her eyes. The slightest blink of an eyelid veiled that glint of joyous light, and with that gesture alone that lovely lady confided in me that he, that good worthy husband of hers, had never for one moment so much as dreamt of understanding what *I* had understood in an instant. And this was no laughing matter! Oh, no! In fact, it was her mortal affliction, because if there was one thing that was quite certain, it was that a woman like her would never belong to any other man. It didn't matter, however. It was quite sufficient that one man at least had understood her.

No, no, I mustn't do it. Not even without intending to. We were alone again, the two of us, walking on, talking away. But I mustn't let my gaze fall on her breast again, and force her surreptitiously to make sure that I couldn't again be indiscreet. It would have been very wrong now, both for me to persist in acting so, and for her again to take delight in it. We'd already come to an understanding. That must suffice. It was no longer a question of us two. It was no longer a question of trying to find out, or to know, or to get a glimpse of what her body looked like. . . . Oh, yes, she was so wholly beautiful! As she herself alone knew herself to be. There would have been so many other things to consider, things that concerned me. Above all, there was this consideration: that, well, to put it mildly, I ought to be twenty years younger, at least, if I was to have anything to do with her. A great melancholy came upon me, and I was filled with useless regret. No, no! It was a beautiful thing that had been revealed to us, amidst all that sunlit splendour, when spring laughed so gloriously around us. It should fill us with the purest joy. For what had been revealed to us was the essential thing here on earth—in all the naked radiant whiteness of her flesh, in the midst of all the green richness of an earthly paradise—the body of woman, given by God to man as the supreme reward for all his pain, all his anxieties, all his labours.

'If it was only a question of you and me, dear. . . .'

I turned. What was that? She'd called me 'dear'! But the lovely Mrs. Anna Wheil had disappeared.

She's beside me now, here in the green light which fills my study, dressed as she was three years ago, in her white organdie frock.

'My breasts! Oh, if only you knew! My breasts killed me. They removed them. A terrible disease viciously attacked them. Twice. The first time was little more than a year after you—— It was there, at those friends of ours—do you remember? That time you caught a glimpse of them? Now I can open the front of my dress with both hands and show you everything, just as it was! Look at them! Look at my breasts! Now that I'm dead.'

I look, but on the settee all that's to be seen is the white patch of the open newspaper.

# THE TORTOISE

*La tartaruga* is among the last stories written by Pirandello. First published in *La lettura* for August 1936, it was subsequently included in the final (and posthumous) volume of the *Novelle per un anno.* (Vol. XV, *Una giornata,* Milano-Verona, Mondadori, 1937.) *Una giornata* now forms part of the Biblioteca Moderna Mondadori, and *La tartaruga* is published in the definitive text in Vol. II of the *Opere.* (*Novelle per un anno,* Vol. II, Milano-Verona, Mondadori, 1957.)

# THE TORTOISE

STRANGE as it may seem, even in America there are people who believe that tortoises are lucky. Nobody has the faintest idea how such a belief came into existence. What's quite certain, however, is that they—the tortoises, I mean—show no sign of having the slightest suspicion that they enjoy this power.

Mr. Myshkow has a friend who's a firm believer in this quality of theirs. He speculates on the Stock Exchange and every morning, before he goes off to do a hard day's gambling, he puts his tortoise down in front of a little flight of steps. If the tortoise makes it obvious that he wants to climb up them, he's quite convinced that the stocks he's thinking of gambling on will rise in value. If it tucks its head and paws in, then they'll remain steady. If it turns away and starts moving off, then he unhesitatingly acts on the assumption that they're going to slump. And he's never once been wrong.

Having said which, he goes into a shop where they sell tortoises, buys one, and places it in Mr. Myshkow's hand. 'Now make your fortune,' he says.

Mr. Myshkow's a very sensitive plant. As he carries the tortoise home, he shudders, 'Ugh! Ugh!' His sturdy, full-blooded springy little body is trembling all over. Maybe it's pleasure he's shuddering with; maybe there's a touch of the horrors too. It's not that he's worried in the least about the way passers-by are turning and looking at him, carrying that tortoise in his hand. No, he's trembling at the thought that what looks like a cold inert stone, *isn't* a stone at all. No, it's inhabited on the inside by a mysterious little animal that's quite capable at any moment of popping out its little wrinkled old nun's head and plonking its four rough skew-whiff paws on to his hand. Let's hope it won't do anything of the sort. Heaven knows what might happen! Why, shuddering from head to foot, Mr. Myshkow might throw it on the ground!

When he gets home. . . . Well, you wouldn't exactly say his two children, Helen and John, went into raptures over the tortoise the instant they caught sight of it—when, that is, he put it down on the carpet in the drawing-room, looking for all the world like an overgrown pebble.

It's quite incredible how *old* the eyes of these two children of Mr. Myshkow look, compared with *his* eyes, which are so extraordinarily childlike.

The two children let the unbearable weight of the four leaden eyes fall on that tortoise, placed there like an overgrown pebble on the carpet. Then they look at their father, with so great a conviction that he won't be able to give them a plausible explanation of why he's done this unheard of thing—putting a tortoise on the drawing-room carpet, indeed!—that poor Mr. Myshkow suddenly feels himself shrivelling up. He spreads out his hands in an appealing gesture. He opens his mouth in an empty smile and says that, well, after all, it's only a harmless little tortoise. And you can even —if you want to, that is—you can even *play* with it.

And like the good-hearted fellow that he is—he's always been a bit of an overgrown schoolboy—he's determined to prove it to them. He throws himself down on his hands and knees on the carpet and cautiously, and with the utmost consideration, he prods the tortoise in the rear in an attempt to persuade it to pop its paws and head out and to get moving. Good gracious, yes, little tortoise, you must—if only so that you can see what a lovely cheerful house I've brought you into—all glass and mirrors. He's quite unprepared for what John does. Suddenly and unceremoniously the boy hits upon a much more immediately successful expedient for getting the tortoise to emerge from that stone-like state in which it's so stubbornly determined to remain. With the toe of his shoe he turns it over onto its shell, and immediately we see the little creature lash out with its little paws and painfully thrust about with its head in an attempt to get itself back into its natural position.

Helen watches all this happen and then, without her eyes becoming any the less old-looking, sniggers. It's like the noise a rusty pulley makes as the bucket hurtles madly down into the depths of a well.

As you'll have observed, there's no respect on the part of the children for the good luck that tortoises are supposed to bring you. On the contrary, they have made it blindingly clear to us that both of them tolerate its presence only on condition that it allows itself to be considered by them as an extremely stupid toy to be treated thus—that's to say, kicked about with the toe of your shoe. Mr. Myshkow finds this very saddening. He looks at the tortoise, which he's immediately put right way up again, and which has now resumed its stone-like state. He looks into the eyes of his children, and is suddenly made aware of a mysterious relationship between the agedness of those eyes and the centuries old stone-like inertia of the animal on the carpet, and he's profoundly disturbed. He's utterly dismayed because he is so incurably youthful in a world which gives such obvious proof of its decrepitude by embracing such far-fetched and unexpected relationships. It dismays him that, without realizing what's happening, he may perhaps be left to await something which may never again happen, since children, now, here on earth, are born centenarians like tortoises.

Once more his mouth opens in an empty smile—it's feebler than ever this time—and he hasn't got the courage to admit why his friend made him a present of that tortoise.

Mr. Myshkow enjoys a pretty rare ignorance of life. As far as he's concerned, life's never really been very clear-cut; nor is he greatly burdened with any real weight of knowledge. Why, it can quite well happen to him too. Yes, one fine morning—just as he's got one leg raised preparatory to getting into the bath—he'll suddenly catch sight of his naked body. There he'll stand, just like that, strangely affected by the sight of his own body, for all the world as if, in the forty-two years he's lived through, he's never set eyes on it before, and is now discovering it for the first time. Good grief, it's not a very presentable body, is it? All naked like that! I mean, you feel thoroughly ashamed about the whole thing, even when it's you yourself that's looking at it. He prefers to know nothing at all about it himself. He makes a considerable song and dance about this fact, however: that he's done all this thinking with this particular body, even if it does look the way it does in one or two places that nobody usually gets a peep at—the bits that have remained hidden under his suit and his socks for the forty-two years he's been a member of this world. It seems quite incredible to him that he's lived all his life in that body of his. No! No! Well then, where have you been living? Go on, where have you been living, without being the slightest bit aware of where you were? Perhaps he's been flying about overhead all the time flitting from body to body, choosing them from among the many shapes that have fallen to his lot since he was a child, because—— Oh no, his body certainly hasn't always been this one! But Heaven only knows what it's been at other times! It really does dishearten him. Yes, it hurts him not to be able to explain to himself why his own body has necessarily to be the one that it is, and not another quite different one. Best not to think about it. And in the bath he starts smiling again that empty smile of his, quite unmindful of the fact that he's been in the bath some considerable time now. Ah, those muslin curtains across the panes of the big window! Look how they seem to catch and reflect the light! Over the top of the brass curtain rods he glimpses the graceful, slight waving-to-and-fro of the tops of the trees in the park as the spring air catches them. Now he's drying that ugly body of his. Oh, it really *is*! Nonetheless, however, he's forced to agree that life is very beautiful, and wholly to be enjoyed, even in that hideous body of his which has, in the period since those childhood days—Heaven only knows how!—contrived to enter into the most secret intimacy with a woman as impenetrable as Mrs. Myshkow his wife.

For the whole nine years that he's been married, it's as if he's been wrapped up—somehow suspended—in the mysterious world of that highly improbable union with Mrs. Myshkow.

He's never dared to take one single step without being left in an agony of doubt, after he's taken it, as to whether he might dare to take another. So he's always experienced a kind of apprehensive wriggling throughout his whole body, and a kind of dismay in his soul, at suddenly finding himself so far from his starting-point, as a result of those halting steps she's allowed him to take. Should he or should he not infer that he was entitled, therefore, to take them?

So it was, one fine day, that he found himself the husband of Mrs. Myshkow, almost without being quite sure that he was.

She, even after nine years, is still so detached and isolated from everything, in her own porcelain statue beauty, so enclosed, so enamelled, as you might say, in a mode of life so impenetrably her own, that it seems absolutely impossible that she's found a way of uniting herself in marriage with a man so carnal and full-blooded as he is. On the other hand, it's only too comprehensible how, from their union, those two withered children have been born. Perhaps, if Mr. Myshkow had been able to carry them in *his* womb, instead of relying on his wife's, they wouldn't have been born like that. But she had to carry them in her womb, nine months for each of them, and so, conceived, in all probability, in their entirety right from the very beginning, they'd been compelled to remain shut up there for the proper length of time in that majolica belly, like sugared almonds in a box. Well, that's the reason why they'd become so tremendously ancient, even before they were born.

Naturally, for the whole nine years that they've been married, he's lived in constant terror lest Mrs. Myshkow should seize upon some thoughtlessly uttered word of his, some unforeseen gesture, and use it as a pretext for demanding a divorce. The first day of their marriage was the most terrible of all for him because, as you can easily imagine, he'd got as far as that without being at all sure that Mrs. Myshkow knew what he had to do before he could effectively call himself her husband. Luckily, she did know. Afterwards, however, she'd never given him the slightest hint that she remembered the consideration and tenderness he'd put into his wooing and taking her that night. It was just as if he hadn't contributed anything at all to making it possible for him to take her; as if there were no tender memories for her to recall. Still, a first child, Helen, had been born. Then a second, John. And never a flicker of tender remembrance from her. Without the remotest sign of emotion on either occasion, she'd gone away both times to the maternity home, and then, a month and a half later, she'd come back home, the first time with a little girl, the second time with a little boy—this second baby even older than the first. It was enough to make you throw up your hands in despair. She'd absolutely forbidden him, both times, to go and visit her in the maternity home. As a result, having failed completely, both the first and the second time, to observe that she was pregnant, and not knowing anything afterwards about either the labour pains or the pains attending the birth itself, he'd found himself in the house with two small children who were rather like puppies you'd bought on a trip. There wasn't any real certainty that they'd been born of her body and that they really belonged to him.

But Mr. Myshkow hasn't the slightest doubt that they are his. In fact he sees in those two children one of the most ancient and time-honoured of proofs—confirmed twice over, what's more!—that Mrs. Myshkow finds in living with him adequate recompense for the agony that bringing those two children into the world must have cost her.

That's why he's completely bowled over when his wife acts in the way she does. She's just come back in from visiting her mother, who's arrived in New York and who's staying for a day or two at an hotel, prior to leaving for England. Finding him still down on his knees on the drawing-room carpet, amidst the cold, coarse derision of those two children of his, she doesn't say a word. Or, to put it more precisely, by simply turning her back on him without a word, and returning immediately to the hotel where her mother's staying, she says everything. About an hour later she sends him round a note. Peremptorily she tells him that either that tortoise gets out of the house, or she's leaving him. She'll be leaving, three days from now, for England, with her mother.

As soon as he's gathered his wits sufficiently to be able to think straight again, Mr. Myshkow realizes that the tortoise can really be nothing but a pretext. And so trivial a pretext, too. Good grief! It's so easily dealt with! And yet, you know, just because it is so easily dealt with it may, perhaps, be much more difficult to get round it than if his wife had made it a condition of their remaining together that he should change his body, or, if he couldn't manage that, to remove that nose from his face and replace it with another that better pleased her taste.

He has no desire, however, that the marriage should fail because of him. In his reply to his wife he tells her that it's quite safe for her to return home. He'll go and dump the tortoise somewhere.

He doesn't care in the slightest whether it remains in the house. He only accepted it because they told him that tortoises were lucky. But—well, when you think how comfortably off he is, with a wife like her, and children like theirs, what need has he got of lucky mascots and things like that? What greater good fortune could he possibly desire?

He goes out, tortoise in hand once again, to dump it in some place more appropriate to the cross-grained little creature than his house. It's evening now, and he's only just become aware of the fact. He's lost in amazement. Accustomed though he is to the phantasmagoric sight of that enormous city in which he lives, he still sees it with fresh eyes every time he looks at it. He's still astounded (and made a little melancholy, too) when he thinks of all those prodigious buildings, and of how they're refused the right to impose themselves on the world as enduring monuments, and are forced just to stand there, like colossal and provisional appearances of reality in some immense Fair, with their multi-coloured, flashing advertising signs reaching into the distance and conjuring up a world of infinite sadness. He's sad, too, as he thinks of so many other things which are equally precarious and mutable.

As he walks along he forgets that he's got the tortoise in his hand. Then he remembers it and reflects that he'd have done better to have left it in the park near his home. Instead, he's set off in the direction of the shop where it was bought. At the bottom of 49th Street, if he remembers correctly.

He continues on his way, although quite convinced in his own mind that, at that time of night, he'll find the shop shut. It's as if, in some odd way, not only his sadness but his tiredness, too, makes him feel a positive need to go and bang his head against that closed door.

When he reaches the shop he stands looking at the door. Yes, the shop's well and truly shut. Then he looks at the tortoise in his hand. What's he to do with it? Leave it there on the doorstep? He hears a taxi coming along the street and gets into it. After it's gone a little way, he'll get out, leaving the tortoise inside.

What a pity the little creature, still lurking away inside its shell like that, shows no sign of having a highly-developed imagination.

It would be pleasant to think of a tortoise travelling all round the streets of New York by night.

No. No. Mr. Myshkow repents his intention, as if it were something cruel he'd thought of. He gets out of the taxi. He's near Park Avenue by this time, with its interminable chain of flower-beds down the middle, and its low, hooped railings. He thinks he'll leave the tortoise in one of those flower-beds, but he's hardly put the creature down before a policeman pounces on him—the one who's on traffic duty at the intersection with 50th Street, under the gigantic tower of the Waldorf-Astoria. The policeman wants to know what he's put in the flower-bed. A bomb? Well, no. Not exactly a bomb. And Mr. Myshkow gives him a reassuring smile, just to prove to him how incapable he'd be of doing such a thing. Only a tortoise. The policeman orders him to retrieve it immediately. 'Animals may not be introduced into the flower-beds. By Order!' But surely that doesn't apply to this animal? Mr. Myshkow tries to coax him into agreeing that it's more of a stone than an animal. Surely he doesn't really think it could cause any trouble! What's more—*for serious family reasons*—he simply must get rid of it. The policeman thinks he's trying to take the mickey out of him and turns nasty. Whereupon Mr. Myshkow immediately retrieves the tortoise from the flower-bed. It hasn't budged an inch.

'They tell me they're lucky,' he adds with a smile. 'Wouldn't *you* like to take it? Here you are—it's all yours!'

The policeman shakes himself furiously and imperiously gestures to him to get the hell out of here.

So here once again is Mr. Myshkow, with the tortoise in his hand and in a state of considerable embarrassment. Oh dear, if only he could leave it *somewhere,* even in the middle of the road, just so long as it was out of sight of that policeman who'd looked on him with so unfavourable an eye—obviously because he hadn't believed in those serious family reasons. Suddenly an idea flashes into his mind. Yes, this business about the tortoise is unquestionably a pretext on his wife's part, and, if he gets past her this time, she'll immediately find some other excuse. It'll be difficult, however, to find one more ridiculous than this one, and for it still to provide her with sufficient cause for complaint in the eyes of the judge and of the whole world and his wife. It would be foolish, therefore, to let this opportunity slip. There and then he decides to go back home with the tortoise.

He finds his wife in the drawing-room. Without saying a word to her he bends down and puts the tortoise on the carpet in front of her. It looks just like an overgrown pebble.

His wife leaps to her feet, rushes into the bedroom, and reappears with her hat on.

'I shall tell the judge that you prefer the company of that tortoise to that of your wife!'

And out she sweeps.

It's just as if that little creature down there on the carpet had understood every word she'd said. It suddenly unsheathes its four little paws, its tail and its head, and, swaying from side to side—you'd almost swear it was dancing—moves about the drawing-room.

Mr. Myshkow can scarcely refrain from rejoicing—but only rather half-heartedly. He applauds very quietly. He gets the feeling, as he looks at the tortoise, that it's telling him something. Only he's . . . well, he's not really convinced that . . .

'I'm in luck! I'm in luck!'

## A DAY GOES BY

*Una giornata* was first published less than three months before Pirandello's death—in the *Corriere della sera* for 24 September 1936. It was then reprinted in the last (and posthumous) volume of the *Novelle per un anno.* (Vol. XV, *Una giornata,* Milano-Verona, Mondadori, 1937.) The book is now part of the Biblioteca Moderna Mondadori, and the definitive text of the story is in Vol. II of the *Opere.* (*Novelle per un anno,* Vol. II, Milano-Verona, Mondadori, 1957.)

# A DAY GOES BY

RUDELY awakened from sleep—perhaps by mistake—I find myself thrown out of the train at a station along the line. It's night time. I've got nothing with me.

I can't get over my bewilderment. But what strikes me most forcibly is that nowhere on myself can I find any sign of the violence I've suffered. Not only this. I have no picture in my mind of its happening, not even the shadow of a memory.

I find myself on the ground, alone, in the shadowy darkness of a deserted station, and I don't know who it is I ought to ask, if I'm to find out where I am and what's happened to me.

I only got a quick glimpse of a small bull's-eye lantern which rushed forward to close the carriage-door through which I'd been ejected. The train had left immediately. And that lamp had immediately disappeared again into the inside of the station, its wobbling, flickering light struggling fruitlessly with the blackness. I was so utterly astounded by everything that it hadn't so much as passed through my mind that I might rush after it to demand an explanation and lodge my formal complaint.

But, formal complaint about *what*?

With boundless dismay I perceive that I no longer have the faintest memory of having started off on a journey by train. I haven't the slightest memory of where I started from, or where I was going to. Or if, on leaving, I really had anything with me. I had nothing, I think.

In the emptiness of this horrible uncertainty, I'm suddenly seized with terror at that spectral lantern which had immediately retreated from the scene, without paying the slightest attention to my being ejected from the train. Am I to deduce that it's the most natural thing in the world for people to get out at this station in that particular way?

In the darkness I have no luck with my attempts to decipher the name of the station. The town, however, is quite definitely one I don't know. In the first grey, feeble rays of the rising sun it looks deserted. In the vast pale square in front of the station there's a street lamp still alight. I move over to it. I stop and, not daring to raise my eyes—so terrified am I by the echo roused by my footsteps in the silence—I look at my hands, I look at the fronts, I look at the backs. I clench them, I open them again. I tap and prod myself with them, I feel myself all over. I even work out how I'm made, because I can't even be certain of this any longer—that I really exist and that all this is true.

Shortly afterwards, as I penetrate farther and farther into the city centre, at every step I see things that would bring me to a standstill with utter amazement, if an even greater amazement didn't overcome me. I observe that all the other people—they all look like me, too—are moving along, weaving in and out past one another, without paying one another the slightest attention; as if, so far as they're concerned, this is the most natural and usual thing in the world for them to do. I feel as if I were being drawn along—but, here again, without getting the sensation that anyone's using violence on me. It's just that I, within myself, ignorant of everything as I am—well, it's as if I were being held somehow on every side. But I consider that, even if I don't even know how, or whence, or why I've come there, *I* must be in the wrong, and the others must quite assuredly be in the right. Not only do they seem to know this, but they also know everything that makes them sure that they never make a mistake. They're without the slightest hesitancy, so naturally convinced are they that they must do what they're doing. So I'd certainly attract their wonder, their apprehension, perhaps even their indignation if, either because of the way they look or because of some action or expression of theirs, I started laughing or showed how utterly astounded I was. In my acute desire to find out something, without making myself look conspicuous, I have continually to obliterate from my eyes that something akin to irritability which you quite often see fleetingly in dogs' eyes. I'm in the wrong—I'm the one who's in the wrong, if I don't understand a thing, if I still can't succeed in pulling myself together again. I must make an effort and pretend that I too am quite convinced. I must contrive to act like the others, however much I'm lacking in all criteria by which to appraise, and any practical notion even of those things which seem most commonplace and easy.

I don't know in which role to re-establish myself, which path to take, or what to start doing.

Is it possible, however, that I've grown as big as I have, yet remained all the time like a child, without ever having done anything? Perhaps it's only been in a dream that I've worked. I don't know how. But I certainly *have* worked. I've always worked, worked very hard, very hard indeed. It looks as if everyone knows it, moreover, because lots and lots of people turn round and look at me, and more than one of them even goes so far as to wave to me. I don't know them, though. At first I just stand there, looking perplexed, wondering if that wave was really meant for me. I look to either side of me. I look behind me. Were they, possibly, waving to me by mistake? No, no, they really were waving to me. I struggle (in some embarrassment) with a certain vanity, which would dearly like me to deceive myself. It doesn't succeed, though. I move on as if I were suspended in mid-air, without being able to free myself from a strange sense of oppression which derives from something that is—and I recognize it as such—really quite wretched. I'm not at all sure about the suit I've got on. It seems odd that it should be mine. And now I've got a suspicion that it's this suit they're waving at and not me. And, just to make things really troublesome, I haven't got anything else with me except this suit!

I start feeling about myself again. I get a surprise. I can feel something like a small leather wallet tucked away in the breast-pocket of the jacket. I fish it out, practically certain in my own mind that it doesn't belong to me but to this suit that isn't mine. It really is a small leather wallet, a faded yellow in colour—with a washed-out look about it, as if it had fallen into a stream or down a well and then been fished out of the water again. I open it—or rather, I unstick two bits of it that have got stuck together—and look inside. Buried among a few folded sheets of paper, which the water has rendered illegible by staining them and making the ink run, I find a small holy picture—the sort they give children in church. It's all yellowed with age, and attached to it there's a photograph, almost of the same format and just as faded as it is. I detach it and study it. Oh! It's the photograph of a beautiful young woman in a bathing costume. She's almost naked. The wind is blowing strongly through her hair, and her arms are raised in a vivacious gesture of greeting. As I gaze at her—admiringly, yet with a certain feeling of pain (I don't know quite how to describe it, it's as if it came from far, far away)—I sense, coming from her, the impression, if not exactly the certainty, that the greeting waved by those arms is directed at me. But, no matter how hard I try, I can't recognize her. Is it even remotely possible that so lovely a woman as she can have slipped my memory? Perhaps she's been carried away by all that wind which is ruffling her hair. One thing's quite definite: in that leather wallet, which at some time in the past fell into the water, this picture, side by side with the holy picture, is in the place where you put your fiancée's photograph.

I resume my rummaging through the envelope and, more disconcerted than pleased—because I'm very doubtful about whether it belongs to me—I find a huge banknote tucked away in a secret hiding-place. Heaven only knows how long ago it was put there and forgotten. It's folded in four, all worn with use and here and there on the back it's so cracked by folds that it's positively threadbare.

Unprovided as I am with anything, can I provide myself with a little help by using it? I don't know with quite what strength of conviction, but the woman portrayed in that little photograph assures me that the banknote's mine. But can you really trust a charming little head like that, so ruffled by the wind? It's already past midday. I'm dropping with weariness. I must have something to eat. I go into a restaurant.

To my amazement I find myself greeted like an honoured guest. I'm obviously most welcome. I'm shown to a table that's already laid, a chair is drawn aside and I'm invited to take a seat. A scruple holds me back, however. I signal to the proprietor and, drawing him to one side, I show him the huge threadbare banknote. He gazes at it in utter astonishment. He examines it, filled with compassion for the condition to which it's been reduced. Then he tells me that it's undoubtedly of great value, but that it's one of a series which was withdrawn from circulation some time ago. I'm not to worry, however. If it's presented at the bank by someone as important and respectable as myself, it will certainly be accepted and changed into notes of smaller denomination which are currently legal tender.

Saying this, the proprietor of the restaurant accompanies me to the door and out on to the pavement, where he points out the nearby building that houses the bank.

I go in, and everyone in the bank is just as happy to do me this favour. That banknote of mine, they tell me, is one of the very few of that series not yet returned to the bank. For some time now, in this part of the country, they've no longer been putting into circulation notes other than those of minute size. They give me masses and masses of them, so that I feel embarrassed, even oppressed by them. I've only got that shipwrecked leather wallet with me. But they urge me not to let myself get worried. There's a remedy for everything. I can leave that money of mine in the bank, in a current account. I pretend I've understood. I put some of the notes in my pocket, together with the passbook which they give me in return for all the rest that I'm leaving behind, and go back to the restaurant. I can't find any food there to my taste. I'm afraid of not being able to digest it. But already the rumour must have got about that, if I'm not exactly rich, I'm certainly not poor any longer. And, in fact, as I come out of the restaurant, I find a car waiting for me, accompanied by a chauffeur who raises his cap to me with one hand, while with the other he holds the door open for me to get in. I don't know where he takes me. But since I've got a motor-car, it's obvious that, without knowing it, I must have a house. Why yes, a very lovely house. It's an old house, where quite obviously lots of people have lived before me, and lots more will live after me. Is this furniture really mine? I somehow feel myself to be a stranger here, a kind of intruder. Just as this morning at dawn the city seemed deserted, now this house of mine seems deserted. I again feel frightened at hearing the echo of my footsteps, as I move through that immense silence.

In winter, evening's soon upon you. I'm cold and I feel tired. I buck up my ideas, however, and start moving about. I open one of the doors, quite at random, and stand there in utter amazement, when I see that the room's ablaze with light. It's the bedroom, and there on the bed . . . There she is! The young woman in the photograph, alive, and with her two bare arms still raised in the air, but this time they're inviting me to hasten over to her so that she may welcome me and joyously clasp me in them.

Is it a dream?

Well, this much is quite certain: just as would happen in a dream, when the night has passed and dawn has ushered in the morning, she's no longer there in that bed. There's no trace of her. And the bed which was so warm during the night, is now, when you touch it, freezing cold, just like a tomb. And the whole house is filled with that smell which lurks in places where dust has settled, where life has been withered away by time. And there's that sensation of irritated tiredness which needs well-regulated and useful habits, simply in order to maintain itself in being. I've always had a horror of them. I want to run away. It's quite impossible that this is my house. This is a nightmare. It's quite obvious that I've dreamt one of the most absurd dreams ever dreamt. And as if seeking proof of this, I go and look at myself in a mirror that's hanging on the wall opposite, and instantly I get the terrible feeling that I'm drowning. I'm terrified, lost in a world of never-ending dismay. From what remote distance are my eyes—those eyes which, so it seems to me, I've had since I was a child—now looking wide-eyed with terror at this old man's face, without being able to convince myself of the truth of what I'm seeing? What, am I old already? So suddenly! Just like that! How is it possible?

I hear a knock at the door. My heart turns over. They tell me my children have arrived.

My *children*?

It seems utterly frightful to me that children should have been born to me. But when? I must have had them yesterday. Yesterday I was still young. It's only right and proper that I should know them, now that I'm old.

They come in, leading several small children by the hand—*their* children. They immediately rush over and tell me to lean on them. Lovingly they reprove me for having got up out of bed. Very solicitously they make me sit down, so that I shan't feel so weary. Me, weary? Why yes, they know perfectly well that I can't stand on my feet any longer and that I'm in a really bad way.

Seated there, I look at them, I listen to them. And I get the feeling that they're playing a joke on me in a dream.

Has my life already come to an end?

And while I sit there looking at them, all bent so solicitously over me, I mischievously observe—almost as if I really ought not to be noticing it—right under my very eyes, I can see, sprouting there on their heads . . . Yes, there's a considerable number of white hairs growing there. Yes, white hair's growing there on their heads.

'There, that proves it's all a joke. *You've* got white hair too.'

And look, look at those young people who came through that door just now as tiny children. Look? All they had to do was to come up to my armchair. They've grown up. One of them—yes, that one—is already a charming young lady. She wants the rest of them to make way for her so that she can come and be admired. If her father hadn't grabbed hold of her she'd have thrown herself at me, climbed up on to my knees, put her arm round my neck, and rested her little head on my breast.

I feel the urge to leap to my feet. But I have to admit that I really can't manage it any more. And with the same childlike eyes that a little while before those children had—oh, how grown-up they are now!—I sit there, looking at my old children, standing behind these new ones, and there is great compassion in my gaze.

# SELECT BIBLIOGRAPHY

THE bibliography of Pirandello is vast. It is not easy to discard any publication on him, for many trivial articles contain a piece of information about his life or his work, or an arresting comment, not available elsewhere. Only in the last few years have we had anything like a systematic study of him, either as a man or as an artist. My choice here is of a few recent books which I have found valuable as comprehensive appraisals, a few older works which tried with considerable success to 'place' him while he was still writing and even more controversial than many people find him even today, together with one or two essays (old and new) which, in their examination of an aspect of his *opera,* illuminate all that he achieved. Since critics have stressed his career as a playwright, some of the books I mention will be primarily concerned with this side of his work. Fundamental now is Giudice's book; I mark it with an asterisk, as I do other studies I most recommend.

## THE LIST


Giovanna Abete, *Il vero volto di Luigi Pirandello*. Roma, A.B.E.T.E. 1961.

*Corrado Alvaro, 'Prefazione' to Vol. I of the *Novelle per un anno*. Milano-Verona, Mondadori. 1956. (He also contributed an excellent article to the *Enciclopedia italiana*.)

Luigi Baccolo, *Luigi Pirandello*. Torino, Bocca. 1949. (This is the 2nd edn. of a discriminating short assessment.)

*Sandro D'Amico, edited a group of 'Lettere ai famigliari' in *Terzo programma,* n. 3, 1961; and the first of the *Quaderni del Piccolo Teatro*. Milano, 1961 : *Pirandello ieri e oggi*.

*Arcangelo Leone de Castris, *Storia di Pirandello*. Bari, Laterza. 1962. (May's review: 'Quando stavamo là . . .', *Italian Quarterly,* Vol. VI, Nos. 23–24, Fall-Winter, 1962, pp. 90–94.)

*Gaspare Giudice, *Luigi Pirandello*. Torino, U.T.E.T. 1963.

Arminio Janner, *Luigi Pirandello*. Firenze, La nuova Italia. 1948.

Frances Keene, 'Introduction' to the Lily Duplaix translations. New York, Simon and Schuster. 1959 (with a paperback edn., 1960).

Federico Vittore Nardelli, *L'uomo segreto*. Milano-Verona, Mondadori. 1944. (This is the 2nd edn.—with little change.)

Ferdinando Pasini, *Luigi Pirandello (come mi pare)*. Trieste, La vedetta italiana. 1927.

Luigi Russo, *Il noviziato letterario di Luigi Pirandello*. Pisa, Il paesaggio. 1947.

'Pirandello e la provincia metafisica.' Melfagor, XV. 1960, pp. 389–401.

*Leonardo Sciascia, 'Pirandello' in his *Pirandello e la Sicilia*. Caltanissetta-Roma, Sciascia. 1961, pp. 7–124.

Walter Starkie, *Luigi Pirandello*. London, Murray. 1937. (The 2nd edn., considerably revised.)

Aldo Vallone, *Profilo di Pirandello*. Roma, Edizioni di *Dialoghi*. 1962. (A brisk survey, translated from his earlier Spanish text.)

Domenico Vittorini, *The Drama of Luigi Pirandello*. New York, Dover. 1957. (The 2nd edn., with some useful material in appendix.)

J. H. Whitfield, in his *Short History of Italian Literature*. London, Penguin, 1960, is acute and stimulating in his comments on Pirandello.

Nella Zoja, *Luigi Pirandello*. Brescia, Morcelliana. 1948.

Vallone, on pp. 124–5, notes several bibliographies which may be utilized (Fucilla, Prezzolini, and so on). Comments by Croce and Gramsci may be pursued, whil Lo Vecchio-Musti, Mignosi, and Tilgher can still yield something.

# PIRANDELLO'S STORIES IN CHRONOLOGICAL ORDER

THE following list, which must be regarded as in many ways tentative, is substantially that published by Manlio Lo Vecchio-Musti in *L'opera di Luigi Pirandello* (Torino, Paravia, 1939, pp. 268–70). The stories are grouped according to the known or probable year of composition. Where a title is printed in italics, the date is conjectural. The numbers against those stories which have been put into English correspond with the series adopted in the note given later (*Translations of the Short Stories*), together with the sequence used for the previously untranslated tales in the present volume. The stories are referred to by their *final* titles.

## THE LIST

1884. (92) Capannetta.

1894. (93) I galletti del bottaio. La signorina. L'onda. L'amica delle mogli. (60) *Concorso per referendario al Consiglio di Stato.*

1895. In corpore vili. (54) Il 'no' di Anna. Dialoghi I: Nostra moglie. *Pallottoline.*

1896. (31) Sole e ombra. Chi fu? Visitare gl'infermi. (90) Sogno di Natale.

1897. (94) Le dodici lettere. Dialoghi II: L'accordo. (95) La paura. Le tre carissime. Vexilla Regis . . . Il giardinetto lassú. Acqua e lí.

1898. La scelta. Se . . . Padron Dio.

1899. (4) Dono della Vergine Maria. (29) La maestrina Boccarmè.

1900. (37) Lumíe di Sicilia. Prima notte. Le levata del sole. *Un' altra allodola.* (30) *Un invito a tavola.* (73) *Scialle nero.* Alberi cittadini.

1901. Nenia. Prudenza. Notizie del mondo. Il vecchio Dio. (84) Con altri occhi. (85) E due! (91) Marsina stretta. Lontano. Gioventú. *La paura del sonno.* (88) *Quand'ero matto. Il valor civile.* (55) Il 'fumo'.

1902. La berretta di Padova. (25) Il figlio cambiato. Tanino e Tanotto. Alla zappa! (83) Amicissimi. (10) Il corvo di Mizzaro. Come gemelle. (14) *Il vitalizio. La signora Speranza.*

1903. Il marito di mia moglie. (8) La balia. Il ventaglino. (16) Il tabernacolo. La disdetta di Pitagora. (58) *Formalità.*

1904. Nel segno. (82) Le veglia. Sua Maestà. (41) La buon'anima. (49) Le medaglie. Una voce. (22) La mosca. (62) La fedeltà del cane. Fuoco alla paglia.

1905. (48) L'eresia catara. (1) L'altro figlio. Senza malizia. (39) La casa del Granella. Tirocinio. Pallino e Mimí. (19) Va bene. Le sorprese della scienza. (50) Acqua amara. In silenzio. (66) *Lo scaldino. Il sonno del vecchio.*

1906. L'uscita del vedovo. Tutto per bene. La toccatina. Tra due ombre.

1907. Dal naso al cielo. (26) Un cavallo nella luna. Volare. (78) La cassa riposta. (15) La vita nuda.

1908. La guardaroba dell'eloquenza. (45) Due letti a due. (59) *Di guardia. Il dovere del medico.*

1909. Stefano Giogli, uno e due. Difesa del Meola. Mondo di carta. (3) La giara. L'illustre estinto. (35) Il lume dell'altra casa. (69) L'ombrello. (11) Non è una cosa seria. (40) *Distrazione. Pari.*

1910. L'uccello impagliato. Musica vecchia. (23) Benedizione. (2) Pensaci, Giacomino! Il professor Terremoto. (24) Lo spirito maligno. (56) La lega disciolta. Leviamoci questo pensiero. (79) Lo storno e l'Angelo Centuno. Leonora, addio! (27) Il viaggio. (12) La morta e la viva. Paura d'esser felice. *Ignare.*

1911. Felicità. Zafferanetta. L'uomo solo. La patente. I fortunati. (21) Il libretto rosso. (38) La tragedia d'un personaggio. 'Ho tante cose da dirvi. . . .' (7) Canta l'Epistola. (5) *Richiamo all'obbligo.*

1912. I nostri ricordi. Risposta. L'avemaria di Bobbio. (42) Certi obblighi. Nenè e Niní. La trappola. Superior stabat lupus. Il coppo. (43) La verità. Notte. Maestro Amore. (57) Chi la paga. (33) L'imbecille. Tu ridi. I due compari. Ciàula scopre la luna. *Nel dubbio.* (75) *La corona.* (9) *La liberazione del re.*

1913. Il bottone della palandrana. La veste lunga. Requiem aeternam dona eis, Domine! La vendetta del cane. Quando s'è capito il giuoco. Tutt'e tre. (70) L'abito nuovo. (96) Nel gorgo. (20) La Madonnina. Male di luna. (13) La rallegrata. Rondone e Rondinella. Da se. (34) Il capretto nero. I pensionati della memoria. *I tre pensieri della sbiobbina.* (72) *Candelora. L'ombra del rimorso.*

1914. Il treno ha fischiato . . . Zia Mivhelina. Sopra e sotto. (63) Filo d'aria. Un matrimonio ideale. (80) Un ritratto. (17) Servitú. Berecche e la guerra. La realtà del sogno. (71) La rosa. *O di uno o di nessuno. Visto che non piove. . . .* Mentre il cuore soffriva. Zuccarello, distinto melodista. (81) La fede.

1915. Colloqui coi personaggi I e II. Il signore della nave. (76) *Nell'albergo è morto un tale. Romolo. La mano del malato povero.* (46) *La signora Frola e il signor Ponza, suo genero.*

1916. La camera in attesa. Piuma. (86) Donna Mimma. *La carriola. Frammento di cronaca di Marco Leccio.*

1917. (28) Il gatto, un cardellino e le stelle.

1918. La maschera dimenticata. (6) La cattura. (47) *Quando si comprende.* (97) *La morte addosso.* (32) *Un 'goj'.*

1919. (64) Ieri e oggi. (89) Il pipistrello.

1920. (74) Pena di vivere cosí.

1921. (98) La distruzione dell'uomo. (18) *Rimedio: la geografia.*

1922. *Niente.*

1923. (65) Fuga. (77) Ritorno. (36) Un po' di vino.

1924. (61) Resti mortali. Sedile sotto un vecchio cipresso.

1926. (99) Pubertà. *Guardando una stampa.*

1927. (87) *Spunta un giorno.*

1931. Uno di piú. Soffio.

1932. Lucilla. (68) Cinci.

1933. (100) Sgombero.

1934. (67) I piedi sull'erba. Di sera, un geranio. Un'idea. C'è qualcuno che ride.

1935. (101) Visita. (51) La prova. La casa dell'agonia. Fortuna d'esser cavallo. Una sfida.

1936. Il chiodo. Vittoria delle formiche. (52) La tartaruga. (53) Una giornata. Effetti d'un sogno interrotto. (44) Il buon cuore.

# THE COLLECTIONS OF THE SHORT STORIES

I LIST the volumes in chronological order, departing from Lo Vecchio-Musti's arrangement by placing revised volumes and reconstituted volumes, not with the parent work, but in the place determined by date of issue. *Quand'ero matto . . .* is a case in point: the Streglio gathering of 1902 is related to the book of the same name put out by Treves in 1919, but is differently made up.

## THE LIST

1. *Amori senza amore,* Roma, Bontempelli. 1894.
2. *Beffe della morte e della vita,* Firenze, Lumachi. 1902.
3. *Quand'ero matto . . . ,* Torino, Streglio. 1902. (See also No. 16.)
4. *Beffe della morte e della vita,* 2a serie, Firenze, Lumachi. 1903.
5. *Bianche e nere,* Torino, Streglio. 1904. (See also No. 12.)
6. *Erma bifronte,* Milano, Treves. 1906.
7. *La vita nuda,* Milano, Treves. 1910.
8. *Terzetti,* Milano, Treves. 1912.
9. *Le due maschere,* Firenze, Quattrini. 1914. (See also No. 19.)
10. *La trappola,* Milano, Treves. 1915.
11. *Erba del nostro orto,* Milano, Studio editoriale lombardo.[1] 1915. (See also No. 18.)
12. *Il turno* [*e*] *Lontano,* Milano, Treves. 1915. ('Lontano' is one of the *novelle* originally included in *Bianche e nere*—No. 5.)
13. *E domani, lunedì . . . ,* Milano, Treves. 1917. (This volume is of especial interest, in that it includes 'All'uscita', a play—which would seem to underline the interpenetration of Pirandello's *novelle* and his works in dramatic form.)
14. *Un cavallo nella luna,* Milano, Treves. 1918.

[1] Later Facchi. (cf. No. 18.)

15. *Berecche e la guerra,* Milano, Facchi. 1919.
16. *Quand'ero matto . . .*, Milano, Treves. 1919. (A reconstruction of No. 3.)
17. *Il carnevale dei morti,* Firenze, Battistelli. 1919. (See also No. 33.)
18. *Erba del nostro orto,* Milano, Facchi. 1919.[1] (See also No. 11.)
19. *Tu ridi,* Milano, Treves. 1920. (A reconstruction of No. 9.)

We now come to the series of the *Novelle per un anno,* which is broken into only by No. 33.

20. Vol. I, *Scialle nero,* Firenze, Bemporad. 1922.
21. Vol. II, *La vita nuda,* Firenze, Bemporad. 1922. (A slightly reconstructed version of No. 7.)
22. Vol. III, *La rallegrata,* Firenze, Bemporad. 1922.
23. Vol. IV, *L'uomo solo,* Firenze, Bemporad. 1922.
24. Vol. V, *La mosca,* Firenze, Bemporad. 1923.
25. Vol. VI, *In silenzio,* Firenze, Bemporad. 1923.
26. Vol. VII, *Tutt'e tre,* Firenze, Bemporad. 1924.
27. Vol. VIII, *Dal naso al cielo,* Firenze, Bemporad. 1925.
28. Vol. IX, *Donna Mimma,* Firenze, Bemporad. 1925. (No. 14 reconstructed.)
29. Vol. X, *Il vecchio Dio,* Firenze, Bemporad. 1926. (Nos. 3 and 16 recast.)
30. Vol. XI, *La giara,* Firenze, Bemporad. 1928.
31. Vol. XII, *Il viaggio,* Firenze, Bemporad. 1928.
32. Vol. XIII, *Candelora,* Firenze, Bemporad. 1928. (No. 13 recast.)
33. *Il carnevale dei morti,* Venezia, La nuova Italia. 1928. (A reissue of No. 17, with a new title-page and new covers.)
34. *Novelle per un anno,* Vol. XIV, *Berecche e la guerra,* Milano-Verona, Mondadori. 1934.
35. Vol. XV, *Una giornata,* Milano-Verona, Mondadori. 1937.

[1] Pirandello told Scott Moncrieff that this 2nd edition was never actually published. (See Luigi Pirandello, *Shoot!* translated by C. K. Scott Moncrieff, London, Chatto and Windus, 1927, p. 356.)

36. *Novelle per un anno,* Omnibus edition, Vol. I, Milano-Verona, Mondadori. 1937. (Contains Vols. I–VIII of the Bemporad series.)
37. *Novelle per un anno,* Omnibus edition, Vol. II, Milano-Verona, Mondadori. 1938. (Contains Vols. IX–XV of the Bemporad-Mondadori series, together with 21 added stories recovered from earlier volumes, periodicals, and Pirandello's papers.)

In preparation for this Omnibus edition Pirandello had started work on a major revision of the stories, but he had completed hardly a third of what he had to do when he died. Angelo Sodini provides an appendix containing the principal variants.

The work of evolving a critical edition of the *novelle* has only just begun. Pirandello left a number of indications of revisions he would wish to make. Unfortunately, he also failed to note how errors had escaped him in earlier editions, and been transmitted from text to text.[1] (The plays also exhibit some oddities of this kind, nortoriously *Enrico IV*, with its persistent 1071—instead of 1077—for the date of Canossa.)

The *novelle* have been reprinted many times, but until we have the critical edition, no re-publication is of bibliographical importance. In my list I have omitted almost all reprints and 'new editions'. Those I have left in are bibliographical oddities. For the rest, the situation is so confused that to reprint the evidence already published would be as misleading as it is unnecessary. The gaps are many and much turns on detail. For instance, Lo Vecchio-Musti is silent about the peculiar circumstance that some copies at least of the first text of *Quand'ero matto* . . . (see Nos. 3 and 16) are dated 1902 on the title-page, but 1903 on the cover. Again, what is one to make of a copy of *Il turno* [*e*] *Lontano* (see No. 12) which is described on both cover and title-page as '1915—Secondo migliaio' when, according to Scott Moncrieff,[2] the second thousand belongs to 1919?

A problem of a different kind, and one not yet completely

[1] See Luigi Pirandello, *Novelle per un anno,* Vol. II, Milano-Verona, Mondadori, 1957, p. 1177.

[2] Op. cit., p. 342.

investigated, is that of status. For the purposes of No. 12 *(Il turno [e] Lontano), Il turno* is a *novella*—some 195 pages long. According to the list of works 'Dello stesso Autore' given on p. [2] of *Bianche e nere* (No. 5), it was a novel when published originally by Giannotta of Catania in 1902.[1] It was certainly a novel once more by 1932, when Mondadori put out a new edition. Conversely, *Pena di vivere così,* which was first published in *Il nuovo romanzo mensile* for 15 December 1920 and enjoyed (in theory,[2] if not ascertainably in practice) a separate existence as a novel, turns up as a short story in Vol. VI—*In silenzio*—of the Bemporad series of the *Novelle per un anno* (see No. 25). That Pirandello finally saw it as a short story seems a fair conclusion, since he was revising it for the Omnibus edition of the *novelle* when he died.

Everyone interested in Pirandello owes an enormous debt to Manlio Lo Vecchio-Musti for what he has done towards the creation of a check-list of his works. We are not at the stage, however, where we must attempt to transform this list into a comprehensive bibliography. One thing is certain: it is never likely to be complete. Pirandello kept few records, though fortunately others have recorded what he told them about his career as a writer. Further to bedevil our investigation he had a habit of contributing works and parts of works to occasional publications—typical is his allowing *La cattura*[3] to be included in *Italian Activities of the Inter-Mountain Region* (as the cover has it; the title-page reads: *Attività italiane nella Intermountain Region,* International Publishing Company, Salt Lake City, Utah, [1930]; *La cattura* appears on pp. 247–56). Such texts not only give us an insight into the processes of diffusion of Pirandello's work—and its impact on expatriate Italians is a major topic which (like the interest in Verga of earlier Sicilio-Americans) has yet to be studied —but may even be important in establishing the genealogies of the *stesure.*

The bibliography of Pirandello in translation is in its babyhood. For instance, the section devoted to Germany, Austria, and

[1] Or was it 1901? See Scott Moncrieff, op. cit., p. 341.
[2] See Scott Moncrieff, op. cit., p. 345.
[3] See A(6) on p. 243.

Switzerland in the Lo Vecchio-Musti bibliography,[1] does not include two translations which, according to Pirandello's own notes, were made and paid for in 1904.[2] Again, is Nardelli correct in saying that *Il fu Mattia Pascal* appeared in instalments in the *Echo de Paris*,[3] when Lo Vecchio-Musti has no record of such a publication?[4] Certain areas are understandably rather sketchily mapped—post-war Russia, Poland, Hungary, and Bulgaria come to mind—but even here concern with Pirandello has continued or revived. Significant is the publication in Moscow in 1958 of a volume containing thirty-seven short stories by Pirandello.[5]

We can well begin at home, with the English and American versions. In offering my list of the translations of the short stories (pp. 242–51) I feel how probationary it is. If we think of the many departments of Pirandello's work, we can—*must*—only be cheered by the prospect of what needs to be done, and what may be discovered or reappraised.[6]

[1] *Saggi, poesie, scritti varii*, ed. cit., pp. 1305–12.
[2] Op. cit., p. 1206.
[3] Federico Vittore Nardelli, *L'uomo segreto*, Milano-Verona, Mondadori, 1932, p. 164. (The page reference is the same for the 2nd, slightly supplemented, edition of 1944.)
[4] Op. cit., p. 1302, is where one would expect to find it.
[5] Новеллы. Переводы с итальянского.
[6] There is, for instance, Pirandello's review of the New York presentation of Shaw's *St. Joan*. Originally published in the *New York Times* for 13 January 1924 it will shortly be reprinted in the *Shavian*, with annotations by Frederick May. Noted by Vittorini (*The Drama of Luigi Pirandello*, New York, Dover, 1957, p. 349) is the article he wrote for the *Fortnightly Review* on 'Tendencies of the Modern Novel'. As Vittorini listed it under criticism *of* Pirandello, it seems to have mystified his bibliographer, who excludes it from the list of the critical articles. The article appeared in Vol. CXXXV (n.s.), April 1934, pp. 433–40, and has been reprinted (with an introduction and notes by Frederick May) in *Italian Quarterly*, February 1963. The brief comment on Moravia has special interest now.

# TRANSLATIONS OF THE SHORT STORIES

THE following list has, of necessity, no claim to finality. It is highly provisional: until very lately no systematic record has been kept of translations into English of Pirandello's short stories; and only during the last few years has any serious attempt been made to trace the early versions. When Manlio Lo Vecchio-Musti revised the Pirandello bibliography in 1960, I was able to supplement his previous entries under this head. (All references to Lo Vecchio-Musti in this list imply: *'Bibliografia', a cura di* Manlio Lo Vecchio-Musti, in Luigi Pirandello, *Opere,* Vol. VI, *Saggi, poesie, scritti varii,* Milano-Verona, Mondadori, 1960, pp. 1251–346.) I now add about thirty further items, but I would emphasize that I have still to complete my search through English and American periodicals, in which there may well be dozens of translations yet to be noted.

The volumes of stories are listed first in sequence of publication and then in chronological order, the stories published separately, either in periodicals or in anthologies. Each story is numbered, so that it may be traced through the various renderings. As far as possible I have followed the general style of the entries in Manlio Lo Vecchio-Musti's bibliography, so as to facilitate reference to that work. I have, however, revised the order in which he listed the stories in the volumes where it conflicts with the actual order. Throughout this list items marked with an * have not been seen by F.M., but are quoted on the authority of Lo Vecchio-Musti. The description of each item is as complete as possible. Since, on occasion, I have had to work from microfilm or from secondary sources, uniformity has been unattainable.

## Collections

### A. *Better Think Twice About It!*

*Translations by* Arthur and Henrie Mayne. London, John Lane, 1933; 2nd edit., 1940*: New York, Dutton, 1st printing, 1934; 2nd printing, 1934*; 3rd printing, 1935. *The volume contains versions of:* (1) L'altro figlio. (2) Pensaci, Giacomino! (3) La Giara. (4) Dono della Vergine Maria. (5) Richiamo all'obbligo. (6) La cattura. (7) Canta L'Epistola. (8) La balia. (9) La liberazione del re. (10) Il corvo di Mizzaro. (11) Non è una cosa seria. (12) La morta e la viva. (13) La rallegrata.

*The English titles are:* (1) The Other Son. (2) Better Think Twice About It! (3) The Jar. (4) The Madonna's Gift. (5) A Call to Duty. (6) The Captive. (7) Chants the Epistle. (8) The Wet-Nurse. (9) The King Set Free. (10) The Crow of Mizzaro. (11) It's Nothing Serious. (12) The Quick and the Dead. (13) Black Horses.

### B. *The Naked Truth*

*Translations by* Arthur and Henrie Mayne. London, John Lane, 1934;* 2nd edit., 1940;* 3rd edit., 1947: New York, Dutton, 1934.* *The volume contains versions of:* (14) Il vitalizio. (15) La vita nuda. (16) Il tabernacolo. (17) Servitú. (18) Rimedio: la geografia. (19) Va bene. (20) La Madonnina. (21) Il libretto rosso. (22) La mosca. (23) Benedizione. (24) Lo spirito maligno. (25) Il figlio cambiato.

*The English titles are:* (14) The Annuity. (15) The Naked Truth. (16) The Wayside Shrine. (17) The Spirit of Service. (18) The Rivers of Lapland. (19) Va Bene. (20) The Wax Madonna. (21) The Red Booklet. (22) The Fly. (23) The Benediction. (24) The Evil Spirit. (25) The Changeling.

### C. *Horse in the Moon*

*Translations by* Samuel Putnam. New York, Dutton, 1st printing,* 1932; 2nd printing, 1932. *The volume contains versions of:* (26) Un cavallo nella luna. (27) Il viaggio. (28) Il gatto, un cardellino e le stelle. (29) La maestrina Boccarmè. (30) Un invito a tavola.

(31) Sole e ombra. (32) Un 'goj'. (33) L'imbecille. (34) Il capretto nero. (35) Il lume dell'altra casa. (36) Un po'di vino. (37) Lumíe di Sicilia.

*The English titles are:* (26) Horse in the Moon. (27) Adriana Takes a Trip. (28) A Cat, a Goldfinch and the Stars. (29) The Schoolmistress's Romance. (30) A Dinner Guest. (31) Sunlight and Shadow. (32) Goy. (33) The Imbecile. (34) Miss Holloway's Goat. (35) The Light Across the Way. (36) A Wee Sma' Drop. (37) Sicilian Limes.

### D. *A Character in Distress*

*Translations by* [Michele Pettinati].[1] London, Duckworth, 1938. (The American edition is entitled: *The Medals,** New York, Dutton, 1939.) *The volume contains versions of:* (38) La tragedia d'un personaggio. (34) Il capretto nero. (39) La casa del Granella. (40) Distrazione. (41) La buon'anima. (42) Certi obblighi. (43) La verità. (44) Il buon cuore. (45) Due letti a due. (46) La signora Frola e il signor Ponza, suo genero. (47) Quando si comprende. (37) Lumíe di Sicilia. (48) L'eresia catara. (49) Le medaglie. (50) Acqua amara. (28) Il gatto, un cardellino e le stelle. (51) La prova. (52) La tartaruga. (53) Una giornata.

*The English titles are:* (38) A Character in Distress. (34) The Beauty and the Beast. (39) The Haunted House. (40) An Oversight. (41) The Husband's Revenge. (42) A Wronged Husband. (43) Sicilian Honour. (44) Mother. (45) A Widow's Dilemma. (46) A Mother-in-Law. (47) War. (37) Sicilian Tangerines. (48) Professor Lamis' Vengeance. (49) His Medals. (50) Bitter Waters. (28) A Cat, A Finch and the Stars. (51) When a Bear went to Church. (52) Tortoises . . . For Luck. (53) My Last Journey.

### E. *Short Stories*

*Translations by* Lily Duplaix. New York, Simon and Schuster, 1959. Paperback edition, 1960. *The volume contains versions of:*

[1] The translator's name is not given in the Duckworth text, and from the entry in the Catalogue of the Library of Congress I deduce that it is also missing from the Dutton volume. Lo Vecchio-Musti attributes the versions to Michele Pettina. My evidence is that they are by Michele Pettinati.

(54) Il 'no' di Anna. (55) Il 'fumo'. (56) La lega disciolta. (57) Chi la paga. (58) Formalità. (59) Di guardia. (60) Concorso per referendario al Consiglio di Stata. (61) Resti mortali. (62) La fedeltà del cane. (63) Filo d'aria. (64) Ieri e oggi. (65) Fuga. (66) Lo scaldino. (67) I piedi sull'erba. (68) Cinci. (69) L'ombrello. (70) L'abito nuovo. (71) La rosa. (72) Candelora. (73) Scialle nero. (74) Pena di vivere cosí. (75) La corona.

*The English titles are:* (54) Lost and Found. (55) Fumes. (56) Bombolo. (57) Who Pays the Piper. . . . (58) A Mere Formality. (59) Watch and Ward. (60) The Examination. (61) Mortal Remains. (62) Man's Best Friend. (63) A Breath of Air. (64) Yesterday and Today. (65) Escape. (66) The Footwarmer. (67) The Soft Touch of Grass. (68) Cinci. (69) The Umbrella. (70) The New Suit. (71) The Rose. (72) Candelora. (73) The Black Shawl. (74) Such is Life. (75) The Wreath.

## F. *Quattro Novelle*

*Translations by* V. M. Jeffrey [Violet M. Saunders] of four stories, with the original Italian texts on facing pages. Published London, Harrap, [1939];[1] November, 1942;[2] February, 1943;[3] December, 1943; January, 1944;[3] 1945;[3] June, 1948;[4] February, 1953;[4] July, 1957;[4] May, 1960. *The stories included are:* (76) Nell'albergo è morto un tale. (35) Il lume dell'altra casa. (46) La signora Frola e il signor Ponza, suo genero. (37) Lumíe di Sicilia.

*The English titles are:* (76) Someone's Died in the Hotel. (35) The Light from the House Opposite. (46) Mrs. Frola and her Son-in-Law, Mr. Ponza. (37) Limes from Sicily.

[1] Undated. The year of publication is assumed by the Catalogue of the British Museum Library. *ECB* quotes as July 1939. *CBI* prefers 1938. Lo Vecchio-Musti opts for 1939. On p. [2] of the December 1943 text, the first edition is assigned to November 1942. This, I think, refers to a rearranged reprinting of the 1939 text. On p. 2 of the issue of 1960, we are told 'First published in Great Britain June 1939'.

[2] Not seen by F.M. Information taken from p. [2] of the December 1943 text.

[3] Given by Lo Vecchio-Musti. No confirmation in 1960 text.

[4] Not seen by F.M. Information taken from p. [2] of the 1960 text. There is discord between the statements of this page and the corresponding note of December 1943.

## Stories Published Separately

G. (32) A Goy *(Un 'goj')*. *Translation by* Arthur Livingston, *Menorah Journal,* Vol. X, No. 1, February 1924, pp. 15–20.

H. (22) The Fly *(La mosca)*. *Translation by* Rita Wellman, *The Forum,* Vol. LXXI, No. 2, February 1924, pp. 220–8.

I. (76) The Shoes at the Door *(Nell'albergo è morto un tale)*. *Anon. translation* (from the French), in *The Living Age,* 8th series, Vol. XXXVI, 15 November 1924, pp. 371–5.

J. (77) Return *(Ritorno)*. *Translation by* Ada Harrison, *The Calendar of Modern Letters,*[1] Vol. I, No. 5, July 1925, pp. 337–42.

K. (58) A Mere Formality *(Formalità)*. *Anon. translation,* in *The Golden Book Magazine,* Vol. II, No. 9, September 1925, pp. 339–410.

L. (21) The Red Book *(Il libretto rosso)*. *Translation by* C. K. Scott Moncrieff, *The Calendar of Modern Letters,*[2] Vol. 2, No. 9, November 1925, pp. 163–70.

M. (78) The Reserved Coffin *(La cassa riposta)*. *Translation by* J. E. Harry, *The Golden Book Magazine,* Vol. III, No. 13, January 1926, pp. 122–7.

N. (23) The Blessing *(Benedizione)*. *Translation by* Francis M. Guercio, *The Bermondsey Book,* Vol. III, No. 2, March 1926, pp. 22–31.

O. (58) A Mere Formality *(Formalità)*. *Anon. translation,* in *Great Stories of all Nations,* edited by Maxim Lieber and Blanche Colton Williams, New York, Brentano's, 1927;[2] Tudor Publishing Co., 1934;[2] 1942;[3] London, Harrap, 1927;[2] pp. 262–82 (with a brief note on Pirandello on pp. 261–2.) A reprint of K.

P. (79) The Starling and the Angel One-Hundred-and-One

[1] Seen by F.M. in microfilm.
[2] Unknown to Lo Vecchio-Musti.
[3] Not seen by F.M. Not recorded by Lo Vecchio-Musti. Quoted on the authority of the Catalogue of the Library of Congress.

*(Lo storno e l'Angelo Centuno). Translation by* Francis M. Guercio, *The Bermondsey Book,* Vol. IV, No. 3, June–July–August 1927, pp. 43–52.

Q. (80) The Portrait *(Un ritratto). Anon. translation* (from the French), in *The Living Age,*[1] 1 November 1929, pp. 300–6.

R. (22) The Fly *(La mosca). Translation by* Miss M. Lankester in *Great Italian Short Stories,* edited by Decio Pettoello. London, Benn, 1930,[2] pp. 480–9.

S. (8) The Nurse *(La balia). Translation by* Miss M. Lankester in *Great Italian Short Stories*[2] (see R), pp. 489–518.

T. (81) Faith *(La fede). Translation by* Miss M. Lankester in *Great Italian Short Stories*[2] (see R), pp. 518–25.

U. (82) By the Bedside *(La veglia). Translation by* Miss Grace Gill-Mark in *Great Italian Short Stories*[2] (see R), pp. 526–44.

V. (83) Close Friends *(Amicissimi). Translation by* Miss Joan M. Wilson in *Great Italian Short Stories*[2] (see R), pp. 544–53.

W. (36) A Little Wine *(Un po' di vino). Translation by* Miss M. Lankester in *Great Italian Short Stories*[2] (see R), pp. 553–8.

X. (23) The Blessing *(Benedizione)* and (79) The Starling and the Angel One-Hundred-and-One *(Lo storno e l'Angelo Centuno),* in the versions by Francis M. Guercio, were republished in *Anthology of Contemporary Italian Prose,* London, Scholartis Press, 1931, pp. 22–37 and pp. 37–52.

Y. (84) Through the Other Wife's Eyes[3] *(Con altri occhi). Translation by* Joan Redfern, *The Fortnightly Review,* Vol. CXXXIII (n.s.), April 1933, pp. 503–10.

Z. (85) Here's Another! *(E due!). Translation by* Joan Redfern, *The Fortnightly Review,* Vol. CXXXIV (n.s.), November 1933, pp. 599–606.

[1] Seen in microfilm by F.M. [2] Not recorded by Lo Vecchio-Musti.
[3] Wrongly indexed as 'Through Another's Wife's Eyes'.

AA. (45) Two Double Beds *(Due letti a due). Anon. translation,* in *The Spectator,* Vol. CLI, No. 5,500, 24 November 1933, pp. 764–6.

BB. (23) The Blessing *(Benedizione),* in the version by Francis M. Guercio, was reprinted in *Seven Years' Harvest,*[1] compiled by Sidney Gutman. London, Heinemann, 1934, pp. 130–41.

CC. (39) Granella's House *(La casa del Granella). Translation by* Joan Redfern, *Lovat Dickson's Magazine,*[2] Vol. 2, No. 5, May 1934, pp. 620–40.

DD. (34) Miss Holloway's Goat *(Il capretto nero). Translation by* [Samuel Putnam],[2] *The Golden Book Magazine,* Vol. XIX, May 1934, pp. 586–91.

EE. (43) The Truth *(La verità). Translation by* Joan Redfern, *The Fortnightly Review,* Vol. CXXXV (n.s.), June 1934, pp. 658–65.

FF. (84) With Other Eyes *(Con altri occhi). Anon. translation,* in *Esquire,*[1] Vol. II, No. 2, July 1934, pp. 54–5. Reprinted in *The Armchair Esquire,*[3] edited by Arnold Gingrich and L. Rust Hills, New York, Putnam, 1958; London, Heinemann, 1959, pp. 14–21. There is an introductory note on p. 14, while on p. 375 a bibliographical comment is provided by E. R. Hagemann and James E. Marsh.

GG. (30) A Dinner Guest[4] *(Un invito a tavola). Translation by* [Samuel Putnam],[2] *The Golden Book Magazine,* Vol. XX, July 1934, pp. 50–7.

HH. (28) A Finch, a Cat and the Stars *(Il gatto, un cardellino e le stelle). Translation by* Joan Redfern, *The Listener,* Vol. XII, No. 295, 5 September 1934, pp. 418–19.

[1] Not recorded by Lo Vecchio-Musti.
[2] This fact is unknown to Lo Vecchio-Musti. (cf. the text published in C.) Seen in microfilm by F.M.
[3] Lo Vecchio-Musti confuses this with Y. The texts differ.
[4] 'The Dinner Guest' is on the cover.

II. (34) The Little Black Kid *(Il capretto nero). Translation by* Joan Redfern, *The Listener,* Vol. XII, No. 306, 21 November 1934, pp. 876–7.

JJ. (70) The New Suit *(L'abito nuovo). Translation by* Joan Redfern, *Lovat Dickson's Magazine,*[1] Vol. 3, No. 6, December 1934, pp. 605–13.

KK. (37) Sicilian Limes *(Lumíe di Sicilia). Translation by* [Samuel Putnam],[2] *The Golden Book Magazine,* Vol. XXI, January 1935,[3] pp. 1–9.

LL. (18) Geography—A Remedy for Happiness[4] *(Rimedio: la geografia). Anon. translation,* in *The New Statesman and Nation,* Vol. X. No. 250, 7 December 1935, pp. 847–8, and re-published in *New Statesmanship,* selected by Edward Hyams. London, Longmans, 1963, pp. 131–5.

MM. (51) The Miracle of the Two Bears *(La prova). Anon. translation,* in *The Living Age,* January 1936,[5] pp. 427–30.

NN. (41) The Husband's Revenge *(La buon' anima). Translation* by [Michele Pettinati],[6] *The Spectator,* Vol. CLVII, No. 5,660, 18 December 1936, pp. 1078–9.

OO. (46) A Mother-in-Law *(La signora Frola e il signor Ponza, suo genero). Translation by* [Michele Pettinati],[6] *The Spectator,* Vol. CLIX, No. 5,711, 10 December 1937, pp. 1046–7.

PP. (53) My Last Journey *(Una giornata). Translation by* [Michele Pettinati],[6] *The Spectator,* Vol. CLIX, No. 5,713, 24 December 1937, pp. 1142–3.

QQ. (86) The Diploma--A Sketch *(Donna Mimma).*[7] *Translation by* Joan Redfern, *The Fortnightly Review,* Vol. CXLVI (n.s.), July 1939, pp. 61–6.

[1] Not recorded by Lo Vecchio-Musti.
[2] This fact unknown to Lo Vecchio-Musti. (cf. the text published in C.) Seen in microfilm by F.M.
[3] Following Vittorini, Lo Vecchio-Musti wrongly ascribes this to 1934.
[4] An odd use of 'remedy'. Not recorded by Lo Vecchio-Musti.
[5] Seen in microfilm by F.M. Corrections made to Lo Vecchio-Musti's entry.
[6] The text is the same as in D. Not recorded by Lo Vecchio-Musti.
[7] Lo Vecchio-Musti erroneously assumes this to be a version of *La patente*.

RR. (87) A Day Dawns *(Spunta un giorno)*. *Anon. translation,* in *The Spectator,*[1] Vol. CLXIV, No. 5,822, 26 January 1940, pp. 105–6.

SS. (88) When I Was Mad *(Quand'ero matto)*. *Translation by* Joan Redfern, *The Listener,*[1] Vol. XXIV, No. 611, 26 September, 1940.

TT. (49) Garibaldi Veteran *(Le medaglie)*. *Translation by* Joan Redfern, *The Listener,*[1] Vol. XXV, No. 629, 30 January 1941, pp. 167–8.

UU. (39) The Haunted House *(La casa del Granella)*. *Translation by* [Michele Pettinati],[2] in *Strange to Tell,* edited by Marjorie Fischer and Rolfe Humphries, New York, Messner, 1946, pp. 39–54.

VV. (52) Tortoises . . . For Luck *(La tartaruga)*. *Translation by* [Michele Pettinati],[1] in *Strange to Tell* (see UU), pp. 228–32.

WW. (38) The Tragedy of a Character *(La tragedia d'un personaggio)*. *Translation by* Frederick May, *The Lodestone,* Vol. 38, No. 2, Spring 1946, pp. 11–15.

XX. (83) Close Friends *(Amicissimi)*. *Translation by* [Miss Joan M. Wilson],[2] in *The World's Greatest Short Stories.* London, Odhams, 1947 (reprint) pp. 397–404. (No translator is named, but the text is the same as V.)

YY. (78) The Reserved Coffin *(La cassa riposta)*. *Translation by* J. E. Harry, in *The Art of Modern Fiction,*[2] edited by Ray B. West, Jr., and Robert Wooster Stallman. New York, Rinehart, 1949;[3] 9th impn., 1960. (A reprint of M.)

ZZ. (13) Black Horses *(La rallegrata)*. *Translation by* Arthur and Henrie Mayne, in *A Treasury of Horse Stories,*[2] edited by Margaret Cabell Self. London, Hutchinson, 1953. New York, Barnes, 1954.[3]

[1] The text is the same as in D. Not recorded by Lo Vecchio-Musti.
[2] Not recorded by Lo Vecchio-Musti.
[3] Not seen by F.M. Not recorded by Lo Vecchio-Musti. Source: *CBI*.

AAA. (89) The Bat *(Il pipistrello). Translation by* Frances Frenaye, in *Modern Italian Short Stories,*[1] edited by Marc Slonim. New York, Simon and Schuster, 1954, pp. 22–9.

BBB. (34) The Black Kid *(Il capretto nero). Translation by* W. J. Strachan, in *Modern Italian Stories,*[1] London. Eyre and Spottiswoode, 1955;[2] New York, Philosophical Library, 1956;[2] Toronto, McCelland;[2] London, Ace Books, 1961, pp. 165–70.

CCC. (26) Horse in the Moon *(Un cavallo nella luna). Translation by* Samuel Putnam, in *A Treasury of World Literature,*[1] edited by Dagobert D. Runes, New York, Philosophical Library, [1956], pp. 994–9.

DDD. (38) A Character in Distress *(La tragedia d'un personaggio). Translation by* [Michele Pettinati],[3] in *Great Italian Short Stories,* selected and introduced by P. M. Pasinetti. New York, Dell (Laurel Edition), 1959, pp. 286–93.

EEE. (47) War *(Quando si comprende). Translation by* [Michele Pettinati],[3] in *Great Italian Short Stories* (see CCC), p. 294–8.

FFF. (49) The Medals *(Le medaglie). Translation by* [Michele Pettinati],[3] in *Great Italian Short Stories* (see CCC), pp. 298–319.

GGG. (90) A Dream of Christmas *(Sogno di Natale). Translation by* Frederick May. Leeds, Pirandello Society, 1959;[4] *The Listener,* Vol. LXIV, No. 1656, 22 December 1960, p. 1151;[4] *Harper's Bazaar,* No. 3,001, December 1961, pp. 71–2, 141 and 154;[4] *English Digest,* Vol. LXVII, No. 2, December 1961, pp. 111–14.[4]

HHH. (91) The Tight Frock-Coat *(Marsina stretta). Translation by* Robert A. Hall, Jr., in *Italian Stories: Novelle Italiane.*[4] New York, Bantam Books, 1961, pp. 190–223. (Italian and English texts on facing pages.)

[1] Not recorded by Lo Vecchio-Musti.
[2] Not seen by F.M. Not recorded by Lo Vecchio-Musti. Source: *CBI.*
[3] The text is the same as in D. Not recorded by Lo Vecchio-Musti.
[4] Published too late for inclusion in Lo Vecchio-Musti.

# THE STORIES AND THE PLAYS

It cannot be too emphatically stressed that there is no real discontinuity between the world of the stories and that of the plays. It is interesting, therefore, to observe how many of Pirandello's theatrical works are derived by him from earlier—sometimes virtually contemporary—*novelle*. *Sgombero* may be seen as marking a climax in the process, with Pirandello writing it as a tale, but immediately seeing it for what it is—a one-act play—and discarding it when making up the later volumes of the Mondadori series of *Novelle per un anno*. In some cases the story is important merely because it offers the seminal idea—(42) *Certi obblighi* and (43) *La verità* both contributed significantly in this way to *Il berretto a sonagli*, which had its *première* (in the author's Sicilian translation) in 1917, some five years after the first publication of the stories. In others it determines the narrative line upon which the plot is elaborated, contributing in addition, perhaps, small patches of dialogue. Typical is (46) *La signora Frola e il signor Ponza, suo genero* (?1915), the dramatized form of which, *Così è (se vi pare)*, was also given initially in 1917. In another group it is recognizably a decisive formative element in the resulting play, but has been considerably modified and supplemented, as we see in the transition from the story (2) *Pensaci, Giacomino!* (1910) to the work for the stage of the same name (first played, in Pirandello's Sicilian translation, in 1916), or, even more excitingly, when three tales are drawn on in the making of *Non si sa come*. This drama, which had its *première* in Czech in 1934, absorbs material from (93) *Nel gorgo* (1913),[1] *La realtà del sogno* (1914) and (68) *Cinci* (1932). Finally, there are those instances where it is a play already—

[1] In 1913 it was known as *Il gorgo*.

or a substantial part of one. *La paura* (1897) is *La morsa*[1] (1898), less the husband-wife confrontation and the return of the lover as Giulia (=Lillina) shoots herself, while *L'uomo dal fiore in bocca* (1923) is only a few words and stage-directions removed from *La morte addosso* (as it had become by 1923, in the collection *In silenzio,* after having appeared originally—in 1919, as one of the stories in *Il carnevale dei morti*—under the title *Caffè notturno*).

Here is a note of the relationships between the stories and the plays. (They are examined more in detail by Manlio Lo Vecchio-Musti: *L'opera di Luigi Pirandello,* Torino, Paravia, 1939, pp. 154–8 and then *passim* to p. 253.)

| | Play | Drawing on the Stories |
|---|---|---|
| 1898. | *La morsa* | *La paura* (1897) |
| 1910. | *Lumíe di Sicilia* | (37) *Lumíe di Sicilia* (1900) |
| 1911. | *Il dovere del medico* | *Il dovere del medico* (?1908[2]) |
| 1916. | *Pensaci, Giacomino!* | (2) *Pensaci, Giacomino!* (1910) |
| 1917. | *Il berretto a sonagli* | (42) *Certi obblighi,* (43) *La verità* |
| | *La giara* | (3) *La giara* (1909) |
| | *La patente* | *La patente* (1911) |
| | *Cosí è (se vi pare)* | (46) *La signora Frola e il signor Ponza, suo genero* (?1915) |
| | *Il piacere dell'onestà* | *Tirocinio* (1905) |
| 1918. | *Ma non è una cosa seria* | *La signora Speranza* (?1902[3]) (11) *Non è una cosa seria* (1909[4]) |
| | *Il giuoco delle parti* | *Quando s'è capito il giuoco* (1913) |

[1] Then known as *L'epilogo.* It received the title *La morsa* in 1910, though a reference to *La morta* [*sic*] in the *Marzocco* for 23 April 1899 suggests that Pirandello was already contemplating the change.

[2] So in the list in chronological order. In his *Play-Story* list Lo Vecchio-Musti suggests 'intorno al 1910'. This, however, was before I had pointed out to him that the volume of stories in which *Il dovere del medico* first appeared *(La vita nuda)* belonged to 1910, and not to 1911 as he believed.

[3] Published in *Beffe della morte e della vita,* 2 ser. Firenze, Lumachi, 1903.

[4] Published in the *Corriere della sera,* 7 January 1910.

| | | |
|---|---|---|
| 1919. | *L'uomo, la bestia e la virtú* | (5) *Richiamo all'obbligo* (?1911) |
| | *Tutto per bene* | *Tutto per bene* (1906) |
| 1920. | *La signora Morli, una e due* | *Stefano Giogli, uno e due* (1909), (12) *La morta e la viva* (1910) |
| | *Come prima, meglio di prima* | *La veglia* (1904) |
| 1921. | *Sei personaggi in cerca d'autore* | (38) *La tragedia d'un personaggio* (1911), *Colloqui coi personaggi* (1915) |
| 1922. | *L'imbecille* | *L'imbecille* (1912) |
| 1923. | *L'uomo dal fiore in bocca* | *La morte addosso* (?1918[1]) |
| | *La vita che ti diedi* | *I pensionati della memoria* (?1913[2]), *La camera in attesa* (1916) |
| | *L'altro figlio*[3] | (1) *L'altro figlio* (1905) |
| 1924. | *Sagra del Signore della Nave* | *Il Signore della Nave* (?1915) |
| 1927. | *Bellavita* | *L'ombra del rimorso* (?1913[4]) |
| | *L'amica delle mogli* | *L'amica delle mogli* (?1894) |
| 1928. | *O di uno o di nessuno* | *O di uno o di nessuno* (?1914) |
| 1929. | *Questa sera si recita a soggetto* | *Leonora, addio!* (1910) |
| 1933. | *La favola del figlio cambiato* | (25) *Il figlio cambiato* (1902[5]) |
| 1934. | *Non si sa come* | *Nel gorgo* (1913[6]), *La realtà del sogno* (1914), (68) *Cinci* (1932) |

*It is relevant, I think, to note that:*

1921. *Enrico IV* draws upon Fileno's notion of the inverted telescope, as it is put forward in (38) *La tragedia d'un personaggio.*

[1] Published in *Il carnevale dei morti*. Firenze, Battistelli, 1919.
[2] Published in *Aprutium*, January 1914.
[3] Presented in Ferdinando Paolieri's Tuscan translation.
[4] Published in the *Corriere della sera*, 25 January 1914.
[5] Originally published as *Le nonne* in *La riviera ligure* for April 1902.
[6] Originally entitled *Il gorgo* (in *Aprutium* for July–August 1913).

1924. *Ciascuno a suo modo* absorbs an episode in the novel *Si gira . . .* (1914–15).

1933. *Quando si è qualcuno* is in many ways a *rifacimento* of the novel *Il fu Mattia Pascal* (1904).

## Unfinished Works

The following plays, which remained uncompleted at Pirandello's death, also derive from short stories:

| | Play | Story |
|---|---|---|
| 1925. | *Pari*[1] | *Pari* (?1909) |
| | *Commedia senza titolo*[2] | *Zia Michelina* (1914) |

[1] Manlio Lo Vecchio-Musti provides the (tentative) date on the evidence of the author's friends. It was first published in the *Almanacco letterario Bompiani*, 1938, pp. 51–62.

[2] Manlio Lo Vecchio-Musti's hypothesis. Internal evidence suggests a date before 1928. It was first published in the *Corriere della sera* for 5 June 1947.

# PIRANDELLO'S WORKS OTHER THAN THE SHORT STORIES

THE following is a list of the principal works of Luigi Pirandello, other than his short stories. There is no complete edition of his writings, but the *Opere,* published in six volumes by Mondadori (Milano-Verona) approaches nearest to this ideal.

## POETRY

1. *Mal giocondo*. Palermo, Clausen, 1889.
2. *Pasqua di Gea*. Milano, Galli, 1891.
3. *Pier Gudrò*. Roma, Voghera, 1894.
4. *Elegie renane*. Roma, Unione cooperative editrice, 1895.
5. *Elegie romane*—a translation of the poems by Goethe—Livorno, Giusti, 1896.
6. *Zampogna*. Roma, Società editrice Dante Alighieri, 1901.
7. *Scamandro* (a verse play). Roma, Tipografia 'Roma' (Armani e Stein), 1909.
8. *Fuori di chiave*. Genova, Formiggini, 1912.

## ESSAYS

9. *Laute und Lautentwickelung der Mundart von Girgenti*. Halle a.S., Druck der Buchdruckerei des Waisenhauses, 1891.
10. *Arte e scienza*. Roma, Modes, 1908.
11. *L'umorismo*. Lanciano, Carabba, 1908. A new and extended edition is: Firenze, Battistelli, 1920.
12. *Saggi, a cura di* Manlio Lo Vecchio-Musti. Milano-Verona, Mondadori, 1939. (In addition to Nos. 9 and 10 there is a useful gathering in of material from periodicals, etc. The work on Verga and Dante is especially valuable.)

## Novels

13. *L'esclusa*. Roma, *La tribuna,* June–August, 1901.
14. *Il turno*. Catania, Giannotta, 1902.
15. *Il fu Mattia Pascal*. Roma, *Nuova antologia,* April–June, 1904.
16. *Suo marito*. Firenze, Quattrini, 1911. (The 2nd edition—with a substantially revised first part—is published in the 1941 *Tutti i romanzi* put out by Mondadori (Milano-Verona). It has the new title *Giustino Roncella nato Boggiòlo*.)
17. *I vecchi e i giovani*. Roma, *Rassegna contemporanea,* January–November 1909. (It was thoroughly re-worked for the 1931 edition put out by Mondadori (Milano-Verona).)
18. *Si gira . . .* Roma, *Nuova antologia,* June–August 1915. (It gained the new title *Quaderni di Serafino Gubbio operatore* for the Bemporad (Firenze) presentation of 1925.)
19. *Uno, nessuno e centomila*. Milano, *La fiera letteraria,* 1925–26.

## Plays

Where a play was performed in a year earlier than that in which it was published the date is signalized thus: (*P*. 1910.)

20. *L'epilogo*. Roma, *Ariel,* 20 March, 1898. (The final title is *La morsa*.)
21. *Lumíe di Sicilia*. Roma, *Nuova antologia,* 16 March 1911. (*P*. 1910.)
22. *Il dovere del medico*. Roma, *Noi e il mondo,* January 1912.
23. *Cecè*. Milano, *La lettura,* October 1913.
24. *Se non così*. Roma, *Nuova antologia,* January 1916. (*P*. 1915.)
24. *Se non così*. Roma, *Nuova antologia,* January 1916. (*P*. 1915.) (Its final title is *La ragione degli altri*. It was written in 1899.)
25. *All'uscita*. Roma, *Nuova antologia,* 1 November 1916.
26. *Pensaci, Giacomino!* Roma, *Noi e il mondo,* 1 April–1 June 1917. (*P*. 1916.)
27. *Liolà*. Roma, Formiggini, 1917. (Both Sicilian and Italian texts.) (*P*. 1916.)
28. *Così è (se vi pare)*. Roma, *Nuova antologia,* 1–16 January 1918. (*P*. 1917.)

29. *La patente*. Roma, *Rivista d'Italia*, 31 January 1918.
30. *Il piacere dell'onestà*. Roma, *Noi e il mondo*, 1 February–1 March 1918. (*P*. 1917.)
31. *Il berretto a sonagli*. Roma, *Noi e il mondo*, 1 August–1 September 1918. (*P*. 1917.)
32. *Il giuoco delle parti*. Roma, *Nuova antologia*, 1–16 January 1919. (*P*. 1918.)
33. *L'uomo, la bestia, e la virtú*. Milano, Comoedia, 10 September 1919.
34. *Ma non è una cosa seria*. Milano, Treves 1919. (As part of Vol. II of the first collection of *Maschere nude*.) (*P*. 1918.)

From now on, where a Roman numeral precedes the title of the play, the text belongs to the second series of *Maschere nude*.

35. I. *Tutto per bene*. Firenze, Bemporad, 1920.
36. II. *Come prima, meglio di prima*, Firenze, Bemporad, 1921. (*P*. 1920.)
37. III. *Sei personaggi in cerca d'autore*. Firenze, Bemporad, 1921. (The IVth edition, 1925, is very important, for the play was recast and given a valuable preface.)
38. *L'innesto*. Milano, Treves, 1921. (As part of Vol. IV of the first collection of the *Maschere nude*.) (*P*. 1919.)
39. *'A vilanza* (in collaboration with Nino Martoglio). Catania, Giannotta, 1922. (In Sicilian. Part of Vol. VII of Martoglio's *Teatro dialettale siciliano*.) (*P*. 1917.)
40. *Cappiddazzu paga tuttu* (in collaboration with Nino Martoglio). Catania, Giannotta, 1922. (In Sicilian. The rest of VII—see No. 39.)
41. *Enrico IV*. Firenze, Bemporad, 1922.
42. VI. *La signora Morli, una e due*. Firenze, Bemporad, 1922. (*P*. 1920.)
43. VII. *Vestire gli ignudi*. Firenze, Bemporad, 1923. (*P*. 1922.)
44. VIII. *La vita che ti diedi*. Firenze, Bemporad, 1924. (*P*. 1923.)
45. IX. *Ciascuno a suo modo*. Firenze, Bemporad, 1924.
46. *Sagra del Signore della nave*. Milano, *Il convegno*, 30 September 1924.

47. *L'altro figlio*. Firenze, Bemporad, 1925. (As part of Vol. XII of the second series of *Maschere nude*.) (*P*. 1923.)
48. *La giara*. Firenze, Bemporad, 1925. (As No. 47.) (*P*. 1917—in Sicilian.)
49. *L'imbecille*. Firenze, Bemporad, 1926. (As part of Vol. XIX of the second series of *Maschere nude*.) (*P*. 1922.)
50. *L'uomo dal fiore in bocca*. Firenze, Bemporad, 1926. (As part of Vol. XX of the second series of *Maschere nude*.) (*P*. 1923.)
51. XXI. *Diana e la Tuda*. Firenze, Bemporad, 1927. (*P*. 1926—in German.)
52. XXII. *L'amica delle mogli*. Firenze, Bemporad, 1927.
53. XXIII. *La nuova colonia*. Firenze, Bemporad, 1928.
54. *Bellavita*. Milano, *Il secolo XX*, July 1928. (*P*. 1927.)
55. XXV. *O di uno o di nessuno*. Firenze, Bemporad, 1929.
56. XXVI. *Lazzaro*. Milano-Verona, Mondadori, 1929.
57. *Sogno (ma forse no)*. Milano, *La lettura*, October 1929.
58. XXVII. *Questa sera si recita a soggetto*. Milano-Verona, Mondadori, 1930.
59. XXVIII. *Come tu mi vuoi*. Milano-Verona, Mondadori, 1930.
60. XXIX. *Trovarsi*. Milano-Verona, Mondadori, 1932.
61. XXX. *Quando si è qualcuno*. Milano-Verona, Mondadori, 1933.
62. *La favola del figlio cambiato*. Milano, Ricordi, 1933. (As the libretto for Malipiero's opera.)
63. XXXI. *Non si sa come*. Milano-Verona, Mondadori, 1935.
64. *I giganti della montagna*. Milano-Verona, Mondadori, 1938. (As part of the Xth volume of the third series of *Maschere nude*. Parts of the play had appeared in periodicals from 1931 on.) (*P*. 1937.)

## Notes

1. The breaks in the run of Roman numbers indicate that the intervening volumes were published earlier in another format.
2. *Scamandro* (No. 7) was performed in 1928.

*A Translation*

65. *'Il ciclope:* THE CYCLOPS of Euripides. Only the first scenes were published (*Messaggero della Domenica,* 13 November 1918). The translation was produced in 1919.

*Scenari*

66. *La salamandra,* a pantomime, Milano-Verona, Mondadori, 1960. (In *Saggi, poesie, scritti varii,* pp. 1145–50.) (*P.* 1928.)
67. *Sei personaggi in cerca d'autore* (in collaboration with Adolf Lantz), published as a *film-novelle*, Berlin, Hobbing, 1929. (In German.)

## QUARTET ENCOUNTERS

The purpose of this paperback series is to bring together influential and outstanding works of twentieth-century European literature in translation. Each title has an introduction by a distinguished contemporary writer, describing a personal or cultural 'encounter' with the text, as well as placing it within its literary and historical perspective.

Quartet Encounters will concentrate on fiction, although the overall emphasis is upon works of enduring literary merit, whether biography, travel, history or politics. The series will also preserve a balance between new and older works, between new translations and reprints of notable existing translations. Quartet Encounters provides a much-needed forum for prose translation, and makes accessible to a wide readership some of the more unjustly neglected classics of modern European literature.

Aharon Appelfeld · *The Retreat*

Translated from the Hebrew by Dalya Bilu
with an introduction by Gabriel Josipovici
'A small masterpiece . . . the vision of a remarkable poet'
*New York Times Book Review*

Gaston Bachelard · *The Psychoanalysis of Fire*

Translated from the French by Alan C.M. Ross
with an introduction by Northrop Frye
'. . . he is a philosopher, with a professional training in the sciences, who devoted most of the second phase of his career to promoting that aspect of human nature which often seems most inimical to science: the poetic imagination . . .'
J.G. Weightman, *The New York Review of Books*

Robert Bresson · *Notes on the Cinematographer*

Translated from the French by Jonathan Griffin
with an introduction by J.M.G. Le Clézio
'[Bresson] is the French cinema, as Dostoyevsky
is the Russian novel and Mozart is German music'
Jean-Luc Godard, *Cahiers du Cinéma*

Hermann Broch · *The Sleepwalkers*

Translated from the German by Willa and Edwin Muir
with an introduction by Michael Tanner
'One of the greatest European novels . . .
masterful' Milan Kundera

E.M. Cioran · *The Temptation to Exist*

Translated from the French by Richard Howard
with an introduction by Susan Sontag
'Cioran is one of the most delicate minds of real power
writing today. Nuance, irony, and refinement are the
essence of his thinking . . .' Susan Sontag

Stig Dagerman · *The Games of Night*

Translated from the Swedish by Naomi Walford
with an introduction by Michael Meyer
'One is haunted by a secret and uneasy suspicion
that [Dagerman's] private vision, like Strindberg's
and Kafka's, may in fact be nearer the truth of things
than those visions of the great humanists, such as
Tolstoy and Balzac, which people call universal'
Michael Meyer

Grazia Deledda · *After the Divorce*

Translated from the Italian by Susan Ashe
with an introduction by Sheila MacLeod
'What [Deledda] does is create the passionate complex
of a primitive populace' D.H. Lawrence

Marcellus Emants · *A Posthumous Confession*

Translated from the Dutch and
with an introduction by J.M. Coetzee
'Since the time of Rousseau we have seen the growth
of the genre of the *confessional novel*, of which
*A Posthumous Confession* is a singularly pure example.
Termeer [the narrator], claiming to be unable to keep
his dreadful secret, records his confession and leaves it
behind as a monument to himself, thereby turning a
worthless life into art' J.M. Coetzee

Carlo Emilio Gadda · *That Awful Mess on Via Merulana*

Translated from the Italian by William Weaver
with an introduction by Italo Calvino
'One of the greatest and most original Italian novels
of our time' Alberto Moravia

Martin A. Hansen · *The Liar*

Translated from the Danish by John Jepson Egglishaw
with an introduction by Eric Christiansen
'[The Liar] is both a vindication of religious truth
and a farewell to the traditional modes of extended
fiction. It is haunted by literary ghosts, and English
readers will recognize the shadowy forms of Hans
Anderson . . . and Søren Kierkegaard' Eric Christiansen

Gustav Janouch · *Conversations with Kafka*

Translated from the German by Goronwy Rees
with an introduction by Hugh Haughton
'I read it and was stunned by the wealth of new material . . .
which plainly and unmistakably bore the stamp of Kafka's
genius' Max Brod

Ismaïl Kadaré · *The General of the Dead Army*

Translated from the French by Derek Coltman
with an introduction by David Smiley
'Ismaïl Kadaré is presenting his readers not merely
with a novel of world stature — which is already a
great deal — but also, and even more important, with
a novel that is the voice of ancient Albania herself,
speaking to today's world of her rebirth' Robert Escarpit

Miroslav Krleža · *On the Edge of Reason*

Translated from the Croatian by Zora Depolo
with an introduction by Jeremy Catto
'Paris had its Balzac and Zola; Dublin, its Joyce;
Croatia, its Krleža . . . one of the most accomplished,
profound authors in European literature . . .'
*Saturday Review*

Pär Lagerkvist · *The Dwarf*

Translated from the Swedish by Alexandra Dick
with an introduction by Quentin Crewe
'A considerable imaginative feat'
*Times Literary Supplement*

Henry de Montherlant · *The Bachelors*

Translated from the French and with an introduction by Terence Kilmartin
'One of those carefully framed, precise and acid studies on a small canvas in which French writers again and again excel' V.S. Pritchett

Rainer Maria Rilke · *Rodin and other Prose Pieces*

Translated from the German by G. Craig Houston with an introduction by William Tucker
'[Rilke's] essay remains the outstanding interpretation of Rodin's œuvre, anticipating and rendering otiose almost all subsequent criticism'
William Tucker, *The Language of Sculpture*

Lou Andreas-Salomé · *The Freud Journal*

Translated from the German by Stanley A. Leavy with an introduction by Mary-Kay Wilmers
'Lou Andreas-Salomé was a woman with a remarkable flair for great men and . . . it was said of her that she had attached herself to the greatest men of the nineteenth and twentieth centuries Nietzsche and Freud respectively'
Ernest Jones, *The Life and Work of Sigmund Freud*

Stanislaw Ignacy Witkiewicz · *Insatiability*

Translated from the Polish by Louis Iribarne with an introduction by Czeslaw Milosz
'A study of decay: mad, dissonant music, erotic perversion, . . . and complex psychopathic personalities'
Czeslaw Milosz